BOOK **THREE** OF
JOURNEY TO ZION

FIRE *of* ZION

JOHN PONTIUS

Latter-day
Legends

Salt Lake City

ISBN 13: 978-1-964978-34-5

Published by Latter-day Legends, a division of Digital Legend Press & Publishing Inc. Salt Lake City, UT 84121
www.digitalegend.com

Inquiries or Permissions: info@digitalegend.com

Cover design by David Christenson
Interior design by Jacob F. Frandsen

Printed in the United States of America

INTRODUCTION

Fire of Zion is the third and final book in the print and audio series "Journey to Zion" series [originally called "Millennial Quest" series] which were all initially written in the in the summer of 1995.

This second book took Sam through the purifying fires of his journey and sets the stage for the dramatic and glorious conclusion captured in this book *Fire of Zion* which takes the reader through his mortal life, and into the millennial age with Christ's return.

The stories and characters in this book are fictional. Although some of the experiences described within are based upon the author's own life, most are a faith-filled product of my hopes and imagination. The spiritual occurrences, visions, visitations, conversations and events in this novel are fictitious, and should be considered as such. As well, references to world events and possible end-time scenarios are merely my attempt to contrast the tragedy of wickedness with the transcendent joy and deliverance available to those walking in obedience to the Lord's voice.

No attempt is being made to define Church doctrine or to describe events as they should, or even might occur in someone's life. Having so said, may I also note that many of the events of spiritual impact in this book are based upon scriptural accounts of similar events in the lives of the ancient faithful, as well as upon prophecies regarding the challenging and exciting pre-Millennial future ahead.

I have great faith in the idea that Father did not cause these great epiphanies to be recorded in scripture simply for our entertainment. I believe that these magnificent events were included in holy writ to show us that we, too, can walk the path of holiness, drink freely from the waters of the Atonement, and receive equally glorious blessings as the ancient faithful did. I believe these blessings are at our fingertips, as achievable today as in any period of antiquity.

I invite you to read *Angels of Fire* with a light and hopeful heart, with an eye focused upon Jesus Christ, and ponder, as I have, the incredible power of what lies just beyond the veil, and your place in it all.

John Pontius

1997

EDITOR'S NOTE

I am pleased to release this never-before published conclusion of the "Journey to Zion" series by my late husband, John Pontius. This is a compilation of John's last three fictional novels all written in the summer of 1995, now entitled *Fire of the Spirit* (Book 1) *Angels of Fire* (Book 2) and *Fire of Zion* (Book 3) print and audio series. I have edited this text so that some events described herein have been resequenced and refined to capture what I know were John's intent and core beliefs.

The reader should be aware that while this book features glorious scenarios involving rich relationships and spiritual joys, it also includes some graphic and potentially disturbing situations. As he states in his introduction, John was attempting to portray the consequences of evil, along with the peace and deliverance that the Lord promises to the faithful.

Readers of "Journey to the Veil" may also notice that there are some similar stories told in that book as in this series. John felt free to embellish these events for his fictional novels, but recounted them accurately in his personal blog "UnBlog My Soul" and as published in the subsequent book "Journey to the Veil."

Another note of interest is that fifteen years after he had written these novels, John met "Spencer" and eventually interviewed him in preparation for compiling the book "Visions of Glory." John was struck by similarities of some of Spencer's true experiences and what John had penned in this fictional series years before. This was surprising to him, and something that we concluded was the obvious workings of the Spirit.

I wish to clearly state that John was completely faithful to The Church of Jesus Christ of Latter-day Saints, and a member in good standing all of his life. He wholeheartedly supported the Church's positions, doctrine, and those in authority. In "Journey to the Veil" John wrote, "I am now and always will be a warrior in defense of the Latter-day Church. Not only is it 'true' but it works. It brings to our lives the very blessings we are seeking . . . I think one of the missions of the UnBlog has been to say over and over that The Church of Jesus Christ of Latter-day Saints is not broken.

It is not somehow true-but-not-functioning, or a kindergarten class one must enroll in and then graduate from to go beyond. The voice of the UnBlog is that this Church is profoundly true, that it is operating as Jesus Christ directs it, and that it will be the organization through which He finally authorizes and orchestrates the building of the latter-day Zion."

This novel is not an attempt to establish Church doctrine or to imply that anything would, or even should, happen as described. That said, I pray that *"Angels of Fire"* and the concluding book *"Fire of Zion"* may ignite your spiritual imagination and draw you closer to Jesus Christ, our Savior and the Rock of our Salvation.

Terri Pontius
July 2024

Page numbers continue from book two with... page 286

Theo shook his head. "That's far more charitable than what he said about you all these years. And, infinitely more charitable than what I said to him this morning," he said emphatically.

"I hope you weren't mean to him," Melody said gently.

"Why would you care? I would think we owe him some meanness."

"No, no Theodore. Don't stoop to meanness. That's what drove me out of his life. Don't make the same mistakes he made."

"You really are my mother, aren't you," Theo said quietly, his voice rich with emotion.

"I am," she said slowly. Her eyes were tender. "I'm so sorry I wasn't there to raise you. Did you have a good childhood?" She really wanted to know. She realized it was an odd question for a mother to ask, but it was something only he could answer.

"I think so," Theo said a little more kindly. "Papa was strict, but he raised us to be good. I was happy, but I think George never got done being angry that you left."

"But, I didn't leave."

"I know, Mama," he said. Hearing him call her Mama again sounded so good to her that her eyes misted with another wave of tears. He laughed, pulled a handkerchief from his jacket, and wiped them away. "No more tears now. I'm not going to let you leave me again. Let's get that settled here and now. I know you didn't leave me on your own. I had to think a long time, but I do remember Papa beating you, and driving you out. I remember the police, and screaming as they pulled us out of that apartment. I remember you fighting the police, and my wondering why you didn't stop them from taking us."

"It was an awful time, now long past," she soothed.

"I know, mother. But, even after reading your letters it took me a couple days to remember. Papa had told us the story another way so many times that I actually remembered it the way he said. It wasn't until I read your account of that day in one of your letters, that I began to remember."

"I'm so sorry..." she began.

"You need to quit saying that. It's not your fault. Quit apologizing for something that was beyond your control. Let's just move on with our lives."

"That's good counsel," she admitted. "I'm just sorry... I mean, I just regret this chapter of my life more than any other. I have thought about you boys constantly, and longed to be with you. But I thought it was useless to try to get you back. Now, I'm not prepared for how big you've become, and how handsome!" she exclaimed.

"Spoken like a true mother," Theo proclaimed happily. "There's some- thing else. You remember Uncle Tennison?"

"Yes, certainly," Melody said guardedly.

"Well, I remember great-uncle Tennison saying awful things about you after you left. I know Papa spoke to him after you left, and I know for a fact that Uncle Tennison is petitioning the court today to have little Sammy here DNA tested, and to have you deported! It is going to be ugly again," he concluded sadly.

Melody thought about this for a moment. "I have tickets to go back to America tomorrow evening. Your father won't have time to do anything that soon. The thing that really concerns me is that I only have today to find George. I'm worried about him. I was told he's living on the street."

"Surely not!" Theo protested. "Papa says he's sending George money every week. He constantly complains about still having to support him."

Melody shook her head. "Your father told me he hadn't been in contact with George and doesn't know where he is. Both statements can't be true. I was told by someone I trust that he's destitute and living on the street. Will you help me find him?"

"Certainly!" Theo cried, jumping to his feet. I know a few places to try. Can we begin right away? I have a car downstairs."

"I'm ready," she said.

Theo turned to his brother. "Come on Sam, the game's afoot!"

"Cool!" Sammy cried, and grabbed his coat.

They hurried through the small lobby to observe traffic inexplicably at a standstill outside the small hotel. What should have been a melee of swirling traffic, screeching tires and blaring horns was an eerie scene of almost total silence. The people seemed to be sitting in their cars stunned to immobility.

"What's news, chum?" Theo asked the first man who hurried passed on the sidewalk. He looked up as if in a daze of disbelief.

"The Russies are invading Europe! They're in cahoots with the Chinee'!" he said in a stunned voice. "The whole bleedin' world's goin' te war!"

With the news of war, the pandemonium in the community hall grew so all-consuming that Vladimir quit interpreting for Samuel, and joined into the shouting. Samuel had no choice but to wait for Vladimir to begin translating again. All he really knew was that the Soviets expected every able-bodied man and woman to report to active duty, immediately. The news of the war was disturbing enough, but the fact that Russia was drafting everyone with two legs made their situation grim if they did not comply.

Samuel longed to be able to switch on CNN and learn what was going on, but had no such luxury to indulge in. He only knew that the events of the last days had just jumped from a holding pattern, to a terrible war destined to eventually end in the death of as many as two-thirds of mankind.

At the center of all this shouting was the old man whom they revered as their spiritual leader. Though Samuel had never asked, he knew his name was Alexei. He was Islana's uncle. It was Islana who had come to him, and given him her intimate knowledge of their lives. Islana was Vladimir's oldest sister. One day, Samuel would tell them about meeting her, but for now, they had more than they could assimilate as it was.

Finally some order was restored, and they fractured into small groups, still arguing among themselves. It was then that Alexei came to Samuel. Vladimir translated for them.

"Did you hear the news?" he wanted to know.

"I did. It is not good."

"It is a desperate time. The prophecies speak of a terrible war at the time of our departure from this land. But we could not have known it would be so soon."

"What will you do?" Samuel asked, trying to keep his questions short to facilitate translation.

"That is an odd question from you," the old man said.

"Why?"

"Because it is you who will lead us away to our new home in Zion."

"Do you believe this?" Samuel asked him pointedly.

"You know I do," he replied, then said, "We must leave immediately. What shall we do to prepare?"

As if a window had suddenly opened in his soul, a burst of understanding flooded into Samuel's mind so vivid it included details, visual images and sounds. He had, in reality, seen in vision the answer to their question. Seconds before he knew nothing of this mission; now, having been asked by those he was to assist, he knew the answer.

"You have stored food," he said. It was not a question.

"Some."

"Gather the people. They must prepare all through the night. Collect everything necessary for the trip. We will leave no one behind who wishes to come. Bring nothing but food, clothing, bedding, and necessary items. If you have any livestock or dogs, bring them. Other pets stay behind. Leave all else here. We will not take weapons of any kind. We will not take furniture or other possessions. We meet at first light tomorrow outside this building. This is what you must do," he said.

Alexei seemed energized by Samuel's words, and immediately turned toward the others in the room. He began shouting orders as people began running in various directions to begin their preparations.

The following day's first light found a long line of people assembled outside. Samuel estimated there to be upwards of 2500 people of all ages. Under Alexei's direction, several dozen men began at the near end, and inspected every parcel. Under their leader's direction they took toasters, VCR's, TV's, radios, pictures, portraits, jewelry, and a host of possessions—mostly worthless, some priceless—and set them beside the road. Among those things left behind was a Faberge egg of intricately wrought gold worth a king's ransom. They were not picked up again. Even stuffed animals and children's toys were abandoned.

By midday they were ready. They began loading into old trucks and cars; even a tractor was driven with a wagon behind it. People packed inside the vehicles until they were over-full. Samuel, Vladimir and Alexei climbed into the blue Honda, and Vladimir started the engine.

"Which way do we go?" Alexei asked. As if he had always known, Samuel answered with great certainty.

"East, then north to the sea," he said.

Alexei shouted the word from the car, and it passed quickly down the long rag-tag caravan. Vladimir gunned the engine and they pulled away, a long line of homeless refugees behind them.

Vehicles began breaking down almost from the start. However, the people proved adept at making them run on almost nothing. They came to the first small town an hour later. The owners of the tractor and trailer were not able to purchase fuel, and were obliged to leave their vehicle behind. The remaining vehicles became more crowded, and children began to cry for want of food and sleep. Just outside the city Alexei signaled them to make camp. They parked the vehicles off the road in a circle, and tents were pitched inside. The wind picked up, and it snowed for the first time that year. It was just September.

Samuel slept in the Honda, and was aware of Vladimir shivering in his sleep. Samuel was not cold, and he almost gave his friend his own thick down coat to put over the top of him. He did not. Anyone without a coat would have frozen to death in a short time. Samuel could not raise anyone's suspicions in such a way.

Morning was still just a gray smudge across the horizon when they were awakened by the honking of a horn. Samuel sat up and stretched. Vladimir struggled to make his stiff limbs move.

"What is going on?" Alexei asked from the back seat.

"Someone is honking a horn," Samuel said. They climbed from the car and found a young man jumping on the running board of one of their trucks, honking the horn and pointing down the road. They looked in the direction he was pointing to see a row of headlights heading toward them. It quickly became apparent they were military vehicles.

"What does it mean?" Alexei asked.

"They are definitely military. What do you think? Are they coming after us?" Vladimir asked.

"They were probably alerted by the townspeople of the last city," Alexei surmised. At this point a spotlight blazed to life, and flooded across their tattered convoy. The lead truck slowed, then sped ahead. After a moment a loud speaker blared.

"Identify yourselves," the voice boomed in Russian. "Be prepared to show your papers!" the voice called.

"We have no papers!" Vladimir said to Alexei urgently. "We are fleeing the country, and we'll all be considered traitors!"

"I know, I know," Alexei said. "We need help from God, and we need it now!" he said. He turned to Samuel. "What should we do?" he asked urgently.

Samuel bowed his head in a silent prayer. "Cheer!" he cried as he looked up, almost before the thought had materialized in his mind. "Cheer them, and curse the Western pigs. Quickly!"

"Pass the word, raise a hearty cheer," Alexei told Vladimir, then began spreading the word. In a few seconds a small cheer arose from a few voices, then was joined by many others. By the time the trucks roared to a halt the people were screaming and dancing up and down, their faces streaked with tears. The military men could not know they were tears of stark terror.

"Who is in charge?" he demanded over the speaker. "Come forward!"

Alexei trotted forward clapping his hands and thrusting his fist into the air. "I am leading this people," he said loudly. "Power to the union!" he cried.

"What?" The man asked, his voice booming across the snowy landscape. The speaker clicked off and he climbed from his truck. He walked toward Vladimir, his hand on his revolver. "What did you say?" he asked.

"Power to the Soviet people, and damn the Western pigs! We cheer you and our certain victory!" he cried enthusiastically.

"Well, yes," he stammered. "We will stomp them into the ground, and send them back to their filthy homeland."

"Yes!" the people cried. "Hurrah, Hurrah. Victory, victory, victory!" they chanted.

"We will destroy the Western pigs!" the soldier shouted triumphantly.

"Destroy them, destroy them, destroy them!" the chant came up.

"You people, where do you go?"

"To fight the war!" Alexei cried.

"All of you?" he asked incredulously.

"We all come to this glorious cause. Drive them out. We will drive them out!" he cried.

The people echoed. "Drive them out, drive them out, drive them out."

"Do you have travel papers?" he demanded.

"Our hearts are our travel papers. We travel to the aid of our country!" he shouted.

"You are true patriots. I wish you were younger, and I would take you with me and make you my general. You people, follow your leader, and he will bring you glory!"

"Glory, glory, glory!" they cried with one voice.

"Victory!" the soldier cried as he climbed back into his rig.

"Victory, victory, victory!" they screamed as he drove away.

As soon as the last taillight disappeared from view they fell to their knees as if on a signal, and voices that had seconds before cried for victory, now prayed for thanksgiving. They were delivered, and every soul knew it was a miracle.

"We can't remain here," Alexei suddenly said, his head jerking up from his prayers. "Our deception will not last for long. We must leave now! Signal the camp. We must travel cross-country from here. We will only take the farming roads. We depart in ten minutes!" he cried.

Melody's first thought was of Samuel when she heard the news that Russia was invading Europe. She immediately tried to dial his number in Russia, and after repeated attempts, was told by an operator with very poor English that the number had been disconnected. A moment of panic swept through her, then she concluded that it was in fact a good sign. They must have closed the office, and her beloved husband would be coming home. He might even be home already! She dialed her own home, and got nothing but prolonged ringing.

It was impossible to estimate how many Eastern Bloc citizens had died in the two weeks of invasion. The international uproar was tremendous and immediate. Every country on earth condemned the action in the most violent possible terms. Nations formerly friendly to Russia, including the U.S., withdrew all ties and unforgiving economic sanctions were slammed into place. NATO ponderously swung its dragon head toward their new enemy, and fire screamed from Russia in billowing threats of absolute destruction. The great Soviet bear stood on its borders and roared to shake the whole earth, and the world trembled.

International opinion confirmed the absoluteness of the Russian conquest, and the resulting sanctions and threats should have calmed the Russian blood-lust to which their invasion had given life. However, it seemed almost as if someone had shot an arrow into the great beast, only wounding it, and feeding its fierce anger to white-hot intensity. Feeling justified beyond discussion, Russia cut all diplomatic ties and communications in or out of Russia, throwing great clouds of dirt into the air in its rage. As the world watched in stark terror, Russia unleashed their arms build-up which mobilized its vast citizenry as never before. Their great, once-hidden military machine pushed their advanced weaponry forward at unmatchable speed.

While the world tried to respond in kind, the United States found itself politically unable to match the pace of rearmament. Recently returned from expensive and emotionally crippling campaigns in the middle-east and North Korea, the people of America could stomach war no longer. Not wanting to spark a nuclear holoaust, the U.S. tried to remain neutral for as long as possible.

———————————

As the minutes ticked into hours, one thing seemed immediately obvious to Melody: she absolutely had to find her missing son and return to America. Even though England had no logical reason to fear a military assault from the frothing giant, they were a paltry thousand miles away— the blink of an eye from possible total annihilation.

She didn't dare miss her flight out, for prices and availability were already astronomical. They searched all that day and late into the evening, all without success, and returned late that evening to the hotel. Theo was as devastated as Melody, but for a different reason. They had spoken to enough people who knew George to come to the inescapable conclusion that he was living on the street. With the outbreak of war, George would be one of the first to be swept into the conflict if England joined the war. Assuming war in Europe was inescapable, England's involvement was guaranteed.

Theo feared for his brother's life. As for himself, he would almost surely get a deferment due to his divinity studies. The churches and their ministers were considered untouchable during times of war. Popular opinion would quickly turn against any government who began drafting "men of God" to do their killing.

"I'm so sorry, Mum," Theo was saying. He had begun calling her Mum, and her heart warmed every time he did so. "I had no idea he was on the street. I just don't know where we might look, especially this late at night."

"We'll begin again first thing tomorrow," Melody said quietly, with little hope. There were only a few hours in the morning before she had to hurry to the airport or miss her flight. With her husband no doubt on his way home, she surely didn't want to miss the flight. "Would you like to spend the night with us?" she asked almost without thinking. Then she realized he was twenty-two years old, and hardly in need of her putting him up for the night. His own home was a short drive away. She drew a breath to apologize, but he interrupted her.

"Thanks," he said. "I would like that. What do you say Sam, my good man? Should we have a sleepover?"

"Yipee!" Sammy cried, and began jabbering and dancing from foot to foot.

"Come on Sport," Theo said putting an arm across his shoulders, "let's go get a bite to eat."

They arranged for a trundle bed to be moved into their room. Sammy got the "bed with wheels," and Theo and Melody took the two twin beds. Theo was about to switch the light off when Melody and Sammy knelt beside her bed. It took him a moment to realize what they were doing, and he quickly joined them.

"Heavenly Father," Melody began after a moment of silence. "We thank Thee with all our hearts for bringing us together again. Oh, Heavenly Father, Thou knowest how deeply I have missed my boys, and how dearly I love them. Now Theo is here, and he's so wonderful, and handsome, and good. I'm so proud of him, as I know Thou art. Please bless him Father, and fill his heart with all the love I was not able to give him..." her voice cracked here, and she had to wait.

"Father, I know Thou knowest all things. And I know that Thou will keep George safe. I pray that we can find him tomorrow, if for nothing more than to say goodbye. I love him Father, and I miss him, and as the world seems on the brink of war, I pray Thou will allow us this last farewell.

"I pray for my beloved husband in Russia, that Thou wilt keep him safe, and bring him home to my arms. Forgive us for our weaknesses, I pray in Christ's holy name, amen."

"Amen," Theo said quietly. He clicked off the light, and slid onto the mattress. They lay in the darkness for a long time in silence.

"Mum?" Theo asked.

"Yes honey?" Melody's voice was sweet with love.

"When you prayed just now, you closed your prayer in the name of Christ."

"That's right."

"But, why? Why use Christ's name if you aren't a Christian?"

"Why do you say I'm not a Christian," she asked, her voice a little wounded.

"Because Mormon's aren't Christians, they're... Mormons, I guess."

"Who told you that?"

"Well, Papa, and my seminary professors. It's pretty common knowledge, I'd say."

"Then, it's false common knowledge."

"Why would you say that, Mum? How could so many good religious people be mistaken about Mormons?"

"What would you say is the definition of a Christian?" Melody asked.

"Well, one who believes Jesus is God, and that he died for our sins, and that he is part of the Trinity. I would also say that a Christian believes in the Bible, and tries to keep the commandments of Christ. There are probably other things, but those are the basics, I think."

"Sammy, are you awake?" Melody asked quietly.

"Yeah," a small voice said in the darkness.

"Do you remember the first article of faith?"

"Yeah," he said again.

"Say it, would you?"

"We believe in God the Eternal Father, and in His son Jesus Christ, and in the Holy Ghost."

"Thanks, honey," she said warmly. "That's what we believe about Jesus Christ. Even a nine-year old knows what we believe. And, I have a deep and personal love for my Savior. I owe him everything! It is my fondest desire to live with him again someday."

"Do you believe he died for your sins?"

"The ones I repent of, absolutely." she replied.

"Well, I do know Mormons try to keep the commandments; their commitment is almost legendary," he said with a tone Melody interpreted as approaching reverence. He fell silent, thinking.

"What about the Bible? Haven't you replaced it with the Mormon gold bible?" he asked suddenly.

"There's no such thing as the Mormon gold bible," his mother replied cheerfully. "We read and love the Bible, both Old and New Testaments. We also have the Book of Mormon."

"That's what most people call the gold bible," he informed her. "You believe it over the Bible, don't you?"

"No," she said. "We believe them equally. The Book of Mormon has clearer teachings in some subjects, and the Bible in others. The two harmonize with one another, and both testify of Christ. They are both deeply important to my faith. The Book of Mormon is also called 'Another Testament of Jesus Christ.'"

"I didn't know that," Theo admitted. "So, you consider yourself a Christian," he said a little stiffly.

"Even more importantly, Christ considers me a Christian. I joined the Mormon faith because I felt it brought me closer to Christ. I did it knowing full well that I would meet severe opposition from my husband, your father. I never expected that it would make me lose my boys…"

Theo thought about this. "Had you known it would do that, would you still have joined the Mormon church?"

She paused for a full minute before answering slowly. "It would have been much harder, but I think I still would have. I knew it was true, and I trusted Christ to make everything else work out right if I did His will and was baptized. In a way, I really had no choice. It was simply what I had to do."

"That's more faith than I would have," Theo said, a note of wonder in his voice. Then, his voice grew accusatory. "I find it hard to accept that any mother who loved her children could leave them, for any reason, even for God."

"I agree with you, Theo," she said gently, her voice rich with love. "I couldn't have left you boys for anything."

"But, you said…"

"Perhaps you don't perceive faith the same way I do. I believe if God asked me to leave my children, or anything else for that matter, both I and my babies would be better off for it. It is only this great hope, this faith that I have, that allows me to believe that good will comes of every act of obedience, without exception. Without that inner peace, I could never have joined the Church—not in a million years."

"You are certainly right about the fact that I don't perceive faith at all like you do," Theo conceded. "As a matter of fact, I am slowly coming to the conclusion that I don't understand it at all. I have spent countless hours sitting before the most learned men of theology, and heard every conceivable description of faith the human mind can conjure. I must draw the somewhat disheartening conclusion that not one of them ever described faith in this way. When you talk of your faith my heart burns, and my soul listens. When they spoke of faith, my mind burned, and my fingers took notes."

Melody laughed at his unexpected humor. "Don't be too hard on yourself, son."

"I know I'm keeping you up, but I may watch you get onto a plane tomorrow and depart out of my life forever.," he said softly. "Would you mind terribly explaining to me how you came to possess this great faith?" he asked.

"I would be thrilled to explain it to you. It all began in 1820 in upstate New York. A young man by the name of Joseph Smith had questions quite similar to your own…"

Dim morning light was coming through the small window of their hotel room before they fell asleep in a room filled with the Holy Spirit, and enormous amounts of love. The last words she heard her son say were, "I promise you this, before I die, I will have this great joy of which you speak, even if I have to become a Mormon to get it."

Her last words were, "Before I die, I want to be sealed to you in the holy temple." A few hours earlier this would have elicited from him a snort of disdain. Now it brought a feeling of warmth which seemed to wash over him from head to toe.

A few hours later they sleepily awoke to a gentle but insistent knocking at their door. Theo awoke first, and opened it part way. It was an older gentleman whose name he did not know, but who seemed to have a familiar face.

"I have something for your mother," the kindly old man insisted. Theo relented, and opened the door. By this time Melody was awake.

"I'm sorry to awaken you so early, but I felt impressed to bring you something," he said, holding out an old violin case. Melody gasped as she took it from him, and snapped it open.

"My old violin!" she cried. She turned to her sons. "I brought this with me from Rhodesia to England, and then took it with me to America, but it mysteriously disappeared during our move to Utah. How in the world did it ever get back in England?"

Helaman shrugged. "I can only tell you that it came into my possession a while back. Can you imagine my pleasure when I found your name written on the underneath side. Why, I felt compelled to acquire it, and bring it to you. Imagine after all these years, what miraculous circumstances must have transpired to bring it back into your possession," he said amiably.

Melody hardly heard his explanation before she was tuning the violin. She blew the dust from the strings, paused, and brought down the bow in a long, sustained note whose tonal quality seemed like liquid joy. She closed her eyes, and with a sudden motion the bow danced across the strings in a fiery Bach quartet. She played for nearly five minutes before lowering the beloved old violin. She stroked it as it lay in her lap.

"Ah, it seems like only yesterday when I first saw you playing that very violin in the park," Helaman said wistfully.

"It was a long time ago," Melody said. "As a matter of fact, I first met your father in that park, Theo."

"He told me the story," Theo said happily. "Both George and I used to go to the park and sit in the bowery where you used to play. We went there when we were upset. It helped us to know you were there once." His eyes lit up. "Mother—do you suppose!?"

"The park!" Melody cried.

"George," Theo said suddenly. They grabbed their jackets and ran for the door.

When they arrived it was still early, and few people were in the park. The bowery was just as Melody remembered it, though it had seemed somewhat larger in her memory. George was not to be found.

"Please, my dear," Helaman urged. "Play for me as you did once before. Perhaps George will hear, and it will call to him. Play, my dear. Play with all the love you possess."

Melody removed the violin from its case, and stood just inside the bowery. The music wafted sweetly across the park, and like the rising of the sun, brought sweetness and warmth to all who heard it. She sent her love in those notes, wrapped in eloquent ribbons of harmony which pierced the darkness lurking in the dirty corners of the streets, and into the ears of their ragged inhabitants.

Theo and Melody saw him at exactly the same moment. George walked slowly toward the bowery, drawn as if by a magnet to the delicate lace-like beauty of her music. He found a spot on the first bench, and sat in rapt silence. His hair was tangled, his face smudged with dirt, and his clothing rumpled. Yet, his face was pristine with sweetness as he listened to her. He did not see his brother, and certainly could not have recognized his mother. He had only come because his soul hungered for beauty, and here it was freely given, and hungrily consumed.

She played on for nearly a half-hour, her heart content that he was here, and that he had found beauty in her. She remembered Theo's comments that George harbored great ill will for her. So, before he knew who she was, it thrilled her that he thought of her, at least in terms of her music, as someone of inner beauty.

As was her habit of many years, she closed her concert with a medley of beloved church hymns, the last being "Come, Come Ye Saints." As soon as she started, George sat bolt upright, and stared at her with great wonder. As soon as she lowered her bow, while people were still clapping, he raced to the steps of the bowery, then climbed them deliberately until he stood immediately before her. She struggled to keep a cascade of emotions from her face. She could hardly believe he was actually standing there, completely unaware of who she was.

"Your music," he said, his voice grave, "touched my soul."

"Thank you. May I ask your name?" she said, not quite sure what else to say.

"George Tennison, Ma'am," he said politely, and bowed slightly.

"A pleasure to meet you, George. My name is Melody," she said quietly, and began putting away her violin.

He seemed to ponder this in deep silence as others came up to compliment her on her music, and to offer her coins. She accepted them graciously, so as to not damage the impression she had begun. When she turned back toward him, his eyes were intently upon her.

"My mother's name was Melody as well," he said with heaviness of heart. "She also played the violin in this park. People say she was very good, and very beautiful as well. I can't imagine anyone playing as beautifully as you though..." his voice grew almost inaudible as he spoke.

"You sound as if your memories of your mother are sad for you," she said, and immediately wished she could take her words back.

"Sad?" he asked. "I don't think sad is the right word. Bitter, perhaps? A little angry, possibly a lot angry. But, I didn't intend to burden you with my memories. I just wanted to thank you for the music. I don't have any coins to give you. I'm sorry," he said as he turned to go.

"Please wait," Melody said hastily. "Please tell me why you are angry with your mother. You see, I'm a mother too, and I'm sorry to say that I have a son who is angry with me too. I feel so tragic in my heart. Please tell me. Perhaps it will help us both."

He turned back toward her, a hard look in his eyes. "There's not much to tell. She left me suddenly when I was quite young. I was devastated by it. My father told me that she simply walked away because she was deceived by the Mormons. That's about it. She apparently loved the Mormons more than her own sons."

"That sounds terrible! Do you believe that?" she asked, struggling to keep from bursting into tears.

"I did for years. I'll admit that I went through periods of hating her. But not anymore."

"I'm glad to hear that," she admitted with obvious relief. He looked at her oddly.

"Why?" he wanted to know.

"I told you, I'm a mother too." He nodded. "What caused you to stop hating her?"

"Well, it's because my memories of her, though sketchy and incomplete, made me not want to believe she could ever walk away from me. I just didn't believe it."

She waited for him to continue. "So what did you do?" she finally asked.

"I found some Mormons, and I asked them to teach me about their religion."

"Why would you do that? Weren't you worried you would be deceived, just like she was?"

"No. My father's a minister, and I had heard so many things about how to resist Mormon lies that I knew I could handle any argument they had."

"Oh, well that's good. But why would you study with them?"

"I wanted to know what was so enticing about the Mormons beliefs that she would leave her own children. I wanted to discover if they were capable of enticing a young mother to leave her family. I'm not sure what I wanted to find. I think I was just looking for truth."

"What did you find?" she asked quietly.

"I found a group of people with great humility and faith. I found people who love the Lord, and who would never entice a young mother to leave her baby. But I also found further rejection, and I found deep, utter confusion."

"I can see why that would be confusing," Melody admitted.

"I went to talk to my father about it, and instead of speaking to me gently and reclaiming me, or convincing me of my error in loving words, with logic and scripture, he confronted me with violent anger. I was so utterly taken aback that I lashed back at him, and told him he was less of a Christian than the Mormon missionaries." Melody had to suppress a smile. She could well imagine how her former husband reacted to that.

"What did your father do?" she asked.

"He threw me out of the house," he said bitterly. "And, my rich great-uncle has seen to it that I can't find any work unless I return to my father and renounce what I think is true. I'm daily forced to decide between eating, and living a lie."

"I'm so sorry, George. How long have been living on the street since then?"

"Nearly six months now," he admitted. "But, I've completed my studies of the Mormons, and I think I'm going to be baptized." Then he gave her a wilted smile. "Does that make you think less of me?" he asked.

"Certainly not!" she replied forcefully.

He smiled wearily. "You're a Mormon, aren't you."

"I am. How did you know?"

"From your music. You know, I recognized one of the Mormon hymns you played! And also from the fact that you aren't against my wanting to join the Church."

Melody blushed at his detection. "So, are you going to try to find your mother?" she asked, and again wished she hadn't.

"No," he said with finality. It caused her heart to sink.

"Why not?" she asked, unable to keep despair from her voice.

"If she loved me, she would have come back years ago. My father was right about the fact that she did leave me. And for whatever reason she left, she hasn't even attempted to come back. My father..."

"Lied to you," a young man's voice said behind them. George spun around to see his older brother. George ran into his arms, and they slapped one another on the back with gusto.

"Big brother!" George cried. "I have missed you, Sport! How did you find me? Why did you come looking? I thought you and Papa had disowned me."

"Never!" Theo said. "We came looking because we finally heard the truth, that you were destitute. Melody and I had to find you before she left back to the States."

"You're with Melody? How odd. We were just..." Then he stopped amid sentence, his mind quickly piecing together the elements of their former conversation.

"But... I'm... are you...?" he stammered.

"I am, George," Melody said sweetly, quietly. "I *am* that Melody, your mother. I never wanted to leave you, and I've come to take you home," she said, and held her arms out to him.

George stood there staring at her with open mouth and blank eyes. For the longest time he merely stared as emotions drifted across his features: anger, fear, distrust, grief, and finally, love. During all this time she held open her arms until her shoulders ached. Finally he lowered his head, sobbed once and walked into her arms, lowering his head onto her shoulder. He stood there and sobbed like a little child. She wept silent tears of sadness, and tremendous relief, all the while stroking the back of his head and humming a tune that leapt happily into her heart. It was the tune she used to hum when she rocked him to sleep so many years ago.

It was Helaman who interrupted their reunion. "I'm sorry to intrude," he said. "But your plane leaves in but a few hours. I'm afraid you need to get packing."

"You're leaving? But you just got here. You can't leave now!" George cried, his eyes brimming with tears.

"I have to leave. I must. There's a war on, and I may not be able to get out later. My husband's at home waiting for me."

George lowered his head as if someone had shot him through the heart, and his body had yet to fall to the ground. "I understand," he said, and turned away to walk back into the park.

"No you don't!" Melody cried, and grabbed his elbow. "I'm leaving, but not without you. You're coming with me!"

"But, I can't leave. I don't have tickets. I don't have a passport. I'm certainly going to be drafted into the military. And, I'm not sure I want to go with you anyway. England is my home, and she needs me now that there's a war."

"I can't make you come, of course. But you must understand that I came back to get you. I couldn't come all these years for fear that your father would take away your brother. Now I..."

"Our brother?" George asked.

"Yeah," Theo said. "Come here Sam, old chum. Come meet your other big brother George. Well, your half-brother," he said as Sammy came forward and shook George's hand. George was so stunned to find out he had a little brother that he could scarcely shake hands. Sammy was in heaven. Two big brothers!

Melody motioned to Helaman, and he immediately took the boy's hand and said, "Come on, buddy, let's go throw some coins in that fountain. I think your Mum needs some time with your big brothers."

When they were beyond hearing distance Melody turned to her sons. "You're only half right," she said.

"About what, Mum?" Theo asked.

"He's not your half-brother."

"So, he's really not our brother now?"

"No. You're going the wrong way. He's your full brother. You all have the same father, as well as the same mother."

"What!" Theo cried, and looked from Melody to George, and back again. "He's our father's son! If Dad finds out about this he'll go friggin' bonkers. He'll have the army attack you instead of the Russians!"

"I know," she said. "That's why I never came back all these years. I knew if he ever found out Sammy was his son, he'd never rest until he had him, too. He'd have taken him away to spite me, even though he didn't know or love Sammy. With his uncle's help, he has enough money to do it, even from England. I couldn't stand the thought of losing my youngest son. He was all I had to remind me of you two."

George turned toward Melody with sudden determination. "Mother," he said, his voice catching on his own words. Melody began to cry again, and held open her arms to him. George rushed into them with a strangled sob. His voice was muffled against her shoulder. "Mother, I understand, and I'm so sorry. I don't know what happened all those years ago, but I know you did what you had to do." He stopped suddenly and took her hand. "Mother, I want to come to America with you. Please, can't we work it out? Are you coming Theo?"

Theo spoke slowly. "I must be bonkers myself, but I think I do want to come. I want to go to America, and maybe even become a Mormon, I think. That'll fry Father's tongue in acid," he said in bitter humor. "But, I'm under the same constraints you are. I doubt we can leave."

Helaman and Sammy were just walking up to them, a big smile on Sammy's face as he reached out his hand for Theo. Melody turned to her friend. "Is there any way you can help me get these boys to America? They want to come. Oh, I know it's asking an awful lot, and you have no great compelling reason to come to our aid, but if you are able, I beseech you for help. I'll pay you back anything it costs, and more."

"My dear Melody, I have every reason to help. I promised your husband I would stay near you until you no longer needed me. That is as compelling a reason as any on earth. I'll see what I can do. I'll meet you at your hotel room in an hour. I suggest you boys do not return home to pack. If you say anything to your father it will greatly reduce your odds of leaving the country. Your only hope is to apply for exit visas on the strength that your mother is an American citizen. I believe they will let you out on that alone. Let me work on the passports and tickets. In one hour then!" he said, and marched away toward his home.

It was more of a miracle than either Melody or her naïve sons could have known that Helaman produced two additional serviceable passports and tickets. He handed them to her and urged her to flee to the airport. They arrived just forty-five minutes before departure, every second of which was spent in passing the heightened security now everywhere imposed. They barely succeeded in getting her two English-born sons on the plane, and only their American parentage and the fact that their tickets seemed to have been purchased prior to the outbreak of the war, finally secured their passage. In fact, had the harried officials thought to look up the new customs laws but hours old, they would not have let them leave at all. As it was, they passed through on the barest of margins, which margin was nothing less than divine intervention on their behalf. Helaman remained by their side, calm, determined and unflappable.

They boarded the plane mere moments before it taxied away. They were still shoving bags under their seats and tightening belts as the big jet roared into the sky. Their departure was so hasty that the stewardess had already given the safety briefing and instructed them to buckle their seat belts. The plane pointed at the sky, and pushed home the throttles.

THE WAR OF WARS

Scarcely a week had passed. Each day the caravan of refugees traveled another thirty miles or so on muddy, rutted farm roads. Every dozen miles another vehicle either ran out of fuel, or broke down. Those vehicles still operating were loaded beyond capacity, and sure to not survive such rough service for long. Alexei sent word that all the camp should gather together prior to supper. He looked over his small group with sad eyes as they gathered before him. Their heads were wrapped in rag scarves, their coats patched and worn, their faces gaunt with fear and hunger.

"My dear people," he called to them loudly, his voice filled with confidence that even Samuel had not anticipated. Again Vladimir translated for him, although Samuel assured him that he was slowly learning the language. "We have made a goodly trek today, and I wanted to speak with you before you retire.

"We are still in danger of being discovered by the military. Our vehicles will not last much longer the way we are using them, and we have no more fuel. Tomorrow we will select four of the best trucks. Onto these we will load our food and those who cannot walk. We will drain the fuel from all other vehicles and abandon them here. The trucks will go in their slowest gears, and take every precaution to use the smallest amount of fuel possible. All of us will walk beginning tomorrow. We will continue in this manner until God opens before us a new way."

The murmur that arose from the people was more of disappointment than disagreement. Samuel surveyed their faces and saw less fear than resolve in a sturdy people who had grown tired from a hundred years of soviet oppression—not from this sudden exodus.

Alexei continued, his voice resonating sharply in the harsh cold. "I feel compelled to caution you to strict obedience to our beliefs. Whatever people we encounter along the way, and whatever villages we enter, we will not steal their food or fuel. If we have more, we will share with them. If they have extra, we will trade for it, but we will not steal. Anyone caught breaking this commandment will be exiled from our group, and will not reach Zion. Remember your prayers. Our people will make it to Zion, of this I am sure."

His voice grew silent, and not a soul made a sound. He looked at the ground as he continued. "You all know the prophecies. Many of us will

not survive the journey." He looked up, his eyes sober. "So, let us be humble and prayerful. We are on God's errand, a journey we have anticipated
with longing all of our lives. Now, go eat your meals and sleep safely. God
bless you," he said and stepped down from the log on which he had been
standing.

The people turned away slowly, talking quietly among themselves.
Samuel did not detect murmuring or dissent, but he also detected very little hope. Their faith was largely centered in long-held dreams, rather than
the workings of the Spirit, and consequently it brought them no peace.

They possessed few tents, and what shelter they had was scarce.
Accordingly, Sam gave up sleeping in the Honda to allow some children
the luxury of sleeping out of the wind. It had always been the case among
these people that they slept in unheated, or at best, poorly heated homes.
As a result they traditionally slept together: husband with wife, brother
with brother, sister with sister, friend with friend. Those who had no one
either slept cold, or were assigned someone to be their bedfellow. This was
known to Samuel, and was of some concern to him. He could not think
of a situation where he could be comfortable sleeping with anyone. And
besides, he actually did not need to—even if they did not know why.

Alexei, however was of another opinion, and not willing to let one sent
from God to lead his people suffer while he had anything to say about
it. As a result, the first night Sam slept outside the Honda he and Alexei
had a spirited, though friendly argument in Samuel's broken Russian on
this very topic. Alexei concluded his part therein by turning around and
walking briskly away while growling, "We'll talk about this later."

Since sleep was not a necessity for Samuel, he stilled himself and
prayed. Except fleetingly while yet a mortal man, it was prayer unlike
anything he had experienced, and it caused his heart ascend nigh unto
heaven. It was far more than speaking humble words, it was communication of the highest order of spiritual attunement; it was a two-way
interview with Heavenly Father on a celestial scale, and something which
relaxed, warmed and healed, and gave him the courage to carry on.

His translated status notwithstanding, he was still Samuel, and what
courage and resolve he called upon came from within the reserves of his
soul. His was not a walk in the blinding light of perfect understanding.
His was not to know every answer, to solve every sorrow and concern
with piercing insight. His was often a walk in the shadows of faith. Except
for when Alexei asked, and pure knowledge flowed, he spent much time

seeking answers. These came during the nighttime hours when his soul soared upon the wings of sweetest prayer.

About the time Samuel could hear the Northern Lights crackling overhead in the far reaches of morning he finally fell asleep. The first sound he heard was a distant thrumming of the wind. Yet, far more disconcerting was the instantaneous cry of alarm that arose from the camp. Instantly awake, he slipped from the blanket and stood.

Having never heard the distinctive sound of a Soviet-armored ground-assault helicopter, he did not appreciate the sudden terror that swept across the hapless refugees. He watched with little understanding as they dived for cover beneath vehicles and whatever safety the rugged terrain offered.

When the first chopper arrived, its very appearance struck fear into his heart. It was larger than any craft he had seen in American skies, and was flying low and fast. For a moment it looked as if it might simply fly past them, but then it swung in a wide arc to come about. When it finally faced them it was fearsome. Its nose was studded with guns, its stubby wings were heavy with a double row of rockets, their red tips plainly visible in the first light of morning.

Alexei and several others ran up to Samuel. "We have been discovered! They believe we are traitors!" Alexei cried, while his people watching the helicopter in terror.

The craft hovered there until another identical chopper thundered over them and swung around to join its brother of death. They menacingly remained there for a full thirty seconds, which seemed an eternity. All around him people screamed and scattered. The question of what they intended to do ended abruptly with a burst of machine gun fire that roared in a prolonged explosion. Samuel could plainly see fire belching from rotating barrels on either side of the narrow ship. The bullets cut a path of death and destruction through the refugees, killing hundreds of innocents in mere seconds.

As if on cue, the remaining survivors bolted helter-skelter across the snowy landscape. At this point, a rocket belched flames and roared into a cluster of vehicles. Samuel watched his blue Honda leap into the sky as it came apart into a thousand fragments which spread further death. He knew for a fact that a little family with three small children had taken refuge there. It caused his heart to cry out in anguish and anger. He had never seen such violence, such wanton destruction. The helicopters were close enough that he could clearly see the bug-like helmet of the forward pilot. For a moment he forgot himself, and looked around for a weapon to fight back. There was none.

Samuel realized with a start that he was not alone. Both Vladimir and Alexei stood beside him as if rooted to that spot by his own refusal to flee. He turned toward them to urge them to seek cover.

"My people die like pack dogs," Alexei said with deep sadness. "Pray to God, Samuel," he said, his eyes filling with tears, "and ask him for our deliverance. Tell me, man of God, what shall we do to escape utter destruction?"

Samuel waited for Vladimir to translate. The answer came to him with startling clarity, yet it made no sense. Still, he shouted the message above the roar of incoming rockets. "Tell them to run toward the enemy!"

No sooner had he given these instructions than both Alexei and Vladimir bolted simultaneously toward their people. They began shouting in Russian. All who were not too frightened to hear, obeyed their words, and in less than one minute, all those who could run were surging forward. Those who did not obey, turned and ran away from what appeared to be a dash to certain death.

At that moment in the frenzy, Samuel looked down and saw Sarah, Alexei's little granddaughter who had befriended him. She had been critically shot and was crying weakly. In a single move he cradled her under one arm, and began to run. He caught another terrified young woman under his other arm, and literally lifted her off her feet as he ran. She looked down in amazement at her feet off the ground, touching the ground once for every three of his strides. Samuel was surprised at his speed, strength and endurance. This was his first experience with pressing his body to its limits, and he found to his amazement that those limits were well beyond his present urgency.

For a terrifying second the choppers seemed to not understand their utterly foolish response to their attack, and they hovered there without firing. The people were too close now to come under direct fire, and the choppers began backing up in a jerky, zigzag effort to stay ahead of the fleeing people. Several bursts of fire flew over their heads, killing those disobediently fleeing from the scene of death. This had the dramatic effect of flooding life into winded lungs and exhausted legs. The people flew forward on the wings of abject terror. The choppers continued to back up, trying to get a better shot.

Finally, the chopper on the left grew weary of trying to fly the big machine in a direction it was not well-designed to go, and banked hard to his left. At that exact moment, the other banked hard to its right. Their intent was to circle around the fleeing people and get behind them where they could complete their destruction. Mere seconds of life remained for the people, except for the strange fact that as the big ships swung ponderously around their tail rotors passed within one another's arc, and in a flash of sparks and tortured metal, they ground each other's tail rotors into flying slag.

Both machines spun out of control immediately. One chopper gunned his big jets to try to regain control. It vanished from sight, quickly rising into the sky in tight circles. The other machine quickly cut his engines and crashed to the ground with a solid thud that Samuel felt in his legs and feet. Oddly enough, the big machine sat there in a billow of dust and smoke, but it did not explode as all were expecting.

Still pointing toward them, it fired another burst of bullets that ripped a path through the survivors, killing more dozens of them. The people ran away from the path of the big guns. Dozens of men dashed toward the downed chopper, quickly covering the two-hundred yards separating them. Samuel watched them pounding on the windows with rocks and moments later, they were pulling the two pilots from their seats. The shooting stopped immediately. By the time Samuel arrived at the big chopper, the two pilots' bodies were already being dragged away.

Samuel felt his stomach turn as he surveyed this gruesome scene. He was saddened the two pilots had been killed; yet he also knew their deaths were justified. These two had killed hundreds of innocent men, women and children for reasons that were not fathomable to Samuel. Their death machine, which towered as high as a two-story building, was now still and foreboding.

Samuel released the frightened woman he had been carrying; she walked away in a daze. He kept wounded little Sarah cradled in his arms as he looked for Alexei or Vladimir. He could not see them. People were returning to their dead families, and wails of grief began to rise from the camp behind him. Still carrying Sarah, he trotted to the scene of carnage and felt a sickness in his soul that would have otherwise translated to an urge to retch, which was gladly not possible for him.

He soon located Vladimir, who was holding Alexei in his arms. A large red stain was spreading around a gaping hole in the old Russian's abdomen. From the ashen color on his face Samuel knew there were mere seconds of life left for him. Samuel had never been exposed to such carnage, and the incredible stench of death was so overwhelming that he fought the urge to run away. Even in his altered state, it was almost more than he could endure.

He carefully placed Sarah on the ground and knelt beside the old man,
who immediately took Samuel's hand. His hand was slick with blood as
he clasped Samuel's tightly. "My people," he rasped, his words thick with
pain.

"Many survived," Samuel told him in broken Russian, with as much
optimism as he could muster.

"They will scatter without me," Alexei said through clenched teeth.
"You must lead them on. You must take over for me," he said urgently.

"I cannot!" Samuel said. "It is forbidden."

The aged Russian narrowed his eyes at Samuel, and skipped all the
questions his statement must have generated in his old heart. What was
impossible was just that— impossible.

"Then heal me!" he cried, and coughed. The sudden movement caused
blood and stench to spurt from the gaping wound in his gut.

Samuel waited, unprepared for the old one's request. He was not waiting for faith, or courage, or anything like unto it. He was waiting for
permission to honor this request.

"Do you have the faith to be raised up?" Samuel asked.

"I know God sent you to us. If God wills it, I have the faith. Tell me
what is God's will, and I will rise up and lead this people to their home.
Speak the words of God, my brother, and I will…" His words died in his
throat as his spirit departed his body.

"No!!!" Vladimir cried in deep anguish. "Don't die! Not now! We need
you! Oh, God, God, why have you allowed our only hope to die. Oh
please…"

Samuel slowly straightened as Alexei's bloodied hand grew slack and
slipped to the ground. He turned to Vladimir, and felt the power of truth
flow into him. Vladimir looked into Samuel's eyes with deep anguish.
"Why did God let him die?" he demanded. "His faith was strong enough!
I felt it! I knew it! Why must he die?"

"It was not Alexei's faith that was the deciding factor," Samuel told
him quietly. "It was yours."

"What?" Vladimir demanded. "It was his life, not mine! Why would
God abandon him because of my lack of faith?" he asked with a quiv-
ering voice, tears freely flowing onto his friend's face over whom he yet
crouched.

Samuel spoke calmly. "It was God's will that you should lead this people with Alexei. Your faith was not ready to see him raised up. Tell me
something. Set aside your grief, and reason with me a moment,"

"I will try. I will try," he said between sobs.

"Consider with me that God cannot show something unto his children which gifts them with something He does not give to all other of His children. As one who lived under communism, perhaps you can understand that God gives equally to all of his children. He could not give to you the vision of Alexei rising from his wounds."

"But why? I do not understand this!"

"What would you have done had you watched the wound in his belly heal, and seen him restored to perfect health before your eyes? Would you have reordered your life, and sought God with greater diligence than ever before?"

"Yes!" he cried. "What is wrong with such a thing?"

"What is wrong is that to do this would change you and make you greater than you would otherwise be. This would give you an advantage that others of God's children have not received. This would not be just, and God can do nothing that is not flawlessly just. Can you see this?"

Vladimir looked away. "In a way I can. If this is true then I have killed him as surely as the bullet that passed through him."

"No! He isn't dead, he yet lives. Don't you understand that it is no more miraculous to close the wounds of a dying body, than to raise the same body from the dead? The reason for his death is irrelevant. The reasons he cannot come back are extremely important, and they all have to do with you!"

"What must I do?" he asked, his head lowered, his chest heaving in silent sobs.

Samuel spoke the words that filled his mouth, marveling as he said them. "Look at me!" Vladimir raised his head as if it weighed several tons. "This day, this moment in time must be the pivot point in your life. If you will set your whole soul in the service of God, and covenant with Him to walk unerringly in His path all the remainder of your life, just as you might have had you seen this great miracle, then seeing a great miracle will not change the outcome of your life. Do this, and there will be no difference in whether Alexei lives or dies. Can you do this?"

"I can." he said simply. "I have always known that one day I must. Now is the moment of my greatest need. Alexei is dead, and I must take his place. I will walk in his shoes, and in God's light." He placed a hand on his beloved friend's body. "Forgive me my Uncle, my brother, that my faith comes too late. Forgive me," he said. He stood slowly, took a deep breath and turned his face toward his people. Samuel watched him square his shoulders and arrive at a decision. He walked to the nearest grieving survivor and knelt beside a young father rocking back and forth with a

teenage girl in his arms. Samuel could hear faint words of comfort being
spoken at a distance.

"Samuel," a voice said nearby. He looked up to see Helaman standing
on the opposite side of Alexei's corpse.

"Helaman," Samuel said quietly. "Assist me, please."

"I am here to strengthen you. But, you must do this alone."

"It overwhelms me, Helaman," Samuel groaned. "I have never before
seen such carnage, such useless slaughter." Samuel looked up across the
bloodied remains of an already-fragile people. "My soul is grieved, and I
feel so inadequate. I am only one, and it is not enough," he cried quietly,
but urgently.

Helaman fixed his eyes upon him and urged him: "See, Samuel, open
your eyes, and see." Samuel bowed his head and prayed until power flowed
through him, he looked up and saw the snowy fields of carnage filled
with heavenly beings leaning over the grieving and dying. All around him
stood a dozen men and women, adorned in glorious white, their faces
serene and glowing with righteousness.

"I see them," Samuel said. One of them he recognized instantly, partly
because he was the only one not in billowing white garment. Though
many years younger in appearance, Alexei stood just beyond the ring of
angels. They were all there for a purpose, and as firmly as he had ever
known anything in his life, he suddenly knew what that purpose was.

Samuel picked up the bloodied hand he had just dropped and in a
quiet voice of authority said, "Alexei, In the name of Jesus Christ, and
by the power of his eternal Priesthood, and through his infinite grace, I
command you to return to your body. Arise. Arise and lead your people
to Zion."

Samuel plainly saw one of the heavenly beings step aside. Alexei hastily finished a conversation with a woman and turned his attention to
Samuel. He stepped past the others, and paused before his body. He
glanced at Samuel, then in the blink of an eye seemed to enter the lifeless corpse through the crown of the head. Samuel watched the wound
close. The body took a breath, and seconds later, he sat up. Alexei placed
a hand on his abdomen, and finding himself completely healed, looked
into Samuel's face.

"I know you now," he said quietly, a look of significance on his face.
"Thank you for being here. And, thank God," he said in a fervent whisper,
looking up into the sky. Samuel wondered if he could see the many angels
who stood rejoicing around them. If fact, he could not, but he clearly

remembered what had been for him a long and empowering visit to his heavenly home. His eyes sparkled with joy, peace and purpose.

"You will need a clean shirt," Samuel smiled matter-of-factly.

Alexei shook that off. "A shirt can come later. For now, my people need me."

Samuel watched as Alexei walked over to Vladimir and placed a hand on his shoulder. The younger man glanced up at his uncle, and for a long moment suppressed the urge to stand and cry out in joy. His heart was filled with exquisite gratitude and praise to God for this miracle of miracles, but here in this place he could not call attention to anything extraordinary; in front of the others, there could be nothing more than a nod. Vladimir glanced at Samuel in gratitude, then up again at his uncle, a look of new-found faith on his face.

Then Samuel turned his attention back to Sarah, who was lying on the ground near them. She was not breathing, and two large pools of blood had gathered near her lifeless body. Alexei felt for a pulse, and cried out. "My precious flower, my little Sarah! She is gone!"

Alexei looked up at Samuel, his face grim and streaked with tears, but calmly resolute. "I know my faith, that it is sufficient to ask you to heal my granddaughter. But, I do not know the will of God." Alexei said solemnly.

Samuel closed his eyes and poured out his heart to God. He knew if he asked with all his heart that God would heed his call, and the child would live. But, more than the life of this faithful child, he feared to ask amiss. His prayer was for understanding, for sanction to exercise the vast powers that had been granted to him. When the answer came it thrilled him.

Taking Sarah by the hand he said, "Daughter of Israel, in the name of Jesus Christ, I call you back. Your mission is not finished in mortality. Sarah, come back. Come back and be whole," he said with quiet authority. Sarah's eyes flickered open. She smiled at her grandfather, and then at Samuel, the color returning to her cheeks. She looked down at her wounds, and gasped as she watched the holes fill with smooth white flesh. It was a manifestation of the power of God she would never forget.

Alexei cried out "Hosanna!" and gathered his granddaughter into his arms. She embraced him for a long moment before he straightened.

"We must soon leave this place," Alexei said as he stood, tenderly releasing Sarah. He stretched his back, and with a sly grin said, "Too bad you didn't heal my old age, too." Then he grew serious. "I was overjoyed to be free of my body for a time, and coming back was startlingly painful.

But, my people need me, and I thank God for His mercy!" he said, and
walked stiffly away with Vladimir.

Samuel walked side-by-side with Sarah until she stopped beside the body of her mother. Words of tragic sorrow spilled untranslated from her young lips.

"I know, Sarah," he said. "I know it hurts, it really hurts," he whispered to her, hugging her tightly. As if she understood his every word, she listened, nodded, and understood.

Then Samuel saw the spirit of Sarah's mother. She was bending over her daughter, whispering words of comfort and instruction. "Your mother is happy now," he told her. "She is warm and safe, and has left me to take care of you."

Again Sarah nodded, and stood, her hand in his. They turned aside to comfort and bless others. He was never sure why, or how his words passed the barrier of language, but they did, and from that moment on, Sarah stayed by his side.

Samuel's eyes remained opened to the world of spirits for several hours afterward, as he walked among the dead and wounded, and healed everyone that the Spirit directed. As he assisted the survivors in their grief, he marveled at how many from the other side of the veil also labored in their own way to comfort those who suffered.

Of the four hundred wounded or dead, one-third were restored to perfect health. All the others passed on, their reward glorious and sure. Word quickly spread through the camp of the healings that had occurred, and a feeling of solemnity settled over them as they pondered this powerful example of God's deliverance.

But the most dramatic effect of this encounter occurred with Vladimir. The changes within him were powerful. A deep inner confidence previously unseen in him now seemed to illuminate his entire frame. He strode forth with confidence, and worked among the people with gentleness and compassion. Probably the most startling of all was that his faith was now absolute.

In much less time than Samuel would have dreamed possible, Alexei got his people loaded and ready to go. They carefully laid their dead inside the very machine that had brought them death. A fire was set, and they walked away slowly, their pathway brightly lit by the funeral pyre of their loved ones.

Having just arrived in Utah, Melody began the joyful task of finding room for her three sons. Their home was not large by American standards, merely three bedrooms and an unfinished basement, but to her older sons, it was a mansion at least five times the size of their childhood home.

Her greatest disappointment was in arriving home to find Samuel still gone. Her heart had danced with happiness all the way home from England, anticipating their joyful reunion. When he was not to be found, and with his phone in Russia still disconnected, she began calling his employer in Texas. After the third call she could no longer get past the switchboard operator. She knew something was terribly amiss. But the joy of having all her boys home comforted and soothed her.

One might assume a general state of economic chaos would swamp the nation, but such did not immediately occur. Slowly at first, then in increasingly greater steps, inflation began to influence the cost of everything from a can of beans, to homes. Though the inflation quietly eroded the value of the dollar, it was not nearly as dramatic as the increase in real property values. People who at one time owned a one hundred-thousand dollar home, now owned a two hundred-thousand dollar home. People who were making seven dollars an hour were now making seventeen.

Contrary to inflationary trends of the past, interest rates remained relatively low. Businesses flourished, were built upon and expanded. Personal wealth appeared to expand as everyone seemed to have money to spend. No one really minded that they were paying more, because they had more. Work was plentiful, and easy to find. War related industry was everywhere. People were offered half a year's salary up front just to come to work. It was not uncommon for skilled craftsmen and blue-collar workers to change jobs every six months due to offers they felt they could not refuse.

A spirit of speculation gripped the entire nation, as well as the Saints across America. People with any type of nest egg, and even a little foresight, parlayed their holdings into considerable sums of money. The Prophet warned the Saints to avoid the temptation to enter into speculation, to borrow or expand their businesses by borrowing. He urged the people of God to get out of debt, prepare spiritually, and store food. Yet with few exceptions, like the click-clack of a train rumbling by, his words became background noise to the happy chatter of a people fully engaged in mammon.

Almost with a united shrug of indifference, the world ignored his counsel. Few within the Church understood why they should not ride the gravy train to financial safety. The minority who heeded the Prophet's counsel were slowly left behind economically. They became an underclass who were seen as stupidly choosing poverty in a time of prosperity.

Class distinction and division seemed to take a thundering step inside the Church.

The news hit the world like a nuclear explosion, and it had nothing to do with the war. The U.N. passed a resolution not unlike the US Freedom of Information Act, but much more forceful. The law was drafted and supported by certain parties in the US as critical "progress" to allow the world to benefit from private stores of knowledge held by religions, governments and private persons alike. No longer would modern, historical or technological secrets be withheld from public scrutiny. It seemed like a noble idea at the time, and the loss of privacy and freedom loomed small against the mass of knowledge and truth potentially gained.

Without even breaking stride, with the new international law passed, the U.N. targeted religions first and descended upon the vast libraries sequestered in the Vatican at Rome and even those maintained by the Church in Salt Lake City. There was an outcry from everyone from the Pope to the President of the United States; yet it seemed that although it violated our sovereignty and our constitution, it was justified in the name of freedom of information and social progress and little harm was actually done. Soon the matter was if not forgotten, at least dramatically minimized in the media and the minds of the people.

However, the actual effect of this seemingly minor storm brought high-water floods of confusion, and eventually proved devastating to almost every living Christian on earth.

Not many weeks after the U.N. researchers forced their way at gunpoint into the LDS Church libraries, they began publishing documents long considered too sacred to share. Aside from members and critics of the Church, few people took notice. Of far greater interest were the Vatican archives. The U.N. began publishing discovered documents, and their translations, that had apparently not seen daylight in thousands of years—if ever. What emerged was a scandal that built in crescendo until the resultant clamor was heard around the Christian world, which actually drowned out the noise of war.

The researchers published what appeared to be conclusive, irrefutable, undeniable, and incontrovertible evidence of a vast Christian conspiracy. Thousands of documents from around the time of Christ spilled across the world proving—not just accusing, but *proving*—that early Christian authorities did not believe Christ was divine. Beyond this, the ancient conspirators privately spoke among themselves that Jesus, the man, the lowly prophet of Galilee, never himself claimed to be anything more than a man whose gentle soul and unique perspective on human relations were peace-giving and uplifting.

Found among the archives were the original, hand-written accounts by Matthew, Mark, Luke and John, Joseph the father of Jesus, James the brother of Jesus, and many others. Without exception these documents painted a much less-positive picture of Jesus than the biblical versions of their stories. They spoke of Mary and Joseph's plan to cover up the un-planned pregnancy that resulted in Jesus's birth. They pressed their clever deception to great success because of the fervor and heightened desire for a Messiah of the day.

To their complete surprise, their little son believed them, bought into the ruse, and lived the life of the "Son of God" as authentically he could. All the gospel writers spoke glowingly of Jesus the man, and darkly of their own dismay at finding him to be little more than the farcical outcome of a lie. He was actually insane, they said, and believed himself to be the byproduct of a virgin birth; and though he was hardly divine, they deemed him a prophet nonetheless. After Jesus died, those seeking power over the growing Christian movement greatly embellished the stories removing any flaws and inserting so-called mighty miracles and worked to ensure the original documents were never found. Acclaimed academic researchers authenticated the documents and verified they were from antiquity. Renowned psychologists confirmed Jesus suffered from acute schizophrenia with many documented episodes of delusions of grandeur.

Many letters of Paul, the supposed Apostle, were widely published. It became apparent that Paul wrote two sets of letters, one to his proselytes to Christianity, and another set to his Jewish puppet masters in Jerusalem. Paul, it turns out, was a plant, a spy of sorts, whose mission was to spur the early Christians to such fervor that they would incur the wrath of Rome, so that eventually Rome would annihilate them as they did all their enemies. Paul's final letter to his handlers in Jerusalem was a bitter cry for rescue. Paul, it seems, had played his part too well, and was about to join his victims in their destruction. His friends at Jerusalem decided the net "effect" of Paul's efforts would be enhanced by his own martyrdom, and asked their contacts in Rome to ignore any "information" they might have received earlier that Paul was innocent. Thus, Paul was abandoned by his Jewish friends and killed along with the other early Christians.

But, perhaps more damning than any of these was an official report written by the hand of Pontius Pilate himself, relating not one, but four interviews with Jesus of Nazareth. The first three were almost word-for-word transcripts of Pilate's conversations with Jesus, whose worldly views Pilate considered to be partly, if not wholly insane. The only reason Pilate washed his hands and pronounced him innocent at their final, much publicized trial, was because Pilate considered the man beyond rational thought, and innocent by reason of insanity.

The broad effect of this drama was one of nearly decapitating Christianity. In less than a year, entire sects of Christianity folded and evaporated. Christian megachurches emptied across the U.S.. All remaining Christian groups were dramatically marginalized and even considered dangerous. Traditional Christian schools of thought and philosophy were at first suspect, then publicly decried, then abandoned en masse, and in time—outlawed. Persecution against Christians became so severe that it became dangerous to say anything in favor of it. Violent beatings were common in the cities and churches were constantly vandalized and the target of arsonists. Secularism and atheism swept the nation as scientific enlightenment finally seemed to triumph over the deluded and dangerous so-called yoke of religion, for which atrocities have been committed against mankind for millennia.

Among the members of the Church of Jesus Christ of Latter-day Saints, a full one-half simply threw up their hands in despair and ceased to consider themselves either members or Christians. Among the other churches that actually survived, the toll reached as high as seventy-five percent.

During all this dissemination of such damning information, the Prophet and Quorum of the Twelve repeatedly urged their faithful to ignore the growing tide of negative information. Before long they openly claimed the information false, fabricated, and Satanic in origin. They labored day and night, visiting the Saints, praying with them, reasoning, quoting scripture that prophesied this very thing, all with little effect. Those without a personal relationship with Christ and acquainted with His voice were simply unable to stand against the unrelenting avalanche of scientific proof, persecution and unrelenting opposition.

Before long many wards simply dried up and blew away. Every stake lost large blocks of their members, and many lost their entire leadership. Some stakes collapsed. Of those remaining, those who chose to pay a full tithing fell to fewer than one in a hundred. Temples closed from lack of volunteer staff and patrons and lack of funds. Several stakes filed claims of ownership of their church buildings and won in civil court. Seventeen temples in the U.S. and most temples overseas were likewise lost into private ownership. In a year's time the Church membership lurched to a stop, reversed itself, and almost faltered entirely. From a worldwide membership of twenty-plus million, fewer than two million would publicly count themselves LDS. The Church finally lost its tax-exempt status, and within a short time, financial ruin gripped the Church in an iron vice.

At this very moment in time, those few who had faithfully remained true to the Prophet's warnings grew deeper in their convictions. Buffeted from every side, they sought greater blessings, and an outpouring of faith overlaid their sorrows. Priesthood power increased. Miracles became commonplace, and it was widely known that angels walked and talked with many.

In a short time the flood of miracles met head-to-head with the calamitous flood of lies and persecutions, a spiritual detonation occurred.

It had been nearly a year following their return to Utah. Melody had found herself unexpectedly in the front lines of a civil war— not a war of bullets and bombs, but a war of faith and ideology. When she perceived the perils around her, Melody quietly aligned herself with the Prophet. To her joy, so did her three sons.

Sacrament meeting was nearly empty, with fewer than one hundred people in attendance. Bishop Snow was newly called, a young man of great faith, though still in his twenties. He had no counselors to assist him.

"Brothers and sisters," he began following the opening song and prayer. "I apologize that we don't have a sacrament meeting program today. Brother and Sister Prevost informed me last evening that not only would they not be speaking, they would not be returning to church."

A murmur of sadness rolled across those assembled. Melody fought back tears, as she sensed Theodore shaking his head in disbelief. George had been baptized almost as soon as they had returned from England, while Theo had decided to wait.

At that moment the doors in the back of the chapel opened and an older man and woman, and their teenage son entered the room. Seeing Bishop Snow's eyes flicker up, all in the chapel turned toward them. Melody recognized them as Brother and Sister Huntington and his son. They had lost their home months ago, and had moved from the area. It was good to see them again.

"Forgive us," the man said quietly. "We ran out of gas and had to walk the last couple miles."

Bishop Snow smiled. "Brother and Sister Huntington! Come up here," he said happily. "Come up here and address us. Would you be so kind?" he asked with obvious relief, and then took his seat.

Brother Huntington straightened, but did not register surprise. He 319
simply led his little family to the stand, and then himself to the podium.

As his family took a seat, Brother Huntington slipped off his battered coat and laid it across the seat behind him, then turned to the podium. Brother Huntington was all of seventy years old. He had a full head of white hair, and an equally white beard several inches long. His clothing was tattered, but his face was bright with faith. Melody could not remember him having served in any visible capacity in the ward or stake. It seemed as if the Huntington family had merely lived a quiet life somewhere on the outskirts of LDS society.

Their aged speaker steadied himself with both hands upon the pulpit, yet remained silent for almost a minute. When he finally spoke his voice was quiet, yet strong. "I left for church with you this morning feeling a deep urgency to worship with you today. We knew we didn't have enough fuel to arrive here, and merely trusted in God to get us here. By the way, I had no idea I would be speaking," he said with a smile, "or I might not have been in such a rush to get here."

This elicited some laughter from the audience.

Brother Huntington ran his fingers through his perfectly white hair, then smiled, seemingly at a loss as to what to say. His eyes fell upon a young woman in a wheelchair three rows back. He seemed to gaze at her for a long time. The young lady was fourteen, and had spent her entire life as an invalid. She had long, light brown hair that her mother had carefully combed and braided. Hair clips shaped like butterflies held her hair out of her face. Though her body was wasted and withered, her face was astonishingly beautiful. Melody realized everyone present had turned to look at the young woman.

"I think I'm going to speak about miracles," Brother Huntington said, and promptly walked from the stand until he stood before the young girl.

He knelt before her and took both her hands in his. He turned to her mother. "What is her name?" he asked, his voice trembling.

"Her name is Vicky Ann," her mother replied.

"How long has she been like this?" he asked, looking back into the child's eyes.

"All her life," came the quiet reply.

Brother Huntington stood, still holding the youngster's deformed hands. His voice was soft and utterly calm. "Vicky Ann, in the name of Jesus Christ I command you to arise," he said, and gently lifted her hands.

Vicky's head lolled back, her mouth open and wet with saliva. The sounds of the congregation's polite concern were unheard by Brother

Huntington, who merely stepped back still holding her hands. The chair rolled forward. Someone coughed poignantly.

"Come on, Vicky," Brother Huntington said with a kindly nod. "Hold her chair," he said to the mother, who quickly set the brake. Whispers of disbelief arose all around them.

"This is ridiculous," someone said and was greeted by a murmur of agreement. A dozen people stood and with flailing arms and stomping feet, left the chapel.

To everyone's surprise, Brother Huntington smiled broadly. He looked down at Vicky. "OK, the faithless ones have left, and you can do it." With a sound something between a growl and a laugh, Vicky stood, looking down at her feet. A look of joy lit her face. She looked up and rushed into Brother Huntington's arms.

"Well done!" Brother Huntington cried. "I knew you had the faith! We just had to wait for a few doubters to leave." He turned her toward her mother who was gasping in utter amazement.

Brother Huntington looked around and saw a large woman nearby who was stooped with age, sitting next to a portable oxygen bottle. "Sister Abigail Foster, aren't you about tired of lugging that bottle around with you?" he said forcefully.

"I surely am!" she said, and stood painfully, her back deeply bowed.

Brother Huntington raised an arm to the square and placed the other on her shoulder. "Sister Abigail Foster, in the name of Jesus Christ, I command you to be healed," he commanded in a voice Melody could only describe as utter joy. He stepped forward and slipped the mask from her face, then taking her hands, quietly said. "You have to do your part, Abigail. Stand up straight. Just do it," he instructed. Melody was close enough to see a look of determination on Sister Foster's face give way to a look of faith. Sister Foster straightened to her full height. Melody was startled to see her clothing collapsing around her.

"Praise God," Brother Huntington cried, his voice cracking with emotion. "I'm sure the Relief Society sisters will help you tailor your wardrobe," he said with a joyful laugh.

Sister Foster gasped, and turned toward the audience. Her face was devoid of the ravages of weight and disease. Some began to weep openly.

Brother Huntington returned to the pulpit where he stood for a long moment in complete silence. He gazed out across the faithful whose faces were now streaked with tears of joy. He nodded once, then spoke. "All done through the grace, power, and merits of Him who is mighty to save. In the name of Jesus Christ, Amen." Then he sat down beside his wife.

The battlefield whereon human lives were being lost paused to catch its breath, and the world waited to see what Russia would do next. Some years earlier the so-called "struggling democracy" in Russia had ceased to exist, if it had ever really existed anywhere but in U.S. newspapers. All the foreign missionaries were expelled. Every church, temple and other Church-owned property, LDS and otherwise, was absorbed by the state, and religious meetings were strictly outlawed. As the fear of war in Europe grew, air travel became severely overbooked and ticket prices skyrocketed.

In the threat of imminent war, other countries ordered the missionaries to leave. The first missions affected were the former Eastern Bloc nations, then France, Italy, Germany and Spain. The missionary force fell from a high of nearly 100,000 to less than half that number overnight. The Church could no longer bring so many missionaries home with limited airtravel and now-astronomical plane fares. When families in the U.S. could not finance their return, young men and women had to take jobs and earn their own way home, many on ships.

Completely against the odds, with miracles attending, all the missionaries eventually made it home. None were lost. Many were blessed by the charity of beleaguered local members in their missions. Most worked as much as a full year for their ticket home, daring to share their testimonies to those who would listen. As they arrived home, they knew there was no likelihood of ever completing their formal missions, but every likelihood of being sucked headfirst into a world-wide war.

What was strange about all this was that these returning missionaries came home with fire in their souls impassioned by the Spirit of God. Their sense of loss in their missionary assignments was turned to rekindling the waning faith of their families and wards. It was, in fact, the thousands of miracles Heavenly Father had wrought to bring His sons and daughters home that kept the remaining saints' eyes opened to belief. Had the Church been able to simply bundle them all onto aircraft and bring them home, these faith-anchoring miracles could not have occurred.

What appeared to be a tragedy was in fact theirs and the Church's salvation. Nobody could explain away the awful riptide of so-called proof against Christianity. Neither could they explain away the powerful deliverance they had beheld in their miraculous return home. As much as any miracle wrought by the hand of God, this tidal wave of faithful missionaries returning home saved not just the Church, but its floundering population from impending spiritual extinction.

The stage for world war set, Russia relentlessly advanced their vast armies and weaponry into Eastern Europe, while China had its eye fixed on South Asia and ultimately the United States. As NATO allies cried for help, and under threat of worldwide domination, the U.S. was finally forced to enter the war. They began an involuntary draft, instituted liberal rationing, and began enforcing laws against hoarding food. Stock markets including the Dow Jones Industrial Average were rocked amid rumors and global speculation and fell nearly four thousand points in a single day. Long-abused entitlement programs and even some food stamp programs were discontinued as riots erupted around the country, with many larger cities forced to enact martial law. The Church "suggested" all members bring their food storage beyond three months necessities to their local Stake Centers, where it would be stored and redistributed to the needy. The government immediately insisted the Church turn over all collected food. The Church refused.

Melody found herself in greater difficulty as each day passed. At first her two older sons were able to avoid going into the military simply because they were not U.S. citizens. She watched as thousands of young men and women were conscripted into the army, or went underground to escape. A general conscription order was issued for all able-bodied persons ages sixteen through forty-five. No longer was gender or citizenship an issue. The penalty for avoiding the draft was death. Eventually, the penalty was enforced on the front lawn of the offender's home. As soon as this became general practice, the mood darkened further and ranks of the armed forces swelled with reluctant conscripts.

Never before had so many nations combined for so great a unified cause, or so great a threat. World opinion soared in favor of the war, and national pride became the religion of the day. The old ethnic dividing lines flared in hatred. Food distribution centers were set up in former grocery stores, and armed troops checked ration stubs.

In a last-ditch attempt to avoid defaulting on its staggering national debt interest payments, the U.S. devalued the dollar beyond the breaking-point and runaway inflation ensued. The bond market imploded as the nation's national credit plummeted. Soon money became worthless, and unemployment was rampant. Huge companies folded overnight, or switched their production to wartime needs. Everything became scarce. Millions of families lost their homes when payments could not be made. The black market roared to life, and food became of far greater value than money. Barter became commonplace as people avoided the distribution centers except for items available nowhere else.

Laws were enacted to stem unemployment and put every citizen to work. Factories bustled with labor paid largely in food and housing rations. To ensure that food was distributed only to those employed in the factories or other "authorized" jobs, a small microchip was implanted under the skin of the right hand or just above the hairline on the forehead. Nearly overnight it became nearly impossible to obtain food unless one had the chip implanted. For a short time, a government-issued credit-card type ID card was allowed instead, but most chose the implants simply out of fear or sheer convenience.

The Church issued a general announcement urging their members not to get the chip implants. They said nothing about carrying the ID card. A full two-thirds of the members ignored their leaders' warnings and got the chip. Those with faith understood its significance and considered it the mark of the beast.

To heavily entice conformity, a law was passed erasing all mortgage debt for those who accepted the implants and worked in war preparations. Black-marketers were hunted down and imprisoned until the underground barely existed.

Soon after however, receiving the chip became absolutely mandatory. Even worse, membership or allegiance to any organization not approved by the government had to be denounced in order to get the chip and receive food and housing.

It became easier and easier to tell the "Good Mormons" from the "Bad Mormons" by the fact that everyone without the chip implant weighed an average of 25 pounds less. The "Bad Mormons" were those who obeyed their leaders, and refused the chips, in the face of massive pressure and fear of survival.

At this time the former economic structure of the world finally collapsed. State currencies became worthless overnight. The value of gold and silver coins skyrocketed but could not be traded without significant risk. Everyone, not just some or a few, but everyone who had refinanced and expanded their homes, or purchased larger homes with remaining high mortgages, inevitably lost their properties. But those who had the chip implanted were told they had nothing to worry about. The government-influenced banks still repossessed their home, but they were "given" another home to live in. It was generally a smaller home, but it was a roof over their heads. The government allowed them to occupy it as long as they remained productively involved in the new economy and the war effort.

Only those who had no, or very small mortgages on their homes escaped the loss of their properties. The "new socialized economy" eventually required that all banks turn their assets and functions over to the government. With all homes with outstanding mortgages now in government ownership, the new socialized banks did not have the will or manpower to search out the few who were still privately owned or with small outstanding balances. Those who had obeyed the Prophet's warnings to become debt-free quietly retained possession of their homes.

Small businesses that could adapt to the emerging barter system and who had not used the hyper-inflationary years to build and borrow remained somewhat intact and in private ownership. Those owners, especially among the saints who had ignored the Prophet's warnings about debt, lost everything.

One morning, Melody received a letter from Samuel's employer in Texas. They regretted, the letter said, to inform her that her husband had been found dead in Russia. The letter was a mere two curt sentences.

Melody shook her head in disbelief, and then anger. Life these days it seemed was incredibly cheap—not worth more than a few casual words! She did not tell Sammy, but took the letter and burned it. Though anguish tugged at her soul, Samuel's last words to her to not believe his employer if they reported him dead, sustained her. Fear often haunted her dreams at night; but when she awoke, her faith in Sam and pure trust in God kept her hope alive for one more day.

A few weeks later, largely because the Church had refused to enforce the chip implants and to turn over it's food and assets, the U.S. government passed a law targeting all dissenting organizations, considering the Church of Jesus Christ of Latter-day Saints now to be an enemy of the State. Many local Church leaders were arrested or killed. The First Presidency went into hiding, and the Quorum of the Twelve scattered underground. All Church property was confiscated, and the Salt Lake Temple was seized by the state and permanently closed.

Melody was never entirely sure why the government simply gave her small home to another family. Most people in her circumstances kept their homes. Melody had refused to let Sammy be implanted with the chip, and he could no longer attend school. And although Melody had an ID card, she had refused to receive the implant. She had a chair in the Utah Symphony, but was told she was not contributing sufficiently to the war effort to have a four-bedroom home and had refused to get the chip. The new family awarded her home had five kids, all of whom were implanted and the father was working for the government.

Melody and Sammy, who was now eleven years old, were given 24 hours to move out of their home and into the street. The new family who moved in had been civil enough to let them stay in the garage a few days until they could make other arrangements. She was not allowed to take anything away except a few personal items. Theo and George had left months ago, at Melody's insistence, to avoid fighting in the war. She had no idea where they were now, but firmly believed that the Lord would protect them, and they would meet again. They had both joined the Church by then, their faith burning brightly. Both had refused the mark of the beast, and had been forced underground to survive.

It was late in the day when Melody and Sammy were finally forced to leave the relative safety of the garage. Except for one small bag of clothing, a journal and a few photos, they left everything behind. It was October, and the weather had turned cold that night. Melody could think of nowhere to go, so they just sat down on the curb outside their former home, shivering as they clung to one another, and prayed a fervent prayer for deliverance.

Moments later an old school bus with darkened windows screeched to a stop before her. The door clanged open to reveal her father-in-law sitting in the driver's seat.

"All aboard!" he announced cheerfully.

Melody cried out with joy, and climbed in with Samuel's aged parents, his sisters and their children. She praised God for this merciful answer to their prayers. All phone communication between the family had been cut off months ago, and only the Lord's intervention could have brought Jim Mahoy to her rescue. Melody looked around at her beloved inlaws, and smiled as Sammy talked excitedly with his cousin across the aisle. This was a happy bundle of exiles, though mostly women and children, since their boys had been drafted for the war. Melody boarded that bus solely upon faith, but was so overjoyed that she did not even ask where they were going. Jim aimed the bus northward.

Jim had heard that a few faithful members of the Church were eking out a safe existence in the rugged hills of Northern Idaho. They had no choice but to attempt to find them. Besides the refugees, the battered old bus held large containers of water, emergency supplies, quite a bit of bedding, a small stack of books, a few cans of gas, and a few meager boxes of canned food. The gas had been collected from motorcycles, lawn mowers, chain saws, even a few kerosene lamps.

Melody was surprised to find everyone cheerful, upbeat, and full of faith. The fountain of their hope flowed almost exclusively from Jim Mahoy, her husband's righteous father. He actually seemed to be filled with joy that they were worthy to be persecuted for their faith. Anyone who did not understand the kind of faith Grandpa Mahoy possessed might quickly think him quite insane. Yet, he was rock solid in both his faith, and his sensibilities. Besides all this, he was perfectly willing to ignore any "proof," incontrovertible or otherwise, that flew in the face of his burning testimony of Jesus Christ, and a lifetime of profound experiences with the Spirit.

They drove past every government checkpoint without much trouble, even though the guards knew they were likely "Bad" Mormons because they didn't have the chips. Persecution of Christians and especially members of the Church had been severe, but now there really was no longer a Church for them to belong to. Though they could detain or kill anyone without the chip, those who manned the gates finally waved them through. After all, it was their own foolish choice to be poverty-stricken and starving. If they had received the chip, they would have food like everyone else.

Somewhere near the Idaho border they heard over the radio that Washington D.C., New York, Boston, San Francisco and Los Angeles had been attacked by tactical nuclear weapons, wiping out the majority of elected government officials. No one was sure who had launched the attack. All civilized life in the United States came to an immediate halt. An emergency shadow government took control, which had been prepared for such an event. Martial law was declared, and all civil liberties were suspended.

People began desperately pouring from the major cities into the suburbs and farmlands. Looting, murder, and ruthless gangs became commonplace. So many people tramped into the farmlands of California and the Midwest what little remaining food was stripped from the land and there was serious doubt there could be a crop the next year.

In the face of starvation, people went berserk in search of food. Those wielding true power in the world had carefully worked to weaken and polarize the United States for decades. With society now in chaos, the new President called upon the Secretary-General of the United Nations to deploy U.N. troops to help, who had been pre-staged all throughout the country over many years. These troops emerged almost as if from the woodwork wearing the blue helmets and began patrolling the streets in armored vehicles, shooting suspected looters on sight. Troops wearing the blue helmets did not speak English and appeared to be Asian. Most claimed they were Chinese; in fact, many were North Korean.

The righteous raised their voice to the heavens, and pleaded fervently for divine intervention. God was their only hope.

THE CAMPS OF GOD

A thunderclap was heard around the world as a vast Russian army breached its southern border into Turkey and swept across Syria and Iraq in a surprise attack. Nobody could believe their sudden aggression and advanced nuclear weaponry. All three countries immediately surrendered their armed forces when threatened with annihilation. Russia captured their supplies and troops and thundered toward their former ally, Iran. All U.N. attempts at diplomatic negotiations with the Russians were summarily rebuffed.

Within days, Russia and China and their close allies suddenly left the U.N., announcing their new "Eastern Coalition." Struck with fear, the United States and the rest of Europe created the hastily-formed "Western United Nations."

Threatened with war, Iran amassed troops on its borders and declared a potential nuclear attack against Russia, Israel and the United States. Israel vowed a preemptive strike if the word "nuclear" were ever used in the same sentence with "Israel" again. The whole world hoped the collapse of Turkey and Iraq would placate the Russian juggernaut. For about a week it appeared to do so.

However on the first day of May that year, and completely without warning, Russia leveled Tehran and Baghdad in a shower of nuclear warheads and then swept across Iran with little opposition. They paused long enough to install a puppet government and outlaw the practice of Islam. Russian soldiers began going from city to city looting and demolishing mosques who opposed them. Wave after wave of Arabs surged against the Russian desecrators in what they saw as the greatest "holy war" ever fought. All resistant Muslims were slaughtered by the thousands.

As a matter of survival, the Muslim tide of resistance fled the homeland of their fathers and poured into Saudi Arabia. Refugees were given food, guns and hasty training. In less than three months, Saudi Arabia commanded the third largest standing army in the world.

With the fall of Iran and almost all radical Islam in general, Israel considered this the fulfillment of prophecy and immediately began dismantling the sacred Dome of the Rock mosque, and reassembling it on another site. Muslims around Israel revolted and attacked in all-out hatred. They were summarily repulsed and slaughtered without even slowing the construction project. Construction of the Third Temple at Jerusalem be- gan immediately. In less than a month's time the outer walls were standing at their full height, and the wall around the temple compound was nearly completed. Materials for the temple had been carefully prepared for decades. Such fervor gripped the souls of the Jews to build the temple anew that quotas were set and passes allotted for those with skills to join the holy construction project. Tens of thousands of Jews and Gentiles, including willing laborers were kept out by sturdy, electrified fences.

Once free of the Islamic occupation of the temple mount, excavation began in earnest. Since the days of Rome, no Jew had been allowed to excavate beneath the historic temple site. The system of underground caves and tunnels was far more extensive than ever imagined. The tunnel leading to the Holy of Holies was finally discovered, and a free-flowing well directly underneath the temple was found and uncapped. Water quickly filled the three man-made caverns beneath the temple and flowed outward for the first time since it was capped by the Romans nearly two thousand years earlier.

During all this, Russian troops simultaneously blitzed into former Soviet Bloc nations and quickly reestablished themselves in absolute rule. Martial law was declared, labor collectives rebuilt, major-city factories refurbished, grocery stores were restocked—and the people rejoiced. The state religion of labor was once again elevated to godhood, and the Soviet communist machine groaned to life. With a renewal of red pride, the new Soviet state began churning out munitions at an unimaginable pace. A full 75 percent of their national budget was poured into the war.

It was then that China finally unleashed its unending hordes into Asia. Nearly one million Chinese soldiers on a vast number of ships left their eastern shore and headed straight for an easy victory in Taiwan which they had been planning for decades. With no time to respond, they took the island in mere days. China and their long-time puppet North Korea then joined forces, and three million combined troops with tanks and warheads surged across the border of South Korea.

The Western Coalition fired a pre-emptive tactical nuclear missile into the oncoming surge. The vast enemy army was temporarily reduced, but more waves of troops surged behind them. Within two weeks of warfare, the reinforced Chinese-North Korean army still outnumbered the coalition four to one in manpower. Unable to use more nuclear weapons without fear of killing themselves, the Coalition was forced to meet wave after wave of heavily-armed Chinese and North Korean troops on the ground.

Day after day the hordes came. Day after day the Western Coalition forces released an unending stream of conventional bombs, trying to avoid getting in the way of their own death. The Chinese died literally by the millions. But because of their sheer numbers, in less than three days the Chinese broke through; hand-to hand-fighting ensued, and the seemingly endless Chinese troops surged forward. By the end of the week there was not a single organized Western Coalition survivor left in South Korea. The loss of Chinese and North Korean life had been staggering: more than seventy-five percent of their army was dead.

Having secured the entire Korean Peninsula, the combined Chinese forces cheered their immense victory over the West. Because the military takeover of South Korea was over so quickly, nearly every Western Coalition military machine there had remained intact. The Chinese picked up these weapons and with two million new reinforcements from home, they continued to sweep into the remainder of Asia in unrelenting conquest. Executing their plan for world domination, China then surged into vulnerable ports all over Africa which they had purchased and secured over decades.

With Russia's overthrow of Iran, the rest of Islam soon surrendered to the brutal Eastern Coalition. Their only condition was that their combined forces would first focus on destroying Israel, and all else later. Russia was by now in need of more armaments and reinforcements, and they called upon their Chinese allies who readily agreed. The vast combined Russian and Isalmic forces then moved toward Jerusalem.

The line was drawn in the ancient sands, and soon every nation on earth would gather outside the Holy City.

The world economy was in shambles. To sustain their war effort, the remaining Soviet economy was now completely occupied in supporting the war. As every able-bodied citizen had been recruited into the army, many of the smaller Russian factories were abandoned to funnel enough workers to man the massive military production plants in Moscow and St. Petersburg. As a matter of survival, families were obliged to leave the empty factory cities and migrate to the country. Mercifully, after that time Samuel and his little band of refugees encountered no further attacks from the military.

It was full-blown winter when Alexei's band of rag-tag refugees arrived outside such a factory city. As they had been trudging onward for three months, exposure and starvation had dwindled them from over 2,500 souls to fewer than 750.

No one bothered to tell Samuel the name of the city, or even if it had a name. All he knew was that it sat in a narrow mountain pass, with a river against its eastern wall, and a mountain against the western side through which they needed to pass. It was an old-style factory city, built not only to contain the factory, but to form a compound for imprisoning the workers. From the outside it looked like the backside of massive, windowless warehouses a half-mile or more wide. The buildings were constructed of sturdy gray concrete. The only way into the city was through a large gate which was now piled deep in junk vehicles and rubble.

There was no sign of life within the walls, and much damage was evident on the outside of the buildings as if they had been under sustained attack, and yet had somehow endured. Alexei stopped a short distance from the towering walls and pondered their options. Snow was falling heavily as the people milled around, miserably looking for anything to make a fire.

A large hole about fifteen feet above the ground had been blown through the wall near the gate. After some effort a makeshift ladder was constructed and Vladimir, Alexei, Samuel and three other men climbed the rickety ladder.

"It's an old flour mill," Vladimir told him after looking around in the darkened interior. Though no milling equipment remained, Samuel could see the metal chutes that once guided the grain on its journey through the mill. The floor on which they stood had been used to bag the flour and prepare it for shipping.

"Hey, look at this," Samuel said in broken Russian as he stumbled over something soft on the floor. "Flour bags," he said as he picked up several dusty, gray bags. Others helped search until they had literally hundreds of fine-linen flour bags. They were in better shape than the clothing most of them wore. They tossed them out the opening to those waiting on the ground. The people received them with a cheer and immediately began cutting them into badly needed clothing.

They discovered that the only doorway leading from this room had been solidly blocked. They were about to give up when Alexei turned to Samuel. By now Samuel felt he could comfortably carry on simple conversations in Russian, without bringing undue attention to the language gifts he had acquired with his "change." He asked Vladimir to translate only when the conversation grew complex.

"We need guidance once again," Alexei said. "What shall we do? We can't go around the city, and therefore must pass through. It is unlikely we shall do so without resistance."

The familiar feelings of truth flowed, and an answer presented itself in his mind. Samuel walked to the right until he found a large ramp covered with sheet metal. The metal had been worn shiny from years of sliding bags of flour down it. He pointed down the chute. "This is the way out, or inside, in our case."

Alexei was the first one down the ramp. He sat on the edge and shoved off. He zipped from sight into the darkness. Samuel heard him swishing around corners, then he came to a stop. Alexei called back up to say he was now on a street. Vladimir went next, then Samuel, and six other men.

They found themselves standing on a loading dock about four feet above a concrete street. It was dusk, and snow was falling heavily. Samuel jumped to the street and immediately saw the flicker of a torch a short distance to his left. The street was blocked by two huge pieces of factory equipment. They were covered with chipped green paint with rollers and large gears on them as if they may have been used for rolling steel. They had been pushed end-to-end across the street so that they formed an impenetrable barrier a dozen feet high. Samuel doubted that even an army tank could push its way past. As they watched, some men climbed onto the machines carrying torches and rifles. When they were assembled there were about ten of them. One of them fired a shot which hit one of the refugees in the shoulder. He spun to the ground with a cry of pain.

"Go back!" one of the men yelled. "We will not let you into our city. If you do not leave immediately we will kill you where you stand and eat your bodies for food!" he said. This produced a demonic howl from the rest of those on the machines. Samuel heard several more rifles cock.

Alexei stepped forward. "We only want to pass through and be on our way. We will not take your food or bother you. Your factory entirely blocks the road!"

Their answer was another shot which chipped the pavement in front of Alexei and lodged in the leg of another of their men.

"Please, we have women and children who will perish if..." he was cut short by a bullet whizzing past his head. He ducked, but did not run. He turned to Samuel.

"God moves mountains. Pray to God, and ask him how we shall move these mountains," Alexei begged him.

Never in his life had Samuel felt what next flowed into his soul. As if he were immersed in liquid fire, the power of God swept through him.

He stepped forward with a perfect knowledge of how God would deliver them. A gun fired, and the bullet slammed into his chest. He took a step back and looked at the wound in his chest. In less than the blink of an eye it closed up and the bullet rattled on the pavement.

Sam looked again at the monstrous machines before him, and raised his left hand before him. A feeling of peace settled over him so powerful that he felt compelled to close his eyes. He slowly moved his hand to the left. Immediately a terrible screeching and grinding noise assaulted his ears. He opened his eyes and watched the machine on the left quickly slide out of the way. He raised his right hand, and moved it to his right. The huge machine scraped to the right so quickly that sparks flew off the pavement. Those who had been on the machines either fell off, or were too terrified to speak.

Now visible, nearly a hundred men with guns and clubs were standing in the street. There were only six with Alexei, two of whom were wounded, and none of them armed. Alexei stepped forward once again and raised his hands in peace. The men on the machine screamed in terror, and many of those in the street dropped their weapons and fell to their knees.

"We mean you no harm," he said in a loud voice. "But, as you see, the power of God is with us, and we must pass through your city. Please make way, and we will shortly leave you in peace. You know this is true, or our God would not give us the power you see."

A cry of fear arose from those in the street. People began running in various directions until only a few remained. When the street was nearly empty a group of four men walked toward them. They were all carrying guns.

A stocky man who appeared to be in his sixties took one more step after the group stopped. He was wearing a tattered coat that came to his knees, a fur hat and boots lined in fur. His hands were wrapped in strips of cloth that seemed to be an attempt at homemade gloves. He stood there a moment, apparently collecting his thoughts, or bolstering his courage.

"I am Motyvich, the mayor of this city. I have never seen the power of God before, but know this is what it must be. Besides, I felt my old heart sing within me with great joy. I will grant you passage through our city if you will teach me of your God, and why you have this power. I wish to know where you are going and why. Will you bring your people inside our protection and take dinner with us? I will trade you food for wisdom. My food, your wisdom," he added with a smile.

"It is a good trade," Alexei said and shook the old man's hand vigorously. "Vladimir, go bring the people into the city."

"How many of you are there?" the mayor wanted to know.

"Besides us, about seven hundred fifty."

Samuel glanced back at Vladimir who had turned and knelt beside their wounded men, praying. Samuel felt a flow of the power of God coming from their direction, and a moment later both men stood. Samuel smiled. Vladimir's faith truly was growing.

Motyvich was still speaking to Alexei. "We are also about that number. Come, I will show you something that will make your old eyes pop from their sockets," he said merrily. As Vladimir and the others climbed back outside, the old man led Samuel and Vladimir down the street. A short distance later they stopped before an iron door large enough to drive a truck through. There were four guards with machine guns standing before it. They unchained and pulled open the big door. A sweet, wholesome smell rolled out of the dark room.

Motyvich took a flashlight from his pocket and clicked it on. In the dim light it made they saw pallets stacked to the ceiling full of sacks of flour and grain.

"It is a beautiful sight, is it not?" their guide exclaimed happily.

"I am having trouble keeping my eyes inside my sockets, as you said," Alexei proclaimed.

"I told you such would be the case."

"How came you into all this food?" Alexei asked.

"We grew much of it with our own hands and brought it here and milled it. When the war broke out more was brought here on its way to Saudi Arabia. When the army ceased to exist, everyone forgot about it, and here it sits."

"Someone will eventually remember it, and come after it." Samuel said in broken Russian.

"You are English, yes?" Motyvich asked.

"No, American," Samuel replied.

"Ah, our old friends the Americans. I will say we are more lucky to be in Mother Russia than in New York today," he said solemnly.

"Why is that?" Samuel asked. He had heard no news of America for months.

"Because the nuclear bombs have leveled it to the ground!" he said emphatically.

Samuel thought about this and the prophecies that it would be destroyed. "It was bound to happen sooner or later," he said.

"Ha!" the mayor cried. "I like this American already. Come, we must make arrangements for your people." He began walking briskly down the street. "We have much food, but very little coal or wood. So, I think we must put you into our homes with our people. Not so comfortable, but much warmer, I think."

"We appreciate your hospitality," Alexei said.

Motyvich leaned close to Alexei and whispered quietly. "It was the American who moved the great machines with the power of God, was it not?" he asked as quietly as he could.

Alexei leaned back and whispered. "His name is Samuel. He is the man of God whom the prophets said would come to lead us to Zion."

"I have heard of these prophets, and of this 'Zion'. But, never have I believed it could be true. Always I thought it was stories from the hearts of superstitious old dreamers," he said more loudly.

"I will tell you the prophecies, and you will see that they are all true!" Alexei proclaimed.

"After you have told me all this, will Samuel, the man of God not teach us also?"

This struck Alexei almost as mightily as a baseball bat between the eyes. He stopped walking suddenly. It was as if the idea had never occurred to him that Samuel might have more knowledge of God that he had not yet taught.

"But, of course it is so," Alexei marveled, as if answering several questions he had asked himself in silence. He turned to Samuel. "You are a man of God and must know the true words of God. How stupid of me to not know this. Samuel, forgive me! But, why did you not tell me? Why did you not teach me? With all my soul I seek the things of God, and day after day I walk next to one who lives with God, and you say nothing?"

"I'm sorry, Alexei. I could not," Samuel replied earnestly. "In all things you lead this people. I am here to assist only you. If you ask, I will teach you. If you do not ask, I can do nothing."

"This I will remember!" Alexei proclaimed. "We waste no more time. Tonight we sleep, tomorrow we assemble the people, and tomorrow evening, you will teach us. If it pleases God, that is."

"It pleases God," Samuel assured him.

The following evening they built a large fire of broken crates in the middle of what appeared to be a large parking lot near the center of the city. Other smaller fires were built beyond to warm the surrounding area. About dusk the people came slowly and found seats on pieces of wood and chunks of concrete. A few brought chairs from their homes not far away. There were about twelve hundred people sitting with expectant faces turned toward him. Samuel could see them all plainly in the flickering light of the fire. There were very few old or very young people. In harsh conditions such as these, only the strongest had survived. Besides a few older people like Alexei, they were mainly in their teens, twenties and thirties. More than two-thirds of them were women. Besides Samuel, Alexei and the mayor were the oldest ones there.

"My fellow citizens," Motyvich called out loudly. It was unlikely those further back could hear. "Our friends have brought with them a prophet of God, and one who possesses the power of God. You all know of the moving of the big machines. It was the prophet Samuel who moved them, and God who gave him the power. He has agreed to teach us. Hear him, my people. Hear the words of God from one who knows Him well!"

Samuel waited as those words were relayed to the people further back. "Thank you, and God bless you," Samuel said, not knowing for sure what to say. He spoke in English, and waited for Vladimir to translate, and for the translation to be relayed back. "I wish to correct only one thing your mayor said. There is only one prophet, and I am not he. I am a servant of God, and one whom he has tasked with aiding this great people in returning to Zion. In time I will teach you who the prophet is, but it is not I."

"I perceive that you are a noble people, long oppressed, and long lost from your heritage. You are the children of Israel, and those whom God has taken in His heart to bring back after their long dispersion. If you wish, I will teach you how to come home." He waited until all had heard the message.

"Oh, yes! Teach us!" they cried almost with a single voice.

Samuel nodded. The crowd grew still. Only the crackling of the fire broke the stillness of the night. As he spoke his voice was punctuated by puffs of vapor in the harsh cold of the night. "There are two great gatherings happening here today. One is of the soul, and the other is of the body. Alexei has been given the job of taking your bodies to your rewards in Zion, and I to assist him. I have been given the great honor of leading your *souls* to Zion."

"Tonight you will come to understand that your body cannot go to Zion and receive your reward there until you have gathered your soul to Zion first."

"What this all means is that you must learn the truth, and embrace it completely in your hearts. You must be baptized and receive the priesthood of God. Then, when you at long last return to the doorsteps of God's temple, you will be permitted to enter. Only then will your journey will be completed, for your body and your soul will have both come home."

"What does Zion mean?" someone cried out, giving voice to the question of a thousand people.

Following Vladimir's translation, Samuel replied. "Zion is God's people, the pure in heart. The people of Zion dwell in the presence of God. They are safe and use the power of God to defend themselves, much as you have seen in your own journey. By the time we arrive at His holy temple, we will be a part of Zion."

"Is Zion then a people, or is there one place called Zion?" the same man cried loudly.

Samuel's voice rang strong. "We will be Zion when we become pure in heart, and when you are each baptized by authority into the gospel. There is also a place called Zion. It has been prepared for all those who become Zion people. When the time is right, I will tell you, and I will take you there, if it pleases God." A spontaneous cheer came from those assembled.

"Then let us be baptized!" someone cried, and hundreds of voices agreed.

The fire seemed to burn hotter at his side for a moment. Samuel rejoiced as he waited for their voices to grow still. He finally held up both hands and a hush fell over them. "You shall, but first you must be taught. First you must know where the power of God resides. You must understand His latter-day work, His true church, and His true doctrine. After you know this, then I will baptize you for the remission of your sins, and you shall receive the gift of the Holy Ghost, and thereafter, His priesthood power. When we arrive at the holy temple each of you must be full of truth, and cleansed of your sins in order to enter and receive the blessings of the temple, including marriage for all eternity, and the sealing of the family so that it will endure forever."

"You must teach us!" they cried, their voices almost desperate.

Samuel waited as their anxious cries grew still, and then paused in the resulting silence as the warmth of the Spirit spread across them and peace healed their fears. When all that could be heard was the crackling of the fire, he spoke again.

"In the spring of 1820, in a state within the United States called New York, there lived a young man whose name was Joseph Smith…" he began. His final words tapered into the night three hours later. The fires had burned to embers, and the people were shivering. But they hardly noticed their frozen limbs for they were alive with the fire of testimony bourne of God.

Samuel prayed in love with them, then sent them to their beds with the promise that they would meet again tomorrow. His heart sang with great joy as he slowly walked back beside Alexei, Vladimir and Motyvich.

"It is a great day," Motyvich said quietly.

"A glorious day," Alexei agreed.

"A blessed day," Samuel proclaimed.

Alexei quietly motioned for Samuel to follow him as they left Motyvich at his door. They walked a short distance to where one of the trucks was parked, carefully guarded by faithful members of Alexei's people.

"I have something you should see." Alexei stepped onto the bumper of the truck and lifted a large metal chest from the truck which he handed down to Vladimir. They carefully set it on the crumbling concrete street. Alexei undid six screw-type clamps with large wing nuts. From the symbols on the box, Samuel surmised it had at one time contained nuclear material. It was both water and airtight. Samuel hoped for their sakes it was free of nuclear contamination.

Upon opening the box Alexei removed a delicately carved wooden box, which he then opened with a key hanging from a silver chain around his neck. Inside was a leather-bound book of obvious antiquity. He lifted it carefully and handed it to Samuel.

"These are the writings of our prophets," he said with reverent awe in his voice.

The book was quite heavy, and apparently fragile. Vladimir stepped up and held the book so that Samuel could examine it. One of the guards switched on a bright loading light attached to the rear of the truck and aimed it at the book. The ancient book itself was about the size of a photo album, approximately twelve inches square. They were bound with leather-covered wood of very skillful craftsmanship. It had a hand-sewn binding. The cover bore bold script completely illegible to Samuel.

Samuel carefully opened to the first page containing writing. The pages crackled ominously as he turned them. Samuel looked up from the book into Alexei's eyes, which were sparkling with happiness. The pages were unexpectedly thick. A moment's inspection suggested they were animal skins rather than paper. The book gave off a peculiar smell, a mix of cedar and antiquity. The rest of the smell was something akin to mothballs.

The book was written in a language Samuel could not read. The lettering was small and careful, with flourishes at the beginning of the sections of text. The flow of the text appeared to be in three columns from left to right. There were occasional hand-drawn pictures scattered among the text. Most of these graphics were skillfully executed. Others were little more than line drawings that could as easily have been crude maps as something else.

"What does it say?" Samuel asked after many minutes pondering. The Spirit was burning brightly within him, and his every sense told him this was a volume of great worth to the Lord and this people. He longed to know what its message was.

"We do not know," Alexei replied with a carefully studied response that Samuel was true. "We have lost the old language."

"But, I heard you quote some of it earlier," Samuel replied.

"We have an oral version which has been passed down from father to son for many generations. Even those who possess this knowledge have great doubts concerning its accuracy."

"Why?"

"Because it is so fantastic, so utterly unbelievable," Alexei answered

"Yet, you believe it," Samuel added.

"I do," the old patriarch replied emphatically. "It seems to be a part of me to believe. I always have."

Samuel pulled the book open midway, and found the flow of the text had changed, as if the writer, or scribe had changed. He studied pictures on the pages and thumbed to the end. There was a score of blank pages at the end as if the scribe had intended to write more. He closed the book carefully and held it out to Alexei, but Alexei did not reach for the book.

"Part of what I do know about this book," Alexei said instead, "is that you are to help translate it for us."

Samuel blinked in surprise, and retained possession of the book. Though completely unexpected, his words had the ring of truth. He opened the book again, and still the pages clung to their message with a tight fist. Then, suddenly, he knew what to do with the book. "Our living prophet is a seer," he said as much to himself as to Alexei.

"This I know. You must take him the book," Alexei said with finality. "He will read its words to us. Will you do this?"

"Alexei, we will hand it to him together. Until then, your fathers have kept it safe for over a thousand years. I suggest you continue to guard it until we come to Zion."

"This is a good thing," Alexei said, and took the ancient volume with obvious respect. He rolled it back into the black cloth, closed it in the wooden box, and packed it away in its airtight chest.

At this same moment on the opposite side of the globe, Melody's first hint that something was terribly wrong was when the old motor home suddenly screeched to a halt. She had been holding one of her little nieces, and the sudden stop started the child crying again. She carefully set the little one down and made her way to the front. The road before them was blocked by old cars and trucks. A group of men was doing something on the ground not far from the bus. With a start she realized they were beating someone. From the energy they were putting into their work she was forced to assume their victim was either dead, or shortly would be.

"We can't let this continue," Grandpa Mahoy cried, and jumped from his seat. At 87 years old, he was just barely able to walk, let alone fight. A dozen hands restrained him. He was the only adult male in the motor home, and he was desperately needed where he was. They urged him to wait, even to back up and find another way. Certainly, it was not their fight.

"All right," he said, shrugging off their hands. "I'll handle this another way. Everybody sit down." They just barely had enough time to take their seats before the boxy old vehicle lurched forward. He laid his hand on the horn and roared toward them. A dozen startled faces looked up, then bolted for the sides of the road for safety behind their barrier. He swerved and slammed on the brakes, just barely missing the body in the road.

"Grab him!" he ordered, and Melody and several others jumped from the door. They yanked up the unfortunate soul and hauled him inside. Before the door was even shut Grandpa backed the motor home up and then raced forward. At the last instant he swerved off the road, through a barbed wire fence, and then back onto the road. People, bedding, babies, pots and pans flew in every direction. They lurched back up onto the road, and roared down the street. For a few minutes it looked as if the men were going to chase them, but they gave up, apparently thinking it not worth the gas it would take to catch them.

"Help me," Melody ordered as she and Grandma Mahoy struggled to roll the person they had picked up onto his back. He appeared to be an older man, his hair sprinkled with gray. The man was unconscious, his face bloodied and smeared with mud. Melody carefully dabbed away the grime to survey the extent of his injuries. No limbs were broken, and no serious cuts could be found, though his flesh was black and blue everywhere they looked.

As Melody was wiping his forehead his eyes flickered open. They were the deepest blue she had ever seen.

"Hello, Melody." The old man said happily in a British accent. The combination of the eyes and the accent suddenly brought the impossible truth full force.

"Mr. Helaman!" she cried, and wrapped her arms around him. "Thank God we stopped, and that you're all right!"

"Why yes, thank God. And, thank you, sir," he said, turning stiffly to address Grandpa Mahoy in the driver's seat. He had slowed the motor home back to a slow pace to conserve fuel.

"You're sure welcome. I'm glad we came in time. Melody, do you know this man?" Grandpa asked.

"Oh Grandpa, yes, I know him very well! This is the man who helped me get my sons out of England. He bought us tickets both ways, and got us passports on a moment's notice. I practically owe him everything in this world!"

Grandpa smiled warmly at his new passenger. "Melody has often spoken of you, brother Helaman. God bless you for all you have done for this family," he said as he continued to drive.

"The debt is repaid," Helaman said with finality. "Here, would you help me stand, please?" he asked, and the women clustered tightly around him helped him up. "I hate being on my back surrounded by people. It seems to happen to me a lot," he added ruefully.

"I can understand that," Grandpa empathized. "Those folks back there didn't seem to like you very much, brother. Why were they beating on you?"

"I had nothing to give them. They said I either had to give them food, gold, or my life. I told them I had none of the former, so they proceeded to take the latter."

"The world is falling apart," Grandma said with disgust.

Helaman snorted meaningfully. Melody interpreted it to mean something similar to "You ain't seen nothin' yet." She was exactly right.

"Helaman," Melody said, suddenly curious. "The last I saw of you, you were getting on a plane for England. Shortly thereafter all international travel was suspended. Now, here you are in Idaho. I don't mean to pry, but why are you here, and where were you going?"

"Why, I was coming to see you," he said matter-of-factly.

"What? Why?"

"Because I made a promise to assist you if you needed me while Samuel is away."

"You've more than fulfilled your promise," Melody assured him earnestly.

"It won't be fulfilled until Samuel returns to you. Until then, you need me again."

"What makes you say that?" she demanded, not willing to believe she was once again in desperate straits.

"The truth," he replied simply.

She had to think about that for a moment. "Okay, the truth then. But how did you know I was headed to Idaho, and then found me even before I got there! You would have never met up with me...."

"And.... here we are," she echoed weakly.

Helaman laughed and sat near her, facing the back of the bus. "Since I'm here to help you, may I make a suggestion?"

"Certainly," Melody replied without enthusiasm. She was still pondering his former words.

"Good. Ask Brother Mahoy to take the next dirt road to the right."

"What? Why? How do you know there's a dirt road. What's the reason?"

"So many questions," he responded, then would say no more. All the women stared at him in wonder.

Melody called up to the front. "Grandpa?"

"Yes dear," Grandpa replied, unable to hear the conversation going on.

"Grandpa, is there a dirt road on the right up there?" Melody asked, trying to see out the windows.

"Don't see one, Melody."

She looked back at Helaman, whose eyes were closed as if to block out the pain of his bruises. She continued, "Grandpa, if you see one on the right in the next few minutes, will you please turn off on it?"

"Why Honey? We won't make much time on a dirt road, and we need to get further away from those men."

"I'm sorry, but I need to go to the bathroom," she said. It was a truth, but not *the* truth. Helaman opened one eye briefly, then closed it. A small smile formed on his old face.

"Here's a dirt road," Grandpa suddenly called from the front. Melody still could not see out the windshield from where she sat. The motorhome veered right, then bounced down the road a short distance and screeched to a halt.

"Farther," Helaman said quietly.

"Go a little farther please, Grandpa," Melody called. They moved ahead slowly as the lane grew more rutted. After a little farther they suddenly dropped down a short hill and came to a stop.

"Well, I'll be! Look at that!" Grandpa said loudly.

Melody made her way to the front. "It looks like an old barn," she said, staring in disbelief at the low structure built into the hillside. It had a dirt roof overgrown with weeds. Heavy timbers defined a door large enough to drive the motor home through.

"It's an old potato cellar," Laura Mahoy said from the passenger seat. "We used these when I was a girl. We kept potatoes in them through the winter and sold them in the spring. They were completely underground just like this one. I wonder if…"

"These things haven't been used in nearly a hundred years. Are you thinking there might be potatoes in it, Mama?" Grandpa asked. "No way. No possible way."

"I suppose you're right," she said. "Besides, if there were, whoever put them there would have come back for them already with this food shortage we've got going. Silly idea," she said mirthlessly.

Grandpa looked at Melody and asked, "So girl, are you going to use the bathroom?"

Melody looked up in surprise, then smiled sheepishly. "Oh, sure. I'll be right back. Let's let the kids run a bit while we're stopped, okay?"

"Good idea," Grandma said.

"Stay within sight of the motor home, kids." Grandpa Mahoy urged. The children streamed out the door and across the snowy ground. As open as it was here they could wander for miles and still be visible.

Melody was nearly the last one out the door when something occurred to her. She turned back to Helaman. His eyes were upon her intently. She took a step backward toward the outdoors. "I'll check the root cellar," she said, and stepped onto the ground. His only reply was a small smile.

Melody found the big doors old and battered by time. They were padlocked shut with a very large, but surprisingly new padlock which had been painted brown to look old and rusty. Her curiosity got the better of her and she searched until she found a big rock. She raised it up and heaved it against the lock. The rock bounced off sharply and nearly landed on her foot. She did this several times before Grandpa came up behind her. She showed him the lock, and he grew curious as well.

It took most of an hour to batter-open the lock. They pulled the heavy door open to reveal a cavernous room with a dirt floor wide enough to drive the motorhome and several others into. It was completely empty. Melody felt devastated, angry, and hungry. It had taken energy she did not have to help batter open the door. She was about to return when she remembered all Helaman had done for her, and how he had never let her down. Still, it did seem horribly unfair. In frustration she picked up the big rock and heaved it into the empty room. It hit the dirt floor and bounced with a hollow *thunk*.

"Hey, that didn't sound like a dirt floor," Grandpa observed, his eyes wide. He walked to the spot and scraped with his heel. About six inches down he scraped across wood—new wood. They dug away the thin layer of dirt and found an access door, which they pulled it up to reveal a wooden stair. Someone fetched their only flashlight from the motor home, and Grandpa descended slowly, flashing the dim beam back and forth. He disappeared from sight, but they could hear him bumping into things down there.

He returned suddenly with a bag in his arms. "Potatoes!" he cried, and pushed them over his head. A dozen eager hands grasped the bag and pulled it up. "Carrots!" he yelled. "Cabbage and pumpkins!" A cheer arose from every throat. He passed an armload of each up to those above then climbed the stairs.

"Is that all of it?" They asked almost in unison.

"No, there's a lot more," he proclaimed happily.

"Let's get it all!" someone yelled.

"No!" he said forcefully.

"Why? We're practically starving!" they cried.

"It's not ours. We will take enough for a few days, and we'll leave something in exchange, and a thank you note."

"But!" they cried.

"Go get that big quilt Grandma made, and those extra flashlight batteries. I think we can spare a shaker of salt and some pepper too. And bring me that piece of paper and pencil."

Someone hurried off to do his bidding. They carefully buried the trap door and closed the big cellar. They rubbed old grease mixed with dirt on the door and lock to make it look old again. It was still battered open, but the cellar was as invisible as before.

The women were just gathering twigs to light a fire when Helaman lowered himself painfully to the ground. "What did you find?" he asked.

"Food!" the little ones cried happily. "We're going to roast potatoes and carrots," they exclaimed.

Melody looked at her old friend with misty eyes. "Thank you, Helaman. I'm sorry I ever doubted you," she said as she slipped an arm through his.

"You think I knew this cellar was here?" he asked, amazement in his voice.

"What I think is that you always show up when I need you most," she said lovingly.

"A pretty good coincidence, I'd say!" he laughed. Then he became solemn. "What *I* think is that building a fire isn't such a good idea," he
warned, nodding toward those kneeling around the brush. A small fire
was already sending bluish smoke into the air.

Melody understood immediately. "Hey wait!" she cried out to the others. "No fire! Put it out! Those bad men will see it and follow us here.
Hurry, put it out!" Everyone immediately hustled to extinguish the fire,
and then watched anxiously as the last black puff of smoke curled into
the sky. They knelt and offered a prayer that no one would see the smoke.

"Back into the motor home, everyone," Grandpa announced, clapping his hands to hurry them along. In a few minutes they were back on
the highway and making their way toward Idaho. As they drove they ate
sweet, crisp carrots, raw potatoes and cabbage wedges. Melody could not
remember eating anything so delicious. Mothers chewed pieces of carrot
until they were very soft, then gave them to their babies, who ate it like
candy. Even Helaman exclaimed how wonderful it tasted as he nibbled
on a carrot.

Besides food, their next pressing need was fuel. They were probably
going to travel upwards of 500 miles during this trip, much of it up and
down hills. They had begun their journey with a full tank and about ten
gallons in cans. Now the cans were all empty, and the tank read less than
one-quarter full. Except for when they were deliberately putting distance
between them and those who had attacked Helaman, they drove around
forty miles an hour to get the best gas mileage possible. The miles crept
past slowly, but the heavy vehicle's gas gauge seemed to move steadily
downward with perceptible speed.

They made it as far as Hazleton, Idaho before they ran out of gas. They
coasted into town on the last fumes in the tank, and the old bus died
before an abandoned filling station and garage. It was just before noon,
yet the town was completely deserted. Hazleton's main drag consisted of
a single narrow street about four blocks long, with ramshackle businesses
on both sides. It was evident that the little town had not fared well economically for many years prior to the present collapse. Still, it did them
little good either way, since there was no fuel to be found or purchased—
even if they had had any money.

The children jumped out and started exploring the abandoned buildings, carefully avoiding those locked tight and shuttered. They saw no
one for over an hour, and the kids were glad to have a chance to play. It
was almost three in the afternoon before one of the teenage girls came
running back.

"I found an LDS church building," she said between breaths, "and there are people inside."

"What were they doing?" Grandpa asked with interest.

"Singing," she cried happily.

Grandpa looked at his wife and shrugged. "I guess that's not against the law," he muttered.

"Grandpa, they were singing "Come, Come Ye Saints!"

He straightened up. "Really? Church meetings have been outlawed for years! Lead us to them, will you? Come on everyone, let's go to church!" He had no difficulty convincing even the smallest among them to come along. Some of the younger ones couldn't even remember going to church in their entire lives.

The chapel was a large rock and brick structure about six blocks from the center of town. The grass was brown and frosted with snow. Oddly, the windows of the church were all intact. In Utah, most every church building had been vandalized. They pulled on the doors and found them unlocked, and without the usual red placard declaring that this church property had been seized.

There was indeed music coming from the chapel, and the sound of an out-of-tune piano. Of course, all the lights were off, but the smell of candle smoke was strong. They quietly opened the chapel doors and found about a hundred people near the front singing with full voices. As soon as those inside heard the doors open, about half of them stopped singing and looked back toward them suspiciously. Upon seeing the family, they soon turned back and resumed their singing. The whole Mahoy clan quietly took the first empty seat behind them, and began singing as well— first, with a feeling of doing something, if not wrong, at least illegal, and then with as much vigor as they possessed. It felt so good to feel the power of that beloved hymn again.

The music came to an emotional end, and a young elder stood at the pulpit. In the dark interior of the chapel only the candle he set on the podium illuminated his face.

"Brothers and Sisters welcome to Sacrament meeting, and a very special welcome to our weary guests. May God grant us peace this day while we worship the Lord. Sister Anderson will offer the opening prayer, and then we'll bless and pass the sacrament. Do any of our visitors hold the priesthood?" He smiled when several heads nodded. "The two older brethren, would you bless? Thanks. And you young man," he said, indicating Sammy. "Do you hold the Aaronic Priesthood?"

"No, sir," Sammy said quietly. "I turned twelve last year, but there's no more..." his voice tapered off.

The young man at the podium surveyed Sammy carefully before he spoke. "There will be a slight modification to the program," he announced. "After the opening prayer, the Spirit directs that we ordain this young man to the Aaronic Priesthood. Are you worthy, young man?"

"Yes sir!" Sammy cried in delight.

"Are his parents here?"

"I'm his mother," Melody said, tears of unrestrained joy gathering in her eyes.

"Is this alright with you then, sister?"

Melody nodded vigorously. "It certainly is. Thank you."

"Sister Anderson," he said and sat down.

The sister in question was old and feeble and had to be helped to the stand. Though feeble of limb, her faith was not, nor was her relationship with her Heavenly Father.

"Our Father who art in heaven," she began, then paused as if awaiting Him to answer. "Great and glorious art Thou, and unto Thee we give all praise and all glory, and confess before Thee our great love, and utter dependence upon Thy goodness to sustain and succor us.

"Beloved Father we bow our heads in most humble reverence to worship Thee, and partake of the sacraments of Thine only begotten Son. It is with the fondest hope of being worthy of that great atonement that we do this, and we beseech Thee in the name of our dear Lord that Thou would forgive us of our sins, and consecrate this day of worship unto our souls.

"Forgive us dear Father for our sins, and sanctify our hearts and souls before Thee that we may find the courage to live a righteous life, even when it is illegal to mention Thy precious name in public.

"We pray for those who oppress us, that Thou would bless them, and through the workings of Thy Holy Spirit, call them to repentance and cause their hearts to swell with compassion regarding us, Thy children.

"Father, we trust Thee, in all things cast our lives at Thy feet, and..."

She got no further than this before the doors of the chapel burst open and two asian armed men in blue helmets stomped into the room. One of them aimed an automatic weapon at the floor and let off a deafening burst of fire. The roar of the weapon was like a sustained explosion. When it suddenly stopped only the tinkling of brass casings hitting the ground came to their ears, ironically like sleigh bells at Christmas time. Acrid smoke filled the room as people screamed and gathered loved ones into their arms.

The soldier's faces were twisted in anger, and their stance was belligerent and threatening. The one who had fired the gun screamed at them, "What you are doing here is *against the law!*" he bellowed. His voice was so twisted by rage that his words were barely understandable. "I have authority to execute anyone who defies the law and meets in a Mormon church. I will give you one minute. Anyone who is not willing to die has one minute to leave. After that, all who remain will be shot down where you stand, and the building burned to the ground!" he screamed.

For a full two seconds people sat rigid with terror. Finally a young woman cried out, gathered her two small children and ran from the room, heedlessly dragging her screaming babies. The guards stepped aside. Thereafter, a few more left, then an old man, then a young couple with a baby.

"Thirty seconds left!" he screamed, and cocked his weapon. About a dozen more people left the room. Melody looked at Sammy, and saw fear mingled with faith. She held out her hand and he laced his fingers into hers in an almost iron grip. Neither of them even looked at the exit, and their only hope of life.

She watched Helaman scratch his head, then turn around and sit so that his back was toward the intruders. He pulled a hymn book from the rack, thumbed to the very song they had just sang and began to sing in a surprisingly beautiful tenor voice.

"And should we die," he sang, "before our journey's through…"

A woman's high soprano joined him. "… happy day, all is well." Melody joined in the sacred hymn, and sang the words with such meaning as they had never before held for her. "Happy day, all is well!" the words kept ringing through her heart. "Happy day, all is well!" Others joined in, and as they joined, they also sat back down, until all were seated with their backs to those who in seconds would take their lives.

"Brrrrrrrrttttttt!" the machine gun belched with a deafening roar above them. It made everyone jump, but they looked at one another and continued singing louder than before. This last burst drove three more adults and one child from the room at a hard run.

"Close the doors!" the one in charge cried. "Close the doors, and let's get this business over with!" With weapon lowered at the backs of the heads of those still singing he stomped forward, his boots falling heavily on the floor. He and his comrade stood for several seconds, and then stepped into the bench just behind Helaman. They laid their still-smoking weapons on the floor at their feet, and began singing in heavily accented voices.

"And if our lives are spared again, to see the Saints their rest obtain,
Oh how we'll make this Chorus swell, all is well. All is well!"

The music ended, but the strains of praise lifted heavenward. Every person in the congregation turned to look at the two soldiers seated behind them.

The one who had fired the weapon smiled weakly, and in broken English said. "We are so sorry to make loud scaring noise. We from Korea. But, we wish to worship with only true saints of God."

A stricken silence endured long moments before the soldier tried to explain further. "You who stayed to die are true saints who love God more than life. It is necessary that we know you will not betray us. It is the only way we can be in army, and also worship Jesus Christ in Restored Gospel.

He stared at them, chagrined and apologetic. "Please to see, we shoot only guns with big noise, and not bullets. Not to make much bullet holes in God's church. Please, forgive. But, we have but a short time. Let us worship God."

A bewildered silence followed, and would have continued except that Sister Anderson, who had remained at the pulpit during all this, bowed her head and continued as if she had never stopped.

"… and we thank Thee for those whom Thou hast sent here to join with us this day, and ask Thee to bless and prosper them in their sorrows, their needs, and their journey.

For a moment her voice grew silent, then in an entirely different, very personal and familiar tone of voice, inserted, "Father, just speaking for myself, I want to thank You for sending the soldier boys and allowing me the privilege of choosing to shed my blood for Thy Son. I was ready to die…and happy…and yet I live…" she concluded, her voice filled with wonder. Twin trails of tears glimmered on her cheeks in the candle light. She sniffled, and after a moment her voice returned to formal prayer.

"Father, into Thy hands we consecrate our lives, and give unto Thee to preserve us or call us home. Either way we shall with grateful hearts ever cry unto Thee, All is well! All is well! In the name of Jesus Christ, Amen." A cry of "Amen" echoed with such vigor as to make one wonder if the only voices speaking this holy benediction were mortal, or if angelic voices had joined them.

The young elder who had opened the meeting stood. "Would the young brother please come to the stand? Do either of you soldiers hold the priesthood?"

"We both do," the one who had not yet spoken replied. "We are both Elders in the Church. If our commanders ever found out we would be executed. This is the first time we have dared meet with the Saints for three years. Please forgive us."

"Would you like to help us ordain this young man?"

They looked at each other as tears sprang to their eyes. They quietly, meekly walked to the stand. Grandpa Mahoy clasped each of their hands as they came toward him. The second of them fell on his neck and held him in a prolonged embrace as he openly wept. When they finally separated they all laid their hands on Sammy's head, and Grandpa ordained him a Deacon in God's true church.

Melody had never felt such a profound outpouring of the Spirit in a sacrament meeting. There were no assigned speakers, and it was not a testimony meeting; but the spontaneous worship they experienced was something entirely new to her. After the sacrament, which Sammy helped pass, the young brother stood at the pulpit again, and pointing at Helaman said, "The Spirit directs that this brother here will please address us on the subject of Christ's atonement." He then pointed at a teenage girl. "Sister Linda Phillips will then bear her testimony on the power of prayer. Then we will hear from our two soldier brothers, and ask them to bear their testimony, and tell us briefly of their conversion. Then, young brother Timothy will bear testimony. We'll go to that point," he informed them, and sat down.

Every talk was extemporaneous, and so energized with faith, testimony, and humility that Melody felt as if her heart might burst open. She sensed the periphery of her vision growing white, almost as if she might pass out, but felt gloriously well. Brother Helaman's talk was like nothing she had ever heard before. He spoke with such deep love for the Savior that the congregation wept. He quoted scripture after scripture with such joy that her heart leaped into her throat. He bore testimony with such power that she wanted to stand on her feet and shout "Hosanna! Hosanna! Hosanna!" and barely restrained herself from doing so. He spoke with deep, penetrating understanding, and in so few words, laid open the atonement of Christ to her view, and what it meant to her personally, in such a way as she had never contemplated. Again and again, she felt herself rejoicing and inwardly crying, "Of course. Of course this is true!"

When Helaman finally drew his remarks to a close, her heart was pounding with inexpressible joy, and her testimony was aflame such that her entire body felt engulfed. Her skin tingled from the tips of her hair to her toes, and she felt as if she understood the gospel of Christ for the first time in her life. She would have run to Helaman and fallen into his arms had not decorum restrained her. As it was, a smile to him was her only communication of the deep emotions within her. Oddly, Helaman did not smile back at her. As soon as their eyes met he jumped as if he had been stabbed from behind by a needle. His eyes grew wide as he studied her face. She caught this strange reaction and raised her eyebrows in query, to which he smiled, and forced his eyes away from her. She longed to ask him what he had seen that so startled him, but which he could not, at least for the moment, divulge to her.

Sister Phillips stood and with trembling hands told of the day when her home was searched by the blue helmets for illegal food. They had a basement room stacked with food and canned fruit. Her husband, and most likely all her family, would have been killed on the spot had they found it. The soldiers repeatedly walked right past the food as they uprooted furniture and smashed holes in the walls in search of food and weapons. During all this time she had prayed for deliverance with great fervor, and faith such as she had never before experienced, and knew this was a miracle of salvation for her family.

The two soldiers bore testimony in deep humility. They told of the death of their families because they would not deny their membership in a Christian church. They told of the destruction of everything Christian, and their brutal induction into the army as the Chinese swept across North and South Korea. Only by pretending to be communists had they escaped execution. For reasons they could not fathom, they had never been asked if they themselves were Christians, for they surely would be dead now if they had. They told of tens of thousands slaughtered for no crime greater than having a picture of Christ in their homes, or bearing a non-Korean first name such as Paul.

Young Brother Timothy was barely fourteen. He stood and bore powerful testimony, speaking briefly of the loss of his family who had been arrested and then killed by the blue helmets. Their crime was that his father had been the Bishop of their ward. There was no bitterness in his voice, only peace. He spoke longingly of the day when they would be together, and expressed deep faith that the day of resurrection was not so far away. He wept as he bore his personal witness—not testimony, witness—that Jesus was the Christ. Melody felt electrified as the Spirit bore witness to her that this young man's sacrifice had prepared him to receive the most supernal of all mortal blessings.

The small congregation then sang "The Spirit of God Like a Fire is Burning" with such volume that Melody and many others looked around the room toward the source of invisible voices. At times she could even hear a mighty organ joining in the joy of that celestial anthem.

When it was time for the closing prayer Melody felt as if she had been to church for the first time in her life. Her heart was aflame with faith, and bursting with joy. So significant was her glorious faith that had the Spirit directed her to raise the dead by her faith, she would have done it, and watched death flee in the face of unshakable faith. It came as no surprise to her when she heard their young leader ask her to give the closing prayer.

"Oh God, our Eternal Father," she raised her voice in perfect prayer and love. "How glorious, how precious, how divinely perfect it is to worship Thee this day. Our hearts are filled to overflowing, our souls rejoice, our minds expand to the very heavens, and our faith fills us with perfect hope. As if the veil had burst open, and heavenly angels had filled the room, we feel ourselves consumed by Thy glory, and overpowered by Thy love."

"Father, we pour out our hearts unto Thee in the greatest strivings of worship we can express, and dedicate our lives unto Thee in the presence of Thee, Thine angels, and these witnesses. Ever after, in all things, in every walk of life, at every hazard, in every circumstance, throughout time and for all eternity, regardless of the cost to ourselves, we covenant and consecrate all that we are, all that we possess, all our time, our talents, our very lives unto Thee, for Thee to do with us as Thou wilt. With joy do we stand with open arms to deliver unto Thee our all!

"All this we do in the holy and beloved name of Thine only begotten Son, our beloved Savior, Jesus Christ, Amen I say, Amen!" The congregation shouted Amen in a single voice, a virtual detonation of praise.

She stood there at the pulpit, her face awash with tears, her eyes tightly closed, her mind lifted up on high, her heart burning with pure fire. It took her a moment to realize her arms were raised over her head, and her face was turned toward heaven. She was not aware that no one in the room had stirred, and every eye was likewise bathed in tears of joy. She did not move until someone placed a hand on her shoulder. She lowered her arms and turned to look into Helaman's eyes.

"Come," he said. "I have someone I would like you to meet."

JOURNEY OF FAITH

Helaman led Melody to the Relief Society room, allowed her to enter alone, and closed the door between them. She was too caught up in the joy of the Spirit to even wonder who she was going to meet. She assumed this would be some local person who might be able to help her family on their way. The room was warm and dim, full of sweet feelings and quietude.

"Melody!" a familiar voice said with such love that she spun around to gaze at a person she had not noticed standing in the shadows near the piano.

"Samuel!" she cried, and ran toward him with outstretched arms. After two steps she drew up short, unsure. He held out his arms to her and smiled, and she slowly stepped toward him, never taking her eyes off his, until their arms were around one another but not touching, their faces inches apart.

Slowly, carefully, as if fearing he might not be real, Melody closed her arms around him until at last they touched ever so lightly. With a cry of joy she hugged him in an embrace fierce with happiness and relief. She kissed him long and passionately, drinking deeply from the well of his love. At long last their lips parted, and she laid her head on his chest. He held her tightly, almost fiercely in his arms, the familiar contours of her body causing his blood to boil with longing.

"You *are* real!" she exclaimed in joy. "I was afraid you were a spirit! They said you were dead!"

"I know," he whispered. "I'm sorry for your sorrow."

Melody was laughing and crying at the same time. "I didn't ever believe you were dead though! You promised me that you would be OK, and I believed you, not them." She looked back up at him questioningly. "But why didn't you contact me sooner?"

"I couldn't," he answered softly.

"I suppose things were pretty bad, huh?"

"Things are really difficult over there," exhaling deeply.

Suddenly she stopped, her brain finally realizing how illogical it was that he was actually there in front of her. "How *did* you find me?" she wondered. "We're way out here in Idaho, lost and hungry. How *did* you find us?" she said out loud.

"Helaman brought me to you," he said simply.

"But he's been with us for the last week or so!" she protested. "How could he . . ."

"He gets around," Samuel said with a chuckle.

At that Melody nodded and laughed with him. "Wow, isn't that the truth!" she giggled. Then she spoke in earnest. "But—how did you get here? Oh, Samuel! You should have come sooner to the meeting with us! The Spirit was *so* powerful, and I gave a closing prayer that is *still* giving me goosebumps."

"I know," he said. "That's why Helaman came to get me. He knew I'd want to be with you on this glorious day."

Melody was now more confused than ever. "How could he have come to get you? He was sitting next to me all during the meeting. What are you talking about?" she asked him in a daze.

"The prayer—you don't know what it was, do you?"

Melody thought for a moment. "Well, it was glorious, but other than that…"

"Do you remember the covenant?"

"Well yes, I do. But …"

Samuel took her face in his hands. "Melody, it wasn't just an ordinary prayer, or a simple covenant. This covenant is the one every person must eventually make to be sealed up unto eternal life."

"You mean in those exact words?" she questioned, trembling.

He shook his head. "No, sometimes there are no words involved. It's not the words, it's the intent. The rock solid, unchangeable covenant, in the face of all hazards. You did it!"

"I don't know what it means," she said, quietly perplexed.

"Search your heart, honey. How do you feel? What does the Spirit whisper about your relationship with God; about your place in his kingdom?"

Melody pondered this briefly and slowly said, "I know as surely as I know you are standing here that my place in His kingdom is assured," without pausing to think about it.

When Samuel didn't reply she thought upon her own words. "Oh my…" she said. "Do you mean this was my calling…"

"It was, my Love. It was! And that's why I was able to come to you. I am so very overjoyed to be able to come back, and to share this joyful moment with you. Don't you see? I have been allowed to come to you to confirm this great blessing, this marvelous change that has occurred in your life."

Melody's voice trembled as she looked up at him. "If such a thing were even possible," she said, "your being here makes it doubly sweet. It adds a dimension to my joy I cannot describe, but which makes this the most perfect day of my life!" she cried.

Samuel released her and began to search his pocket. "I brought you something in honor of this occasion," he said, retrieving a stunningly beautiful white flower. It looked like an orchid, but larger, with a brilliant pink center. Its fragrance filled the room with sweetness, and she took it with wonder.

"It's beautiful! Where did you get it?"

"I picked it just before I arrived," he said.

"But, you're talking as if you just got here."

"I did. Just a minute ago."

"Where were you just a minute before that?" she asked, her voice a little suspicious.

"Somewhere just beyond Siberia," he answered truthfully.

Melody sat down on a nearby chair, and contemplated this for a long moment.

"That's what the change was that day in the Salt Lake Temple, wasn't it?" she said slowly. "You have been . . . what is it called?"

"The scriptures call it being translated. We refer to it as the 'Mightier Change,'" he said softly, then added: "I couldn't tell you back then."

Melody cried again, this time with tears of relief and understanding. "That's all right, my darling. I finally, finally understand! And, I confess, I love you now more than ever before!" She stopped to brush the fresh tears from her sunburned cheeks. "Oh Sam, tell me all about it! Is translation truly marvelous? I mean, do you feel very much different? Is it everything a mortal can hope it could be?"

"It is far beyond wonderful," Samuel said, then added thoughtfully, "yet really in some ways, not all that different. I am the same. I think, I hope, ponder, pray and yearn just as always. I am physically very different, but my soul is as it always has been." He scooped her back into his arms. "Oh my sweet Melody, I love you, and have missed you with all my soul," he said fervently.

"I love you with all my soul," she replied with deep feeling. She gazed into his eyes, searching his face and finding joy mingled with sadness. She understood. "You will be going back," she said. It was not a question.

"In just a few minutes," he admitted.

"Oh Sam, I have missed you terribly. I am happy in the Lord, yet I feel so incomplete without you," she said softly, her eyes pooling with tears of love.

"Not for much longer, my love," he said. "Only for a little longer."

"But now that I understand, I think the waiting will be less painful …" she replied a little dispiritedly.

Samuel straightened up. "I have some instruction to give you before I must leave." But Melody was not interested.

"I just want to go with you," she said, burrowing into his chest again.

Sam stroked her auburn hair. "I wish you could. Just remember that I am perfectly well. Remain utterly faithful and obedient, my precious wife. Stay near my family, and let Helaman help you."

"Is Helaman also…?" She didn't know what word to put there.

"You'll have to ask him that question," he replied.

Melody shook her head. "I really don't need to. I already know the answer."

Sam wrapped his arms around her in one last embrace, and kissed her lips tenderly. "I must go, sweetheart. Give my love to Sammy, but please don't tell him I came here. He must also be ready before he can know. I love you … forever," he said. Then he slowly took a step back and simply faded from her sight.

She was sitting on a chair holding the beautiful white flower when Helaman quietly opened the door and entered. Melody knew full well nothing like it grew in Siberia. It was a delicate tropical flower, and it had been picked mere minutes before. With a deep sigh that was far more happiness than regret, she stood and followed Helaman. She was so lost in thought that Helaman silently looped his arm through hers and led her gently from the darkness of that unlit building. When they emerged into the dimming light of evening, a wisp of candle smoke swirled behind them as if they had emerged from another world.

When she rejoined her family they were talking with the two soldiers who had driven an armored vehicle onto the church lawn.

"Melody, the Korean brothers have given us fuel and food. We should have just enough fuel to reach our destination! It is a great blessing," Grandpa Mahoy exclaimed joyfully, and turned again to thank their Korean brothers, who brushed aside his gratitude with confessions of humility and regret.

"It *is* a day of miracles," Melody agreed quietly as they walked together towards the motorhome still a few blocks away.

"Who did Helaman take you to meet?" Grandpa asked.

"Oh, just another miracle," she said wistfully, and held up the tropical flower still vivid and glorious in the chilly afternoon.

Samuel returned to his frosty blankets in the bitter cold of Mayor Motyvich's small apartment. Sarah, Alexei's granddaughter, was tossing and turning on the cold floor a few feet from him; Samuel draped his warm coat over her and she soon slept contentedly. The night dragged on endlessly as he listened to the others sleep. Himself lacking that need, Samuel lay awake the rest of the night, his heart fondly rehearsing each moment of this evening's great joy. He and Melody had been separated for a little short of two years now, without any communication between them since he left the job site a year ago. Helaman regularly brought him word of their welfare and had been faithful in watching after them. But Samuel could send no message to her, nor could Helaman even mention they often met.

Now that she had pierced the spiritual veil separating all mankind from God, he knew he could be with her as occasion allowed, and as the Lord willed. As a translated being, one of his main functions was to minister to those—especially those of his family— who were heirs of salvation, and whose calling and election had been made sure. What a glorious blessing it was that Melody had succeeded against such incredible odds! Yet, in a broader sense, he knew of no one who had gained this great blessing who had not done it against seemingly insurmountable odds, willing to sacrifice all. This was the only way it could be done.

Helaman often commented on the general condition in the world, and being involved with aiding and ministering to the saints, especially those very recently blessed with this great gift, he was quite aware of the condition of mankind, and of the Church. His reports were startling. Since the Church had been outlawed nearly eight months ago, the number of individuals qualifying for their election had quadrupled. Extra heavenly beings were being assigned to minister to them as their numbers steadily increased. Far from tearing down the work of the Lord, this great persecution had the unexpected effect of exponentially spurring the faithful onto greater glory. Humbled by their circumstances, those whose hearts were true found their full spiritual greatness, and the heavens opened extra lanes on the highway between heaven and earth to accommodate this great outpouring of faith and righteousness.

As the faith of the faithful grew, so did the occurrence of miracles. Healings, restoration of life and limb became daily occurrences. Visions, dreams and angelic visitations were commonplace. In a matter of a few months first the Church, then the world, became polarized into diametric opposites.

Of course, there were those who could not face the opposition, and who ran to join the forces of evil to preserve their lives at all costs. As opposition in all things must remain equal, with the great increase in miracles and manifestations of God's power, so a corresponding increase occurred among those whose damnation was evident as well. As the weeks slowly clicked by, those whose faith had once been bright now took intense delight in persecuting those whom they had formerly called brother and sister. Many innocent lives were lost, both spiritually and physically, and innocent blood shed by those whose hearts had once been at least content with the religious status quo. It was tragic now to see a great sifting take place when the names blotted from the book of life were friends, loved ones, admired ecclesiastical leaders, and beloved family. Many of the persecutors were incensed by the miracles taking place, while others drew lines in regard to social issues, which were hotly contested by those who felt they were more enlightened than the Prophet.

However, one report Samuel delighted in was concerning the Brethren. Helaman reported that the Quorum of the Twelve and First Presidency had all remained faithful and true, and were in fact secreted away, very much engaged in running the Church, and preparing the people for the Lord's triumphant return. Helaman spoke of them in first person, having often met with them. He said they daily communed with angels, and with the Master himself. All was as it should be, he said, and no unhallowed hand could stay the Lord's return.

Alexei decided to allow his people to spend the winter in the great factory city. There was food there, shelter and new friends. He did not ask Samuel what the Lord desired, and Samuel did not volunteer to say. Had Alexei asked and obeyed, they would be trudging through knee-deep snow making their way slowly toward Zion. That would have brought them the greatest blessings, and poured out miracle after miracle upon their heads—marvelous blessings not otherwise available. Staying in the city gave them time to become comfortable, to lose their determination, and to succumb to the temptations that idleness brings. Samuel silently grieved for them, knowing that when they left that next spring their hardships would be greater, even though the weather would not be the source of it.

The one great blessing staying in the city afforded them was the opportunity for Samuel to teach the people. Each evening that it was not snowing or blowing they met in the great open square at the center of the city. It seemed odd to Samuel that they met in the open when surrounded by cavernous factory floors and warehouses. But, he soon learned that only non-Russians see the indoors as preferable. None of the buildings available to them were heated, and during the day they radiated the intense cold of the night before, making them colder inside than it was outside. Inside it was dark, musty, and often dirty or greasy. Outside, the sun lit their days and large fires lit their nights. No one would be foolish enough to build a large fire inside a building and not expect it to fill with smoke and burn to the ground. It was common understanding among them that if one building burned down, so did every building, since they were joined side by side to form the large square compound that was their city.

Each night was an excursion into faith and righteousness. Samuel oftentimes arrived at the bonfire with no knowledge of what he was to teach them, only to be filled as he opened his mouth. These were the best times, and the Spirit of truth was poured out upon them in rich measure. As the evenings progressed, however, fewer and fewer attended, until less than half of those in the city seemed interested anymore. Most of those who came each evening were Alexei's faithful refugees. Most from the city lost interest, or took offense, or simply grew weary of the routine.

Samuel rejoiced as he taught the faithful. He rejoiced in the great truths that came forth, but as much as this, he rejoiced in their simple faith and believing hearts. He praised God for their growing testimonies, and in the blessing of being their trumpet call to truth. His all-night prayers were symphonies of praise for the Lord's tender mercies to all His far-flung children, and joyous marveling that God would use the weak and simple, such as Samuel knew he was, to help accomplish this mighty work.

Weeks passed, and still they came faithfully. Samuel organized a special Sabbath meeting where they met earlier in the day. He selected those of the strongest faith to stand forth and testify before their brethren. As they did so their own faith was magnified a hundred fold, and those who heard their own revered loved ones testify were changed as well.

By the time the days grew longer, and the winds turned warm and sweet with the scent of new life, the band of wanderers were anxious for one simple rite of summer to occur: they desperately wanted the river beside the city to flow ice free that they might dam it up, and be baptized. It was the desire of every faithful heart, including Samuel's.

When the day finally came that the ice gave way and clear waters flowed, a cry of joy arose from the people as if food had arrived for the starving. Men, women and children labored to stack logs and rocks in the rushing stream that formed beside the larger body of ice still remaining to make a pool deep enough. Samuel tested the water, and found it far too cold to endure. Yet, they would not wait. "Tomorrow," he told them. "Tomorrow at noon, come with fasting and prayer, and I will baptize you into God's true Church, and you will take upon yourselves the name of Christ. Then after you have been warmed and built fires in the square, I will give you the gift of the Holy Ghost." They cried aloud for joy, and danced in one another's arms like children.

When the appointed hour drew near, the people moved in a great congregation to the water's edge. Samuel pulled off his shoes, walked across the ice still on the bank, and waded out into the water. He looked up into a sea of faces standing above him at the water's edge. For almost half a minute no one stirred.

"Who will be first?" Samuel asked in a loud voice. "Who comes first to the waters of purity?"

"I will," a small voice said from far back in the crowd. Samuel watched the sea of people part for the person who walked toward him. His heart radiated with joy to see that it was Sarah, Alexei's granddaughter. It was she who had first befriended him that night when he had been forced to sit at the children's table. It was she who had been raised from death at the helicopter attack. It was she who now walked toward him with sure steps. She stopped by the water's edge and stepped out of her shoes. She unfastened her coat and dropped it to the ground. She had made rough baptismal clothes from flour sacks. The cut and stitching were crude, yet Samuel had never seen so gloriously pure a vestment even on an angel, and he had seen many angels.

Samuel held out a hand. Her eyes fastened on his, she walked through the flowing ice water without any indication she felt its stunning cold.

He turned her toward the people and raised his hand over her head.

"Sarah Caterina Antoyov, having been commissioned of Jesus Christ, I baptize you in the name of the Father, and of the Son, and of the Holy Ghost, Amen." He lowered her into the water, and as he did so he heard a great cry of "Hosanna! Hosanna! Hosanna!" go up from a hundred thousand angelic voices. He knew the people on the riverbank had not raised the shout, but those who loved little Sarah from the world of unseen family. He pulled her from the frigid waters as quickly as he could. The warmth of her body caused the cold water to evaporate suddenly, letting off a billowing cloud of steam which curled slowly around her head.

At that very moment a cloud parted in the heavens and a brilliant shaft of sunlight fell upon her, illuminating the mist. People on the bank gasped, and held hands to their eyes. For a full minute Sarah looked as if she were engulfed in billowing waves of fire which seemed to form into the shape of a dove alighting upon her.

No one dared move until Alexei stepped into the water and led his granddaughter to the shore. Others quickly wrapped her in blankets. She refused to leave the water's edge.

"Pray God," Alexei said quietly, "and ask him if a sinful old man may beg a remission of his sins in the waters of Christ's sacrifice."

"What you ask is the very desire of your Savior's heart," Samuel said in a voice that only Alexei heard. Tears sprang from the weathered old face, and he bowed his head in strong emotion.

"Then if it pleases God let it be so, and for all eternity ..." thereafter he spoke a phrase in Russian that was unfamiliar to Samuel. He looked with puzzlement at Vladimir who stood on the very water's edge, his torn coat removed in preparation for his baptism.

"Roughly translated," Vladimir said with great significance, "it means Phooey the Darkness."

Samuel baptized Alexei, who too was greeted into the kingdom by a halo of fire. Samuel saw people on the bank looking around them, or gazing up into the sky trying to determine the source of the spiritual fire. They did not understand what eternal significance this event held in the heart of God. He had long awaited this very moment when His scattered people once again came unto Him with humble hearts and true faith.

This was the gathering of Israel that was in the Father's heart, when they took upon them the name of His beloved Son and entered into the kingdom via the straight gate of baptism. Their journey to Zion was but incidental to this, the greater gathering. God had held this day in His heart for millennia, and today was a grand day of days, on both sides of the veil.

Samuel baptized over a hundred people before Alexei insisted he come from the waters to save his life. They had built a fire upon the bank, and Samuel rubbed his blue legs until they turned pink again. It was somewhat amazing to see his flesh chilled to solidity, and still feel no pain or stiffness. When Alexei was content, Samuel returned and baptized another hundred, then another, until all who desired it were washed pure and holy in the blood of the Lamb. It was indeed a glorious, glorious day!

By the time the big fires were crackling in the square they had all dried and changed. Samuel brought a chair and set it before the people. He spoke to them briefly about the gift of the Holy Ghost, and then motioned for Sarah to be the first. Samuel was certain all present could hear the angels singing as he spoke the sacred words bestowing upon this faith-filled child the greatest gift God grants the living, second only to the bestowal of eternal life. She stood and turned toward him.

"Did you hear them, great one?" she asked breathlessly, her eyes sparkling in the firelight. "Did you hear the angels singing?"

"They sing for joy, Sarah," he told her. "They sing for you."

"I wish I could sing with them the song I hear in my heart," she said, her eyes bright with joy.

"They can already hear the song in your heart," he whispered.

"Thank you, great one," she said, and stepped aside for the next. Samuel had had a difficult time allowing them to call him 'great one.' It was actually a compound word which as near as he could tell meant "the one whom God sent, but is not a prophet." Vladimir told him to think of it as an honorific, and not an undue homage. Samuel had trouble seeing the difference, but it was apparently clear to them. He restrained himself from out-and-out forbidding them to use the term. Had he done so, they probably would have persisted anyway.

It took three evenings to confirm them all. Each blessing was recorded word for word by several people Alexei had instructed to do so. When all the baptisms and confirmations were done, a detailed record existed.

Alexei's people reluctantly left the walled city soon thereafter. They began their journey ankle-deep in mud, and filled to overflowing with profound faith and hope.

Just as Alexei's people had wintered in the factory, Melody's family had wintered in Hazelton. There was such love and faith here that they immediately accepted the first offer they received to stay. This had come from Sister Anderson, who lived alone in a small home not far from the chapel. Her little home had been built prior to central heating, and still had a cookstove in the kitchen. Sister Anderson's quiet grace and genuine hospitality was so marvelous that before they were all tucked in that first evening, they knew they were not just "at home"—they *were* home. Here they healed both physically and spiritually as they awaited the advent of spring.

Spring had already broken in Idaho, and a skiff of green was visible across the abandoned fields when the Mahoys began their journey once again. It was hard to leave, yet they knew they must. Reasons uncertain, and Helaman's gentle assurance drove them on. Their slow journey through Idaho was much less eventful the farther north they came. The smaller the town they passed through, the more helpful and accommodating were the people there. In one small town they had to drive down several residential streets to pass through. Several times they were stopped and given a few wrinkled apples, a quart of old motor oil, or much-needed encouragement. These country people seemed much less oppressed by the hatred all around them. When they passed the small LDS church there, they found it had been burned to the ground; only the spire remained standing as a stark testament to the fact that even here they had not escaped persecution.

Their journey took them beside a river. They were never sure what its name was because all road signs had been destroyed. They gradually descended as the canyon walls grew taller and further apart. As they traveled along the river for several days, it had grown to be almost a mile across, the walls of the canyon hundreds of feet above them. They believed this to be the Columbia River. The family came to two large cities on opposite sides of the river. The big bridge that used to connect them was gone. They could see ocean-going barges sunken in the harbor. They passed through without incident, grateful to be beyond any large population center.

They left the Columbia and turned toward the mountains. The canyon narrowed almost to nothing, then opened back out again. Nearly vertical cliffs miles apart surrounded them. Above the cliffs stretched the great Idaho desert for hundreds of miles. Down in the protection of the cliffs the rolling hills were just turning green with approaching spring.

The first major building they came to was an LDS church. They found it standing and in good repair. The most remarkable thing of all was that an electric light burned brightly in the foyer. They had seen no electricity anywhere for at least a year. Two men stood by each door. They had no weapons in their hands, but their expression was determined.

The family stopped in the church parking lot and climbed out wearily. They stretched their legs by walking to the front door of the church.

"Good afternoon," one of the guards said. "Have you come a long way?"

"We have been on the road since last fall. We started just outside of Salt Lake City," Grandpa Jim Mahoy told them.

"Would you mind if we asked you a few questions?" the guard said.

"Of course not."

"Who was the last prophet in the Book of Mormon?"

"Moroni," Grandpa replied.

"Who was his father?"

"Mormon."

"What position did Mormon hold in the Sanhedrin?"

"He was a general in their army, and a prophet of God. There was no Sanhedrin."

The guard smiled. "Would you please bear us your testimony?" he gently asked.

Grandpa squared his shoulders and paused to collect his thoughts. Tears came to his eyes as he said, "I know…"

"That will be sufficient," the guard said. "I don't mean to be rude by interrupting you, but there is a testimony meeting going on inside right now. Perhaps it would be more enjoyable bearing your testimony in there rather than standing out here. Please come into the Lord's house, all of you! You may remove your shoes just inside the door." Then he paused and said with a smile, "Welcome home."

Samuel and the "Camp of God," as the people began to call themselves following their baptisms, left their winter home in the spring with confidence they did not feel upon entering. Almost two hundred people from the city joined their march to Zion, swelling their ranks to a little over 900. They took with them sufficient food to sustain them for almost six months. They could have taken more had they the means of carrying it. As it was, they were afoot, with only two military trucks, with a good supply of fuel. Both trucks were ruggedly built and in excellent condition, but they were hardly sufficient to carry so many people's basic supplies. They were loaded until their springs groaned under the weight.

After leaving the factory city they turned north, and avoiding any obvious roads, traveled cross-country, intent on encountering as little civilization as possible. Small factory cities and villages dotted the landscape, so they moved as far away from these as possible. They frequently met small bands of people moving without purpose across the wilderness of Northern Russia. These bands brought disturbing news of the world's perilous condition. They willingly shared their food with these wanderers, taught them the Gospel as opportunity afforded, and moved on. Almost all of those they encountered joined their migration, probably as much for the food on their trucks, as for any hope of actually reaching the mythical place called Zion.

The terrain was vast with dense birch forests hugging surging rivers of water, ice cold and clear. These forests quickly gave way to vast stretches of sparse brush lands and tundra that was spongy underfoot. They followed the rivers as much as possible, only crossing the open ground when the geography they encountered demanded it. They were forced to choose a route that their two trucks could traverse. Even so, they frequently found themselves pulling the trucks from dense mud bogs.

It was early one afternoon that both trucks became stuck in mud up to their floor boards. Every effort to free them only dug them deeper into the mud. The men strung ropes onto the chassis of the vehicles, but even with enough people pulling on the ropes to snap them in two, the trucks would not budge. With great reluctance Alexei ordered that the trucks be unloaded of their precious cargo. They would be left behind. Samuel watched all this from the near bank, his own sense of the situation declaring them hopelessly stuck. By now the heavy mud was so high that one could only enter the cab through the windows.

For the first time since leaving the factory city Alexei approached him. "I have endeavored to do all in my power without calling upon the Lord for deliverance. I know all I need do is ask, and God will speak to you. What shall we do that we may continue our journey with our trucks?"

As if viewing a motion picture in his mind, a complete vision arose wherein he watched the trucks being easily freed from the mud. Even seeing it with his spiritual eyes, he could hardly believe it was possible. Yet, his faith was absolute, and he began describing how the Lord would have them retrieve the trucks.

They went to a nearby stand of birch and cut long narrow trees. They trimmed the limbs from just one sides. They laid these on the mud, limbless side up, parallel to the truck on both sides, then tramped on them until they settled into the mud. They laid another layer, and another, until they could tramp them no deeper into the mud. They next cut long poles and cleared them of all branches. These they forced under the trucks until a pole extended from both sides of the truck every few inches from bumper to bumper. A hundred strong men got a grip on the poles and upon Alexei's cry, lifted the truck above the mud.

At that moment Samuel wished he had a video camera with all his heart. It was one of the most incredible things he had ever seen: that truck suspended upon poles held up by a hundred men barely straining their muscles. A cry of joy escaped every lip in the camp as they walked forward on the logs beside the truck, and set the big truck on solid ground. They quickly carried the second from the mud in the same manner.

Afterwards they all knelt and thanked God for their deliverance. It was a miracle in their eyes, and in Samuel's as well. He tried to calculate the weight of the big truck, and quickly discovered that rather than being a miracle of levitating the trucks by the power of God, it was a miracle of obedience. Each of the men on the poles was lifting a little more than fifty pounds each. Yet, without the aid of a loving Heavenly Father, they all would have walked away from them, never having even considered such a means of deliverance.

Every evening Samuel taught the people more of the Gospel. He allowed his Russian now to be excellent, and no one suspected that he had known it all along. Alexei spent all his time walking among his people, encouraging them, praying with them, answering their concerns, and weeping over their losses. Every day there were losses, and each loss devastated someone.

Hardly a day went by when they did not bury some faithful soul. Usually it was the very old, or the very young who could not endure the rigors of the march. Babies began to be born along the trail. Mothers often did not survive, and their babies usually did not. The cry of a baby in camp became a talisman, a sign of life, survival, and continuity. When one of these tiny voices of hope was stilled, all mourned.

A division was slowly developing in the camp. There were those who rejoiced in the outpouring of truth that God delivered via Samuel's tongue. And there were those who listened curiously, hesitantly, suspiciously, even skeptically. The greater the truths he taught them, the greater the dichotomy grew, until there were those who openly opposed, even debated what he taught. When the spirit of dissension was present, the Spirit of God departed. Thus, as time went on the moments of teaching grew fewer and fewer, and the truths grew less and less profound.

It was now mosquito season with a vengeance. It was almost as if the jaws of hell had snapped open and vomited demonic mosquitoes to eat them alive. Thick swarms of thirsty insects attacked with single-minded hunger. All suffered, their exposed skin puffy with accumulated venom from thousands of bites. Morale grew at first feisty, then rebellious. First they complained, then they rebelled—not so much against Alexei, or their new faith, as against the whole concept of their bitter experience. They entirely forgot their previous joy in having repeatedly escaped destruction through the providence of God in the face of powerful enemies they could not combat.

Against Alexei's urging they stopped, made camp, covered themselves with blankets, and wept loudly. Nothing Alexei or Vladimir could say would move them from their smoky fires which kept the mosquito hoards at a distance. They would not come to hear Samuel teach, and fought to pull supplies from the trucks in quantities that would quickly exhaust the group's provisions and render their onward trek impossible. Short of beating them off with clubs, there was nothing Alexei could do. Those who would still obey Alexei's voice were becoming a dwindling minority.

For three days Alexei went from fire to fire, urging, begging, even threatening, yet the people would not obey. Finally, he retreated to his own fire and knelt in prayer. Samuel joined him, as did a few faithful others. They were still on their knees when the first cry arose. The voice was that of a man, yet so shrill it sounded like a small girl. Above his screams there came a roar as if the very gates of hell had been opened within the camp.

Alexei sprang to his feet and ran toward the sound, dodging tents, fires and screaming children. They came to a stop a mere stone's throw from a scene of terrible carnage. Before them a great grizzly bear stood upon its hind legs, its front paws raking the air as if intent on killing the very air. Samuel had never seen such stark ferocity, such shear rage. The bear's roar was like the scream of a demon mingled with the roar of a hundred lions. It dropped to the ground and charged. Bodies flew into the air as the great beast ripped at everyone in its path. It again reared up and roared.

As if answering a call, another mighty roar came suddenly from their right where a beast even larger than the first was tearing through the people with even greater ferocity. Then a scream of a woman, and an identical roar to their left. In all there were five bears, and all seemed possessed by a demon of terrible wrath. Men grabbed clubs, shovels, knives, anything they could find to fight the threat to their families, and were in a single swipe tossed into the air as effortlessly as one might toss a tissue.

Exquisite terror gripped them all, and the people began to run helter-skelter across the camp seeking any means of escape. There was none to find, and there was no way to get past the bears without suffering the awful wounds of death.

As if on a signal from their collective will, the bears caught sight of Alexei and his small group of faithful. Forgetting for the moment their rage against those surging all round them, they fell to their fours and bore down upon the small band of men. Samuel watched in astonishment as the people fell back, ran and then as if pricked in their conscience, turned back to gaze upon the fate of their leaders. Now a double arena had been formed. A large group of men, women and children formed a circle twenty yards in diameter. Inside that ring was a circle of five frothing bears, and inside that, four men.

The largest of the five dropped to its front feet with such force that the ground shook beneath their feet. It roared and shook its head back and forth, spraying the men with acrid foam. Its fangs bared and snapping, it charged for Samuel. When it was about three feet away it stopped suddenly, screamed, and jumping like a rabid dog, bounded back. Others did the same, coming within a few feet of one of the four under attack. Screams came from the people watching from a distance with each attack. Samuel saw hundreds of them fall to their knees in prayer, others turned on their heels to race even further away. Someone started one of the trucks and began driving it away as quickly as it would go on the rough ground.

A dozen times the bears charged, sometimes getting as close as six inches from tearing flesh. Samuel knew why he felt great calm, for he knew absolutely the bears could not hurt him. Yet, the calm that exuded from Alexei, Vladimir and Karl, Vladimir's teenage son, was so incredibly steady that it astonished even Samuel. They stood facing the bears as they charged, not even bringing their hands up to protect themselves as the enraged beasts fangs snapped inches from their face and foul, foaming spittle sprayed in their faces.

After many minutes of this, Samuel sensed a change in the bears, as if the time had come to make good their threats. Killing passed across the minds of the bears, and the thousand others who watched. Where the bears had until now made their lunging attacks separately, randomly, they now paused, cried with a single collective voice of rage, and charged.

At that very instant Alexei raised his right arm to the square. A voice of complete calm, yet as mighty as a thunderclap rang out across the bears, and fell upon the ears of all.

"In the name of Jesus Christ, I command you to depart," Alexei said. The bear closest to him came to such an abrupt stop that it appeared to have hit the end of an invisible chain. Each of the others did the same. The bears seemed so unnerved by this sudden event they stood immobilized for many seconds. Then they turned their backs to the men they had only seconds earlier intended to rip to ribbons, and walked slowly away. The bears continued to walk, occasionally looking back at Alexei, until they came to the wall of frightened people, who quickly parted as the bears walked down the corridor of human bodies opened for them, and disappeared into the low brush.

Alexei stood without moving for many minutes. Samuel had often tried to imagine the many glorious moments in human history: Moses upon the banks of the Red Sea as it opened before him; Nephi before his rebellious brethren as they fell stunned by the power of God; Samuel the Lamanite upon the walls of the city prophetically crying to the people. But he had actually seen true human majesty but once, as it fearlessly rebuked the jaws of death in the unfathomable power of the Master's name.

The people slowly returned, their faces stunned and shamed. Alexei waited until silence was upon them. "We break camp immediately," he said loudly. "We march through the night and into the next day, and into the following night. God will go with us!" He turned and walked back to his own tent to pack his meager possessions.

As they traveled the little band of seekers grew until their numbers were over one thousand. With the fall of the Soviet empire, hundreds of thousands of Russians took to flight, the vast majority of them heading south toward warmer climates and richer soils. Every day Alexei's group met bands of people moving in the opposite direction. A hundred times they escaped destruction through divine intervention. Each group they passed added to their numbers a little at a time. They fully expected to find the whole northern coast abandoned of human life by the time they arrived.

Of all the obstacles they knew they would encounter, the most impassable was the Eastern Siberian Sea. All Samuel knew of their journey was that they must arrive there before the waters turned to ice.

It took them the entire summer to travel to the Northern coast. They were twice blessed to be able to load their whole band on trucks, busses, or trains and cover as many miles in a few days as they might have in months. The reason such things occurred was that the bands of south-bound refugees willingly traded busses or fuel for food. Oddly enough, those fleeing south seemed to have large supplies of gasoline or diesel fuel, and almost no food. They, on the other had been blessed with abundant food, and no fuel. It made for many interesting evenings of bartering. It was amazing to Samuel to see how many liters of gasoline was worth a liter of wheat or rice.

They arrived at the coastal town of Likhalkin in August. The city was virtually abandoned with no electricity, water, or economy, and very little food. The people who still clung to their city did so with the bleak hope something would change before winter seized them in its icy jaws.

Likhalkin sat on the mouth of the Vladensko river. It was a sprawl-ing jumble of concrete buildings and wharves. Judging by the size of the docks, at one time the sea port must have been quite busy. Now, it stood silently waiting for better times. The few people remaining in the city looked at them suspiciously, yet from a distance. They walked en mass down the main street of town in grim silence. It was somewhat like walk-ing through the bleached ribs of a monster that only a short time ago would have devoured them in a single bloody bite. Now the monster was dead, and with its death they knew safety.

As they approached the ocean with its tumble-down piers and great steel cranes jutting into the sky like the accusing finger of a skeleton, a feeling of desolation came over them. They had come a long way to find the final, and furthest point in their journey so very uninviting. They could journey no further North, as their destination had always been the sea. To turn East and Northward would be to journey into increasingly more arctic territory until life simply could no longer exist. This was as far as anyone, including Samuel, had ever thought of going. Now that they had arrived, their journey seemed futile indeed.

In need of shelter from the winds blowing off the ocean, they searched warehouses and other buildings. Every run-down building they found offered little protection from the wind. They finally settled for a long warehouse tightly enclosed on all sides, which at least housed them from the wind. There they found a large stack of wooden crates and broke them into firewood. As evening closed in upon them, Samuel stood be-side Alexei gazing out across hundreds of small fires. The people were quiet, a few mothers sang quietly to children. Here and there a child cried, or laughed in youthful innocence. It was a bleak time. They had exhausted their food supplies trading for fuel and transportation. They had but little food left, and there was none to find here in Likhalkin. Yet, the people did not complain, and their collective spirit, though subdued, remained faith-filled.

Nearly a year had elapsed since they wintered in the factory city, and Samuel had taught them the gospel as extensively as the Spirit directed they were able to bear. With few exceptions, they had gathered every eve-ning of their journey and had listened sometimes for hours as he taught them the truths of the restoration. Every evening the Spirit fell upon them until they sometimes shouted for joy, or stood up and sang in spon-taneous verse, singing new songs no one had heard before, yet all spon-taneously knew. He had heard people stand up and prophesy in a loud voice, even speaking in tongues. It was all new and unique to Samuel, yet it was how the Spirit manifested great joy in these people. He knew it was of God, and rejoiced in it. They were, after all, the blood of Israel, and they were worthy of the greatest blessings.

In their journey a great sifting had occurred. Those who murmured or rebelled either abandoned them, or in time died. Those who had faith, who sought righteousness, lived. Though this great sifting process was opaque, unobservable to the people, it was not lost on those faithful who now stood beside Samuel gazing across at the people. Of the thousands quietly milling around at his feet, there was not one among them who was unworthy. Acting in the authority he had been given prior to leaving on this journey he had baptized them, and had given them the gift of the Holy Ghost. Now, at journey's end there was a final task he needed to do.

"Alexei, call the attention of the people. I have an instruction to give them," Samuel said. Alexei gazed at him with surprise. In all their journeying Samuel had not once instructed him in anything. Never had he done more than provide guidance when asked to do so. In the many minutes it took to gain everyone's attention they walked until they stood in the midst of the people. More wood was brought and the closest fire kindled bright enough that all could see.

"My people," Alexei said, his voice ringing out in the cavernous interior of the warehouse. "We have come a long distance, and have endured many things. I do not know what awaits us, yet I feel the power of God in my soul, and my faith confirms in my soul that we are on God's errand, and He will take us safely to Zion. It is not necessary to know how this will occur, only necessary to enjoy the peace that it will be." A ripple of agreement drifted up from the sea of dirty faces before them.

"All through this journey Samuel, whom we all love and look to as a man of God, has asked nothing, and given no word of advice or instruction except when I have asked for it. For the first time he has stepped beyond this divinely-imposed limitation, and requested that he might address you. My soul trembles with joy to hear what words God has given him that are so important that he does not wait for us to ask for them. Hear him, my people," he cried softly, and turned toward Samuel, his eyes moist with emotion, his face beaming with anticipation.

Samuel gripped his friend's shoulder in love, then began. "That which I now do is something no man may request," he said. "Yet, the time has fully come, and I am instructed to give unto you one of Jesus Christ's greatest gifts. You understand well the principles of the Priesthood of God. Until this moment I have received no commandment that any of you should receive it. Yet, as the days draw to a close that you will remain upon the soil of your homeland, and as you walk upon the final leg of your journey to Zion, I am given to know that you will not set foot upon your new land until you bear the Priesthood of God."

"Praise God!" a hundred voices cried out in simultaneous joy. Then a thousand, then thousands joined in, until they were all chanting, "Glory be to God, and the Lamb!" Samuel waited for them to grow quiet. As if by a signal the chanting came to an abrupt end.

"The first to receive the priesthood will be Alexei, thereafter Vladimir, Karl, Masik, and others by my own hands. Thereafter, Alexei and those I ordain will go forth among you, and this very evening, all worthy brethren will hold the Priesthood of God. Bring forth the books, and let there be a record of these things kept beside the records of your baptisms."

People scrambled to bring forth the big ledger book they had found in the factory city. Someone brought a small wooden box and placed it before Samuel. Alexei took a seat and a dense silence fell across the people as Samuel placed his hands on their aged leader's head.

"Alexei Antoyov, in the name of Jesus Christ, and by the power of the Holy Melchizedek Priesthood which I hold, and according to the will of God, I confer upon you the Aaronic Priesthood and ordain you to the office of Priest therein. I confer upon you the Melchizedek Priesthood and ordain you to the office of High Priest therein. I give you the authority to ordain others to these two priesthoods as you shall be directed by God. I say unto you to be faithful in all things, and great shall be your reward. I bless you that you will complete your journey to Zion, and live to see the Savior of all mankind standing upon the steps of the Temple in the New Jerusalem. This I do because of your faithfulness, and according to the covenants you made with God before the world was formed. In the name of Jesus Christ, Amen."

The sun was just coming up when the last deacon was ordained and set apart. It was such a glorious outpouring of blessings that few felt tired. With the rising of the sun the final scraps of wood had been burned, the last few bites of food consumed, and the chill of the night held back primarily by the warmth of the Spirit.

"Hey!" a voice echoed back and forth across the vast emptiness of the warehouse. Samuel spun around to see a tall, bearded man stomping toward them, a clipboard tucked under one arm.

"Hey!" he cried again as he grew closer. "You can't stay here! This is a private building, and you must leave!" the man roared as he stopped a dozen feet from Alexei.

"We are children of the motherland," Alexei explained. "We have as much right to be here as anyone. Besides, we are only pausing here before moving on."

"Wrong!" the man roared. "This warehouse and the assets of this company were all sold about five years ago to an American company. This is not Russian property, and you are not welcome here. Look, you have burned up valuable crates, and you are lucky there are no longer police or I would have you all arrested and jailed. You must leave, and take all your crying babies with you!" he bellowed, his voice echoing back and forth across the building.

"We have nowhere to go!" Alexei explained in a loud voice.

"That is not my concern. I go now to get the guards. When I find them, they will return with clubs and guard dogs to drive you out!"

Alexei turned to Samuel. "My friend, I suppose now that I, too, hold God's holy priesthood, I should know within me what to do, but I do not. Pray, ask God what we shall do."

"There is an order to God's kingdom, Alexei," Samuel admonished him. "The order as long as I remain with you is that you ask me. When I am gone, you will know what to do as you ask God. You have done exactly as you should."

"What is your answer then?" Alexei replied, puzzled.

"Ask him the name of the company who owns this building," Samuel suggested.

By this time the man with the clipboard had nearly gained the outer door of the warehouse. Alexei cupped his hands to his mouth and shouted, "What is the name of this American company?"

"Why do you care," he called back, his voice hollow and echoing.

"I may wish to pay rent or restoration for the crates," Alexei replied loudly, and truthfully.

"I do not understand Americans," the bearded one yelled back. "They call the company Princess's Gem. It is a foolish name, but who understands capitalists?" he said loudly.

Alexei again turned to Samuel who was standing with his mouth agape. "What does it mean?" Alexei asked.

Samuel whispered something, and Alexei nodded and shouted back at the man, "Why are you still here in Likhalkin?"

"I was told the American would come and I was to meet him!" the frustrated man bellowed, then turned into the door to leave.

"Wait!" Alexei cried. The man froze with one foot across the threshold. "How were you to recognize this American who is coming?" he asked. "Do you have his name?"

"No!"

"How then?"

"I have only a picture," he replied, shaking the clipboard in the air.

"May we see it?" Alexei insisted. The man seemed undecided, then finally turned back and began stomping toward them. Alexei, Samuel, and a small knot of others moved toward him. As he walked he was flipping pages on the clipboard. When they met he held up a large picture of the American who owned the company.

"Satisfied?" the man demanded, and dropped the pages over the picture.

"Have you studied the photograph?" Alexei asked him, a smile on his face.

"I have, but who understands Americans. They all look alike to me," he said, and flashed a grin that was missing several teeth.

"Would you recognize your employer if you saw him then?" Alexei asked, his voice even more humorous.

"Absolutely," the man insisted importantly.

"Then I suggest you take a look at my companion here," Alexei said, pointing at Samuel. The man turned a bored expression upon Samuel, and after an instant his face dropped. He flipped back to the picture and studied it, his eyes darting between the photograph and Samuel's face.

"What? Is this so?" he finally cried. "I think it *is* you! You are the American. Say something in American!" he demanded.

"Give me a cheeseburger, fries and large Coke," Samuel said in English, and smiled at his choice of words. It was the only thing he could think to say, not having spoken much English years.

The company man dropped the clipboard. It was still rattling on the concrete as he switched to English himself. "It is you!" he exclaimed. "The old man who gave me this picture and my instructions said the first thing you would say in English would be about American food! Thank the patron saint of weary travelers! I am so much crazy to finally have you come. Now, I will go with you to America," he cried. "The man said I could come too, with my family. Is this not true?"

"It is true," Samuel replied, then switched back to Russian. "Where is my ship," he asked, not even sure there was a ship.

"My instructions two months ago by the old man were to anchor it offshore and wait for you. Come. Come. We will light the signal fire, and it will return. The radios do not work without electricity, but we have a signal. Come, you will see!" he urged, taking Samuel's elbow and directing him toward the door. The others followed him down the waterfront for half a mile until they came to a big pile of old furniture. "My name is Andryev Moskov," he explained as he fumbled with a book of matches. "I have waited here for over three years for you to come. But, I have done everything as you instructed, you will see. It is all ready."

He struck the match and a big fire soon was burning on the pier.

"There!" he suddenly cried, pointing at the horizon. "There, they signal back!" Samuel could see a blue light flickering on and off in the early dawn. They stood on the dock as a dark shape slowly materialized. The closer it got the more sure he was that they were looking at a fish processing ship. By the time it was close enough to see the white smoke billowing from its twin stacks, he had decided it was indeed an old floating factory ship.

The ship's lower deck consisted of a ramp like a ferry might have for loading automobiles. Samuel could not see inside that deck, but assumed it was, or at least had been filled with canning equipment. The decks above that were row upon row of small windows. He knew the factory ships had enough room for a full crew to live on the ship. Their numbers would be greater than this ship was designed to accommodate, but with some care, they could make do. The only question was of food and fuel.

As if Andryev had read his mind, he began speaking excitedly. "As I was instructed, the ship has now been fitted to house four thousand. There is food and fuel aboard for a one-month voyage. The factory has been stripped, and the equipment you requested is in the main hold. The food and water were replenished two months ago, waiting for you to arrive. This has been no small task, but the American dollars you gave us speak loudly. It is a good thing you have arrived, though, for the money is all but gone. Yes, it is a very good thing," he concluded happily.

As soon as the ship was tied to the pier they began moving the refugees aboard. Alexei and Samuel went ahead to determine what accommodations they now possessed, and were pleased to find the old ship in reasonably good condition. Much of the upper decks were small ward rooms with a big dining room and kitchen. The kitchen was heavily supplied and ready to begin production. At one time the old ship had been quite nice inside. The walls and floors were all hardwood, and crystal chandeliers hung in the main dining room. Samuel found a plaque stating the ship had been built in 1949 in Boston as a ferry. He could only guess what ill fate had brought it to be a factory ship in the Russian fishing fleet.

The main hold, which was once the parking area of the ferry, was now filled with old gray busses. The large fish freezers in the lower deck were packed full of food, and the engine rooms below were clean and efficient. The big ship had a crew of twelve who had lived on it and kept it in good condition, waiting for their arrival.

There were many pieces of the puzzle missing, but now Samuel at least knew what Helaman had done with the money from the gem he had recovered in Switzerland. He had come to this place and purchased the ship, all in preparation for this very day. It filled Samuel's heart with deep gratitude to see the bigger picture of the workings of the Lord, which had been hidden to him for so many years. He was lost in happy memories when Alexei approached him, and a man in a faded captain's uniform walking beside him.

"Samuel, this is Captain Anestiv, and he wishes to know where we sail, and when."

"When—as soon as we are aboard. Where—to Prudhoe Bay, Alaska."

"To America?" the captain exclaimed in disbelief.

"Yes, to America," Samuel responded quietly.

"But won't the American submarines sink us, or the American fighter planes attack us? The Americans will not let any Soviet ship near, I think not," the captain replied hotly.

"They will not stop us, and we will go safely."

"It cannot be. I will not pilot my ship and these thousands of good people to their deaths!" he insisted, and stomped away.

"What should we do?" Alexei asked Samuel quietly.

"You and Vladimir teach him the Gospel. Take as much time as you need, but we must leave tonight before sunset."

Alexei smiled. "You sound like a Russian now," he said. "We will do as you say. I already feel the power of the Holy Ghost upon me. That Russian captain better look out, for he is about to become baptized," he said earnestly. Samuel gave him a grin and a clap on the back.

The ship pulled away from the harbor a few minutes before sunset, just an hour after the captain's baptism in the frigid waters of the East Siberian Sea.

They sailed northeast, then due east toward the coast of Alaska. Although this was significantly farther than a direct course would have been, it was the route the Lord directed. It took five days to reach Wrangle Island, some 500 miles from Likhalkin. From there they continued east until they crossed into U.S. waters three days later. As the Captain announced their entry into the waters of the Americas, a cheer arose that was heard in every part of the ship. It took three more days and approx- imately 500 more miles to round Point Barrow. From there they sailed through choppy waters for five days before sighting the first artificial oil drilling island of Prudhoe Bay, Alaska.

Far across the boiling gray waters of the Beaufort Sea, the amber lights of Prudhoe Bay's sprawling complex were plainly visible in the night. Seeing those lights brought a surge of happiness to Samuel, for he had once worked there, and their familiar warmth was like seeing the distant flickering of a candle in the window of your home after being lost at sea. Yet, seeing it also indicated it was still in operation, making it unlikely they could land there without difficulty. Since the outbreak of the war, Prudhoe Bay was one of the most secure sites on the North American Continent. They would not welcome a boatload of Russian immigrants, no matter how righteous their cause.

As if to validate his dark ponderings the first mate cried out, "Captain, I have a large shape materializing directly ahead. It is emitting a strong radar signal. Captain, it is an American Submarine!"

"I told you this was foolish!" the captain accused loudly without turning toward Samuel or Alexei. "What do you want me to do now?" he added, his voice lowered. There were countless rumors of the American navy sinking shiploads of fleeing Russian citizens. Sadly, many of them were true.

"Captain, I have a strong sonar blip directly ahead. I believe the sub has fired a torpedo!" he cried.

"Hard to Port! Full speed..." the captain cried, but was interrupted by a commanding voice.

"No!" Everyone turned toward Samuel. "Come to a full stop," he commanded quietly.

"But..." the captain objected.

"Do it, please."

"Full stop," the captain said, then added. "Now, we die."

"Twenty seconds to impact, fifteen, ten, nine, eight, seven, six, five, four, three, two, one..."

WARS IN YOUR OWN LANDS

Melody, Helaman and those with them found the new little Idaho town to be open and friendly, and deeply spiritual. Their initial introduction to their temporary home was like walking into the embrace of a loving family, and they rejoiced to be there. Worship services were held every day, and fasting and prayer brought each soul the comfort and joy they so desperately craved in these hard times. Helaman saw that Melody was settled, he excused himself to work elsewhere. Thereafter, they saw him but seldom. When he finally did return, he brought disturbing news.

A general conference of the Church had just been concluded wherein a few general authorities had urged all present to cooperate with the government forces, and to embrace the new monetary and political systems that were being enforced by the government. These mixed messages confused and divided what was left of Church membership. However, the Prophet stood and boldly declared that Christ is the head of the Church, and he urged the Saints to follow him as the prophet and true mouthpiece of the Lord, no matter the consequences.

Even more frightening was the news that a huge army had crossed the border of Mexico and had invaded dozens of cities in Southern California, New Mexico, Arizona, and Texas. The army was made up of the combined armies of a dozen repressed South American nations, including Mexico. They were well organized, well supplied, well led, and fierce. The reports were that all it took to receive a bullet in the head was to have a white face. Thousands of Americans died within the first month of the assault, and millions of others fled north in stark terror.

With little or no food, the fleeing hordes of American refugees looted as they went, causing nearly as horrific a devastation as the armies behind them. It seemed the "American Liberation" army, as the invaders called themselves, was in no great hurry to proceed, and waited until the fleeing bands of Americans devastated their fellows before moving in to complete the job. They even went as far as to announce which cities they intended to attack next, simply to allow the terrified population to depart. Behind the conquering army came another army of foreign women and children intent upon inhabiting the vacant homes of the vanquished.

With its entire military forces committed to the war overseas, the U.S. government had very little to throw in the path of the invasion.

What small forces they did muster were quickly swept aside by superior weapons and soldiers. A frantic call went out to the front lines for some portion of the committed troops and National Guard to return home to defend their own soil. A reverse convoy was quickly formed and sent homeward. In its haste, it was intercepted en route and destroyed almost without resistance. A dense fog of desperate fear settled upon the inhabitants of the western United States, and without hope, they struggled to throw together whatever rag-tag resistance they might invent.

The invaders split into three forces without warning. One prong continued its conquest up the California coast, another pressed into Texas where it met heavy resistance, and a third headed directly for Salt Lake City, conquering every city in their path. As they rolled across the desert they gathered up American Indians of every tribe, training and outfitting them. Most of them willingly joined in the promise of sweeping the white man from off the face of the land. A great cry of self-righteous vengeance arose from their collective throats, and they marched with solemn hatred toward everything that represented their long oppression and expulsion from their native homelands. Their single watchword was "Purge the land of the white plague, preserve all else." Consequently, their warfare was as much of the mind as of arms.

It was their practice to capture a few hundred of the enemy, publicly execute them in a brutal fashion, and watch the remaining citizens flee in terror. Though reports were everywhere believed to the contrary, the death toll in the recent days of their offensive grew very small compared to the vast reaches of land they conquered almost without opposition. Exponentially greater numbers died from the looting and frantic exodus of the invaded, than from the bullets of the invaders. Almost without opposition they swept northward, clearing the land as they went. Thousands ran from their homes in near nakedness seeking refuge further north. Others sat calmly waiting for the armies to pound on their doors.

Somewhere outside St. George, Utah the great, unstoppable army paused, passed around that city, and following Interstate 15, quickly made their way toward the capitol of Utah without entering any other cities. Their journey to the heartland of Utah's capital that was expected to take weeks in fact took but a few days, and without warning, the invaders swarmed into the valleys of the mountains. Here, their tactics radically shifted; they sought and received an audience with the exiled President of the Church. The meeting lasted several days. Afterward, they departed toward the East in peace. Their army was so large it took two weeks for it to pass through the city. They left a large body of troops just outside Salt Lake City.

Almost immediately, the Church surged back to life. The temple at Salt Lake was cleansed, refitted and rededicated. With the total collapse of government, the Church became the defacto authority in the desert West. Thousands returned to their homes illegally confiscated during the dark days of their persecution. The only utilities restored were sewer and water. However basic medical services became largely available. Cooperative farms were formed to produce food for the people. In less than six months, Utah was one of the few places on earth where hunger and fear were not the norm.

The first general announcement made by the true Prophet was an explanation of why the South American armies had spared them. It was quite simple. For years the Church had loved, fostered, and cherished the South Americans as the children of Lehi. The Mormon Church was one of the few things in North America they did not despise. Hence, they spared it, in fact continued to guard it with their army.

Those who had abandoned their principles and joined in the persecutions had largely left the valley when the Lamanite armies had arrived. Food and missionaries were sent to the armies guarding their borders, with the result that nearly all were baptized.

However, peace was far from settling upon the country. Without warning, ships containing Chinese and Russian troops began landing on both the California coast, and the Eastern seaboard. As they threatened to overthrow the entire nation, they brought with them the terror of foreign invasion. As their numbers grew, the people flocked toward middle America, abandoning most major cities to the invaders without a struggle.

At first there was gladness that these foreign armies did not seem to pursue them, but their elation was soon violently crushed. As soon as a city was subdued or largely abandoned of its people, Chinese planes flew over the huddled masses and dusted them with a pink cloud of death. The Chinese had spent decades developing a powder which slowly decayed to release its deadly toxic gas for this very assault. People took one breath of the pink horror, rolled their eyes into their sockets, and died in a choking anguish just minutes later. Thereafter the pink powder began decaying their bodies until there was nothing recognizable after a mere three days. Thus, without firing a bullet, the depopulation of the American coast lands proceeded in its gruesome wake. The only thing that stopped the invading armies from annihilating every living being was that there simply was not enough pink death to do so.

From that day, people of every area and religion flocked into the Utah
valleys in an unending stream. Those who came were mostly women,
many children, and an occasional pre-teenage male. They came contritely,
not as a conquering army, invading hoard, or roving band of desperadoes,
but as a conquered people beaten into humble, hopeless submission. As
if the Church had always known they would come and had prepared for
years, tent cities were thrown up in orderly chaos. Medical needs were
met, food was provided, productive labor assigned, and peace established.

Then came the missionaries—thousands of them teaching day and
night, comforting, blessing, healing the sick bodies and wounded hearts.
Large groups of baptisms became a daily event, and the Spirit of the Lord
was poured out upon the valleys of Utah as abundantly as during the
dedication of the Kirtland temple.

Priesthood holders were assigned to each tent city. Wards were organized, stakes formed, and order reigned supreme. It was then that the
Church set aside a portion of the BYU campus and reignited the School
of the Prophets. Reignited was the correct term, for those who emerged
from its holy walls were aflame with righteousness. For the first time in
this dispensation, the priesthood was commonly understood in its fullness, and its powers fully enjoyed. Men and women emerged from that
sacred experience with great faith and great power.

It became nearly axiomatic to say upon seeing someone aglow with the
Holy Spirit, "Behold a priest (or a priestess) of the Most High," with a
holy, warm embrace. As the righteousness of the people grew so did their
joy, and their general communion with God. So common did the tales
of great miracles, healings, and outpourings of priesthood power become
that all rejoiced, and all believed. For the first time in nearly two hundred
years, the children of God were in fact one in heart, with no poor among
them. They were Zion.

In her Idaho haven, Melody felt the continual outpouring of the Spirit
like a warm breeze blowing from the south. A kind family had invited
her, Sammy and Helaman to stay in their small home, and for that small
season she had found peace. Now, a restlessness stirred within her so powerfully that she could not stop pacing. The voice of the Holy Spirit whispered constantly in her heart until one evening halfway through dinner
she stood suddenly at the table and announced in a forceful voice, "I leave
tomorrow for Utah."

As if her own words had voiced the restlessness which had settled upon
the entire community, a cheer arose from a thousand throats as multitudes

of righteous were moved upon to speak the same words. Not all left, but those who did went by twos and tens, forming into determined little caravans, heading south. There was no general announcement by the Brethren, no great call, no public debate or discussion; they simply heard the voice of the Spirit, and obeyed.

It was early spring when they departed their cherished mountain home, and mid-summer when they stumbled into the Salt Lake valley, singing songs of joy. They were amazed to see every square foot of that valley covered in tents. Everywhere they looked, s a newness of life had come upon the once-tired people. All was order, peace and righteousness. How glorious it seemed to be home. How strange the cities seemed, being so dark without electricity. Yet, a feeling of security literally bathed the night in peace.

Home! For the first time in years Melody suddenly remembered she had a home of her own in South Jordan. Even with the quiet industry of the valleys of the mountains of God there was very little gasoline, and few functioning vehicles; so she, Sammy, Helaman, and a few others used a little horse-drawn cart to travel the freeway south. A day later, she was standing outside her former home, gazing with gentle longing at what was once hers. It was painfully obvious that another family lived there now. The warm, unsteady light from candles danced softly in the interior of the house. Rippling laughter of children emanated from the walls that had once separated her from the cold. She turned aside, lifted her head to the sky, and laughed. It was a laughter of happiness, and of peace. She strode back to the cart that had brought her and was already seated when a familiar sound told her that someone had opened the door to her home—her former home that is.

"Drive on," she said quietly to Helaman, who held the reigns. He snapped them softly and clucked at the horses who were munching on the unmown grass.

"Wait!" a man's voice cried after them.

"Just keep going," Melody instructed. "We'll find some other place. They need this home now." She smiled as Helaman nodded and prodded the horses again.

"Please wait!" he called. But, Melody did not wish to even discuss to whom this home might belong. It was theirs now.

"Mother! Sammy!" the voice cried in desperation. Melody turned in her seat and gasped.

"Stop! Stop!" she cried, and jumped from the still-moving cart. She ran toward her oldest son Theodore, her arms outstretched. They fell into

one another's arms so passionately it should have hurt, but neither of
them felt anything but joy and wonder.

"What?!" the captain cried. Did they miss us?"

"No, Captain," the first mate replied. "They shot under us! Our draft is too shallow!"

"They won't miss a second time. We must turn about and run. Now!"

"Let me have the radio," Alexei said. The anxious captain handed him the mic. He promptly handed it to Samuel. "Say something amusing in American," he said, and smiled.

Samuel keyed the mic without having a clue what to say. He opened his mouth and this is what came out. "Whoever shot that one's gotta be from New York. No other American would have the gall to shoot another fellow American without even saying hello. On the other hand, I suppose a New Yorker would have at least taken my wallet before blowing me away. I take that back—you've gotta be from California. The last time I was there they were killing each other at stop signs just for smiling wrong."

"Please identify yourself," a flat voice boomed across the speaker.

"Texas!" Samuel cried. "I should have known. I have a brother in Texas."

"Who are you? Identify yourself, or not. Either way I have orders to sink any foreign vessels entering American waters."

"The fact is, we are an American vessel. This is the USS Princess's Gem, registered in California. US Merchant Marine registry 0722515." This he read from a plaque above the radio.

"I never noticed that there," the captain mumbled, rubbing his chin and pondering the plaque as if it had just materialized out of nowhere.

"Please remain at your present location while I check your identification..." silence crackled across the waters.

It took several minutes for the voice to return. "Your ID checks out. I have instructions to order all traffic out of these waters. While we apologize for shooting at you, we still can't allow you to stop here. Please turn around immediately and depart. Have a pleasant journey."

"Captain," Samuel said. But there was no answer.

"Captain?" Silence still.

"Perhaps he does no longer wish to talk to you," the Russian captain said in broken English.

"Captain Bill Hamilton!" Samuel said loudly into the mic.

"How did you know my name?" an angry voice boomed out of their speaker. "Are you a US intelligence vessel? State your business immediately, or I will open fire. My name and the mission of this vessel is classified!"

"Captain. I only wanted to ask you if you set the safety on that torpedo before you sent it into the night."

"That is also classified…." there was some background noise of people speaking all at once that came across as gibberish over the radio. "What…"

"Captain, I only ask because our instruments indicate the torpedo has circled back toward us. It will pass under us as before. Your sub is the next thing on its list. I suggest you…"

"Right full rudder! Release countermeasures! Full…" the radio clicked off to the sound of shouting.

Samuel turned to his captain. "Now, Captain, bring our ship to dock as quickly as possible. This is the only chance we will have to get past the sub."

"Aye," he said, and began shouting orders to his small crew.

Samuel whirled to address Alexei. "Alexei, I suggest you prepare everyone to disembark. We will need to be ready to get off the ship in just a few minutes. Get the buses loaded and running. Load all the extra food and clothing. We have to be off the ship minutes after it pulls to the dock."

Alexei and Vladimir hurried away, shouting orders. About thirty minutes later the old ship nosed up to the concrete pier. The big ramp was lowered to the ground and the gray busses began rumbling off the boat. They didn't even take time to tie the ship, but Captain Anestiv kept the engines running to hold it firmly against the dock. Samuel took his place in one of the buses and they drove off into the sub-arctic night of Prudhoe Bay. They had gone less than three miles when a clap of thunder and enormous explosion of orange fire erupted into the night sky behind them. There was no one on board the faithful old ship when she blew.

Samuel's bus took the lead as they wound their way toward the exit road from Prudhoe's vast complex of oil wells, gathering stations, gasification plants, power generation and pump buildings.

"I remember this place. Turn right here. See that complex over there to the right? That's Pump Station One. I worked there a few times." Samuel felt as if he were giving a tour, rather than fleeing for their lives.

There was a guard gate a short distance ahead. Four marines were standing outside the little building, their guns lowered. The crossing gate was lowered. Samuel could see their breath in the frigid night. They were breathing rapidly, adrenaline coursing through them in anticipation of a fight.

"Let me drive," Samuel said. Vladimir stood up and Samuel slid into the seat while the bus was still moving. He slowed and crawled to a stop beside the first marine.

"Good evening," the guard said. "I have orders to hold you here. As far as we're concerned, you are an invasion force, and we have orders to shoot to kill."

"Good evening Sergeant," Samuel responded, not sure if he was a sergeant or not. "I appreciate your concern. Would you take a look into the window just behind my seat?" The sober face in the helmet nodded once and he took a brisk look into the window. Samuel knew a young mother, a three year-old boy and an infant were huddling in the cold bus. The soldier continued on down the line until he came to the last window. He walked slowly back to Samuel.

"Did you see an invasion force in this bus, Sergeant?"

"I don't know. I'm not responsible for the decisions, I just have my orders."

"Weigh this alongside your orders, then," Samuel replied. "These people have spent the last two years walking through hell to get this far. For every adult you see on this bus, four others have died along the way. For every child on this bus, six others have died. If you stop us, we will either be executed, or sent back to where we came from. We must continue on."

"If I let you pass, I will be executed," he said forcefully, yet with regret.

"That wouldn't be good either," Samuel said. "We wouldn't want that. Where should we wait?"

"I suppose, right where you are." The soldier's voice softened. "Thank you for not forcing us to shoot. We would have shot you, you know."

"Yes, I know. That would be even worse for you than if they had shot you for letting us escape."

"I don't understand how that could be," the soldier said, stomping his feet against the cold.

Samuel flashed a smile at him. "Well, you know as well as I do that killing an innocent man is a no-no with God. Killing one of God's anointed is even worse. I'm afraid you would have had a very unpleasant eternity as a result."

"What do you mean, anointed?" the soldier asked.

"You should understand that. You're a deacon in the Priesthood," Samuel replied. His words surprised even himself.

"Be quiet!" the soldier whispered urgently. "If anyone knew that…" His eyes flashed from side to side, but none of his fellows was paying any attention. Relieved, he looked back at Samuel and cocked his head to one side. "How did you know that I'm a deacon?" he asked.

"The same way you know I'm an innocent man, and one of God's anointed. You sense it in your heart."

The soldier's voice grew brisk. "Look, I'm sorry you're in trouble here, but I can't do anything about it. Who are all these people, anyway?"

"The ten tribes, or at least part of them."

"You mean these are the…"

"Yes."

"But, I always thought they'd come from the stars, or across a highway cast up from the ocean."

"We just came across the ocean," Samuel replied.

"I know, but…"

"Ah, you do know. And you know that my words are true, my young Deacon."

"Maybe I do. But, even if that was so, I still couldn't let you through without getting myself shot for disobedience. There is zero tolerance for such things these days."

"There is a solution to this," Samuel said quietly, almost under his breath.

"What might that be?" the young soldier asked suspiciously.

"Come with us."

The soldier took two steps back as if he had been slugged in the chest. He gasped for breath and blinked his eyes rapidly, pressing a gloved fist to his chest as if his heart hurt.

"That's impossible," he hissed, trying to keep his voice very low.

"It is both possible, and the right thing to do. You know that. As a matter of fact, you already knew you had to leave, you just didn't know how."

"But, how?" he cried under his breath. He stole a look at the three other soldiers who were paying more attention to some teenage girl on the second bus than to this hushed, treasonous conversation.

"How did I know about your decision to leave?" Samuel asked. The fellow shrugged, a look of terror on his face.

"I didn't, actually. But the Lord did, and He just whispered it to me. Come with us. The time is short, and we must leave quickly or we will never reach Zion. Soon, other soldiers will come, and we will be trapped.

Come with us, and take your place in the greatest migration of God's people since Moses departed Egypt."

"I… I…" he stammered. A frowned expression creased his face, then he marched away. He barked orders to his three comrades. "I am escorting these buses to the parking area at Central Control Facility. Have them follow me. Make sure they all follow. Tell the others to meet us behind CCF in the morning."

"Yes sir!" they barked.

The young man marched to the door of Samuel's bus and pounded on it with the butt of his assault rifle. "Open up!" he ordered. Samuel pulled the handle and let the young man aboard.

"Drive straight until I tell you to turn," he instructed as he lowered his weapon at Samuel's head. "Don't try anything."

"All right, son," Samuel said, and put the big bus in gear. He gunned the diesel engine and lurched out as the heavy gate was raised. They turned left two miles later on the road to CCF and ground slowly down the snow-packed road. After they turned, Samuel could see a long line of headlights following them. A few miles later they came to a "T" in the road. They should have turned left to go to the CCF.

"Turn right here," he said, and for the first time, lowered his weapon. "I hope you realize we are now an enemy of the United States of America."

"Son, what's your name?"

"I'm Lieutenant Hollis. Randy Hollis," he replied smartly.

"Brother Hollis, I'm Samuel Mahoy. This is Alexei, the leader of these people. I want you to understand that we are not an enemy of this great country, and in a while they will realize that. For now, we had best put as many miles between us and Prudhoe Bay as possible."

"Yes sir," he agreed.

"Brother Hollis, what's the local time?" Samuel asked.

"Well, it's just a little after five in the morning, sir," he replied after consulting his watch.

"Then daylight will soon be upon us. What do you know about the Mormon Church?" Samuel asked.

The lieutenant shot him a withered glance. "Well, I had just been ordained a Deacon when the Church was outlawed. I haven't been to church for nearly eight years since then."

"Has it really been eight years?"

"Yes sir."

Samuel was misty-eyed as he spoke. "I haven't been home for seven of those eight," he said slowly, his mind filling with a mental vision of Melody, Sammy and the twins.

"So, are you a prophet, or something?" Randy asked.

"I am—something like that," he replied without thinking. His usual modesty would have prevented him saying this, but something about the circumstances elicited a direct answer. He wasn't *the* prophet. But there could be no doubt that he was sent from God. The distinction seemed insignificant at that moment.

"Randy?"

"Yes sir?"

"Would you like to know more about the Church that you just committed everything to, including your life?"

"Well, yes sir, I guess I would. Being as how I'm going to die for my convictions shortly, I'd like to know what they are. Will you teach me?"

"I'm going to drive the bus. Vladimir speaks excellent English. And, he has a powerful testimony."

Vladimir was still bearing testimony when the ice fog settled in upon them. The darkness of night was just giving way to the gray of dawn when it came.

Crystalline ice fog is something difficult to visualize until one actually sees it. The best way to describe it is to imagine a windless cold day, so cold your breath crackles as you exhale, so cold that exposed flesh turns white with frostbite in less than a minute. Now imagine taking a thousand tons of silver glitter made of ice, and suspending it in the air. The headlights of the bus hit the slowly swirling crystalline fog and glared back into Samuel's eyes in dazzling flashes of color. No longer able to see the road, Samuel pulled to a stop and turned off the lights. All the other busses did the same, and their drivers dozed off amid the crystalline beauty surrounding them.

In less than an hour the sun began to rise. As it rose above the horizon it penetrated the ice fog in a burst of light. In the deep arctic winter the sun hardly rises above the horizon, yet, reflected as it was off the ice fog, it was dazzling. A halo formed around the sun in stark white too bright to look at. It was truly a halo, for it completely encircled the sun.

Some distance further out a second halo appeared, then still farther away, a third. Connecting the sun with each of the circles of light was a tapered shaft of light going up and out in all four directions. Each beam of light was broader at the ends where it touched the halos, and tapered in the waist. It formed an image a thousand feet high in the shape of a brilliant, double cross. The bottommost beam of light appeared to continue from the sun directly to the front of the bus, so that they might have stepped on it and walked directly into heaven.

"Is this the Second Coming?" Vladimir asked after Samuel aroused him from a deep sleep. Soon everyone on the bus was awake and gazing in wonder at the spectacle. Still the fog swirled around them so thick that they could not see the bus directly behind them.

"No, it's not the Second Coming, but it *is* our salvation." Samuel said.

"What do you mean?' Vladimir asked.

"Listen!" Alexei said urgently. "Listen." Everyone grew silent so that the low idling of the bus sounded loud and persistent. In the silence another sound thrummed above them.

"Helicopters!" Randy said urgently as he recognized the thrum-thrum of the mighty war machines above them. They listened in stark fear as the sound came toward them, grew very loud, then passed off into the distance.

"They didn't see us," he finally said as the sounds faded. A few minutes later the monstrous helicopters came across from a different direction, and again passed overhead without stopping.

"Why doesn't the radar work? Surely radar can see through the fog," Randy asked Samuel.

"Because God has closed their eyes. They see what He wants them to see," he replied.

"Then, we *are* going to make it safely to Zion?"

"Oh yes, we are going to make it to Zion," Samuel rejoined. The word "safely" was conspicuously absent from his reply.

The ice fog lasted about an hour longer than the fuel in the helicopters. Shortly after their ominous searching ended, the fog lifted to reveal a barren expanse of ice that stretched as far as the eye could see in all directions. Only to the south was a hint of a mountain range visible on the horizon. These were part of the mighty Brooks range. The only evidence of man having been there was the raised roadbed upon which they were slowly driving.

It took them two hours to sight Pump Station Two of the Trans-Alaska pipeline. Built in the seventies, the pipeline still carried crude oil along its 800 mile length to the fresh water port of Valdez, Alaska. Forty-eight inches in diameter with wall thickness varying from a quarter inch to well over a half, the pipeline had outlived its designed life of twenty years by over triple. Not only was it a marvel of engineering, it was a marvel of maintenance as well.

For several years in the nineties Pump Two had been mothballed due to lack of flow through the pipeline. But when the new world war had broken out, all environmental concerns had been tossed aside and the huge oil reserves of the Arctic Wildlife Refuge had been hastily drilled and plumbed. Now, the pipeline carried in excess of two million barrels a day to the ragged remains of the U.S.

With the absolute dearth of middle east crude, the Alaska oil range took on critical importance. The shipping lane from Valdez to Seattle was the most heavily guarded sea corridor on the globe. Given all that, it was not surprising that the road paralleling the pipeline should be the most jealously guarded gravel road in the world. The shivering refugees' only hope of salvation was in divine intervention. But of this they each had personal knowledge; divine providence had stayed with them throughout their journey.

About the time the great plumes from the twin jet engines of Pump Two came into sight, it was beginning to grow twilight again. The ice fog settled in rapidly around them. Samuel directed the buses to remain nearly bumper to bumper as he felt his way past the station. On the left side of the road were white reflectors every hundred feet, and on the right, yellow. By following the closely-spaced reflectors, they could pick their way down the highway using a flashlight rather than the headlights of the bus. As long as the reflectors remained white on their left, they were on the road. If a reflector on their right side was white, they were about to drive off the left side of the road. If a yellow reflector passed on the left, they were about to drive off the road on the right.

They inched their way past the station without being seen, climbed the low hills just north of there and found the ice fog non-existent on the far side of the hill. They gratefully switched on the headlights of the buses and continued on. An hour later they crossed a bridge over an unnamed river, and drove parallel to the river for many miles.

It was deep into the night when Samuel had the strong impression to turn down a sideroad. Though not plowed of snow, the road was passable. They drove up a narrow canyon between low hills, wound past numerous 55-gallon drums scattered along the sides of the road, and finally came to a closed gate. Samuel pushed open the gate with the bus, and drove into a large yard surrounded by large steel buildings. It was a construction camp used recently during repairs to the pipeline. In better times it would have been torn down and cleared away. In these times of pragmatism and financial hardship, they had been left standing.

They opened the doors to the big sheds and found ample room inside for their buses. Crews were sent out to sweep fresh snow over their tracks. The crews were just returning when the thrumming of helicopters was again heard in the distance. They finished their work and pulled the big doors shut on the sheds moments before the big black harbingers of death slid past.

At that moment in time a breeze whipped the yard around the sheds, in mere seconds moving tons of powdery snow. One of the big black birds swung up the canyon and hovered outside the big construction camp complex. With no visible sign of the invaders it shortly lifted higher and roared away. Samuel had watched it hovering a mere stone's throw from the building he was in. The crack in the door was large enough that he could see the big machine guns under its stubby wings, and the dozens of rockets nestled against its side.

"The only problem with being inside the sheds is that we can't idle the engines. We'll soon freeze to death," Randy said, his breath creating ice fog with hung around his head like a cloud. "We can't light a fire. Besides, there's nothing to burn. And if we idle the engines on the buses through the day we'll run out of fuel before we reach the next Pump Station. When we reach the next station they'll see us, and call for the helicopters. And," he drew a deep breath. "we'll starve to death about the same time we freeze to death."

"I must say—it is very refreshing," Vladimir said without looking at Randy, but obviously responding to the young soldier's concerns. ". . . to once again be in the jaws of death."

"I don't understand why that would be refreshing," the younger man replied bleakly.

"Because it gives us the chance to exercise our great faith. And, it gives our loving God the opportunity to show His hand in some great miracle to preserve our lives."

"I can certainly agree it would take a miracle to do that," Randy replied hotly.

"Young man," Alexei said, walking past Vladimir and taking the soldier by both his shoulders. "You must understand that we have been on this journey to Zion for over two years now. We have seen miracles aplenty. We have watched God shut the mouths of bears, destroy helicopters who were slaughtering our people, even raise the dead. In every way we have great faith in our God. In time you will join us in these feelings."

"In time I hope I will still be alive to have faith."

The old man smiled. "It is my opinion that you will be. Now, come and I will show you what we do when it appears we are about to die. Come…"

For himself, Samuel longed to find a quiet spot where he could not be seen for a while.

"Alexei," Samuel called after the old man.

"Yes, my brother?"

"I am going to walk outside for a while, and will return in a few hours. Don't send anyone after me."

"As you wish. God speed," the old man said in Russian.

"And you," Samuel replied with bowed head.

Samuel stepped out into the daylight of the arctic winter, in reality not much more than twilight. The sun was not visible in the shallow canyon they were in. He walked until he came to a very hard patch of ice. He continued walking until his tracks were not visible in the ground. He called upon God in mighty prayer, and in seconds was no longer in Alaska.

Randy followed the old leader between the buses to where a large area remained open. There, in the midst of the busses and abandoned equipment in the sheds a few hundred people knelt on the ground in a circle within a circle within a circle. All waited for Alexei to arrive.

"Vladimir, my son. Since my English is weak, would you lead us in prayer so that our young soldier friend will understand?"

"Gladly," Vladimir replied, and took a position in the center of the people. Randy knelt beside Alexei far back in the crowd.

After a long silence Vladimir raised his hands high over his head and looking up into heaven cried out, "Our Father who art in heaven, hear the pray of Thy children."

All the people repeated in broken English. "Our Father who art in heaven, hear the pray of Thy children." Few of them actually understood the meaning of the words, but the warmth of the Spirit they knew well as it settled upon their collective souls.

Randy looked up with a start, for it appeared to him as if a bright light had formed all around Vladimir and those closest to him. He blinked then lowered his head, thinking it must have been his imagination.

"Oh Father, we give Thee thanks, and honor and praise and glory." Vladimir began reverently, and the people echoed each word. "But most of all we thank Thee for the atonement of Thy Son, and for the deliverance

His great sacrifice has brought into our lives." Again the people repeated, but this time, they began speaking before Vladimir had finished.

"Great is Thy glory, and endless is our joy in Thee, and ever and ever shall we worship Thee, Thou who are most holy above all, and in whom we take infinite delight." Randy was startled to hear many voices speaking in exact unison with Vladimir's. No longer was there an echo of voices, but all seemed to be speaking as one voice.

"Holy Father, we raise our voices in Hosanna's unto Thee, and pray Thou will hear our cries of joy and adoration and worship, that our voices might join with those of the angels in making a joyful sound unto Thee." Randy found his own voice loosened as an intense burning welled up inside his soul. Without knowing how, he knew every word Vladimir would say, for the phrases formed in his own heart as they were spoken by the congregation.

Vladimir raised his hands high. "Beloved Father, we confess before Thee our weakness, our sins, and our impurity, and pray Thou will look down upon us in mercy, and apply the atoning blood of Thine only Begotten Son, to purify us with fire. Especially we pray for our young American soldier…" At that moment a pause in the collective voice caused Randy's own to cry out as if the sound of a trumpet.

Randy's voice reached into the heavens: "… and forgive me, oh Father, and purify me with fire, that I may humbly attend to the great task before me, willing to give my all, my life, my hopes, my very being in service to Thee. Father, beloved Father, unto Thee I consecrate my all, willingly, joyfully, with great longing to be of service unto Thee, and unto this people." These words the people did not echo, but cried in response, "Amen."

Vladimir continued once again, but Randy could not tell the words did not originate with himself. As far as he could feel, his was the only voice in that large temple of steel and snow, and his voice ascended unto the throne of God in mighty worship for the first time in his life. He did not notice the hours pass, nor the stiffness in his body, nor the cold seeping into his flesh, for he was afire with the Spirit of truth, and the power of the Holy Ghost was working a mighty change in his soul. He was literally a different person.

When the young man stood stiffly, his eyes were puffy from prolonged tears of joy, his face was aglow with light, and his soul felt as if it were on fire. He looked around to really see the world for the first time in his life. A new and glorious feeling surged through him suddenly, powerfully, and he fell to his knees again. A dozen people joined him in silence as he poured out his heart in mighty prayer. The feeling that had brought this sudden undeniable urge to commune with his Father was a feeling of love so powerful, so healing and life-giving that the only way his soul could answer was in sweetest prayer and gratitude.

All around Randy the work of caring for so many people, sharing their meager food, and providing for the very demanding rigors of their journey went on unnoticed. For most of that day he remained where he was, surrounded by a handful of fellow worshipers who waited upon him, covering him with blankets, keeping his knees upon padding, making sure he did not lie on the frozen ground. All this was unseen by him, for he was elsewhere. When he finally came back to the world of mortality he was exhausted, unable to stand or walk, and filled with the Spirit to the consuming of his flesh.

"Take him to a place in the bus where he can sleep." Alexei instructed. "See that he drinks and eats a little. He is our brother now."

ESCAPING BABYLON

Melody found it difficult to release Theodore. They were both laughing and crying so loudly that neither of them could speak.

"Mother!" another voice cried from the steps of the house. "Mother!"

"George Alexander?" she cried in wonder. Her younger son from England, much older and taller than the last time she saw him, bolted down the steps three at a time and ran to her. Theodore stepped aside just as George ran into her arms. They embraced and kissed one another over and over.

"Mother! Mother, it's so wonderful you're actually here. I knew you'd come! I just knew it!" George shouted with joy. "I want you to meet your grandchildren. Mama, I have two beautiful little girls, and Theo has two boys and a girl. We're going to the temple just tomorrow to be sealed. Mother! It's just too wonderful!"

Sammy had waited behind his mother until this exact moment, when he strode around her and grabbed both his brothers in his arms. Now a strapping sixteen year-old, he was as tall, and definitely stronger than either of his siblings. They cried out in happy surprise and hugged him fiercely.

About this time, children and wives came pouring out of the little house. In all, over a dozen people were living in her former home. She was amazed to see the changes inside. Someone had completely removed the electric stove. In its place stood a big makeshift wood-burning cook stove. It was the ugliest thing she had ever seen, but it was radiating a warmth that completely redeemed it. The smell of baking bread added to its ugly charm. The furniture was all handmade. The kids slept on three-tier bunk beds. There was one room for boys, and one for girls. A third bedroom had a normal bed with soft mattress. The fourth bedroom had quilts on the floor for beds for the rest of the adults. The married couples took turns in the only private room a week at a time.

One by one Melody was introduced for the first time to her daughters-in-law. She instantly adored them. Their faces were full of love and light, and she found herself completely charmed. The grandchildren were precious beyond gold. It was late into the night before their excited laughter and stories were hushed and put to bed.

Melody finally had some time alone with her boys. After briefly mentioning some of her own adventures in Idaho she asked, "What happened to you boys after you left home? I was so afraid you would be caught and punished by the blue helmets for not getting the mark and joining the army."

Theo spoke first. "Mom, it's a long and wonderful story. We can't tell it all to you now, but when we left here we didn't know where to go. We finally made our way into the mountains, and there we found a large community of Saints. Mother, it was wonderful. They were full of the power of the Lord, and faithful and true. They were living off of their food storage and moving every day or so. They lived there in the mountains. Day after day their numbers were growing. Many times the soldiers would come and walk past our camp without seeing us, or they'd fly right by overhead. Even though we had campfires burning, they wouldn't see us. We were truly living and being preserved by the power of God."

George nodded and excitedly continued the story. "In our group we had one of the members of the Quorum of the Twelve Apostles, Mother. Imagine it! A prophet and an apostle among us! Every day he sent some of us into town to get supplies, and to preach the gospel. In the nearly four years we have been apart, George and I have been on a full-time mission. We have baptized hundreds of people. By the time the enemies of the Church left the Salt Lake Valley, we were Zion, and fully ready to partake of the glories of the Lord."

Melody clapped her hands in joy. "Oh, I'm so proud of you! I want to hear all about that time. As a matter of fact, I feel strongly you two should write it down while it's still fresh in your minds."

Theodore and George looked at one another meaningfully, then back at their mother. "We were instructed by Elder Andrews, who is the apostle I mentioned, to do exactly that," Theo said. "When we're not working to feed our families, we write everything we can remember." He winked at her. "What about you, Mom? Have you written down your experiences in Idaho?"

Their mother chuckled. "So you want to know if I practice what I preach? Well my dears, actually I have. I kept a diary the whole time." Then she grew more serious. "I want to know something else. Have you boys found your joy in the Lord? Have you truly found and dined upon the fruit of the tree of life?"

"We have," came their emphatic reply.

"We are ready and anxious for the Lord to come again," George explained.

"Do you believe in the ministering of angels?" Melody asked.

"Oh, we do. You do too, don't you, Helaman?" Theodore said, directing his comment to the older man sitting a short distance away. Helaman looked up from the Book of Mormon he had been reading all evening.

"Why do you ask?" he wondered.

"Because I have this strong feeling about you. I always have had a strong feeling about you. I think…"

"I think there's someone I'd like you to talk to, rather than my poor self," Helaman interrupted. "Come with me you three."

"But, aren't you going to answer my question?" Theodore asked, already knowing the answer. He had tried many times to pin Helaman down, and had been unsuccessful every time. It was almost a game with them now. Yet, he had known Helaman in England almost twenty years ago. The man was older and walked with a cane then. Now, when Helaman should have been much more frail, he was exactly the same. He still walked with a cane, most of the time without a limp. He still looked ancient, yet still had the ability to move like a cat when he needed to!

Helaman walked to the front door without a word, opened it and walked through. He held it open for Melody who was followed by her two adult sons. Sammy had already gone to bed. They followed Helaman who walked quickly to the edge of the front lawn, then turned around to face them. Since there were no street lights, it was very dark out. The only light on Helaman's face came from a single kerosene lamp in the window of the house.

"Who did you want us to meet …" Melody asked, and gasped. She ran forward and into the arms of the familiar man who was walking briskly down the sidewalk at that very moment. He was dressed in a heavy down coat and thick boots, even though it was hardly that cold in Utah

"Hello, my love!" Samuel cried with great affection. He kissed her over and over as he held her in his arms, savoring the smell of her hair and the warmth of her body against his.

"Sam," Melody sobbed against his shoulder. "Oh darling, I've missed you every single day since you left!" She pulled back to gaze into his face. "Oh my goodness, Sam Mahoy, you are a sight for my sore eyes! Can you stay long?"

"I'm sorry, Angel, I can only stay for a few hours," he replied.

"Dad!" Sam Jr. said, having waited as long as he could before running into his father's arms. "Oh Dad, you are really home! I've missed you so bad!"

The two Sams wept for joy as they held one another, and Samuel ruffled his sixteen-year-old's hair as he had done since Sammy was a child. Then Samuel turned again to Melody. "Will you please introduce me to my other sons?"

Melody put her arms around her boys. "Theodore, George, meet my husband, Samuel Mahoy."

Samuel embraced them each in turn. It was the first time they had met face-to-face, though they had heard much about him from their mother as well as from Helaman. While he held them in his arms, Samuel told each of them he loved them, and thanked them for their care of their mother. They both pulled away from their stepfather with deep affection for the stranger who called them his sons. They knew, as did Melody, that he had now included them in his celestial family.

Perhaps it was this obvious love that put George at ease so quickly, or perhaps it was a question he had wanted to ask for a long time. Whatever the reason, George asked the first opportunity he got. "So, you work with Helaman?"

In fact, he had asked the same question of Helaman, and had received a kindly, but blunt sidestep to his question. Whatever he expected his stepfather to say, it was not what he had heard, and it quite startled him in its directness.

"I do," Samuel replied, his answer given by the Spirit. "And, rather than have you ask questions one after another, let me just answer them here. I am what in some ages is called an angel. I received my commission from the Lord and was translated to my present state many years ago while you boys were still in England. Helaman and I have been working to bring a portion of the tribe of Levi of the lost Ten Tribes from the North. Is there anything else you want to know?"

Both boys stared at Samuel before they found words to speak. Finally, George blurted out, "Heck yes! There's a lot more I'd like to know," he exclaimed. "To start with, why couldn't Helaman just say what you just said?"

"Because I'm not your father. It wasn't my place," Helaman interjected. "However, now that you know, you must also respect the idea that only your father may inform another of his blessings. You may never speak of it, not even to your Mother or each other. Do you understand?"

"Yes, absolutely," they both said.

"This isn't our first exposure to heavenly beings," Theodore replied. "We had many experiences being assisted by strangers who saved us from impossible situations on our missions, and then simply disappeared. We know the importance of sacred silence."

George nodded in agreement as Theo continued. "I have never had the opportunity to actually ask what it feels like to be so blessed, to actually converse with angels and to live so close to Heavenly Father," he explained.

Samuel smiled. "You're talking to an angel now," he said.

"Good point!" Theo replied, somewhat astonished at his own lack of insight. "But I guess it isn't quite the same as having the angel Moroni appear above your bed in a cloud of glory," he observed wryly.

"True," Helaman replied. "It's better! Before you ask why, think about it. Here we are, conversing with you as one friend converses with another, telling you things that few mortals have heard. We are under no mission to appear, deliver a message, and depart. You may actually ask anything you feel is appropriate. The fact that this is the case is a direct result of your worthiness in Christ to receive this blessing, and the great price you have paid to be obedient to His voice. You are both greatly blessed—actually, far beyond your understanding. Don't let the realization that this great man is your father cloud the fact that he is in fact, one familiar with the face of the Lord, upon whom lies the most profound of blessings: an angel in every sense."

This all had the effect of causing the boys to ponder what had been said in deep silence.

Samuel smiled at them warmly. "Your faithfulness in Christ is the main reason I have come today. You two have a great work to do, as does Sammy, your brother. You need to work with him to help get him prepared so I can come to him soon. My coming to him has little to do with his mission, but I miss him very much. So, do all you can to hurry him along. Teach him about your struggles, and your great faith. Teach him about Jesus Christ and the empowerment of His great atonement. Sammy will come around quickly; he has strong faith already. In a short time you all must leave this place and begin your journey to Zion."

"Is it really that close?" Melody asked her husband, gazing up into his face.

Samuel took her hands and kissed the top of her forehead. "Yes, my love! In just a few months the group I lead will cross Canada and head for Missouri. Your leaders here will begin your journey from Utah in a short time. Finalize your preparations now. As soon as word arrives that a group has arrived at the Cardston temple from Alaska, that will be your signal to begin the journey."

"We will, Father," George promised. Samuel smiled at his words, especially his calling him "Father."

"Where is the group you are with?" Theodore wanted to know.

"They are just beginning down the Trans-Alaska pipeline."

"That is a heavily guarded road. It will take loads of divine intervention to bring them safely here," George said knowingly.

"They have great faith," Samuel assured him.

"As do we," Theodore added. "Perhaps we should go inside and let you and mother talk?"

"Thank you," Melody said gratefully. The boys returned to the house with Helaman. They were deep in conversation as the door banged shut.

Samuel turned to face his wife. He bent down and kissed her lips tenderly. "I have missed you, Melody—really, really missed you."

"Oh my darling, I have missed you terribly," she replied sadly.

Samuel paused, then smiled broadly as if a wish had suddenly come true. "If you'll come with me, I'll show you one of my favorite places on earth." She nodded happily as Samuel took her hand. They walked into the darkness of the night.

It was several hours before Melody pushed open the front door and walked inside. Samuel was now gone. She walked slowly into the room and sat softly on the love seat, a faraway look in her eyes. Her face was aglow with happiness, her cheeks flushed and rosy. Her hair was loose around her face, and she smelled of lilacs and exotic flowers.

Even though it was very late, her sons had waited up for her. Though not worried about her, they had been anxious for her to return.

"Where have you been, Mother?" they asked.

"I'm not sure," she replied softly. "To heaven I think..." was all she would say. They never did find out what happened that night. But, until the very end of her life, whenever someone mentioned that evening, the same sweet smile would cross her face, and she would get a faraway look in her eyes.

Samuel returned to the snowy landscape with some regret. His whole being longed to stay with his beloved wife and children, to go with them to Zion. However, the Lord had commissioned him with another task, and with all his heart he chose to obey. He knew Helaman would stay with his family as much as needed, and they would arrive in Zion safely.

He retraced his steps to the big steel sheds only to find the buses loaded with people and backing out into the yard. It was nighttime, and time to journey once again. The air was bitterly cold with a brisk breeze blowing. Had he been able to appreciate the cold as a mortal, he would have buried his head in his coat, and shivered fiercely. The wind chill was nearly seventy below zero. As it was, he pulled his coat around his neck, and trotted to the first bus.

Alexei and Vladimir smiled at him as he climbed aboard. Neither said anything to him about his long absence, nor the possibility that he might not return on time. He took his place behind the wheel and glanced at the fuel gauge. There was less than a quarter of a tank left. They would have to find fuel before the morning came.

The convoy of noisy buses turned left onto the snow-packed haul road, and continued their slow journey toward Pump Three. The road from here was hilly, tucked between a river on their right, now frozen, and hills on their left which grew in height and ruggedness as they pressed forward. They drove slowly, partly to preserve fuel, and partly to ensure that no accidents claimed any of their numbers. The old Soviet buses were at best utilitarian, yet extremely sturdy. The same engine that powered the vast fleet of Soviet (now Chinese) light armory also hummed under the hoods of these old gray buses.

Finally, the gentle rise of the ground dropped away steeply, and they could see Pump Station Three glowing brightly at the bottom of a broad valley. Dense plumes of heat were visible billowing into the sky from the four, square exhaust stacks of the big turbines. Samuel pulled to a stop and turned off the lights.

"From here, we must walk," Alexei said. They had run out of fuel, and there was no other alternative. This came as a terrible shock to those on the bus. They had walked literally a thousand or more miles across their frozen homeland. Now, to be once again afoot in an even harsher world, one unknown and frightening to them, was almost more than their weary bodies could accept. Still, they began gathering up their possessions, and moving toward the front of the bus. None complained, even those who knew their depleted bodies could not make the remainder of the trip afoot.

"Alexei," Samuel said quietly as he watched the people filling the road. "It is unthinkable to see these people afoot again. I'm afraid many of them haven't the strength to go the hundreds of miles we have left."

"I know this," Alexei said, his eyes tearing in spite of himself. "My dear brother, I don't know how, but we must go into the station below us and obtain fuel and food. I need you to petition Heavenly Father again, and gain His word. As so many times before, we need His aid!"

Sam nodded humbly, and waited for the Spirit to accord. When it did, he placed an arm on the old man's shoulder. "You are right. I must go alone into the station. You will wait here for my return," he told Alexei, his mind clear on what he had to do, just no idea yet of how to do it.

"We will wait for your return. God speed," the old Russian said.

Samuel began the long walk toward the pump station without much idea of what he should do. As he topped a hill on his slow journey and dropped over the crest, he realized that the pump station was all but abandoned. As soon as he was out of sight, an odd vision filled his mind. It was of a hallway with a gray steel floor. The hallway was lined with lockers on one side, and fire-fighting equipment on the other. He had seen many like it, but not specifically this one. Suddenly, in as much time as it takes to think a thought, he was standing in that hall. A sudden warmth flooded over him, and he pulled open his coat to let the cold escape. Billows of frigid air rolled downward and across the floor from his frozen clothing. He took a step and slid forward. He looked down to find his snowy boots melting into puddles of water. On the painted steel floor it was quite slick.

He took three careful steps to a rubber mat that ran before the row of lockers. He walked down them slowly reading the names. He came to one which read "GRIZZ." This startled him, because he was quite sure he knew the man who owned this locker. He smiled to himself just thinking about "Grizz", who worked at Pump Two years before. This fellow was a three-hundred pound festering package of profanity. He could insult anyone over anything, find something vile and profane in any situation, and curse in a way few benighted heathens ever considered.

Tonight, Grizz's locker was securely locked with a very large padlock. It was unusual for the locker to be secured, since theft was nearly unheard of at the pump stations; this was because everything they used at the station had been given to them by the company. Nevertheless, this evening Grizz's locker was locked tight. For reasons Samuel could not explain, he felt that the very thing he needed was inside that locker. He took hold of the lock and it simply clicked open in his hand. One of the laws he did not have to abide as a non-mortal was the law of opposition. As long as he was doing God's ordained work, nothing in the material world could oppose him—a sturdy lock as well.

The locker contained a gigantic pair of coveralls, a down parka, two large boots, and a collection of tools. Although Samuel didn't realize it until he had it is his hands, on the shelf under a white hard hat he found what he needed: a clipboard with a maintenance schedule, and a set of keys.

Samuel pulled down the clipboard and was not surprised to note that the service schedule for two remote gate valves was due in the morning. It would not be at all unusual for someone to begin this maintenance the night before. He grabbed the keys and the clipboard, and hurried out into the freezing night.

He marched undetected across the yard to where the fuel trucks were stored in a big garage. The truck he sought was a large red tanker truck with a capacity of four thousand gallons of diesel, and five hundred gallons of regular gas. He found the truck, inserted the key, and the engine coughed to life on the first try. He let it idle as he climbed from the cab and stabbed a finger onto the "UP" button to raise the garage door.

Samuel shifted the big truck into gear. No one at the pump station saw him drive smoothly out into the night; it was a miracle, he knew, as the station would normally be heavily patrolled. When he arrived at the guard gate it was already open; he drove to the haul road and turned left. In less than a half-hour he was trying to figure out how to turn on the pumps to transfer the precious fuel to the buses.

It took most of the night to pump the fuel. By the time Samuel was finished it was just growing twilight. As the morning grew lighter a dense fog had rolled into the low valley. He drove the big truck past the pump station and honked twice on the air horn. Behind him, unseen in the fog, a convoy of refugee buses rolled past, barely able to see more than the bumper of the bus in front of them.

They drove all that next morning and passed Pump Four about midday. They saw no further helicopters. Samuel could only assume that there had miraculously been no reports of strange vehicles on the haul road, or anything unusual the night before.

From Pump Four they began the slow climb toward Atigun Pass. Here the terrain changed dramatically from rolling to rugged. To their left the rock formations were breathtaking. A great jutting of granite in one spot formed a jagged mountainside. Right next to that another great peak jutted in the opposite direction, and between them a giant stone dome as smooth as a bowling ball. The combinations of stone formations seemed impossible to all exist in the same place. As they climbed the air grew colder, and the road more treacherous. Near the summit, the visibility was nearly zero. Samuel slowed the fuel truck as much as he dared without going so slow that he could not start again on the slick road.

The only thing that gave it away was a single flash of light that caught his eye. Samuel stopped and studied the blinding snow where he had seen the dim flash. In a moment he saw another, and realized it was the unsteady movement of a dim flashlight off to his right. He pulled a little farther ahead and stopped. Unwilling to stop on the long slope, the busses passed him and continued up the hill until they reached a flatter area. By that time Samuel, Alexei and others were climbing through a deep drift toward the light.

"Thank God you saw my light!" a weary voice cried as they pulled open the passenger door of a big supply truck leaning on its side, stuck on the side of the road. "I've been here for nearly 24 hours, and had just about given up hope."

"Come on, we'll help you get warm. I have a bus here," Samuel told the man.

"Who are you?" he demanded through chattering teeth. "I didn't think any buses were running up here anymore."

"Well, if I told you we were the ten tribes returning from the North, would you believe me?"

"No, I'd say you're insane," the half-frozen driver asserted.

"Right," Samuel chuckled. "The bus has my crew in it. We just left Prudhoe on our way to Fairbanks. Our fuel truck is just a few yards away. We'll drop you off at Pump Five on the other side of the pass. The crew in the bus will see if they can get your truck out of the snow. It doesn't look like it's damaged, mostly stuck I think."

The driver was beyond relieved. "That would be wonderful," he gasped between coughs. "I'm afraid my feet are almost frozen. I can hardly feel them anymore."

Samuel helped him into the cab and climbed in himself. "Pull your shoes off and let me rub your feet," he instructed.

The driver looked at him suspiciously, then began unlacing his boots. He had worn regular work boots in the truck, not expecting to have to endure the fierce cold for any length of time.

Samuel began rubbing his feet and found them frozen solid. His heart lurched in sorrow. He would probably lose both of his feet. Samuel prayed silently and in that moment the Spirit flooded him with peace. He gratefully extended God's gifts to the man. His toes immediately softened and flexed.

The man sighed. "Oh, thanks, that feels much better," he said and lay back in the warm cab. "I guess they weren't frozen after all."

Samuel turned up the heater to full blast. "I think they'll be fine," he said. The driver's eyes closed in relief and he quickly fell asleep. Samuel put the big truck in gear and drove past bus after bus of Russian refugees.

Alexei and Vladimir began examining the cargo of the truck while Samuel took the driver to Pump Five. Samuel already knew what was in the truck. On the door of the truck were the words, "Carr Gotstein," Alaska's largest food wholesaler.

Atican pass wound steeply downward with many tight turns, but the scenery was breathtaking. Samuel enjoyed the drive as the lost driver snored deeply. A few hours later he dropped the tired man off at the base of the hill leading to Pump Five.

"I've got to continue on, but it's just a short walk to the station," Samuel said.

"You can't just drive me up the hill?" the man protested wearily.

"I can't," Samuel told him. "I have to go back to get your truck out of the snow."

"Okay, I do appreciate you doing that," the driver said in a sort of daze.

Samuel looked him in the eye. "I will deliver your truck and its contents to where they need to go."

"Sounds good," the driver told him sleepily. "Thank God you saved my life—I know you did."

"Yes, God *is* good! I am indeed glad we found you," Samuel said. Then he added, "We'll take care of your truck. If anyone asks, just tell them the Lost Tribes of Israel have it."

The driver laughed loudly. "I'll do that. Thanks, and so long."

There was an element of danger in returning the man to Pump Five. He would surely report that he had arrived at Pump Five in a fuel truck. That would put to rest the mystery of the missing fuel truck from Pump Three. The odds were they wouldn't send helicopters after a missing fuel truck. But, they probably would send a security vehicle, or set up a roadblock.

Samuel pondered all this as he found a place to pull off the road just beyond Pump Five. The terrain was less rugged here as the road leveled out quickly. There were once again trees—that is if the stubby, black spruce of the far north can rightly be called a tree. Still, it seemed wonderful to be in less-barren country. When the first trees appeared they were sickly looking, barely alive, and less than the height of a man. In just a few miles they became taller and thicker until the forest was dense with robust spruce.

It took the buses an additional three hours to catch up with him. But, when they did, there was a semi-truck filled with food in the convoy. Now they had more food than any of them had seen in years. It was a miracle, and they all rejoiced.

With plenty of food and fuel the only thing to slow them in reaching their destination was the treacherous journey south. Samuel knew that only the power of God would deliver them once they reached Fairbanks, which housed the largest military base in Alaska.

A pink fog settled over Salt Lake and Utah valleys without warning, and its work of death began instantly. With an almost complete breakdown in communication, people had only heard rumors about the "pink death." What they had heard, even the most horrifying rumors, was less than the reality—because none who actually experienced the pink cloud ever lived to tell about it.

The war waged by the Chinese and Russian forces against the United States was never intended to be easy. They knew before they loaded the submarines that brought them to the American homeland that resistance would be fierce, and strongly doubted they would be able to use their pink horror more than once or twice before they were rebuffed. To their delight, they arrived in the East without opposition and dispensed their death with nothing but isolated, ineffective resistance. When it became evident they had underestimated their chances of actually conquering their hated enemy on their own soil, they had dispatched urgent requests for backup and supplies. In the meantime, they stormed from city to city subduing and killing as many as they could.

Somewhere in the Midwest they came to the startling conclusion that there was almost no one left for them to kill. The deep South was heavily engaged in a war against troops from South America, and far too well-defended for them to engage. The far north was too sparsely populated to waste their dwindling supplies on, and the West coast of California was already in the hands of the South Americans. The major population centers of the West were now teeming with frightened refugees. Salt Lake City made the perfect target.

The Chinese loaded the last of their deadly supplies onto a stolen plane and argued for three days over whether to drop it in sufficient quantity to kill on contact, or to spread it over a vast area in the hopes of killing more in the long run through the lingering death it left in its wake. In the end a compromise of sorts was reached. They would dump sufficient on the city center to kill a few tens of thousands, and spread the rest south as far as it would go. Sick from exposure to their own chemicals, they took off knowing they would not themselves survive long enough to even land the plane.

When the drone of the plane was heard above the quiet city, every eye looked up in wonder. A plane had not over flown their homes in years. As the billowing pink cloud began forming behind the plane, they knew something was terribly wrong. When the first people in the streets died after three choking breaths, the population screamed in panic, ran a few steps and died themselves.

Theodore was rocking his youngest child and humming an English tune to her when his head suddenly snapped up.

"What is it, honey?" Melody asked.

"Do you hear that, George? Do you hear it, Helaman?" he called loudly. The baby in his arms began to whimper. He handed her to his wife and stood. At that moment George came running up from the basement.

"We have to go into town," he was calling. When he saw Theodore he looked at him solemnly. "We have to go into town."

"I know. I was just coming to get you. Where's Helaman?"

"I'm here." Helaman said as he walked in from the back of the house. "We must leave. But first, we need to leave a priesthood blessing on this home."

Theodore nodded. "Mother, Rachel, everyone! Come, gather in a circle and hold hands," Theodore instructed. It was a few moments before all the kids could be gotten from their beds. It was still early in the morning, and the house was chilled from the winter night. They came protesting— but they obeyed.

Theodore surveyed the small group to make sure everyone was present. Thereafter he raised his right arm to the square, as did George and Helaman. Melody had never seen anything quite like it.

"In the name of Jesus Christ, and by the glorious power of His priesthood. I rebuke the destroyer and place a blessing and promise of protection upon all present, and upon those we love no matter where they may be. In His holy name, Amen."

A chorus of "Amens" was followed immediately by a barrage of questions as the three priesthood holders pulled on their coats.

"Please, tell me what is going on," Melody pleaded.

"Mother, the plague is come. I heard the Spirit of the Lord plainly speak in my ears to tell me to make haste into the city. We must hurry before there are none left to help."

"What plague?" she demanded.

Theodore threw open the door. Already a light dusting of pink powder was on everything in sight. "Behold, the hand of death," he said soberly as he surveyed the landscape.

"What is it?" a dozen voices demanded sleepily.

"Get together. Sweep it into the streets. Go help the neighbors, and show them that your faith and the Priesthood has delivered you. Our only hope is in the mercy of God. Go now, there is no time to lose," he commanded. "Come George, we have a long walk ahead of us."

Every house Theo and George passed they pounded on the door and prayed with them, leaving a priesthood blessing. Some of the houses they entered were already filled with choking people. These received priesthood blessings. Many recovered instantly. Many died before their words were finished. Death seemed to be very selective, taking whole households, whole kinships, while completely sparing others.

The nearer they walked to the city the greater the number of dead. They walked up and down the rows of homes, often meeting other groups of priesthood holders doing the same task. They did little more than call a greeting, and pronounce a blessing upon the other faithful brothers they passed, who then joined their ranks. Many of the groups of righteous also included women who went out boldly to minister and heal through their faith, and by power they had received through their temple ordinances.

The outskirts of the city seemed to be the hardest hit. As they walked up the quiet streets they stopped by each body. At each body they paused, listened, and either walked away, or knelt down to bless them.

"My beloved sister in Christ, in the name of His holy Priesthood I command you to return to this world and complete your sojourn here," one of them would say when inspired to do so. Without exception the black, sunken eyes would flicker open as color and vitality returned to the festered flesh. Never once did those restored to life seem surprised, but calmly stood, thanked them in two or three words, sometimes with a hug, then strode off to continue administering to others. But fewer than half of those they encountered were they allowed to heal in this way.

All through the day, George and Theo worked their way closer to the Temple. As they labored up and down each street they were met by more and more who had heard and heeded the call to redeem Zion just as they had. It took most of that day before they came to the outer walls of temple square, and the great granite Salt Lake Temple. They walked into the square to find throngs of righteous in the attitude of singing praises and worshiping in songs of joy. They raised their voices with those already there for hours. As if the veil grew thin at that place, many saw visions, spoke with angels, and prophesied of glorious things to come.

It was well past midnight when the men again climbed the concrete steps of their home. Their walk home had been much more disheartening than their march into town. Almost every front lawn they passed had mounds of dirt marking the graves of loved ones whose faith, or whose destiny had not been sufficient to keep them on this mortal sphere. It was not correct to say that only those who were unrighteous died that day. For all knew of people with great faith who simply were not ordained to survive that experience. It was true to say, however, that none who were not righteous survived the desolating sickness.

For reasons no one quite understood, on the following morning a loud rumbling awakened everyone in the house. Children ran from their beds in terror, wondering if the house had come alive, or was going to be destroyed by another earthquake.

"It's the furnace!" Melody cried. "I can't believe it—the electricity is back on!" It had been several years since a light bulb had burned in the valley. Many children had not seen such a marvel in their young lives, and stared into the lights until their eyes ached. Realizing that light bulbs would be impossible to replace, every fixture with more than one bulb was quickly stripped of all but one, and children were schooled intensely on the evils of leaving a light running for no reason, or even worse, turning on a light during the day, even if it was dark in the room. The family gathered around the radio, anxious to hear any news from the outside.

The following day muddy brown water began burping from the taps. In a few days it became sweet and cold. A few days later someone brought an old television back into the room and plugged it in. They watched as the picture flashed to life. The first image they saw was the face of their Prophet.

"Brothers and Sisters, I repeat. Now that we have running water in most parts of the valley, I urge you to plant gardens in every available space come spring. If you do not have seeds, contact your home teachers. Some will be made available. Every chapel will hold classes on gardening between now and spring. Your gardens must be successful the first time. If you have no garden plot, join with neighbors at their invitation and share their space. Dig up your lawns and flower gardens if necessary. You don't need fertilizer, all you need is faith. Pray for your gardens, do as the Holy Spirit directs, and they will flourish.

"The supplies of food the Church and many faithful members have stored against this very time are nearly exhausted. Come next fall we will live on whatever we raise this summer. Fear not, for all this is known to the Lord, and he will bless your efforts with bounty from the earth. As He did when feeding the 5,000, Jesus Christ will multiply your faithful harvest with food sufficient to feed your families and neighbors.

"I leave you this last prophecy to warm your hearts and strengthen your backs against the times just ahead. In the not far distant future the Lord will sound His trumpet, and a few blessed and chosen ones will begin the journey back to the lands of our inheritance in the East from whence our fathers were driven by the hand of unrighteousness. There they will build a Holy City."

"Many of us will remain here to receive and teach those who will flock to us for aid. It will be a great missionary labor, and we will baptize millions. As we prepare the people they will be gathered to Zion. In time we will all go to Zion. Except for those who go first, we shall not walk, but shall go upon the wings of the Spirit."

"We will build God's Zion and will meet the Lord Jesus Christ as He returns to His temple. There we will watch in awe as He comes in Glory to subdue all enemies under His feet, and to establish the millennial reign of peace so long awaited by the righteous of every age. This I prophecy in the name of Jesus Christ, Amen."

That message was repeated every half-hour throughout the day. In the evening speakers from among the General Authorities spoke on subjects of great interest. The topics were as basic at times as obedience, baptism, faith, and repentance. At others, they were as lofty as the ministering of Angels, the washing of feet, and the second endowment, the fullness of the priesthood, miracles, the law of consecration, and a host of other topics previously unmentioned in such a large forum. It was almost as if General Conference were in permanent session. The Spirit rested upon His people in rich abundance, and Zion began to emerge among them. The temples were open twenty-four hours a day. It was truly a time of rejoicing among the faithful.

Samuel and his convoy of Lost Israelites reached Fairbanks late at night in the last days of January. The air was almost brittle with cold as they lumbered down unplowed roads toward the city they most feared. The nearer they drew to the city the broader the roads became, and road signs counted down the miles before they would arrive. The first street light they encountered was not lit, nor any thereafter. They came to the main gate of the massive military base that now encompassed the city. No lights glimmered in the crystalline fog. Strangely, no one was at the guard gate, and they passed into the city.

Fairbanks was a city of ice. Every structure, every tree, every sign was completely encased in thick frost so that some structures were not even recognizable. Cars were stalled in the middle of the freeway where they had been abandoned, and nowhere was there a light to be seen. Nowhere was a person to be found.

Samuel turned off from the main highway and drove slowly down a wide street, its name obscured by ice. Turning left down another street and then right again they found a row of houses. Buses began stopping as families stomped through the crusty snow up to the front doors and into the empty homes. In less than an hour everyone was inside and snuggled under blankets. Of the hundred homes they occupied that night, not one was missing furniture, beds or bedding. The only things that had been taken were food and photographs.

All else had been left behind.

A ZION PEOPLE

Peace, such as can come upon a people of tremendous faith on the ragged edge of starvation, settled over the Salt Lake Valley and its environs like a down comforter. As food grew more scarce and less varied, the people fasted as many as three days a week, giving their surplus, if they had any, to those without. That which they lacked in physical needs was abundantly replaced in spiritual manifestations such as had not been previously known among the people in this dispensation. It became commonplace for people to see or hear angels in sacrament meeting, for children to speak prophetic words, and for talks given in church to be as powerful as anything that ever rolled from the tongue of a prophet.

Another interesting change was that the Saints did not consider anything they possessed as their own. Most families had not actually built or paid for the homes they lived in; few had purchased the food they ate with any kind of money. All they possessed was "ours," rather than "mine," and a simple equality of stewardship blessed the people. Every day those able to labor did so with all their energy. In return they were given sufficient for their needs, and even some of their wants. The streets were clean, the schools staffed, and the businesses manned. The bishop's storehouses were stocked as much as possible, and public utilities were maintained, all through the Church distribution. There was no jealousy, class distinction, or wealth except as was common among all of them.

For the first time in several hundred years, Zion blossomed upon the desert soil. For the first time in as many years the condemnation was lifted off the Church, which condemnation had been because of their worldly walk and prideful hearts. With the lifting of that heavy burden, the Spirit of the Lord moved freely and powerfully upon the people in all they said and did. The emotions most common among all who dwelt in Zion was peace, and undiluted joy.

When summer finally came at long last all hearts and hands turned to the soil. A hundred thousand gardens produced bountifully, and food was no longer scarce. Trees that had ceased to give fruit for years now sprang forth with limbs heavily laden. Nothing was wasted, all was preserved, and there was enough, and to spare.

The long-awaited call finally came to prepare to trek east to the center place of Zion, but it did not come over the television, radio or any address

given by the Brethren. It came into the hearts of those who listened.
Melody simply began collecting things they would need. As if some internal mechanism had chimed the hour of preparation, the work began in quiet earnest through out every reach of Zion.

Melody was just finishing stitching the border on a quilt when a firm knock came to the door. It was just turning cool as summer gave way to fall. She was sitting in the house with all the windows open, a pleasant cooling breeze moving gently through the house. The children were all at work or play outside. She laid aside her work and walked down the steps to the door. She was not prepared for what she saw.

"Mother!" the tattered visitor cried, and rushed into Melody's arms.

"Lisa! My sweet girl! I can't believe you are here! Oh Lisa, I have prayed so hard that you would come home. Come in, come in." she urged.

Lisa turned around and picked up a little boy two years old, who was hiding behind her. A small girl not much older than four had been holding his hand. "These are my babies," she said happily. "Monica and Timmy, meet your grandmother," she said, holding Timmy forward. Melody knelt down, smiling at him so broadly that he smiled back immediately, and looped his arms around her neck. She then held out a loving hand to Monica, who took a happy skip and slid a small hand into her grandmother's.

"Come inside everyone. Welcome home!" Melody exclaimed with joy. Lisa smiled back at her with relief and love. It was the best thing Melody could have said.

Everyone having eaten and the little ones happily off to play with cousins, Melody turned her attention to Lisa. Her stepdaughter was still lovely, although her tired eyes were puffy and strained. Her hands were severely chapped, her dress torn and tattered, and her short hair looked like it hadn't been washed in months. It broke Melody's heart to see her this way.

"Lisa, the last I knew of you, you were in Texas with your husband," Melody said as she reached out to rub her daughter's shoulders.

"That's right. It's a long, long story," Lisa said wearily.

"I'd like to hear it. When your father returns, he'll be most interested to hear everything that's happened to you. He loves you so much!"

"Oh Mama, how is Papa?" Lisa cried. "Is he well? Where is he? I had so hoped he would be here!"

"Your father is much more than well. I saw him last winter for a few hours. He's off on a mission for the Lord. He's doing fine. Come to think of it, I don't think he's aged much at all in the last dozen years. He sure looked good to me," Melody said wistfully.

"You haven't aged either, Mama."

"You're sweet honey." In fact, Lisa was right. Melody wore her fifty-seven years with elegant grace.

"As a matter of fact, if I didn't know any better, I'd say you're pregnant! Sorry, but it's true," Lisa giggled.

Melody blushed. "You're far too observant," she said, running a hand across her slightly distended abdomen. "I am."

"But, aren't you kind of…" her daughter said, and then stopped, not wanting to be rude.

Melody laughed. "Old? Normally, I would say yes. But, I'm different. Something has changed in my body these last few years, and I feel as strong as when I was twenty. I have simply loved being pregnant again. I'm so happy I can hardly express my joy."

"So, you are all right with being pregnant? I mean, you're happy about it?"

"I'm positively overjoyed," Melody said with such fondness that Lisa was left without a doubt that it was so.

"So, since you're expecting, obviously Daddy came home a few months ago." Lisa winked at her mother. "When is your baby due?"

"Just three months. I can hardly wait."

Lisa thought about that. "So when can I see Daddy again?"

"That depends mostly on you," Melody said slowly.

"What do you mean?"

"I'll explain later," Melody said, trying to avoid a real answer. "He is on a special assignment, and can come back if we have sufficient faith. Otherwise, I'm thinking we will only see him when we finally make it to Jackson County,"

Lisa shook her head. "I don't understand."

Her mother good-naturedly patted her knee. "Oh sweetheart, I'll explain it all to you in good time. Now, tell me about you!"

Lisa settled into the couch, savoring the warmth and security of her new surroundings. Melody joined her. "Well, as you remember, Alvin and I left Salt Lake just before the Church was outlawed. How long ago was that now?" Lisa wondered.

"About five years ago, I think."

"Seems like longer," Lisa said quietly.

"It does indeed."

Lisa sighed and continued her story. "So anyway, we moved to a small town outside of Houston called Huntsville. It was beautiful there. The economy was still good. People were optimistic, the Church was growing, and it was wonderful. Alvin got a job with a small crating company and quickly moved up into management. We bought a house and were doing great—until the Church was outlawed."

Melody nodded in sympathy. "It came as a total shock," Lisa confided. "The changes it made in people's attitudes were severe. Since we were new in Huntsville, few people knew we were Mormons. Alvin decided to try to keep it a secret as long as possible. I was worried about doing that, like it was betraying our faith or something. But, Alvin insisted he'd lose his job if he didn't pretend to not be a member."

Lisa stopped, her voice becoming emotional. Her mother nodded for her to go on. "Everything seemed to go along fine for a few months. But, it was awfully hard for me to stand by and watch as other Church members were persecuted and driven out of their homes. I could hardly stand to keep quiet. The only reason I did was because Alvin insisted. He was adamant that we should not let anyone know we were Mormons. I tried to go along as best I could. I salved my conscience by helping other members, giving them food or clothing, and housing them whenever I could. It was truly pathetic. The members were so destitute. My heart ached for them," she remembered, her eyes pooling with tears.

"The worst part came when the monetary system changed and paper money was outlawed. Everyone was forced to get the microchips in their bodies, or to go hungry. Of course Mormons who wouldn't renounce their religion could not get the chips. Alvin came home one day and announced that he had gotten the chip implanted. He said it was so that he could feed me. At the time I was three months pregnant with Monica. He said it was the only way."

"Your poor husband!" Melody told her softly.

"I was frightened, and didn't know what to do. He pressured me to get the chip also so that I could have the baby in a hospital." Lisa paused with emotion. "I refused," she whispered.

"You are indeed a brave girl," her mother told her with a nod.

"Maybe too brave," Lisa told her. "What happened next was so sudden... I had no warning. It was really bad for the other members of the Church. They were leaving Texas as fast as they were able, but many of them were destitute. I had found three teenage children digging in our garbage can. I convinced them I was their friend, and took them in to hide them and feed them. They said they were Mormons, and that if I took them in I could get in trouble. I told them I was a Mormon too, and not to worry."

Lisa stopped, her voice breaking. "Oh, Melody, but they weren't Mormons!" she cried. "They were spies. They turned me in to the police. Some men came in blue helmets, and without saying anything more than that I was an outlaw, they threw me out into the street. When Alvin came home they let him into our home, but I couldn't go through the door of my own home. The police went inside and talked to him for over an hour. When they came out they loaded me into a jeep and drove me over fifty miles away from my home and dumped me off on the side of the road. They told me not to try to return home." Lisa paused as tears rolled down her cheeks. She looked up tragically. "I have never seen Alvin since, and that was over six years ago."

Melody held Lisa tightly for a few minutes before her daughter could go on. "What happened next, my dear?" stroking her back.

Lisa sniffed and bravely resumed her story. "I was close to the border of Louisiana, and was able to hitchhike to the town called Leesville. When I arrived I was nearly starving. It was a small town and a lady saw me stumbling down the street and gave me food and a place to spend the night. In time I got a job as a nanny and housekeeper for a family named Allen. They were very good to me. I took care of their two younger kids and kept house. They were fairly well-to-do, and seemed to not care that I was homeless, or that I was pregnant."

"Everything went fine until it came time to have the baby. They drove me to the hospital for a prenatal checkup. I hoped to get the checkup in spite of not having the chip. I had been able to do other things fairly easily without a chip in Louisiana, and hoped to get by. When the hospital found that I didn't have a chip, they offered to implant one. I refused, and they reported me to the authorities."

"It was late that night when the police came to the Allen's. I had gone to bed early with light labor pains. They got me up and brought me to the police station. The police grilled me until I finally told them I was a Mormon. The Allens were shocked, and ordered the police to punish me then and there. So the police took me out into their truck. All this time I was in labor, and terrified. It was raining and cold, and all I had on was my nightgown. The only other clothing I owned was the dress I was wearing when they found me, but it was far too small now. The Allens let me keep the nightgown; otherwise I would have left their home naked. As it was, I was shivering in the back of their truck, sitting in the rain in a wet nightgown, terrified, cold, and in hard labor."

Lisa was crying again, and stopped to compose herself. "I was actually hoping they would take me to prison where at least I might receive medical help. My biggest fear was that they would just dump me somewhere. If they did that I was quite certain that I or my baby would die—and probably both of us."

"Oh Lisa, that's terrible!" Laura cried.

"It really was, Mama. The police drove to the outskirts of town and stopped on the side of the road. I could hear them arguing for a while about what to do with me. One of the policemen was actually compassionate. He argued I was young, and pregnant, and that I would die if they left me there as they had been instructed to do. The other said they had no choice. I could hear them arguing loudly in the cab of the truck. They both seemed desperate. Neither wanted to cause my death, but neither knew what to do with me. All the time I was sitting in the back of their truck in the rain. While they were arguing my water broke, and I knew the baby was coming. I had heard of the government taking babies from other Mormon women. I knew I couldn't wait for them to decide what to do with me. I climbed out of the back of the truck as quietly as I could and ran away into the night."

Melody took her daughter's trembling hand. "I was still close enough to the truck to hear their conversation when they realized I had escaped," Lisa continued. "They just shrugged, and said me being gone made it easier on them. They drove away and left me huddled behind a bush. If they had looked for me they could have found me in seconds."

Melody rose to get a handkerchief for her daughter, who was almost incoherent by now. Lisa wiped her tears, then continued. "After they left I knew I was in worse trouble than before. I prayed like I have never prayed before, and suddenly I felt a warm hand upon me. Somehow, Mama, I was guided through that delivery, even though I don't know exactly how it happened! It was a pure miracle, I know that!"

"Praise the Lord!" Melody exulted.

"It was a miracle, let me tell you," Lisa told her. "I was just exhausted, and wrapped little Monica in my nightgown, laying her on my belly to keep warm. Luckily it was a warm night, and I was so exhausted that I slept and fed Monica until morning."

She paused here to reflect, then concluded. "As I look back on those events, I'm surprised I survived, and Monica as well. Actually, I know we survived only because Heavenly Father was watching over us very carefully. Ever since that miraculous experience, I have felt more faith than I've ever had before."

Melody's eyes were brimming with tears, and she put her arm around Lisa. "What happened then?"

"Well, when I could walk, I went back to the Allen's and was able to hide us in their garage for two days," Lisa said.

"What did you eat?" Melody asked.

"I ate from a bag of apples and opened some jars of bottled fruit on the shelf. When Mrs. Allen found me, she screamed and ran back into the house. She began throwing things at me and ordering me to leave at the top of her lungs. She threw shoes, blankets, food, clothing, all kinds of things! She even threw a big laundry bag for me to put them in. She was 'screaming' while I loaded all that stuff into the bag while saying, 'Thank you, thank you.' She was also weeping, and I knew she hated herself for what she was doing. I left with enough food and clothing for a few days. It was nighttime and rain was starting to fall."

Lisa shivered as she thought about it. "That very night I heard the news that Mexico had invaded Texas. Suddenly, the police quit worrying about Mormons. I no longer had to hide for fear of being arrested, or having my baby taken away. I joined the army of people who were leaving Texas. I was able to get a ride up into Oklahoma. There were so many refugees now that I was no longer different from anyone else. It was hard to get food, but when people saw that I had a tiny baby, they usually shared. It was an awful time, and terrifying."

"I can't imagine how you survived," Melody said, her eyes filled with pain.

"I'll tell you how I survived—by divine intervention. I know that now."

Melody nodded solemnly. "I have prayed with great faith concerning you and Bonnie," she told her. "I had no idea you were struggling so! But I always felt you were being preserved."

Lisa smiled in gratitude. "Your prayers were undoubtedly a big part of my survival. Prayers—and an older gentleman I met in Oklahoma."

Melody cocked her head. "Older gentleman? Was his name Helaman, by any chance? Does he walk with a cane?" she asked.

Lisa's eyes grew big. "How did you know? He does use a cane, and his name is Helaman!"

Melody laughed out loud. "He is a friend of your Father's, and seems to be heavily involved in our family's survival," she grinned.

"I had no idea. If it hadn't been for my bumping into Helaman in Oklahoma, I would never have survived," Lisa exclaimed.

"Oh no! Please tell me about it," Melody encouraged.

"It's kind of a funny story!" Lisa began. "I arrived in Oklahoma in
the hot afternoon. It was extremely muggy and unpleasant. Monica was
hungry, and I didn't have much milk for her. I probably would have if my
diet had been better, or if I even had more water to drink. By this time,
Monica was five weeks old and I was pretty much skin and bones."

Melody shook her head. "Oh, you poor dear!"

"The people I was with tried very hard to help, but they didn't have
anything either," her daughter continued. "I had decided I was going to
die about the time we made it as far as the rest stop. We were driving an
old beat-up van, and it overheated and died. We coasted into the rest stop
with steam billowing out of the engine. There were lots of other people
there, refugees like us. When we arrived there was a big fight going on.
It appeared to me as if a big bunch of them were beating someone up. It
made me so mad that I left Monica on the floor of the van and ran toward
them, yelling my head off. Somewhere along the way I had picked up a
branch, and was waving it around. I must have looked insane running
toward them like that."

She stopped here to shake her head. "When I arrived, this poor old guy
was on the ground bleeding. They had worked him over pretty soundly.
I clobbered the guy closest to me with the stick and knocked him to
the ground. That got their undivided attention, and they actually backed
away. I asked them what this man had done wrong. They said he was
a Mormon, and Mormons were responsible for the invasion of Texas. I
asked them why, and they said because everyone knew they were. So I
told them I was a Mormon—as a matter of fact, I screamed it at them!
I told them that I was an advance scout for the Mexican army and that
they were going to be here before sunrise and kill everyone who had ever
touched a Mormon."

"You're kidding!" Melody cried.

"No! That's exactly what I said," Lisa laughed, her face beaming for
the first time.

"What did they do?"

"They believed me! They took off in every direction."

"No!"

"It's true. They did!" Lisa insisted. They laughed together, and Lisa
turned contemplative again.

"I helped the old man to stand up, but it was he who practically dragged
me back to the van. In spite of the beating he had taken, he seemed pretty
strong to me. I tried to clean up his wounds, but he insisted on helping
me. He said his name was Helaman. At that moment the people at the

rest stop started coming back. I knew we were in trouble when the first rock hit the side of the van and broke out a side window."

"Whoa!"

"Richard, the guy who owned the van, jumped back in real quick. It started right up, and we drove away. Whatever had been wrong with the van before, it seemed perfectly fine after that. Honestly, it was another miracle," Lisa said quietly.

"Helaman seems to be surrounded by miracles," Melody observed wryly.

"Well, Richard drove us several miles from the rest stop and pulled over. He told us we had gotten him into trouble, and ordered us out of the van; then drove on with us standing by the road: an old battered man, a sick mother and a baby. I started to cry. Then Helaman says, 'Oh, let him go. He would have just wanted part of my apple.'"

"'Apple?' I asked. So he reaches into his coat pocket and pulls out this big red apple. He handed it to me, and I bit into it after he told me to. Mama, I have never tasted anything so amazing in all my life! I chewed until my jaws hurt and then swallowed. I handed the apple back to him, but he wasn't interested. I finally ate the whole thing. While I ate, he played with Monica. She seemed to love him, and stopped crying for the first time in days. It was strange, too, because I felt the milk flowing into my breasts then, and was able to nurse her for a full year after that. That was a miracle too; I had been dry for weeks."

Lisa took a deep breath and continued. "Helaman stayed with me and began taking care of me. He always was somehow able to find food and transportation, or whatever else I needed. He was very kind. But, he was so solid in his faith that I literally fed upon his love of the Lord. He began inviting me to pray three or four times a day. We never traveled on the Sabbath, and he never passed by a fellow sufferer. He gave of everything he had, no matter who was in need or how little we had ourselves. I learned something new and wonderful from him every moment of every day. If he had been forty years younger I would have fallen hopelessly in love with him right there on the dusty streets of Oklahoma."

"I know what you mean. Helaman is a marvelous man, and a Christian of the highest caliber," Melody affirmed.

Lisa stared at her mother. "How long have you known him?"

"Honey, I've known Helaman for over twenty years. Your father has known him about the same. And, I met him in surprisingly similar circumstances."

"Who is he? I mean, why does he have such a great involvement with our family?" Lisa wanted to know. "I spent years with him, walking from Texas to Utah. And, how could he also have been here with you too?"

"I don't know, but he was." Melody asserted.

Lisa's eyes grew wide. "Well, when I see him again, I'm going to ask him!"

Melody laughed and shook her head. "No, don't ask, it won't do any good. I've asked a hundred questions he just didn't answer, and he may stop coming if we try to pin him down. Just accept him for what he is, and praise the Lord for it. Maybe he's your guardian angel!" she suggested smilingly.

"Yes, I've often thought that maybe he is!" Lisa declared.

Melody got up and motioned for Lisa to follow her into the kitchen, where they began making dinner. "What happened the rest of the time? Six years is a long time to walk," Melody asked as she and Lisa peeled potatoes for the soup.

"Well, we didn't walk the whole time, of course. We spent days, even weeks at a time in some places, waiting for my health to return, or for some opportunity to continue on. During it all he never insisted on anything. If I said I wanted to sleep for several days, I slept. If I would have said I wanted to go to the moon, he would have taken me, I think! But all I could think of was making my way back home to you and Daddy."

"We're so glad you're finally here," Melody beamed at her, leaning across the table to give her daughter's hand a squeeze.

"Where is my twin sis, Mama? Where's Bonnie?" Lisa asked suddenly.

"I…" Melody suddenly interrupted herself as a sudden understanding flooded into her heart.

"Is she OK? Where is she? Is something wrong?" Lisa asked in a rush.

Melody felt the Spirit flood over her. "No, everything is as it should be."

"Where…." Lisa asked, but was cut short by Melody's reply.

"She's with Helaman." Her answer was so powerfully true that Lisa instantly believed her. Of course—Bonnie was with Helaman!

"Where do you suppose they are?" was the only final question to be asked.

"I have no idea. But it really doesn't matter. They'll be here in time."

"In time for what?" Lisa asked, perplexed.

"In time to begin walking back to Zion," her mother answered with a note of wonder and awe in her voice.

"Walking?" Lisa asked, as if she had just heard a death sentence pronounced.

Melody patted her arm. "You'll be up to it, my dear, and filled with joy at the prospect by the time we leave."

Lisa frowned then said, "I kinda doubt it. But I have experienced so many tender miracles, I would do anything the Savior asked."

Melody decided to change the subject. "Since you left your husband in Texas, how is it you have two children?"

"That's an interesting tale."

"I'd love to hear it," Melody said, bringing out some garden carrots for the two to peel and chop.

"Well, I didn't know this, but right after I was taken away from Alvin, he immediately tried to find me. He had no idea where I was, but never gave up looking. He finally left Texas looking for me and headed north. He assumed I would try to go back to Utah if I was still alive. He searched for four years and finally found me just outside Denver, Colorado. We spent one night together, and I got pregnant," Lisa said, rolling her eyes.

"Why isn't he with you now?" Melody asked gently.

Lisa frowned and stopped peeling. Melody felt horrible for having asked, but didn't know how to retract the question.

"When we met again he had no light in his face," Lisa answered. "I knew that he had completely lost his faith. But, he was so overjoyed to see me again, and see Monica too, that my memory of my love for him overwhelmed me, and I let him sweep me off my feet. Literally."

"I see," Melody said quietly.

"The next morning he was angry with me for leaving Texas, and fumed about the four years he had spent searching for me. He insisted we go into Denver, that he could get work and food and medical care for me and Monica. I tried to ask about his faith, but he wouldn't talk about it. When I finally insisted that we talk, he said that he had lost his testimony. He said he had seen too many awful things, and that if God really was alive, he was an awful and heartless being who didn't deserve to be worshipped. He said he just preferred to not even believe there was a God. He told me I was a fool to put myself through all this hardship because of a false belief in a false religion."

Melody shook her head sorrowfully. "What did you do?"

"I bore my testimony to him as powerfully as I could, and he answered by cursing at me, at the Church, and at God. He told me if I didn't come to Denver with him, he would take Monica and go without me. I told him I would think about it, and that I would give him his answer in the morning."

Lisa's voice grew happier. "Late that night Helaman returned from—well you know how he is; he's inclined to come and go without warning."

"I know exactly what you are talking about," Melody affirmed.

"Anyway, Helaman returned quite late and I asked him to take me away from Alvin. He bundled us away that very night. We went way around Denver, and walked across a mountain range on dirt roads. Sometimes we had no roads to follow. When we descended the other side about a month later it was winter, and we were in Vernal, Utah. I had Timmy in Vernal. The odd thing is that when I arrived in Vernal I was in perfect health, and seven months pregnant."

Lisa finished peeling her last vegetable, and rose to get a glass of water. "Sweet little Monica was just two years old and full of energy and happiness," she went on. "She just thought her life of being on the road, sleeping in the open, and never knowing where our next meal would come from, was perfectly normal. Helaman was just wonderful with her, and he treated her as tenderly as any father could have. He was stern at times, but never harsh. Even though I have repeatedly told her otherwise, I know Monica thinks of Helaman as her father. She loves him dearly."

Lisa stopped to think about what she said next. "I have come to the conclusion that Helaman is more than a man, because no mortal in his sixties could have done all he did for me. Still, I can't imagine why I should be so blessed to spend six full years being guided by someone who may in fact have been an angel of God, when all around me millions of people were perishing. I just don't understand why I was so blessed."

"The best I can explain it . . ." Melody began quietly, then changed her mind. "Well, I will just say that Helaman told me he had made your father a promise about our family, and he was going to fulfill it."

"He did all this because of a promise to Dad?" Lisa asked, astonished.

"Maybe it was more than a promise; perhaps it was more along the lines of a covenant."

Lisa sighed. "I think I know what you mean. Well, one day I would sure like to know. In the meantime, Helaman left me before I could thank him properly. I wanted to give him a big hug and tell him I love him."

"I am sure he already knows that," Melody mused.

She was more right than she knew.

Samuel and his little band of refugees left Fairbanks several weeks later. It had been a time of rest and renewal for the weary travelers. Samuel could not imagine what had happened in Fairbanks to cause every man, woman and child to leave so suddenly.

He prayed mightily about where they were to go next. He was instructed that they needed to travel in an almost straight course southeast through Alaska, down through the Yukon Territory, across a corner of British Columbia, through the heart of Alberta and straight south to the Cardston Temple. In all, their remaining journey still involved over 2,000 miles through a foreign country quite possibly unwilling to let them peaceably pass through. Even peaceably, a thousand people eat a lot of food, and the task of feeding them would certainly require drawing upon the local resources. It was unlikely in such a devastated world, that any local economy could stand such a strain for long.

Samuel was still pondering these questions as they were pulling away from Fairbanks in the faithful old gray buses. When he brought his bus to a sudden stop just south of town, several buses behind him actually rammed into his back bumper. Alexei followed his eyes to where he was looking. Through the dense ice fog it was nearly impossible to see what it was.

Alexei let his gaze follow Samuel's out into the frozen world. "What are you looking at, my friend?"

Instead of answering, Samuel turned the heavy bus right and drove a half-block before turning into an Alyeska yard full of ice-covered trucks. There were literally hundreds of Chevy pickups, all of them crew cabs, all of them new, or nearly so, all of them red. There were even two large motor homes, four greyhound-type buses, and a host of trucks, tractors, cranes, generators, bulldozers and numerous other vehicles.

"I think I'm looking at our way through Canada," Samuel said.

Alexei immediately understood. "Of course! We will go through in small groups," he cried, relief in his voice. "In this way we will not threaten anyone, or bring upon us an attack from the Canada army. God truly is wise and good," he said humbly.

"God is good," Samuel agreed. "And the pipeline was very accommodating to leave us all these nice red trucks. Let's go see if we can find keys." Not only did they find keys, but they found a very large repair shop with four more greyhound-type buses inside. In the end they loaded most of the sick and elderly onto two buses. All of the other refugees were given a new truck with enough fuel to make it to Whitehorse without difficulty.

The exodus began two trucks at a time every half-hour. It took most of the next week to get everyone on the road south.

Along with the buses they took two additional fuel tankers. They were empty of course, but Samuel was certain he knew how to remedy that problem. Just outside of Fairbanks was the North Pole refinery. It used to produce most of the fuel consumed in Alaska.

When they pulled up to the main outer gates of the refinery they found the lights blazing brightly. It was a good, and a bad sign—good in the sense that it absolutely meant there was fuel still being produced at the refinery, and bad because it also meant it was manned and guarded, perhaps by the US military.

It was still foggy as they approached. Samuel went first in his bright red tanker and slowly approached the guard gate. Two armed men in US Army uniforms in protective masks stepped out into the cold. By the rapid puffs of frost coming from their masks Samuel could tell they were frightened.

They waited for Samuel to climb out of his truck and approach them. He was still wearing his Alyeska parka, and his stolen ID badge. They didn't even look at it.

"Go back where you came from," one of them said after angling his rifle toward Samuel's chest.

"We need fuel…" he began to explain, but was cut off by the first guard leveling his weapon at Samuel and flicking off the safety with his thumb.

"I'm not going to say it twice," the first guard said.

"All right. I'll leave," Samuel said walking backwards toward his truck. Without this fuel they would still likely make it to Whitehorse. With it, they might have made it all the way to Cardston.

"Wait," the Spirit commanded, and Samuel obeyed. The first officer raised his weapon, his finger tightening on the trigger.

"Wait a minute," the second guard ordered, and held his radio mic to his ear. The guard did not lower his weapon.

After a moment the other guard looked disappointed. "The boss wants to know what your name is."

At that very moment the Spirit brought a memory and flash of knowledge to Samuel's mind. Years ago he had known the man who ran the North Pole refinery. He smiled broadly. "Please tell Brother Richards hello from Brother Mahoy," he said.

The message was repeated over the radio, and a voice radioed back.

The guard looked at Samuel oddy. "You can enter on foot," he said less gruffly. "Just go over to that big building with the flashing red light. Someone will meet you there."

Samuel left the big truck sitting before the gate and walked a considerable distance until he was met by another armed man. He was scanned with a type of beeping device and led through a winding maze of halls until he came to a double set of doors with a plaque overhead labeled "Control Room." Just as he was about to reach for the door it flew open and a familiar face came stomping out to meet him.

"Brother Mahoy!" his old friend cried happily, and scooped him into his big arms. "What in the world are you doing up here?"

"Brother Richards!" Samuel laughed. "It's a long story that you wouldn't believe." He regarded his friend with a smile. "Wow, you've lost some weight, my friend!"

"Well, you can't eat crude oil," Brother Richards chuckled. Then more seriously, "We live on pretty slim rations around here."

The last time Samuel had seen Brother Todd Richards was over twenty years ago. In that era Brother Richards had weighed in excess of three hundred pounds. While not close friends, they had served together on several Stake callings, and Samuel had always liked this big man whose face was always pulled up in a happy smile.

Brother Richards shut the door and motioned for Samuel to sit.

"Where has everyone in Fairbanks gone? The entire city is deserted!" Samuel blurted out.

Brother Richards looked incredulous. "Didn't you hear, Samuel? The military was installing a small nuclear power plant on the base when the power grid was sabotaged. The reactor overheated and resulted in a catastrophic core meltdown." He shook his head sadly. "The city was immediately evacuated, and everyone was ordered not to return because of the danger of radioactive fallout. It took weeks to contain."

"I'm surprised you are still here!" Samuel said.

"So am I," Brother Richards agreed wryly. "I was going to evacuate with my family, but the military refused to let me go. I finally cut a deal that I would stay if they took my family all the way to Utah."

"I'm sorry you have to be separated," Samuel empathized.

Brother Richards nodded sadly. "It's been hard, but at least I know they are safe. The military keeps our skeleton crew safe here as this facility is considered critical to national security. The fallout was largely localized and we have decent protection from the radiation. Also, as soon as air travel out of Alaska was shut down, I was stuck here with no way to leave."

"That's awful, Brother Richards. Is there anything I can do to help?"

"I'm surprised you're still working for the pipeline yourself. I thought you retired a bunch of years ago," Brother Richards said, ignoring his offer for help.

"Well, I'm not actually."

"Then, what are you doing in Fairbanks?"

"I'm on my way south. I've spent the last three years bringing a group of Russian Israelites from their country on their way to Zion. We've been here for a few weeks living in the empty houses in town with no apparent issues. Now we really just need fuel," he finished simply.

"Is that right?" Brother Richards said enthusiastically, and leaned forward in his chair.

"How many of you are there?" he queried.

"Over a thousand."

"None of you have had effects from the radiation? Wow!" he cried, then leaned back again. "Three years you've been traveling?"

"Not quite three, actually."

"Who put you up to this? I mean, how did you get involved?"

"The Lord put me up to it. A prophet of God sent me."

"Holy cow!" he intoned again. "So, this really is it, isn't it? The ten tribes are returning from the North." He looked dumbfounded but pleased. "Where are they at this moment?"

"On their way south as we speak." Samuel replied. The conversation was going faster and faster.

"Where did you get enough vehicles…."

"The Lord, and the pipeline provided."

Brother Richard's eyes grew wide. "You didn't! You took all those trucks in the vehicle pool yard, didn't you!"

"We didn't take them. The Lord gave them to us."

"I doubt if the military will see the fine line there," Richards commented ironically.

"I'm not concerned about the military."

"Why not?"

"Because they that be with use are greater than they that be with them," Samuel replied, quoting the prophet Elisha.

Brother Richards gave him an odd look. "You really believe that, don't you."

"Believe? Is it proper to call an absolute certainty a belief?" Samuel asserted.

"What are the odds you will actually make it to Jackson County, Missouri?" Brother Richards asked with sincerity.

"One hundred percent," Samuel replied quietly. The answer resonated in the office more loudly than if he had shouted it from a bull horn.

There was silence before his friend spoke again. "Do you have room for one more?"

"If that one is a faithful Latter-day Saint, we do."

"Sam, I have to confess that I've not been able to be faithful with the persecution of the Church, and all. But, in my heart I do still believe, and have a strong testimony," Brother Richards told him honestly.

"We need fuel," Samuel said again as if all the intervening conversation had not occurred.

In response, Brother Richards picked up a portable radio and keyed the mic. "Control Room to George, come in?"

"George," the radio crackled.

"Take the trucks parked outside the gate and fill them. Have them ready to leave within the hour."

"Yes sir," was the muffled response.

He turned back to Samuel. "I'm going to go grab a few things. Do you need any warm clothes? We have lots."

"Anything you can spare would be wonderful," Samuel admitted.

After the trucks were fueled, Todd's nerves were calmed by Samuel as they walked past the guards who didn't seem to mind they were leaving. As as soon as they were found to be missing, the guards grabbed as much food and fuel as they could carry, and quickly left themselves. When the pipeline authorities investigated the surprising silence from the refinery, they found the place totally uninhabited.

Brother Richards, or Todd as he preferred to be called, was driving the tanker when they rolled up to the Canadian border guard house two days later. They were startled to find several dozen red trucks parked in long rows on both sides of the road. None of the trucks had passengers in them.

"This doesn't look good," Samuel said.

"Let me handle this, Samuel," Todd requested.

"I would love you to," Samuel said after the Spirit stirred his soul.

Todd pulled up to the gate and waited for the guard to walk slowly out to the truck.

"Where you headed?" the guard asked.

"South," Todd replied.

"We are not allowing any traffic into Canada," the guard said sternly.

"We're here to pay the toll fee for all these red trucks and their passengers."

The guard looked behind him at the parked vehicles, and chuckled. "Those people are all in jail."

"I'm willing to pay five gallons of diesel for each truck you let past."

"I don't need to accept your bribe. All I need to do is shoot you, and all the fuel is mine anyway," the guard threatened, putting a hand on the butt of his pistol.

Todd smiled faintly. "I was fairly certain you'd say that, so I brought you a surprise," he said, and reached into his pocket. He carefully pulled a grenade from his pocket and held it up so the guard could see it. "You see, a truck load of fuel this size would make a crater about a mile across I'd guess."

"What the…" the guard cried and took two steps back as if hit in the chest by an invisible hand. "Wait! Hold on. What do you want?"

"I already told you. I want to pay the toll of five gallons per truck."

"Uhm, ten gallons," the guard said weakly.

"Four," Todd countered.

"All right! All right! Five. But, I'll have to call my boss, and all those people are on their way to jail…"

"Get them back." Todd ordered.

"I can't…"

When Todd pulled the pin in the grenade, Samuel began to doubt his sanity. He had never been a part of a Mexican standoff, and didn't like it at all. He thought grimly that he had come too far and shed too many tears to see these wonderful people die in a mile-wide crater. He was about to intervene when the guard suddenly stammered, "I'll have them back here in an hour."

"You better start rounding up some gas cans, too," Todd said calmly. "I want to be on the road before dark."

"Yes sir. Uhm, excuse me, I've got to make a radio transmission," he said, and hurried away.

Samuel shot a daggered look at his friend. "Put the pin back in that grenade!" he hissed.

Todd smiled cooly. "Okay, don't get so upset."

Samuel was serious. "I have a job to finish here, and I can't let you blow the thing to kingdom come the first few days you're with me!"

"Relax, it's a smoke grenade," Todd assured him. "We drop them from helicopters to mark oil leaks on the pipeline. I think this one is orange."

"It's not—you mean—you were bluffing a man with a gun and taking a thousand people as hostage!?"

"Yeah," he said, and grinned like he had just eaten the canary and gotten away with it.

"Well, you have just alerted what's left of the Canadian military to stop us," Samuel said, more serious now. "We must pray and ask for the Lord's forgiveness for relying on our own strength, and for safe passage."

After the people returned and they were a few minutes beyond the checkpoint, Samuel and Todd humbled themselves and prayed aloud together as a warmth entered the cab. Several times they heard helicopters in the distance but did not seem to come any closer.

This type of situation occurred at nearly every town or village along the Alaskan highway but they seemed to know just what to say and do in the moment. While few towns would only let them pass safely in exchange for fuel, their bountiful supply of fuel turned out to be liquid gold. They were able to purchase nearly everything they needed along the road. In fact, the word went ahead of them as much as the limited communications still allowed, and people lined the roads to offer whatever they had for sale. Samuel thought they might be met by armed men intent on simply stealing the fuel. But, Canada had years ago confiscated every gun the citizens owned. What few guns actually left were far more valuable for hunting deer or moose than for making the unwise choice of shooting at a loaded fuel truck. They made sure that one of the things the rumors included was tales of their generosity.

Their 2,500 mile trek across Canada lasted well over a month. What should have taken five days stretched into weeks as they slowly negotiated their way across Canada. This was true both in the sense of barter, and in making long detours around portions of the Alcan highway that were impassable. But the Lord was with them, and the weather was beautiful by the time they arrived into Cardston.

Nearly the whole city was waiting along the road to welcome them, rejoicing at their arrival. Somehow they knew they were coming. The Cardston Temple was without electricity when they arrived, but had been safely guarded by faithful members. Because of the need to purchase everything with fuel, the three tanker trucks ended up in the lead of their convoy. Thus, Samuel's rig was the second to pull into the large parking lot outside the temple.

This was a historic moment, one foreseen and foretold for thousands of years. He could almost hear Jesus Christ, Isaiah, Ezekial and a host of others speaking the words that would echo through the generations regarding this moment.

As vehicle after vehicle pulled into the parking lot until it was full, Samuel stood facing the Temple of the living God. He pondered the faithful sons and daughters who would now fulfill their spiritual journey, in one of the greatest exoduses ever conducted by mortals. It was not possible to calculate exactly, but his faithful few had traveled in excess of 10,000 miles in a little over three years.

Beloved friends and leaders joined him in his silent vigil: Vladimir, Alexei, Sarah, Karl, and a hundred others. Without preamble or explanation, Alexei knelt upon the brittle grass in front of the majestic temple and raised his arms over his head. The people fell to their knees, their faces streaked with tears of joy.

"Oh beloved Father!" he cried, as if his heart might burst if the great gratitude within was not given voice. "How everlastingly grateful we are for Thy almighty providence, love and gentle care over these, Thy people. Surely, Father, we shall worship Thee and take Thy name upon our lips with reverence all our lives, generation upon generation, in remembrance of Thy great providence in bringing us out of the lands of our long captivity and unto this holy edifice."

"Purify our hearts, O God, that we may enter into Thy house with humble hearts, and partake of those covenants which have long been denied us. Father, into Thy hands we commend our lives, and covenant all that we are, or ever will become, in joy and in honor of these great blessings. Hear our prayer, Holy Father, and accept our offering, we pray in the name of Thine only begotten Son, even Jesus Christ, Amen."

"Amen!" rent the air like the battle cry of a mighty army. Then a sweet stillness settled over them.

The refugees outside the temple grounds prepared to rejoice in this transplendent day of deliverance. "Look!" someone shouted, and they all turned to see a man in a white suit and tie walking quickly towards them. Samuel stepped forward, prepared to explain why these thousands of people were there. But there was no explanation needed.

"Welcome, O House of Israel!" the man said. "We have been awaiting your arrival for many years! After we secure your housing and food necessities, we will ask you to follow the following procedures." He waited for the translators to finish before he spoke again. "Each of you will have two interviews. The first will be to make sure you have been baptized and ordained. If not, these ordinances will be attended to first. The second interview will be to determine worthiness to enter the House of the Lord.

We ask that those who speak English come first. They will then be instructed and set up to help and interview those who do not speak English. We estimate it will take several weeks to complete all these ordinances."

The people stood in humble rapture as his words were again translated for them. The man in white then continued.

"May I ask, which of you is Samuel?"

"I am," Samuel said with some surprise.

"I am President Arkin. I have been instructed by our Prophet to defer to your leadership regarding these people. He asked me to thank you personally for your long and faithful service."

Samuel bowed his head, cleared his throat and answered with a voice made unsteady by deep joy. "I am well blessed for my service, and if you speak to him, tell him thank you for the opportunity to serve in this capacity."

"Actually, I will speak to him this night over the Church's short wave radio. He will be most pleased that you are finally here. We have reports of many others coming after you. It seems as if the floodgates are finally open, and Israel is coming home."

"Praise the Lord," Samuel declared heartily. And as if his words had triggered a blazing fire, the entire congregation cried, "Praise the Lord!" in Russian, as if with a single voice.

President Arkin smiled and gazed around him at the sea of tear-streaked faces. He sighed happily, then turned back to Samuel. "Come, then. We have much work yet to do. I need your advice on many matters. I know of your special status, and I am most honored to work with you." President Arkin stood with his hand outstretched toward the temple waiting for Samuel to follow.

But Samuel stood still. "Give me just a moment to say goodbye, please." he said. Brother Arkin bowed his head, a puzzled look on his face, and stepped back two steps. The faithful temple president had no idea that Samuel would not see his friends again for many years. Samuel spoke in his now-unbroken Russian.

"Alexei, Vladimir, my friends, my brothers and sisters. I must leave you here."

"What!" they cried out, tears starting again in their eyes. "But why? There are still thousands of miles for us to go!"

"It is true, but now you are in the land of Zion, and in the care of the Prophet. You are no longer strangers in a strange land, or wanderers in exile. The curse is lifted, and the long dispersion of Israel is finally over. Your people will no longer be hated, hunted or persecuted. No longer shall you be killed and imprisoned by the Gentiles. No longer shall you lift up your heads under oppression, but shall from this day be protected of God. Now is the long-awaited day of your deliverance. Now, my beloved friends, you are free!"

A cheer arose from the assembled thousands, "Free! Free! Free!"

When it died down, Samuel continued. "I did not realize it until this moment in time, but this is the extent of my mission among you. I have assisted you, taught you, baptized you, ordained you, and brought you to the steps of God's holy temple. My work is done. I have another work to do. I must take my leave of you."

"No, no!" a thousand voices cried at once. "Will we see you again?"

Sam raised his arms in victory. "We will! In Zion! I will be with you when the Lord comes to His temple. We will meet again in Zion! Until that glorious day, farewell my dear friends."

The resulting chorus of "Hurrah for Israel!"and tears was unintelligible, yet heartfelt. From out in the crowd a familiar form raced toward him and ran into his arms with great energy. It was Sarah—not so little anymore, but a beautiful young woman almost fourteen, full of faith and vitality. She was Alexei's granddaughter, and for Samuel, the closest to family he had among them. She was the daughter of Islana, from whom he had learned so much of this people during his training in the Idaho wilderness school. She was also the only survivor of her immediate family. Sarah's devotion and love to Samuel were absolute and unshakeable.

"Samuel!" she cried, her voice almost shrill with fear. "You aren't going to leave me, are you?" she cried.

Samuel opened his mouth to explain when a shimmering light just behind Sarah drew his attention. He looked up to see Sarah's mother Islana standing behind her, a glowing hand upon her daughter's shoulder. Samuel smiled. Sarah sensed something and glanced over her shoulder but saw nothing.

"Dearest Sarah, my task is finished. I promise you will be safe. Your mother will watch over you after I leave, I testify of that to you."

Sarah again glanced over her shoulder. "Is that my mother I feel warming my soul?" she asked breathlessly as peace settled all around her.

Samuel brushed her long blonde hair away from her face with a tender smile. "You look very much like you mother," he whispered. "She has also joined God's true church and is anxious for you to receive your blessings in the temple one day."

Sarah looked at him with belief and adoration, although she was openly weeping. She pulled Samuel down to her and kissed both his cheeks in formal farewell.

"Goodbye," she said almost inaudibly. "Then we will meet again in Zion."

Samuel brushed the tears from his own eyes and struggled to be brave in front of this valiant soul as precious to him as his own daughter. He could not say goodbye easily, and was spared the necessity of doing so by Alexei, who was distraught.

"No! I cannot say goodbye, my brother," Alexei cried, and fell on his neck in tears.

"Then, let us say what your ancestors long ago said. It is a greeting, as well as a benediction. 'The Lord bless Thee, and keep Thee,'" Samuel said slowly, tears now streaming down his face.

Alexei replied in a whisper. "The Lord make His face to shine upon Thee, and be gracious unto Thee:"

Samuel could hardly reply. "The Lord lift up His countenance upon thee, and give thee peace."

Before he was persuaded to remain forever with his beloved people, Samuel spun on a heel and marched with President Arkin into the temple. He smiled to himself as he heard Vladimir's steely voice command someone to bring up a generator and find a way to power the temple.

"So, your mission is complete?" President Arkin asked as they walked briskly together.

"It is. I have loved it, but I am anxious to go home. I haven't seen my family for almost five years."

"You have living family?" President asked incredulously.

"My wife and all my children are living."

He stared at Samuel. "When I heard that you are—well you know—I just assumed you had lived centuries previously, I guess."

"It feels like that long ago," Samuel said, and laughed to himself.

President Arkin nodded and smiled broadly. "I can imagine. Well Brother Samuel, we will take good care of your people. We have been preparing for this very day for nearly a hundred and seventy-five years. We have food, lodging, medicine, temple clothing, and everything but electricity, it seems."

At that exact moment a generator rattled to life and a great cheer from the crowd went up..

"And, now, we obviously have electricity," the President remarked, completely amazed.

Samuel shook his hand. "Thank you, and God bless you, President. You have your work cut out for you."

"I know. We will go with God's hand upon us."

From where they stood, the front doors of the temple were now plainly visible. Two young men stood before the doors, guarding it with great solemnity. Samuel stood facing them for a full minute in contemplation before turning back to the Temple President.

"A word of caution," Samuel told him in parting.

"Please," President said.

"Not all who came with us are worthy to enter the temple. You must not let them enter until they are ready. You will need to hold some church courts and rebaptize some. Not many, but some—more than I had wanted. However, I am confident that before this people leave your area, all who I brought will be in the group of faithful who continue on to Zion."

"I pray to God it is so. Thank you for the warning."

Samuel sighed. "I suddenly feel very tired in spirit. I shall take my leave now. Fare thee well, President."

"And you," President Arkin replied quietly.

Samuel nodded, shook his hand again, then turned and faded quickly as he walked away.

NOW AND FOREVER

Samuel wearily arrived upon the mountain top to find Helaman waiting for him. A young woman and a young man Samuel did not know were standing beside him. A gentle spring breeze was blowing, and the song of a faraway bird was in the air. It was one of Samuel's favorite places on earth, and not accessible by any means other than helicopter or the power of God. As far as Samuel knew, no mortal had ever set foot here.

The fact that other heavenly servants were here was unusual, but not unexpected. Helaman seemed to always know where Samuel was and what he needed. At the end of this long and difficult assignment it was a pleasure to be with his dear friend once again. It brought him peace, and placed an appropriate conclusion to this chapter of his life.

Samuel greeted Helaman silently with a warm embrace. They turned to look out across the emerald-green sea as it rolled steadily toward the long stretch of white sands far below. The scent of exotic flowers greeted his senses like expensive perfume. He had been here only three times prior to this. Once was with his wife, and sudden memories of Melody arose sweetly in his mind.

"Well done, my brother," Helaman said at last.

Samuel sighed deeply and turned toward his Nephite friend. "Thank you, Helaman. And, more than I can express, thank you for your long service on behalf of my family."

Helaman smiled broadly. "It has been a joy," he replied happily. Indeed, it had been exactly that for him. Having dealt with several generations of disbelieving and stiff-necked heathens, it had been a pleasure to work with people whose hearts were tender and teachable, and who wanted with all their soul to be worthy and obedient. In fact, it had been more of a vacation than an assignment.

Helaman turned to the woman beside him. She was as tall as Helaman with dark brown hair to her waist, exquisite brown eyes and luminous skin. Her face was aglow with goodness. She radiated light and had every appearance of being an angel. She possessed that timeless beauty that spoke of youth and great age; the appearance of one yet to be born. She was dressed in a radiantly white gown that reminded Samuel of a temple gown, with the exception that a lei of exotic flowers was draped over her shoulders. She smiled at him with perfect teeth and rich ruby lips, and eyes that twinkled in ways that suggested deep inner peace, and a healthy sprinkling of mischievousness.

"Samuel, I would like you to meet someone who loves you very much. Her name is too complex for a mortal to pronounce. In your language her name would be Star."

"Forgive me that I don't remember you," Samuel said almost shyly, and held out a hand. She did not offer hers, but bowed from the waist. He knew she would not shake his hand. However, Samuel had learned that it was still polite to offer. Had she extended her hand and he felt nothing when they touched, he would have raised his arm to the square and commanded her to depart. Her response was exactly appropriate and indicated her worthiness and the appropriateness of her appearing.

Star had been smiling broadly and recomposed her features into seriousness. "I have long awaited this moment, and have asked this special blessing from Father that I may come and speak to you before my mission begins," she said, her face radiant with joy.

"In what way may I be of service to you, Star?" Samuel asked, his heart fluttering in his chest with anticipation and wonder. He had never known a creature of such exquisite elegance before, and yet he felt a bond and connection with her that confused and delighted him.

She laughed, a sound which came more to his heart than his ears. "You already have blessed me much more than you know. I was granted this great blessing only because of your standing before the Lord, and because my stay on earth would be…" she paused here and smiled. "… brief," she concluded, as if searching for words.

"Who is this young man with you?" Samuel asked her, sensing she had said all she would on the former subject.

"This is my dear brother. He and I go everywhere together," she responded as she turned to smile at her companion. The handsome young man bowed slowly, but said nothing. Samuel felt a great outpouring of love for the young man, and from him back to Samuel.

"We must go." Star said quietly, and immediately began to grow transparent.

"Wait, please," Samuel said softly. They remained with him, neither coming nor going. "I don't remember you, but I feel with all my heart that I want to tell you, both of you, that I love you."

"We love you too, Samuel. When you meet our mother, please tell her I love her and am so grateful for her giving me life. Now and forever…" she said, the last of her words coming into his mind after his eyes could no longer behold her. He wondered what circumstances might bring him to recognize who this precious spirit's mother was. It was a mystery in his heart, but a sweet one.

Samuel turned back to Helaman and taking a deep breath, turned toward the ocean. Helaman never took his eyes off of Samuel. "Who are they?" Samuel asked.

"They said all they could," he replied.

Samuel nodded, familiar with the sometimes cryptic nature of divine things. He knew no more would be said, so he changed the subject. "Is my family well?" Samuel asked. "I'm anxious to return to them if there is time now."

"They are well, and gathered. Your youngest daughter Bonnie is still on her way to join you. I will continue with her until she returns, and until you are ready."

"Ready for what?" Samuel asked.

Helaman smiled mischievously. "Your next assignment, of course."

Samuel squared his shoulders and nodded. "Can you tell me what it is, or do I have to wonder for a while?"

"I can tell you now," Helaman grinned. "Your next assignment will be to accompany your family, and many others, to Zion."

Samuel was elated. "You mean, I get to stay with my family! This makes me so happy! I have missed them very much!" he said with a happy sigh. Then he glanced at Helaman with a smile. "This sounds much easier than my previous assignment."

"In many ways it will be much more difficult."

"Why is that?"

"Because, the more you love those you serve, the harder it is to see them suffer and die," Helaman replied, his voice heavy with emotion, with deep personal understanding of the truth he had just spoken.

"I'm beginning to understand why some ask the Lord to take them speedily into his kingdom when they grow old," Samuel replied, with no hint of regret in his voice.

Helaman nodded. "I know what you mean; I have thought the very same thing. Yet, all you need do is ask to be taken home, and your assignment as a special servant will end immediately."

"I know, my friend," Samuel replied solemnly. "I'm nowhere near ready for that. You have been at this for over two thousand years. Do you ever wish to have another assignment?"

"Never!" he replied forcefully. "I love what I do, and feel the importance of my assignment. I wouldn't want to do anything else. I sense this is also the case with you, my young friend."

"Nobody's called me young for a long while," Samuel replied with a laugh.

"In the work we are both engaged in, you are but a babe—albeit a powerful one."

"I am sure I'm but a child in the eternal scheme of things." Helaman mused, as he thought about the incredible mission he had just completed. "It really is glorious, isn't it, my friend, serving the Lord like this?"

"Beyond anything man can comprehend," Helaman replied, his voice resonant with supernal happiness.

Helaman stepped back slightly. "I need to go now to complete a few things before I bring Bonnie to you. You need to get home to your wife. She needs you."

"Is everything all right?" Samuel asked, suddenly concerned.

Helaman shook his head slightly. "Everything will be fine as soon as you get there."

"Farewell my friend," Samuel said, and immediately departed.

"God bless you," he heard Helaman's voice reverberating back.

Samuel was in the nowhere between everywhere that traveling by the power of God is, when a sweet instruction came to him. Without hesitation he returned to the early morning hours just outside the Cardston Alberta temple. He arrived just out of sight, not three paces from Alexei's tent. He lifted the flap and said a single word, "Sarah."

Sarah was kneeling on the ground beside her bed roll, talking with Alexei. She was fully dressed, making spiritual preparations to begin her day's labors. She turned her head so quickly that her hair flew out in a halo of golden tresses. "Samuel!" she cried with a sound that was both an exclamation of astonishment, and a cry of joy.

Samuel looked at her grandfather's startled face and said the only thing he needed to, "I will take good care of her. May I?"

Alexei nodded silently, fully aware that Samuel would be taking his granddaughter with him, and lovingly embraced her. Then Samuel took Sarah's hand, and they both were gone. Alexei sat there for several moments before he opened the tent flap and followed their footprints in the grass to where they ended without a trace just beyond the trees.

It was early morning when Samuel and Sarah arrived just outside the Mahoy home in South Jordan, Utah. There were street lights glowing in the early dawn, and several lights on inside the home. He could see shadows moving around inside. He stepped up to the door and heard a cry of anguish.

"Helaman! Where is Helaman?" a feminine voice cried out.

Samuel yanked open the screen and grabbed the doorknob. It was locked, but as usual opened without resistance to his twist. He quickly escorted Sarah into the house, and asked her to stay downstairs; then he charged up the stairs, turned right and ran into the master bedroom. He found his wife propped up in bed, her knees elevated. Two women he did not recognize were huddled near the foot of her bed, also on their knees.

"Melody, sweetheart, I'm home," he announced urgently, and sank down beside her.

"Oh, oh, Samuel!" she cried, grabbing both of his hands. "Samuel, I was so afraid. I need a priesthood blessing. The baby is coming, and I'm not able to deliver it. My body won't let this baby deliver, Samuel! I think it's stuck! I need help, or the baby will die. Please, Samuel! Beg the Lord to spare my baby, and take me instead. Please…" she begged on the edge of hysteria.

From her pale and exhausted face he could tell she was beyond endurance, and near collapse. A profound peace flooded through him—sweet, pure peace—and he knew what he should do. He sat on the edge of the bed. His wife rested her head in his lap and cried weakly. He laid both hands on her sweat-soaked head and blessed her.

"Beloved and precious wife, in the name of Jesus Christ I rebuke your fear, your weariness, and your physical limitations. I command your body to function correctly, and to bring forth this child. I promise you in the name of Jesus Christ that you will be delivered of a healthy child this night, and you will raise him to maturity in righteousness. This I do in the name of Jesus Christ, Amen."

Melody's trembling stopped, and she pushed herself up with determination.

"I'm ready," she said to the two women. "Bring towels. The baby will be here shortly," she said. The two women scurried to comply.

"Thank you my love," she said to her husband, turning her now-confident face toward him. "I feel better now. I can feel the baby moving. Thank you—and thank you, Father!" she said, looking heavenward. Then she turned her face away as she moaned with the onset of renewed labor.

"The baby's coming," one of the midwives said. "Wait for the next contraction and push!"

About ten minutes later the baby came into the world with a tiny cry.

"It's a girl!" the midwife cried. Then there was silence as they worked with the little one to open her throat and dry her off.

"Oh, she is glorious!" Melody marveled breathlessly. She turned weakly to her husband, who still held her hand. "Hey, you said I'd have a son," she chided him with a small smile. "But I always wanted a daughter, and she is perfect," she said breathlessly, and lay back against her sodden pillows.

The attending sister appeared anxiously at Melody's bedside. "Melody, there's something wrong with the baby. She's not breathing right. I'm afraid she was too slow in delivering. I'm afraid we're going to lose her. Here…" she said, and brought the little bundle to lay in Melody's arms.

"Oh no!" Melody cried, her face distorted with disbelief and sorrow. "No. No. No!" she repeated over and over. But the child in her arms appeared lifeless. "I tried, my baby girl, I tried to give you life. Please stay with me!" she begged the little soul in her arms. Then she turned to her husband. "Oh, Sam, I know you have power with the Lord. Ask Him for me to spare our precious daughter," she cried, her face streaming with tears. "Bless my baby," she begged, then looked up. "Oh, please, dearest Father, take me instead of this sweet baby, I beg Thee…" she cried in deep anguish.

Samuel, his face coursed with tears, gently opened the bundle to gaze upon the little face ringed with a halo of dark hair. Two little lids flickered open to reveal her clear eyes, and startling intelligence in that tiny face. She gazed deeply at her mother, and then at her father before closing her eyes. Samual placed his hand on her tiny head and prayed.

"Heavenly Father, in the name of Jesus Christ and by the authority of His holy priesthood, I give this child of Thine, and ours, a name and a blessing. The name I give her is Melody Star Mahoy. The blessing I give you, Star, is the knowledge of our love, and the promise that err long, your mother will hold you in her arms, feed you from her breasts, and raise you in a time of glorious peace. Until then, I commend you to Heavenly Father's care and to His love. In the name of Jesus Christ, Amen."

Melody Star took a shallow breath and seemed to relax. She quietly departed mortality.

"Oh, no, no! Oh Samuel! Oh my precious daughter! Don't die, don't die!" Melody mourned. She wept uncontrollably for many minutes before she spoke again. "I don't understand, Sam! I wanted her so badly, and I loved her ever since I felt her inside me. She was the child of my old age, the child of our love, and the witness I had that Heavenly Father loves me and heard my prayers. I have yearned to bear your child, Samuel, to have this binding seal upon our love and our eternal marriage."

Melody's voice gave way to more sobbings, then she spoke again. "Sam, I don't understand why you said she would be a *son!*" She paused as her face contorted with pain while silent tears fell on the still bundle in her arms.

Her face twisted again. "Oh, oh, another contraction!" she said, her attention diverted to her own physical pain. "Why do I have more pain?" she asked the midwives.

"Sometimes there are a few contractions to expel the placenta," one of them replied. "It's nothing to worry about."

"It was stronger than that," Melody asserted. "I think ... oh! Here comes another contraction. This one is strong!" She reached down and palpated her stomach. "My tummy is really firm. I think I'm carrying another baby!" she cried incredulously.

"But there was only one heartbeat," the midwife protested, and lifted a stethoscope onto her abdomen. She listened for a second, moved the instrument to a new location, then pulled them down in wonder. "There's still a strong heartbeat!" she cried in wonder. "You do have twins!"

At that moment a strong contraction bore down, and the ladies scurried to find more towels. In about ten minutes another child entered mortality. "It's a boy!" they cried in unison. "A healthy, strong little boy," they laughed and cried, barely able to contain their happiness sufficiently to perform their office. They bundled the little one up without even wiping him thoroughly, and happily, joyfully, laid him in Melody's arms. They silently took Star's little tabernacle away.

Melody had never felt such exquisite pain, and now such exquisite joy. "God has heard my prayers, and blessed me with the child He promised. Oh, Samuel, oh, my love, we are so blessed!" she cried happily, and laid her head upon her husband's chest in exhaustion and joy. She opened the little blanket so she could gaze upon her son's tiny face; but her thoughts were still with her daughter.

"Why did you name her Melody Star?" she finally asked.

"That was her name," Samuel replied simply.

"When I heard you say it, I knew it was her name; but how did you know?"

"I'll tell you about it later. Just know, darling, that your daughter Star fully understood she would only be in mortality for a few moments, and she accepted that. I also feel impressed to tell you how perfectly she loves you."

"I sensed that while I held her. I wish I could tell her how much I love her," she said wistfully, a note of both joy and sadness in her voice.

"You just did, my love," he replied. He looked to the opposite side of the bed and watched Star smile; with a radiant smile she leaned forward and kissed her mother on the forehead. Then she slowly vanished without straightening from the kiss. In his mind he heard her musical voice say, "Now and forever…"

Melody and Samuel named their son Helaman James Mahoy. With the birth of little Helaman a new sweetness fell upon their home. Melody was radiant with love, and seemed at times to have difficulty deciding which of her boys she should be gazing upon with absolute adoration. Sammy, now eighteen years old, held his little brother hour upon hour.

Samuel pondered the great bond between his sons, and remembered the fierceness of his own love for his little brother Jimmy, just prior to Jimmy's death. The thought was not unsettling to him, for he knew that love was the nectar of life, a sweet fruit he had been blessed to savor many times.

It felt so good to be home.

APPROACHING ZION

It would be a dramatic understatement to say that Melody welcomed Sarah into their home. From the first moment they met, the day that baby Helaman was born, a bond of love formed between them that astounded everyone except Sarah and Melody. In a very healthy way, Sarah became her lost baby girl, and Melody became Sarah's lost mother. They wrapped their love around one another so completely that to see them interact was to be charmed to the core. Melody was no longer young to be the mother of an infant, and Sarah lavished upon her new mother such attention and assistance as few mothers ever experience.

Though Sarah knew little English, and Melody absolutely no Russian, they communicated by the power of love. It wasn't long before Melody's sweet new teenage daughter was mimicking oft-repeated phrases in tortured English and bombarding both Samuel and Melody with myriads of questions. Even something as simple as a flushing toilet had to be explained in detail, and pronounced slowly in English. It was a fun and fascinating time for them all.

For Sarah this was the childhood she had missed, and she followed Melody around like a two-year-old. However, she was anything but childish in her interaction with her new mother. Raised to work, and expected to do so without complaint, she served with quiet zeal, and when not helping take care of baby Helaman, often invented jobs to keep her busy hands occupied. Melody urged her to slow down, a thing she seemed incapable of doing. Yet, for Sarah, these simple chores were a delight, and far easier than anything she had known as a child.

Best of all, Sarah had Melody's complete love. For many weeks Melody was the sun, and Sarah's tiny planet revolved around her in tight circles. As the weeks grew to months and beyond, Sarah's universe expanded to include everyone she found within it. Equally as wonderful was the fact that all who came to know Sarah, loved her.

Samuel and his family spent all that summer growing and preserving food, along with making clothing and gathering other necessities. Some things were impossible to find, among these shoes, medical supplies, and anything mechanical or electronic. Still, these things hardly seemed important in the face of the quest they were contemplating. Spirits were

high, almost jubilant, as preparations were made in a world fast crumbling all around them.

Almost all the inhabitants of Zion saw these times as a period of happy privation. It felt to them as if they had returned to pioneer days, and they struggled to adapt their minds and hands to scrubbing clothes by hand while using their washing machine as the tub of water for doing so. The Zion dwellers learned the art of cooking by fire, sun oven or cook stove, and many began to produce excellent dishes, as the meager ingredients would allow.

Sarah was by this time a scant fifteen-years-old, yet she seemed far older. Had anyone been able to look beyond the immediacy of their own lives, they would have seen the Lord's wisdom in placing Sarah among them. This little girl with broken English and busy hands knew things vital to their survival. Having lived all her life in relatively primitive circumstances, she accepted as the normal what the "saints" saw as hardships.

Sarah quietly demonstrated her skills by simply doing them: baking bread outdoors without an oven, washing a whole family's clothes in just a few gallons of water, cooking, cleaning and bathing with an economy of effort and supplies. She also knew how to sleep warm, which was something most had yet to figure out, and how to make her own thread, needles, soap, yeast for raising bread, treat a wound without medicine, and a seemingly inexhaustible list of other skills desperately needed by her new family. As much as they gave her, she gave more in return.

Without even knowing it, Sarah became the epicenter of a tidal wave of change. What she taught her willing and attentive mother was quickly spread throughout the community. Aided by the Holy Spirit, some essential truths took little time to become common knowledge.

It was tempting to think that because a relative peace had settled upon God's mountain home, that the world had also found peace. Nothing could have been further from reality.

While Samuel had been on his four-year mission to bring lost children of Israel from the north, much had happened in the world, and most of which he had not been aware. The combined armies of South America had invaded the United States and claimed much of California, Arizona, New Mexico, Texas and all of Cuba. They had sent armies as far north as Nevada, Utah and Colorado.

The initial South American zeal to retake what they viewed as the lands of their fathers from the hands of the "white devils," was satiated with their collective capture of countless property. That portion of the army which had invaded Utah was unique in that nearly every member of its forces was a member of the Church. They had quietly banded together and when the opportunity arose, they marched into Utah with the single-minded purpose of ridding their spiritual homeland of those who had banned, outlawed, and persecuted those they revered as their spiritual brothers and sisters.

The South American soldiers in Utah were successful beyond their own hopes. Once having accomplished their self-assigned task, the soldiers took up station outside of Salt Lake City and stood sentinel against armed incursion by any others. In time, food, missionaries, and love called them in from their self-imposed sentry duty, and they became one with the Saints. Even so, they stubbornly remained separate, an autonomous and unique people, retaining their weapons of war and standing ready to use them. When the spirit of preparation settled upon God's people, it landed squarely upon them as well. They positioned themselves to march before the caravans of faithful to clear the way and ensure their safety. It was a noble and needed thing, but unbeknownst to them, one which they could not possibly accomplish with the arm of flesh.

It is probable that the South American armies would have continued northward in their conquest had not the Chinese and Russians landed on both the East and West coasts of America. The only metropolitan area that escaped extermination was New York. With the fall of the American constitutional government, the Western U.N. claimed all of the state of New York as sovereign territory of the Western United Nations. For reasons unclear, the Chinese and Russians bypassed that entire region.

After sweeping the Eastern seaboard clean of most of its population, the combined Chinese armies bypassed most of the abandoned cities of middle America and targeted their fury on the Salt Lake valley with chemicals of death. Having then exhausted their chemical resources, they joined with their forces from California and attacked Arizona's teeming cities, a land now physically and emotionally claimed by the South American invaders. The two forces clashed in the vast deserts of Arizona, and having underestimated their enemy, were caught in a South American surprise attack. This brought an unexpected end to the majority of the Chinese threat on the American continent. Even so, it exhausted both the means and the will of the South Americans to wage war any more. They settled into the impossible task of retaining and living upon the vast regions they had conquered.

Before they could even restore electrical power to their cities, Texas organized themselves into a separate nation, elected a Confederate-style government and attacked their South American squatters, reclaiming all of Texas and large amounts of New Mexico. Demoralized by this unexpected defeat, the South Americans retreated from Texas and after a year of continued bloody conflict, finally signed a treaty with them. Texas boldly annexed Oklahoma, Arkansas, Louisiana, Mississippi, Alabama, Georgia, South Carolina, Florida, and eventually Cuba.

Without opposition or even comment from what little remained of Washington D.C., the new Confederate Nation of Texas began the arduous task of rebuilding. Their first official act was to cut all ties with the Western United Nations.

With the United States in chaos and the Western U.N. weakened, a new face appeared on the European horizon, challenging the domination of the world through his high position as Secretary-General of the Western United Nations. Quiet and charmingly calculating, Secretary-General Aleksander Sarkus suddenly rose to supreme power within a matter of weeks. In a bold move, he and his inner circle secretly launched a covert nuclear terrorist attack on the Western U.N. building in New York City, decimating the area and killing the remaining world leaders who were gathered there for a Western world summit.

At this point forward, any possible threat to Secretary-General Sarkus's domination was eliminated. Now unopposed, he swiftly took control of the Western U.N. and moved its headquarters to Switzerland, renaming the organization the "United World Order" and giving himself the title "Supreme Commander." Using his new position and seductive powers of persuasion, he began meeting with western world leaders to amass an army capable of controlling the remaining splintered nations. He also instigated a cashless world monetary system, which the nations gratefully accepted because their own economies were falling in rapid succession.

After the bombing in New York, the federal government of the former United States ceased to exist in any official capacity. Food was not regularly delivered to the cities, and hungry bands soon began foraging for food. Communities and churches banded together and actually built walls around subdivisions and small communities. Once they felt secure, they themselves roamed out and preyed on smaller communities or farms for tribute of food or young men. Large groups of families gathered into feudal tribes, as local populations began to recover to a small degree.

Only among the Saints in the Mountains of the Lord did the Constitution of the United States, in its pure form continue as supreme law. With happy acquiescence from the remaining citizens of the former United States, the inhabitants of Utah, Idaho, parts of Nevada and surrounding areas elected a new President, Congress and Supreme Court. Their first legislative act was to repeal the many amendments to the constitution. Elections were scheduled again in three years with an eye to the fact that they did not fully represent the population of the land governed, and that changes would occur as greater areas fell under the protection of their peace. Until then, they rejoiced in liberties and freedom unknown since the late 1700's.

Shortly after the reestablishment of the U.S. Constitutional government among the Saints, the now-strengthened Church again called missionaries into the states now occupied by South America, as well as into the new Confederate Nation of Texas. Their commission was to preach unto the house of Israel. The times of the Gentiles were past, the Church proclaimed. They went forth with faith, like unto Ammon and his brethren, into a hostile land, among a bloodthirsty people. The inspiring reports that filtered back from these intrepid missionaries was that the people of Israel were flocking to the waters of baptism. But, the glorious news was not without its cost. Dozens of faithful missionaries died at the hands of evil men, giving their lives in the cause of the Master. They were speedily replaced.

The nations of Europe thus far had fared slightly better than the United States. Though their land was devastated by war, their compact population and smaller land mass made it possible for most local governments to survive somewhat intact, in large part due to governmental and monetary assistance by Supreme Commander Sarkus and the newly-formed United World Order. Unexpectedly, the one thing that did largely survive all this destruction was television—if one had electricity to view it. Every day news agencies both official and renegade, broadcast disturbing news of the world condition.

It was then the unthinkable happened. As China's domination of their occupied countries solidified, their thirst for domination became unquenchable. Under the guise of assisting their Russian allies at the European eastern front, the Chinese marched a massive army north through Ukraine to bolster Eastern Coalition forces. As the army entered Belarus they suddenly swung eastward and unleashed their full might upon Moscow. The Russians were caught completely by surprise, and within two days Moscow was brutally overthrown. Knowing that Russia was now burning with rage at this Chinese treachery, Supreme Commander Sarkus offered military aid and the former Soviet Bloc in exchange for the Russian juggernaut's unconditional alliance.

In the wake of the horrific devastation of worldwide war, a full one-third of the population of the world had died. In the ensuing war another one-third had died either of wounds of war, or of the indirect results of war upon the weakened populations. The land was poisoned by the mindless use of nuclear weapons, chemical and biological warfare, whose poisons were ultimately washed to the sea where they killed vast regions of life beneath the waves. Some estimates placed the death toll in the seas as high as a full two-thirds of all life therein. The very ability of humans to inhabit the planet was at once called into question. To the western world, including many in the U.S., their only hope glimmered in the United World Order, and the promise of help from Commander Sarkus.

It was during this world-wide turmoil that Samuel and his family, and thousands of other faithful Saints turned their heads and hearts toward the east. They had been warned by the Prophet that Commander Sarkus was the prophesied Anti-Christ, and the true followers of Christ were determined to follow Him and none else, no matter the consequences. Amid the world chaos, they began to sing and rejoice as they quickly made preparations for the journey to Zion.

Having brought a small group of refugees through a much longer trek, Samuel could not envision the journey from the valleys of the mountains to Missouri with any great anxiety. This group of Zion people was prepared both physically and spiritually for the journey. They were led by men of God and accompanied by angels and translated beings. Beside himself, Samuel was aware of thousands of sisters and brothers now among the Saints who were likewise translated and endowed with this special calling and power.

Samuel knew that the journey east would be protected and sanctified by God, but also hallowed by the blood of many he loved. It had ever been thus, and would be once again, that the price some would pay to redeem Zion would be their own precious blood. Just as Christ Himself had paid with His blood to purchase redemption, so there was a cost for this redemption. Helaman had taught him that this was a pattern that could not be defied.

The first company left in the early spring of the following year. Their caravan consisted largely of horse or hand-drawn wagons and carts. Even a few ancient handcarts from former days had been pressed into service, more as a matter of emotion than necessity.

Since there were few automobiles upon the nation's formerly grand highway system, Samuel and his group left walking down the middle of Interstate 80 East. As if a silent trumpet had been sounded high above the desert valley, hundreds of groups just like his started that very day for Zion. Their horses hooves clopped steadily on the hard asphalt as they slowly made their way east. Most wagons they pulled were the frames of small cars stripped of their engines to make them lighter. They rolled easily, and proved adequate protection from wind and rain at night.

By far the most popular wagon was the ubiquitous mini vans, now stripped. With everything but one or two seats removed, they held the belongings for several families, and rolled easily on the hard surfaced roads. It became common practice to unhitch the horses at the tops of long hills, and after loading as many people inside as could fit, allow the vehicles to roll to a stop as far as they would go. Besides being a welcome change of pace, it gave the horses a needed rest, and added hundreds of free miles to their trek.

Familiar cities passed slowly: Fort Bridger, Green River, Rock Springs. Each day they felt the Spirit of the Lord strengthen and push them onward. Every day difficulty darkened their journey, but not their hearts.

After two tragic mishaps with vehicle brakes failing while coasting down a mountain pass, it became the practice to chain three vehicles together before allowing them to coast. That way, any brake failure could be overcome by the other two. This backfired one day when the center vehicle blew out a tire, lost control, and caused the other two to crash into the side of the mountain. The three cars rolled side-over-side down the long mountainside, strewing baggage, food and bodies as they rolled. However, for reasons of providence not understood by any present, all survived without injury. Only the vehicles themselves were left by the way. Toddlers who had been thrown from the tumbling vans simply stood up and cried for their mothers. Teens were pulled from the twisted wreckage still laughing from the experience. Old people were dragged from the wreckage, alive and unharmed. It was impossible to understand why they had been miraculously spared, but it was a joyful relief nonetheless. There were special prayers of thanksgiving that night at camp.

The practice changed again, and single vehicles made the dizzying spin down the steep grades alone. However, they were thoroughly checked by someone who understood mechanics and piloted by an adult driver before being allowed to go. Vehicles of questionable quality were chained to a fallen tree at the top of the hill. Once this practice became common they were unharmed—until they approached Cheyenne, Wyoming.

Cheyenne had declared itself an independent city-state, organized a militia and closed its borders to the world. With enough citizens to

provide for their needs, and sufficient arms to enforce their will, they possessed an arrogance and determination on a par with an invading army.

Their terrible demands to pass were simple: one-half of any traveler's food and clothing, one-half of their young men, and all male children under three years old would be required as tribute to ensure safe passage. Any attempt to turn back, bypass Cheyenne, or to fight would be met with deadly force.

The leaders of the caravan to Zion called a council around a large bonfire to consider their options. In their midst were two of the Quorum of the Twelve, including the President of that quorum who now addressed them.

Samuel stood near the fire; though he had no leadership voice for the company, he did speak for his family. He waited with some anticipation to hear what would be decided. Many options were discussed, including fighting. They had with them one hundred armed soldiers, with more coming in groups behind them due to arrive each day for weeks. In time, they would be strong enough to force their way through.

Others were in favor of negotiating a lower settlement, reasoning that some price would be required no matter the solution. Others favored leaving during the night and heading north to Torrington before heading east again, thereby going around Cheyenne. There were even a few who favored slinking back to Salt Lake City and abandoning the journey until a compromise could be negotiated with their enemies.

President Johnson, senior apostle and President of the Quorum of the Twelve, listened with polite interest to all comments. Somewhere in his early seventies, he was spry and energetic. He was of medium build and somewhat tall, bald except for what he called his "putting green" around the sides of his head. He wore a short beard of gray, which was unusual among the Brethren. His appearance was at once noble, yet open and friendly. The saints loved Elder Johnson without exception. Even more importantly, they honored his priesthood keys, and trusted his ability to speak on behalf of the Lord.

After hours of dissertation and some debate had passed, he stood and thanked everyone for their comments.

"Brothers and Sisters," he said with deep affection in his voice, his face luminous, "I understand your concerns, and share them. However, as I have listened to your excellent ideas, I have been struck quite forcefully that none of them are what the Lord wishes us to do. Here is what I propose. We will divide our food so that each brother who holds the

Melchizedek priesthood has three day's supply. They will then go among the people of Cheyenne and preach the Gospel of peace."

A few whisperings and coughs punctuated the air. The President went on. "I believe it was Nephi who observed that the word of God was more powerful in subduing their enemies than the sword. The brethren will preach, bless, prophesy, and share their food with whomsoever they meet. In one week's time they will return. I promise you in the name of the Lord that if they are fearless and faithful to this charge, we will pass through this city at that time without loss of life, and without tribute except as we choose to render.

Samuel's family looked at one another with hope. President continued, "Remember, these people we call our enemies are the Lord's children. They are frightened and hungry, and probably see us as a grave threat. Let us answer those fears with kindness and show them Christ-like love, and they will let us pass."

The sounds of consent and accord arose from all assembled. Samuel felt his heart burn with conviction of the inspired wisdom of this course of action.

"All in favor please signify," President Johnson called out. Every hand arose.

"All brethren who wish to answer this call please remain by the fire to be set apart. All others please attend to your families. We will call evening prayers by the bugle as usual. Go now, and God bless you for your faithfulness."

Samuel joined his sons Sam, Theo and George, and a host of others. One by one they were set apart by Apostle Johnson. When he laid his hands upon Samuel's head, he jerked them back off as if they had been burned. He stepped aside to see Samuel's face and looked down at him.

"I see you have already been given an unusual and glorious mission to perform," he said so quietly that none but he and Samuel understood.

Samuel actually blushed. "I would like to answer the Lord's call through His Apostle," he replied.

President Johnson nodded. "I feel impressed that there is something more you must do in Cheyenne."

"I feel it too," Samuel said.

"Then, let's get you set apart," the President said, and pronounced a brief, but powerful blessing upon him.

When it came time to set apart Sammy, Samuel ordained him an Elder, and President Johnson set him apart as a full-time missionary. It was heartwarming to young Sam that his entire family could be there to witness his ordination.

By the first light of day Samuel, Sam Jr. and others of the Saints were slowly approaching the ramshackle barricade of upturned cars and busses that blocked the road.

"What do you want?!" a woman's voice called shrilly from the barricade. Previously, it had been a man who had made their demands. "Have you come to surrender?"

It was Samuel's voice they heard in answer. "We have come to share our food and to pray with you. Or, if you do not wish to pray, we wish at least to share our food." Samuel pulled a small red apple from his backpack, and held it up for them to see.

There was a long moment of silence before a woman with bright red hair stood up on the side of an old school bus. "Throw me the apple," she demanded. Samuel walked the short distance to the bus and carefully tossed it up to her. She caught the apple in a swift movement and carried it to her mouth.

"What else you got in that bag?" she asked, her mouth full of apple.

"I have some other food, and my scriptures."

"Throw me the whole bag," she ordered.

"I cannot," he replied. "I wish to save some for the others. But if you wish, I can give you a potato."

"I'll take it," she responded hastily. Samuel sorted out a potato not much bigger than the apple and tossed it to her. This she tucked into her pocket. "For my kids," she explained a little forlornly.

"How many kids?" he asked.

"Three," she replied cautiously.

Samuel tossed her two more potatoes which also went into her pocket. Others of his group stepped forward following his example. There appeared to be about a dozen lightly-armed people. Only one of them was male, and he appeared to be in his early teens.

"Thanks," the woman said. She looked at him suspiciously and asked, "Why are you feeding us? We expected you to attack, or to go around."

"We have no desire to attack, and no time to go around. We are the people of God, and feel no malice toward you. We hope to be able to share our faith with you," Samuel replied in complete candor.

"We're not interested in your faith. We know you're Mormons. Mormonism is outlawed in Cheyenne," she replied in an accusatory voice.

Samuel smiled and held out his arms in surrender. "Then, we will baptize you all, so you will have no choice but to decriminalize your own faith," he replied loudly. She could not know that his words were in deep earnest, and profoundly true.

"Haha! A bold plan," she said with a laugh and smirk on her face. She took another bite of her apple. "This apple is the first fruit I've eaten in months."

"What do you usually eat?"

She didn't answer, but gazed at him with wary eyes. "Grass," she finally replied quietly.

"You survive by eating grass? I wasn't aware the human body could survive on grass," he said, somewhat amazed.

"It can't for any length of time," was her reply. "But, it fills the belly, and does have some food value, especially when it goes to seed. It's harder to chew, but makes into a green tea. It isn't so bad once you get used to it." She bit into the apple again and spoke through her chewing. "The city does have a few farms running, but there isn't enough seed to get them producing soon enough, so we eat grass and a little bit of wild game—but not very much."

"I'm sorry for your trials," Samuel responded softly. "We have been a little more blessed in that we had our food storage to fall back on for a couple years."

She stared at him hard. "Yeah, I had heard that the Mormons have a bunch of food. It doesn't seem fair."

"We prefer to be called Latter-day Saints."

"Whatever," she replied curtly. Then her voice softened. "I used to know some Mormons. They were fine people, actually."

"Why do you say 'were'?" Samuel asked.

"They disappeared after the Mormons were outlawed."

"Fortunately, those times are past," Samuel said happily.

"They aren't past here!" she insisted. "The remaining Mormons are being rounded up to be executed, if the rumors are correct. You people should have stayed in Utah. I heard you have your own peaceful government, and even have electricity and running water again. Believe me, if I had a peaceful home with food and water, I'd stay put."

"I see your point," Samuel said. "However, we are going back to Missouri to build the New Jerusalem."

This took the woman back. "I heard of that in my church. Isn't that where Jesus is supposed to rule the world in the Millennium?"

"It is. Who told you that?"

"Oh, I read the Bible," she said nonchalantly. Then her voice lowered. "I even have a Book of the Mormons," she added in a whisper, as if she were revealing some dangerous secret. It was still illegal to own that book, so her whispering was probably a wise precaution.

After some silence, Samuel spoke. "There's something else you want to tell me," he urged.

"Nope."

Another silence. "OK, I'll tell you," Samuel challenged. "You were baptized a member just before the Church was outlawed."

"I was not!" she insisted hotly.

"You left it shortly after that, and even persecuted some other Mormons."

"You are crazy," she said angrily.

"And, now you are sorry."

"I'm not either!" she cried.

"Not guilty, or not sorry?" he asked calmly.

She did not answer immediately. She looked around, and finding her companions totally engaged in receiving food from the other Mormons, turned back to Samuel. Her voice grew soft and regretful. "Okay, I *am* sorry," she said finally. "I was afraid, and I got caught up in the feeling of the time, and didn't want to be identified as a Mormon myself. I did some bad things."

Samuel gazed steadily at her. "The Apostle Peter did something similar when he denied he knew Christ for fear of his life."

"That's right, he did," she replied, and gave her head a toss so that her bright red hair fanned out across her shoulders. If she had been something more than skin stretched over bones, she might have been attractive. "I don't wonder why he did that anymore," she said quietly.

"Then, you've learned something quite marvelous from your experience."

She shook her head vehemently. "I look upon it with loathing, not as something marvelous."

"I suppose," Samuel allowed. "Would you like to know what's going to happen once we get to Zion?"

"Got nothin' else to do," she said with a bored voice. "You fed me, so I'm yours until I get hungry again."

"What's your name?"

"Shirley," she said after some hesitation, as if she were leery of telling him.

"Shirley, do you understand what Zion is?"

"Don't know that I do. Is it a place, or a people?"

Several hours later he and Shirley were deep in conversation while they walked toward town. He accompanied her to her home, which was in fact a small apartment not far from the barricade. There he found over a dozen very hungry people. He gave them all his food, most of which they used to make into a thin stew. They invited him to share their meal. He ate a little while he taught them the Gospel.

That evening more came to hear him, and the following morning they had to move into a larger apartment to make room for all who wanted to hear. He taught with joy and conviction, and bore down in testimony as strongly as the Spirit gave him utterance. By that evening many in the group either admitted they were former "Mormons," or requested baptism. He invited them to join their band in a few days. They immediately began making preparations to do so.

That evening as Samuel lay awake with Melody in their tent pretending to sleep, he was suddenly aroused by a fierce voice.

"Where's the Mormon?" a male voice demanded. A gunshot went off and someone screamed nearby. Samuel jumped to his feet, hoping to act as a decoy for the rest of his family. He walked quickly towards the two men and three women who were waiting outside. He silently prayed that Melody and young Helaman would not be detected; they were miraculously unseen.

"Come with us!" a man ordered him at gunpoint. They escorted Samuel to an army jeep idling by the curb. It was the first running vehicle he had seen since leaving Cardston, Canada. They sped down darkened streets toward the center of town. After zipping around numerous corners they came to a school surrounded by a high fence.

"Out!" the man ordered. Samuel complied and let himself be led through the fence and into the school. The air inside was dense with the smell of body odor and feces. The stench was overwhelming. Through the classrooms and larger rooms were literally hundreds of prisoners kept in squalid conditions. It was the middle of the night but few of those inside were asleep. They looked at him through narrowed eyes.

"Welcome," a thin woman in the near darkness said as she approached him. "Are you one of the Mormons camped outside the city?"

"I am," he replied.

"You should have left rather than come into this city."

"Why is that?"

"Because most of you have been rounded up already. Come with me." Samuel followed her down a hall stepping over bodies all the way. Finally, she turned into a small classroom and stepped aside.

"Father!" a weary voice called. It was Sammy, his son, and many others he recognized and loved. The woman was right: they were almost all here. She was also wrong though; they were exactly where they should be.

"See," the woman said in weak triumph. "You're all in the same sinking ship as the rest of us."

"Who are all these people? Why are they locked up?" Samuel asked.

The woman narrowed her eyes bitterly. "We are the misfits, the out of favor, the ones who dared question or oppose the new government. There are lots of Mormons here who thought it was suddenly okay to be Mormons again. They were sadly mistaken," she said with deep irony.

"Which are you?"

"I fit into several of those categories, even the Mormon one."

"We're here to help you," Samuel said.

She laughed. "You're in prison too," she reminded him, "and not a moment too soon. They told us just today that there were too many of us, and at least half of us would be executed tomorrow morning, starting with the Mormons. Your timing is impeccable," she said, her voice heavy with sarcasm.

"Then, there's still time," Samuel told her.

She shook her head as if Samuel were insane. "Time for what?"

Samuel ignored her question. "First, is there a woman here named Bonnie?"

"I have absolutely no idea," she said with anger in her voice.

"She would be in her late thirties. Blond hair, blue eyes, and probably among the Mormons."

"Do you really think she's in here, Dad?" Sammy asked. He didn't really expect an answer since it was apparent Samuel did think so.

The woman shrugged. "Come with me, and I'll take you to the rest of the Mormons. They stick together, so they're easy to find."

She led the way to a large room with wide raised steps that had once been the band room. When they entered only the very small children were asleep. Everyone else watched them with thinly veiled fear.

Samuel stepped forward. "I'm looking for a woman named Bonnie Mahoy. Do any of you…"

"Daddy!" a hoarse voice cried out. A young woman came running down the steps toward him. She fell into his arms with a cry of joy and wept as if her whole soul had been rent. "Daddy, Daddy," she said over and over. "I knew you'd come for me. I knew it!"

"Are you all right?" he asked, forcing her to look at him.

Bonnie clung to him, nodding weakly. "I am, I think. I'm awfully hungry and sick, but honestly I'm better than most. My husband is really bad off though. He was beaten by the guards for insisting they give us food. He's over here," she said, leading the way around many supine bodies.

She came to a far corner of the room and stopped. "Daddy, I want you to meet Steven, my husband." A young man in his late thirties was huddled in a fetal position on the hard vinyl floor. His only comfort was a rolled up piece of cloth under his head. His face was battered and cut. One eye was swollen shut, and dried blood was visible in his hair and on his face. His skin was pasty and damp. He was obviously in shock and severe pain.

"Steven. I'm Samuel, Bonnie's father. How are you doing?" Samuel inquired, surveying his injuries as much as possible in the semi-light.

He couldn't look up for long before his eyes shut again. "I'm pretty battered, I'm afraid. I've got two broken arms, a broken collar bone, several broken ribs, and probably a concussion," he said with a slur. "I haven't even thought about what internal injuries I might have. But, I'm doing OK other than that," he laughed weakly, and winced from the effort.

"What you did was a very brave thing," Samuel started to say.

"Futile and foolish, you mean," Steven replied. "I just couldn't stand to see my wife and the people starving."

"How long have you two been married?" Samuel asked Bonnie. He hadn't even known that Bonnie was married.

"Less than a year, Daddy," she said. "We were married secretly by our bishop. The authorities found out about it, and killed the bishop," she said, her heart heavy with regret. "He was such a wonderful man, Daddy. You would have liked him. He had tremendous faith. Steve and I feel horrible because it was all our fault!"

"His death was not your fault, Bonnie. It was the Lord's will," Sam comforted her. "So, this was a year ago?" he asked.

"About a year ago, I guess. It's hard to keep track of time," Bonnie replied. "I just wish we had our strong bishop with us now."

But there was only a little time to do what must be done. They would talk of loss and sorrows later.

"Steven, how is your faith?"

"Very strong, sir."

"Strong enough to be healed?"

"Yes sir," he said emphatically.

"Then take my hand, Steve," he directed. With a small groan Steven raised his broken arm high enough to take Samuel's hand.

"Steven, in the name of Jesus Christ, and by His holy priesthood, I command you to be healed, and arise." This he said solemnly, in a calm and commanding voice. He slowly pulled on Steven's hand, coaxing him to a sitting position. Steven grunted in pain as he pushed himself upward with an elbow by sheer willpower. He gave Samuel a look filled with hope, and intense pain. His face was beaded with sweat.

"Stand up Steve, you can do it. It requires faith, not a tolerance for pain. Stand up."

"I will!" Steven cried. He came to his knees with a groan, then pushed himself to one foot, and then to standing. Samuel began undoing the makeshift slings supporting his arms. Steve reached up and stripped a bloodied bandage from his head. There was no wound beneath.

"Don't say anything," Samuel instructed just as he was about to cry out for joy. Bonnie gasped and rushed to her husband. He held her tightly in arms that had been useless and festering just moments before.

Samuel looked around. "Sammy?"

"Yes sir," his son said, coming to stand beside his father.

"You see that lady sitting by the piano?"

"I do, sir."

"She has faith to be healed. You're an elder. Go heal her as you saw me heal Steve. Stay with her long enough to offer a prayer of thanks, then return and report to me."

"Yes sir," Sammy said and marched away.

"Steve, you're an elder as well, aren't you?"

"I am. I am indeed," he replied, keeping his voice as low as he could.

"You take the far side of the room and begin healing people in Christ's name," Samuel instructed.

"Yes sir!" he cried, and hurried away with Bonnie on his arm.

"You, good brother," Samuel said, motioning toward a man lying in a puddle of his own vomit, yet whose eyes were burning with fire at what he had just seen. "Do you have the faith to be healed?"

"I do!" he cried hoarsely.

"Then in the name of Jesus Christ, arise."

The man jumped to his feet as if he had been shocked by a cattle prod.

"I'm a high priest," his face aflame with faith. "Tell me who's next," he said humbly.

"That sister there with the three kids huddling around her. The smallest one there has died. Bring the little one back, then heal the others," Samuel directed.

"I will go and do as the Lord commands," the man said, and turned toward the sister. At that very moment Samuel heard a cry of joy as the woman by the piano received the promised blessing from Sammy. To his left he could hear the quiet words of Steven, and sobs of joy all around him.

Samuel turned back toward the thin woman who had escorted him to this room. She was on her knees praying. He knelt beside her and curved an arm across her shoulders. She laid her head on his arm.

"I don't know your name," he said.

"Grace," she said with some irony in her voice.

"Grace, are you ready to be healed?"

"I'm not sick," she replied without looking up.

"I wasn't referring to your body," Samuel said. "Your sickness is within your soul."

"I know it is. I'm afraid I have sinned too bad to be forgiven. It would be better for me if my sickness was in my flesh. I think I have sufficient faith for my body to be healed. But, the wounds of the soul are more permanent, I'm afraid."

"What makes you think that? Don't you think the Lord is able to heal all wounds, and bind up all sorrows and afflictions?" Samuel asked her gently.

"I do," she said, and looked at his face through tearful eyes, "if the person is worthy." She paused poignantly. "I'm not. I'm the worst of the worst. Don't you wonder why I'm not sick like the other Mormons?" she demanded.

"I know why," Samuel said. "So does everyone in this room."

"What? How? I mean…"

"You sold your integrity for some food," Samuel said.

"I sold more than that. I sold my friends, my self-respect, my body, my very soul," she lamented.

"I know," Samuel replied. "Listen to the sounds of joy in this room tonight. How does it make you feel?"

"Like shouting praises to God," she said honestly.

"Then, you haven't sold as much as you thought. There are those who would order us all shot after what you are seeing. I'm going to leave you here. You seek God, and ask Him to forgive you," Samuel said as he stood up.

"How will I know when He has?" she asked as she looked up at him, tears coursing down her face.

"You will know when peace floods in upon you. Then you will know," he said. She didn't answer, but lowered her head.

Just as the first rays of morning were beginning to light the walls of their prison, the last of those with faith to be healed stood upon solid legs. Sometime during the night Grace had been taken out and released.

"Shortly, the guards will come for us," Samuel said, his voice solemn and steady. "This morning some of you will die. If you are afraid to die, seek help from God those around you. If you are not, then give your strength to others. At some point we will all die. It is a rare opportunity to be able to die for your faith. Lift up your hearts and be glad," he said brightly.

"If we die with our hope bright in Christ, happy day, all is well!" an old man cried. A chorus of "Amens" filled the room.

Samuel gazed at them in love. "You have great faith. Do not fear, but let your hearts be full. The hour is upon us." At that very moment the door banged open and four armed guards stomped into the room.

"All you Mormon vermin—out!" the only man among them ordered. They obeyed meekly. They were led out into a fenced enclosure that surrounded four tennis courts. One wall was made of cement blocks, the others were tall chain link.

"You are to be shot for being Mormons, and enemies to the state," the man cried out, his voice bitter with hatred. "Your only hope of survival is to renounce your religion and swear allegiance to the state of Cheyenne! Anyone who refuses will die! Do you understand?!" He waited until he was certain his threats had reached their greatest possible impact.

You!" he said, pointing at a young woman with a four-year-old girl clinging to her neck. "You and the child. Against the wall!"

The mother adjusted her sobbing child and walked to the wall where she turned to face the four guards. She was one of those healed just hours before. She had been severely afflicted with festering skin lesions. Her face was now clear of all blemishes, and free of all fear. She comforted her baby until she grew still.

Willing to make an example of her, the guard marched up to the young woman and shouted in her face. "Are you still a Mormon? Or, are you going to renounce?!"

"I will not renounce," she said calmly, looking him squarely in the face.

"Shoot her," he said with utter disdain in his voice. "Shoot her and the brat!" he bellowed, and took a step back. The three guards, two women and one man, looked at one another as if unsure what to do. Finally one of the grizzled women stepped forward and pulled a pistol from her holster. She cocked it and aimed it with a steady hand at the mother's heart. She was barely ten feet away. Samuel felt his heart racing. He wanted to run forward and stand between them, but he was constrained by the Spirit. He looked at his son, and saw tears streaming down his face.

"Fire!" the guard cried, and the gun bucked in her hand. The young mother slumped against the wall, followed by her baby.

With a satisfied grin, the guard marched back to the prisoners and pointed his pistol at Bonnie. "You," he cried, "to the wall." Bonnie walked soberly to the wall and stood next to the two bodies at her feet. She didn't seem to notice.

"No!" a young man's anguished voice cried out, and before Samuel could stop him, Steven ran to his wife.

"All right fool, you can join her then," the guard said, and shoved them together. "Will you renounce your false religion?"

"No," they both said in unison.

"Guards take aim," he commanded. The same woman who had shot the first two raised her pistol. Her eyes were glassy and numb, a look of hatred on her face, then a brief wince. The other two guards stood as if paralyzed by shock.

"Last chance Mormons. Renounce your religion, or die."

"No," they said again.

"Shoot her first, then him," he commanded, and stepped back two paces to watch them die. Steve turned them so that he was between Bonnie and the guards. She closed her eyes as he lowered his head to kiss her with great tenderness. This infuriated the guard who screamed, "Fire!"

"He's in the way!" the guard screamed, her voice nearing hysteria.

"Then shoot him first!" he screamed back in demonic rage.

As if sudden understanding had just hammered into her mind, the guard blinked her eyes, turned the pistol slightly and fired. The male guard fell to the pavement. Everyone's eyes were riveted on this unexpected development, and were shocked to hear another gun discharge. They looked around in time to see the female guard who had fired both times slump to the ground from her own bullet. The other two guards quietly took their guns from their holsters, dropped them to the ground and slowly walked out of the building, leaving the doors open behind them.

"Steve," Samuel said, drawing his son-in-law's eyes to his own. Steve was dazed, and not sure that he had not actually been shot himself. He stood looking into Bonnie's eyes with deep shock on his face.

"Yes, Father?" he said meekly.

"God has spared you. Please administer to the young mother and her child. Their death was untimely."

It took a moment for comprehension to dawn. Steve's eyes brightened. "Yes sir!" he replied with certainty, and knelt by their bodies. Two other priesthood holders joined him. Soon the only lifeless bodies left behind were those of the two guards.

Moments later a rattle of gunfire interrupted the quiet of the morning. Shouting and more gunfire came to them from across the yard. Former prisoners began streaming out of the school building. They passed through the gate and out into the city without opposition. Samuel and the others waited where they were, just a little beyond the tennis courts. Finally, a small group of four armed people approached them from one of the buildings. The second among them was Grace. They stopped a short distance away, at which point they holstered their weapons.

"You're free to go," Grace told them happily.

"Where have you been, Grace?" Samuel asked.

"Trying to redeem my crimes," she said.

"That's the Savior's job."

"I know, but I felt like I had to act or my soul would be lost forever. You said I should pray until I felt peace. I pondered every possible way for me to be forgiven by God. When my mind happened upon the idea of going for help from the resistance, I felt such a feeling of peace that I ran the entire way to get them. It may not have been what you were meaning, but it has brought me the peace I had lost. Now, I can begin to petition Jesus to take away my sins with some faith."

Samuel threw his arms around her. "He will hear your prayers, Grace. We are very grateful to you for bringing help," he said, overjoyed.

The woman in front cleared her throat, and all eyes shifted from Grace to her. She was young, perhaps in her late twenties, but her face was steely and hard. Her dark eyes sparkled with keen intellect, but her countenance was nearly devoid of light.

"I'm the leader of the resistance, such as it is," she informed them. "We're going to go from here to the standing government's headquarters and call on them to surrender. They have a lot more people and guns than we do, so I don't really expect to be successful. I suggest you people return to your caravan and find a way around the city."

"Tell me something," Samuel asked as she was about to turn away. His question brought her eyes back upon him. "Why are you doing this? Why are you willing to fight them?"

"Because they are wrong and we are right," she snapped back.

"That is not the right answer, and you will fail," he said solemnly.

"How do you know that?" she demanded.

Grace interjected into the conversation. "Listen to him, Jean, I told you, he's a man of God," she urgently told her leader.

Jean glanced in her direction. "What makes you say that?"

Samuel stepped toward her. "A new era is upon the land, and the times of tyranny are past. God will not allow any form of government to prosper unless it is founded upon righteousness, freedom, liberty, and true constitutional principles. The main reason our own nation was toppled was because as a people and a nation we had abandoned these very things"

"Then, you're saying we should fight for liberty and freedom, and the outdated constitution?" she asked, her voice somewhat ironic, as if such a cause were impossibly naïve.

"Not just fight for it, cherish it, pray for it, and seek God's help in establishing it. Be willing to spill your blood to obtain it, and be willing to step aside and let it rule in your stead."

The woman spat and turned away. "What you suggest is the philosophy of a fool. Others have dreamed, and they have all died."

"Not all," Samuel countered. "Consider that our founding fathers were just a few, yet they changed the course of a whole nation. Their task was more difficult than yours. You fight for something the people already believe in. In their day as well, the majority of the people did not understand freedom."

Jean thought for a moment. "I suppose most people do remember and dream. But, do you really think such a thing is possible? I find my heart yearning for what you say, but I'm too afraid to hope. We are just a few hungry survivors, and there are so many who have a different agenda, who don't trust the old ways. And, it seems they all have the guns," she said, her voice a little hopeless.

"This is not a battle of guns," Samuel assured her. "It is a contest between truth and error, between freedom and captivity. God established this nation and this constitution once in the face of great opposition. If you fight for another form of control, you are outnumbered and you will lose. If you fight for freedom, to establish the constitution and guarantee liberty and freedom of worship, then you fight with God, and they are outnumbered."

"Are you sure you're not a politician?" she asked with mock suspicion,
then added, "I do believe in the constitution. I was studying to be a nurse before the war. All this killing and hatred is toxic to my soul. I detest it, and yearn with all my heart for freedom and liberty. I really do," she said with deep emotion.

"Then, set your goals there. Fall on your knees and pray until you are certain you are doing as the God of all liberty desires of you. Once you are on His errand, you will succeed," Samuel instructed.

"Do you really think so?" she asked.

"I am certain of it," Samuel replied.

Jean pondered these words for many moments before a look of resolution crossed her features. "I will do as you say," she said quietly. Then she nodded at Samuel, turned and walked away. The haughtiness was gone from her gait.

"God bless you," someone called at her back, and a hundred voices echoed the cry. She stopped walking, hung her head for a moment, then without turning around continued on with greater determination and hope. In that brief moment she had come to know that what Samuel had told her was true. They would triumph as long as their cause was just and inspired of God.

Jean did not go directly to battle as she had planned, but returned to her tent where she confronted the Lord for many hours through the night and following day. It truly was a confrontation, for it was the only powerful form of communication she understood. She at first accused, then demanded the Lord get on their side of the war; then after many hours, she finally wept and pleaded for forgiveness. As the Spirit slowly permeated her soul she softened, repented, and humbly asked God to show her what her place was in His war.

When she reemerged, Jean was serene and confident. Her small band of rebels had never seen this fiery leader at peace. Much more than any warbling battle cry, her serene confidence energized them. When they finally made their way to battle, there was no one there to fight. The account of their victory at the school yard the day before had been told and retold with such inflation that they were more fiction than fact.

For those standing in the hijacked seats of power, the delay of the expected attack of the rebels created a state of deep anxiety within their ranks such that during her night of prayer, the military force that gripped Cheyenne had quietly dissipated. When morning came those in command of the city found themselves in command of themselves alone. The transition in power was accomplished overnight, without bloodshed.

Within seven days, the newly-elected democratic government of Cheyenne let the Saints pass through their city unmolested. It had taken exactly one week for the miracle to occur, exactly as President Johnson had proclaimed. President Johnson gave the new government enough wheat, barley, and corn to seed several large fields. If they were careful, in a few years there would be no more hunger in Cheyenne.

Almost as if Interstate 80 had been constructed for the express purpose of transporting the Saints home, they followed it due east across Nebraska, stopping only as necessary along the way. At every major city they encountered, a drama similar to Cheyenne was replayed. Every day they rejoiced, every day was filled with miracles, and every day they buried more faithful saints along the way. They were periodically attacked, robbed, persecuted, ridiculed, or driven away at gunpoint. Each time they responded the same, by teaching the Gospel of Jesus Christ. Each time it cost them more lives; each time many were healed or brought to life; each time it delayed their journey; each time they moved on with more people accompanying them, and more joy than they had had before. The very ones who had persecuted them often begged to join them. These they taught, baptized, and happily embraced.

The further east they traveled the fewer people they encountered, until at Lincoln, Nebraska they found no inhabitants at all. The city was intact, there were just no living people. The streets were littered with human remains. Samuel thought of the Nephites finding and naming the Land of Desolation because of the heaps of bones they found there. It was impossible to describe the feeling of desolation they felt as they passed through, knowing each of those deceased had not so long ago been a loving being, with families, dreams, and lives. As they passed children hid their eyes, women looked away with heavy souls, and grown men wept at the tragic end of so many.

They left I-80 at Lincoln and continued east on side roads until they came to the Missouri River. They found an intact bridge and crossed over into the upper parts of Missouri.

The rolling hills of Missouri were green and lush. Every town, every home, every farm was abandoned. In some places there was evidence of warfare. In others, human bones lay in the streets, undisturbed since they had died from the "pink death" plague years before.

It took seven days to travel from the Missouri River south and east to Adam-Ondi-Ahman, the place where Adam would meet the Lord in the greatest Priesthood meeting of all time. They could feel it's sacredness as they entered the small valley, surrounded with lush trees and rolling hills of verdant green. The valley itself was devoid of any human structures, seeming to them to be as pristine as when it was a part of the Garden of Eden. They camped there for several weeks waiting for the remainder of their people to catch up with them. From there it took six days to travel to Independence, the actual place where they would build the New Jerusalem. They arrived at the ancient cornerstone of the temple late on the afternoon of April 6th, and fell upon their knees and prayed until the shining moon bathed the glorious hills of Zion in light.

They were home at last.

THE NEW JERUSALEM

When the Saints arrived in Jackson County, Missouri, they were the only human inhabitants of the region. They first blessed the land, casting out all disease, darkness, and evil that may have lingered there. Plans were then quickly developed to accommodate the influx of people that must shortly follow. Crews were assembled to lay out tent cities. For now there were enough empty homes and buildings to house all who had come to build up Zion. The brethren set up Church headquarters in the LDS visitor's center which stood a few blocks from the temple site. It served as both an office building and a chapel.

That next day the building site of the temple was staked out, and work was immediately begun to clear the ground. The old corner stone was carefully removed and set aside. It was crudely cut, and though historic, would not serve to support the corner of the structure the Lord intended them to build. It would be laid symbolically at the corner, but it would not bear the weight of the mighty structure.

Through foresight and inspiration, they had brought with them a communications system able to transmit sound, video, and data. It relied on a system of satellites owned by the Church which had been put in service just three years prior to the war. The destruction of communication satellites had been one of the fronts of the war, so the Church's system was rare and highly prized. The equipment was set up and switched on. In a few seconds the link was complete and fully functional. President Andrews, the Prophet of the Church prayed with them, then announced plans for the greatest temple ever built.

While skilled architects studied the plans under the direction of Elder Johnson, crews set out in all directions to acquire building materials. There was a vast plenitude of everything they would need—tools, lumber, and machinery of every type. This was due to the fact that this land had been heavily populated before the war. Their death and destruction had been so swift they had left behind everything of worth. It stood in construction yards intended for other buildings, banks, skyscrapers and homes. It now awaited any hand willing to make use of it.

Others set out to find fuel and construction equipment. Some went in search of a quarry from which to cut the stone. In the meantime, a thousand men cleared top soil and gravel with the power of willing muscle.

Samuel labored day after day to dig the foundations of the new temple. His was a tireless task. Able to work almost indefinitely and recover with little or no rest, he had to pace himself to keep from working the non-translated beings to death.

He was amazed to find that dozens of men and women in the crew were capable of similar feats of tireless labor. He began to suspect that a considerable percentage of their number were, in fact, like himself. It was an odd fact that he was unable to identify a fellow translated being any easier than anyone else. Except on special occasions, and for reasons only known to God, none in that state could discuss their present circumstance; Samuel honesty did not know which of his brothers and sisters were, in reality, angels.

Perhaps as startling as the number of people working faithfully on the temple was the fact that a full two-thirds of them were women. They came each morning and labored side by side with the men, even stepping in front of them to ensure their participation in the fullest extent. What was most odd to Samuel and many others, was the strength they possessed, equal to, and at times greater than a man. Yet, they were not hard, nor masculine. They worked, walked and spoke with gentleness and feminine dignity. In every respect they were saintly and gracious, yet they worked like draft horses for the Lord.

When the plans they had received from the Prophet were fully understood and drawn, they were laid out for all to inspect. Samuel, and a thousand others stared in wonder at the tremendous scope of the mission ahead of them. It was a daunting task that could well take decades to complete. The main building was circular. Radiating outward were twelve rectangular buildings arranged like the spokes of a wheel. Each of these was connected to another circular building at its end which formed a twelve sided building completely enclosing the spoked wheel. The spaces between the spokes held gardens, fountains, outdoor libraries, outdoor ordinance rooms and offices. It was truly magnificent in every respect. When completed the entire structure would be a little short of a quarter mile in diameter.

The main building was to be four stories high with an additional four stories of spires and steeples. At the very top of the temple was to be a statue of the Angel Moroni with his trumpet held by his side, indicating that the trumpet had been blown, that Christ had returned to the earth. Each of the spoke buildings was stair-stepped, beginning at three stories nearest the temple proper, and stepping in graceful arches and flowing lines to a single story at the rim.

The outer rim was two stories tall with row upon row of steepled windows, graceful arches and tall towers. Each of the twelve outer buildings were identical with three prominent steeples above the main arched doorway. The inner hub of the temple was to be paved completely in marble, with an inner Holy of Holies paved on its floor in pure gold. The workmanship was to be exquisite, finer than mortals can build without divine assistance. The materials to adorn its interior were to be brought in from the four quarters of the earth. The building was, in fact, designed by Christ himself.

Not attached to the great Temple of the Living God were twelve buildings for preparation to enter the temple, schools to teach the people the ways of God, and vast "parking lots" that appeared more like parks. An obvious oddity was that none of the parking lots connected to any roads, and could only be accessed from the air. In all, it was a vision of grandeur never before attempted by mankind.

Stone began arriving from the quarry before the crews had dug the foundation to bedrock. A bulldozer rumbled onto the site and finished in but a few days what would have otherwise taken months. The cornerstone arrived, a massive block ten feet square and three feet thick. Upon all six sides were chiseled the words "Holiness to the Lord," in Gothic letters. The great cornerstone was laid a full two stories below the natural level of the ground. There would be a great underground system of rooms with twelve fonts dedicated to baptisms for the dead.

With much effort and manpower, it was lowered into place by a massive system of cables and cranes. Once set, it was at once discovered that it sat several inches out of place. The arduous task of resetting all the slings, cables and pulleys had just begun when four men in white stepped out from among the workmen. No one had noticed them previously. These four walked up to the stone. Each placed a hand upon the stone and slid it the necessary distance. While the stone rumbled its way to its permanent position, the workmen fell to their knees in humble gratitude. They would not build this mighty structure unaided.

The enormous stones began arriving with every hour, each cut to an exactness that defied mortal skill. Each stone was placed with deftness so that the building began taking shape even as they watched. It soon became obvious that every part of the construction process was accelerated. The workers sent three great stones from the quarry, and six would arrive. They would strike the stones with a crude chisel, and a polished surface would emerge. Miracles became so commonplace that a scribe was assigned to attend each phase of the work to document every such

occurrence of divine aid, so that every generation thereafter might give
glory to God.

Weeks, rather than years saw the outer wall rise to ground level. Workman completed the stone floors of native white granite in several weeks and the walls continued climbing toward heaven. Six days a week they labored from sun up to sun down, never pausing for more than a few minutes to eat or drink. Samuel found himself almost outworked by mortals who seemed to have the strength like himself. They sang, prayed, and shouted praises as they worked.

As the outer walls of the Temple grew in height so did the inner structure. After six months the intricate bridge stones were set arching from the inner walls to the outer, and the spires began to rise above them all. The first stone of the center spire was cut from a different vein in the quarry. Where the other stones were uniformly lustrous white in color, the spire stones were brilliant and sparkling, as if with white diamonds. The spire stones required longer to dress. Intricate in design, and delicate in shape, they required special care. A single mistake could cost a week's work by ruining a nearly completed stone.

Each night the workman laid down their tools, and returned the following morning to find some intricate part of their work completed. The precious stones were then carefully transported to the temple and lifted into place. The center spire rose to a certain height, and stopped. A different construction method completely unknown to them would be used to craft the upper spire. Undaunted, they turned their labors to other areas.

Once this sparkling white vein of stone was found they felt impressed to use it to frame every arch, window and doorway. The effect was stunning. The same brilliant stone was also used on all floors, columns and ceilings. The effect was so striking that there was no need to plaster the exterior of the building. The structure was magnificently beautiful.

The architecture was uncommon in that the inner walls, arches and ceiling were to span the full distance from wall to wall without benefit of trussing to hold the outer walls. Not being an architect, the engineering impossibility was lost on most. All arches push outward on the walls that support them; without some means of countering that incredible force, the walls would collapse of its own weight long before the structure was even finished. This miraculously did not occur.

The plans called for an intricate network of long, graceful walls that flowed outward from the main structure in a design so lace-like they appeared almost to be huge doilies cut from stone. The effect was gloriously beautiful, and impossibly complex. No single architect could completely understand how they transferred the incredible weight of the great stone ceiling of the temple through these walls and to the foundation. The construction was similar to the obscure renaissance design called a flying buttress, yet it was an adaptation of that concept never before contemplated, nor attempted by man.

His eyes opened to things of the Spirit that few mortals were able to see, Samuel watched in awe as a thousand angels labored on the Temple. He watched as a mortal would place his shoulder against some task too great for any man or woman, and several unseen angels would gather on each side of him. With a mighty shove and shout of praise, the object would move, apparently against the laws and logic of nature. This explained the phenomenal strength the women possessed. It also explained why once they left the temple site, their strength was once again only equal to their mortal stature.

One beautiful sunny afternoon, Samuel was helping set a long white stone in a broad stairway when he heard a sustained scream. Everyone looked up to see a worker falling head first from one of the highest walls of the Temple. She hit the ground with a low thud while everyone ran to her in great concern. Then she immediately stood up, dusted herself off, and climbed back upon the wall. She was uninjured, undaunted and back at work almost without comment, except for the thousand prayers of gratitude uttered.

Perhaps even more amazing than all this was the steady influx of people into Jackson County. Thousands from many tribes streamed in the course of the summer, and the number of workers swelled. Skilled artisans of every craft and trade arrived. There were carpenters, painters, plasterers, workers of gold, gems, and a hundred other trades.

The Temple was soon expertly wired for electricity. Provisions were made for elevators, escalators, and some designs and constructs within the Temple no one was sure what function they served. The Holy of Holies was built without a ceiling, directly below the center spire. The center spire itself contained a circular cavity exactly twelve feet in diameter which penetrated its exact center. No one was sure why it was there, or how the open ceiling would be sealed, as it was presently open to the sky.

But, by far the happiest moment for Samuel came when the School of the Prophets was once again convened, and he was asked to preside over it. He set down his tools, handed his thick gloves to another, and left the Temple never to return as a workman. His heart was full of gratitude as he walked slowly away, marveling at how much they had accomplished in a single summer.

The central structure was nearly complete on the outside. The system of spires was about half-erected. A thick vein of gold had been discovered at the quarry, and enough had already been mined to cast the Angel Moroni of solid gold. He had seen the plaster model from which the solid gold statue would be cast. It stood twice the height of a man and would eventually weigh more than the structure of the temple spire could normally support. This, however, did not concern them.

The School of the Prophets held its first class in the Visitors Center chapel. Those who initially attended were brothers and sisters in leadership positions, taught and assisted by immortal beings. The class lasted six weeks, during which time they ate and slept at the Visitors Center. The goal, almost universally accomplished, was that each student leave after that six weeks with their Calling and Election made sure. What a joy, a supernal privilege it was for Samuel to stand amidst righteous women and men, angels and resurrected beings, and call upon the powers of God to work the mighty changes within the souls of his students. He considered that no greater blessing could have come to him, or those over whom he presided.

His calling to preside over the school, and his standing before the Lord as a translated being himself, gave Samuel an unusual perspective on things. As the spiritual power of those attending the school grew he was able to gather speakers of great uniqueness. Though they spoke of these things not at all, toward the end of the first session of the school they were taught day after day by glorious visitors from the past. Imagine what one could learn about the law of Moses, when the class was taught by Moses himself! Or, what one could learn about faith from the Brother of Jared! It was a time of such rejoicing that Samuel felt as if his very soul was aflame night and day.

The leaves had turned to shades of yellow, red and orange, and the nip of fall was in the air when a new caravan arrived. Samuel was standing near the back of the chapel listening with great joy to a lecture on love being delivered by John, the disciple whom Jesus loved, when he felt compelled to leave the hall. He passed by the guards standing at the doors and hurried out onto the front steps of the Visitor's Center. The Temple, a dozen blocks away, dwarfed everything around it, its brilliant white spires reflecting the afternoon sun. As he approached, he saw a vast ragged group coming steadily toward the temple.

"Samuel!" a voice cried with such joy that he instantly knew who it was.

"Alexei!" Samuel cried in return and ran toward his old friend. They met halfway across the lawn and fell into one another's arms with great joy. Vladimir and a host of others joined in the embrace until they were laughing out loud in the overwhelming joy of reunion.

"You are finally here!" Samuel cried happily, clapping his back.

"Yes, we are here to build that portion of the great temple dedicated to Levi," Alexei explained. "It was never known to us until we had our experiences in the temple at Cardston, but each of the twelve outer buildings must be built by their respective tribes of Israel. There are twelve, one for each."

"I knew that must be the case," Samuel agreed. For this reason and others like it, the inhabitants of Zion joyfully welcomed each new arrival to Zion.

"We will help finish the center building, then we alone will build our temple," Alexei said humbly, tears of joy gathering in his eyes.

"How many tribes are represented by your people?" Samuel asked.

"We have people from three tribes," Vladimir explained excitedly. "We will build three of the great temples in the outer temple ring."

"How many tribes are we still missing, I wonder?" Alexei asked aloud.

"The Lord will provide," Samuel said with complete faith.

"Of course He will," Alexei agreed.

"We have brought something else of importance," Alexei said urgently, and motioned for something to be brought forward. It was the carved box containing the box of their scriptures. "When can we see the Prophet?" he asked excitedly. "We have something important to give him."

"President Andrews is in Utah, but I believe he will be here in a few days. In the meantime, do you want to give your scriptures to President Johnson?"

Alexei shook his head. "I think not. When President Andrews arrives, he is the Seer; we will give them to the Prophet," he said, then after a moment added, "A few more days out of several thousand years isn't so long." This brought a smile to all their faces.

The following day after Alexei's group was settled, ground work began on three of the outer buildings. Alexei and his people provided all the labor for these structures. Everyone else assisted with technical direction, or in getting them materials.

During this time, industry began to operate once again. Food became plentiful, though basic. Clothing was largely handmade, but cloth was loomed now and easier to obtain. Medicines were scarce, but were rarely sought after. The power of the priesthood was so prevalent that sickness was rarely treated with medicine. Doctors of medicine worked on the Temple and delivered babies, but not much else. Even after community water was restored, there was still no electricity, and no reason to believe it might begin any time soon; there were no working power generation plants anywhere nearby. But the power of the priesthood made up exponentially for any lack of electrical power.

From the day they arrived in the New Jerusalem, a system of consecration and community economy was established. There was no money in circulation. Whatever was needed by a family to live was freely available. There were two large stores in Zion, one which dispensed food, another handling clothing, furniture, and building supplies. It was extremely common to go to the store with one's arms laden with surplus items or items in excess of your own needs, and on the way out to pick up the several items needed.

Samuel's family occupied a house a few miles from the Temple site. It was an older home with four bedrooms. Since they had no gasoline, there was no need for the double car garage, so it was converted into an apartment for Lisa and her two children: Monica, now six, and Timmy, age four. Melody's sons and their wives each had their own homes. Bonnie and Steven temporarily occupied a bedroom in Samuel's home. Since they had no children, their need for a separate home was delayed and many larger families that arrived almost daily were given the much-needed housing first. But Bonnie and Steven loved living with their parents, so they were in no great hurry to have their own home.

Little Helaman turned two that spring. He was the delight of his Mommy and Daddy, who were both shamelessly infatuated with their little one.

Despite the turmoil of the world, for the Mahoys a new season of joy had begun.

BONNIE'S STORY

The one member of the Mahoy family who was yet a mystery was their twin daughter, Bonnie. She said very little about her experiences of the past six years. Steven, her husband, also chose not to say much about those years until his wife finally broke her self-imposed silence. Samuel often wished she would find her peace so they could know what had occurred that still caused her pain.

That day came unexpectedly one afternoon while everyone but Bonnie and her mother were away working at the Temple; the babies were asleep, and they were washing dishes side by side.

"Mama?" Bonnie began." It tickled Melody that her stepdaughters called her "Mama." It was the girls' way of constantly reaffirming their love and acceptance of the woman who had married their father.

"Yes, honey?"

"The reason I haven't said much about the years we were apart is because I'm so ashamed."

Melody didn't look up from her work. "Do you want to talk about it?" she asked as casually as she could.

"I do, desperately, but I'm just so ashamed that I can't." She shook her head. "I don't want to keep it a secret anymore, though! What should I do?" Bonnie asked, her voice soft and pleading.

"Do you need to talk with the bishop, honey? Is there something you still need to work through in that respect?"

"Oh, no. Mother, I've paid the price for my mistakes, and Heavenly Father has forgiven me. I just can't forgive myself."

"Bonnie, if you feel comfortable with telling me, maybe that will help you come to terms with it. I'm a good listener," Melody urged her gently.

Bonnie took a deep breath. "Okay Mama. I'll try and see how far I get." She handed a wet dish to her mother and began. "Well, as you know, I had left Lisa in Rexburg and was attending BYU in Provo when the Church was outlawed. When that happened, I refused to get the microchip implanted, since I was certain it was the mark of the beast. Without even being able to go home to say goodbye, I was then ordered to leave Utah Valley. They drove us about fifty miles north of Salt Lake and dumped us off in the desert. There were about a dozen of us college kids. We began walking along Interstate 80, living off of whatever we could beg from passing motorists. There was still a lot of traffic in those days."

"I feel so terrible, because we didn't know anything about this!" Melody told her sadly.

"Mama, there was no way for you to know; I couldn't get ahold of you! Anyway, we finally made it to Cheyenne without dying in the desert, only because we didn't admit to being Mormons. We had hitched a ride on a semi-truck and got a ride all the way to Cheyenne. The driver said we could probably find work there, so we went that far with him."

Bonnie was washing one plate over and over, her mind riveted on the story. "To avoid suspicion my friends and I parted company in Cheyenne to find work and a place to live. We were afraid that a group of us without the chip implanted would be labeled as bad Mormons and exiled again. It was the most terrifying experience I have ever had. I remember walking down the back streets of town wondering where I would ever find help. I was terrified someone would rob or rape me, or something worse, and was afraid to go near groups of people. I tried begging from house to house, but everyone I begged from asked me why I didn't just go to the food centers? I didn't have a good answer, and they suspected I was an illegal. And it was illegal to give food to someone who didn't have the microchip."

Melody nodded with deep understanding. "It sounds completely awful, Bonnie!"

Bonnie's shaking hand handed the plate to her mother to dry. "It was, Mama, it was. I had gone without food for most of a week, and was too weak to hardly even walk. My clothing was dirty and torn. I was sick. I had lost so much weight I was practically skin and bones. I was certain I would die. Finally, I could stand it no longer and stumbled into a food center and asked them to give me a microchip. They asked me why I hadn't gotten one earlier. I told them my family lived in the country. I told them I had walked into town to get a chip because my family was starving."

Bonnie started to cry in shame. Melody waited. "They happily implanted the chip in my right hand and gave me food and a job. It was so easy and so painless that it didn't take me very long to get over my guilty feelings for having done it. Whenever I was hungry, all I had to do was to wave my hand under the scanner and I could take anything I needed from the store. In a short time I began berating myself for having thought it a bad thing. I actually started to think that those who still refused to get the chip were stupid beyond belief!" Bonnie said.

"I can understand why you would think that," Melody soothed her. Bonnie just shook her head.

"I was pathetic, Mama. Anyway, during this time I met Steven, and fell in love with him. He was my age, handsome and super sweet. He worked at the Food Center and helped me get a job. He had been there longer than me, and worked in management. I was flattered when he showed an interest in me because I was still very skinny and had not yet regained my strength. Nevertheless, he was kind and complimented me, so it was easy to love him. I was terribly lonely, and he was the first guy who saw beyond my awful appearance."

Melody stopped her. "Bonnie, you could never look awful!"

"Oh Mama, if you had seen me, you'd never say that!" Bonnie laughed ruefully, and continued. "So we dated for almost a year, during which time I said nothing about the Church to anyone. I actually began to almost forget it even existed. That's why I was so startled when Steven asked me if I would like to go to church with him. I naturally assumed it was an approved church, and after thinking about it for a day or two, I told him I'd go with him.

Bonnie dried her hands on the dish towel and took a seat at the countertop facing her mother. "Steven took me to a house not far from our work. The meeting was held in the basement, which I thought was odd. But, these were odd times. Imagine my total surprise when we sang an LDS hymn for the opening song! I was both overjoyed, and terrified as it became obvious to me that these were Mormons, and I was stupidly sitting there with them! I sat in stunned silence as the meeting progressed. All this time Steven was watching me with anxiety—I could just tell. The words "Mormon" or "LDS" were never used until the Branch President spoke. Steven told me later that if I would have objected or acted offended in any way, they would have immediately shut down the meeting. They would have moved their meeting place, and Steven would have found other work where I would never see him again. It was super risky for him to take me there."

Bonnie looked down at her hands and frowned. "I am ashamed to say that I seriously considered turning them in, and I actually may have."

"What changed your mind?" Melody asked, her voice subdued.

"The branch president. I don't suppose you knew this, but everyone in the underground Church always used a false name. The branch president went by the name of Helaman."

Melody looked up sharply, her eyes narrowing. "Helaman, huh? Describe him, would you dear?"

"He was perhaps in his fifties, though still very energetic. He had quite dark brown hair and dark brown eyes. He almost looked as if he might have a little Indian, or Hispanic blood in him."

"Did he use a cane?" Melody asked.

"Yes, he walked with a slight limp. Why do you ask?"

"You just finish your story. I'll tell you later."

"Sure. So Helaman was the only speaker at church that night. I have to tell you that I have never felt the Spirit of the Lord more powerfully than I did then. He spoke with such conviction and powerful testimony that I found myself hanging on his every word. He was truly not ashamed of the Gospel of Jesus Christ! He openly and proudly spoke of his love for the prophet Joseph Smith, and bore powerful testimony about Jesus Christ."

Melody took a seat at the counter with Bonnie, listening intently. "Do you know what, Mama?" Bonnie said excitedly. "He said that all those proofs from the Vatican documents disclaiming Jesus Christ were just a clever fabrication by the U.N.—a scheme of Commander Sarkus, and a deception of the adversary! And Helaman said he knew with *firsthand* knowledge that Jesus is the Christ!"

Melody nodded knowingly. "I always believed that someday the real explanation of those documents would come out," she said. "Their deception was the perfect storm, wasn't it? And yet, your Helaman saw through it!"

"Oh yes, Mama, he did. I had the distinct feeling as he bore testimony that he couldn't have loved the Lord Jesus Christ, nor the Prophet Joseph more if he had known them personally." Bonnie paused her as if reliving that sacred evening again in her heart.

"What happened next?" Melody asked after a brief silence.

Bonnie shook her head. "Nothing, really. I started attending church every week after that. It was held on a different night of the week and at a different place every time. Steven and I found great joy in it. My testimony returned and I was so grateful to Steven for having the courage to invite me there. He saved my life that day."

Melody smiled. "He is a wonderful man, that husband of yours! So, you were happy then?"

Bonnie took a deep breath and looked away from her mother. "Well, everything went along just fine until I started noticing that Steven and I were the only two at church who were not thin from hunger. I began seeing the thin, ragged appearance of the children, and the tired look in the faces of their skinny mothers. After that, every time I looked in the mirror and saw my plump, healthy cheeks, I hated myself. Steven and I talked about this for hours, and decided that we had sinned by getting the implants so that we could eat. We concluded that we would remove the implants, but that before we did, we would smuggle food to our brothers and sisters."

Melody's eyes widened. "That sounds pretty brave—and risky!" she noted.

"Well, it actually worked! That very next meeting we showed up with extra food for them. They were very happy, and extremely grateful. However, they begged us not to do it ever again. But you know, Mama, bringing them food seemed to atone for my sin of being full while they were starving. It somehow made my feelings of guilt less powerful, I guess. I talked Steve into taking food each time we met.

"This went on for nearly a month before Steve's supervisor asked him why he had started taking home more food than he could eat. Steve acted surprised, but his boss showed him a computer printout that indicated the number of calories he had been taking home. We had no idea the computer calculated how much each person ate. About a month ago the number had nearly tripled for Steve. The computer had triggered an investigation. They also told him that I was going to be investigated because I was also taking home more than four times the food I needed. Steve told them that we were in love, and that I was pregnant, and eating like a horse."

Melody laughed in spite of herself, but Bonnie did not reciprocate.

"His supervisor said that made perfect sense. He told Steve not to worry about the extra food, but to keep it down to what was absolutely necessary. Steve agreed that he would." Bonnie rolled her eyes.

"Well, now we had two problems. First of all, I was not pregnant, and in a few months it would be obvious that Steve had lied. The other problem was that we could no longer take home enough food for the children. The only solution I could think of was for Steve and I to stop eating so much, and to take the surplus food to our friends. We immediately began to do that. When our supervisor saw that I was losing weight, and pregnant as he thought, he insisted I go see a doctor. I refused, which caused him to really become suspicious."

Melody nodded. "I can see that."

"We were in such a tight spot that we didn't know what to do. Finally we decided that our only course was for me to actually become pregnant. If I did, the people at work would quit being suspicious. If I did not, they would assume we had been hoarding food and come search our apartments. When they found that we were not living together, they would force me to have a pregnancy test, and one thing would lead to another until they found out we had been giving food to Mormons. It was all so ugly…" she said with a shake of her head.

"So, what did you decide to do?" Melody asked with great curiosity.

"We asked Helaman to marry us so that I could become pregnant."

Her mother's eyes widened. "That seems like a drastic solution," she observed dryly.

"It was, but I really did love Steven, and he loved me. We actually wanted to be married, and would have eventually chosen this course. We just felt trapped at the time."

"Well, I'm glad to hear you loved each other, at least," Melody said with relief.

"Yeah, I guess that's true," Bonnie admitted with a small smile, and continued. "So we made arrangements to be married that next Friday right after Sacrament meeting. We were so excited, it must have showed in our faces. Several people asked us what we were up to, and we denied that anything was going on.

"Friday came and we hurried away after work to be married. We told Helaman our plans just before Sacrament meeting, and he became very concerned. He asked us to wait until we could think this over some more, but we were determined. He said he didn't feel good about it for some reason, and again asked us to wait. We pressed him to marry us, and he consented, but said he wanted to do it immediately, rather than after church. We agreed to that."

Melody looked worried. "I wonder why he didn't want you to marry?" she mused.

"You'll see why, Mama. So we met early before church and had a quick ceremony in one of the back rooms of the member's home. We had already begun as people were arriving for church. Brother Helaman gave a beautiful talk on marriage, and pronounced us man and wife. We were just kissing for the first time as a married couple, when we heard the commotion outdoors. The door banged open and the police stormed into the room."

"Oh no!" Melody cried.

"It was just awful, Mama. The officer went directly to Brother Helaman and arrested him. They clubbed him unconscious and dragged him out of the room. Then this guy ordered me to hold out my right hand. I did so and he held a small electronic device over the microchip in my hand. No sooner had he done this than the chip began to heat up. I had heard stories about them doing this, and knew that I had only a few seconds to save myself. I tore away from them and ran. The only thing I could find in the old house was a bent fork in the kitchen. I used one of the tines from the fork and dug the chip from my skin…"

Bonnie sat there for a moment in silence, her face pale. When she began again her voice was bitter. "I dug that thing out of my skin and dropped it on the floor. As soon as it hit the floor it exploded with a tiny blue flame and a liquid oozing out."

"I've never heard anything like that," Melody exclaimed in horror. "What would have happened if you hadn't gotten it out?"

"I would have died! The little battery is made of some material that is really poisonous. It causes the person to die within just a few hours. They actually pronounced a death sentence on me because I was a Mormon!" Bonnie slowly held out her right arm and showed her mother a ragged scar on the back side of her hand.

Melody was repulsed by the size of the scar and the obvious pain it would have caused to create it. "I'm so very sorry, honey," she said softly. "You know, I'm surprised they didn't try to stop you from digging it out."

"Oh, no! They did at first but then stood there and laughed at me thinking I would fail."

"That's so cruel. What about Steve?"

"They did the same thing to him. He had a pocket knife, and insisted that I use the knife and give him the fork. To be honest with you, I don't even remember him saying a thing to me, I was so focused on saving my life. He finally took care of himself and got his out just in time too."

"What happened next? What happened to Helaman?" Melody asked with some urgency.

Bonnie sat quietly for a few long moments, rubbing the scar on the back of her hand absent-mindedly as she relived the horror of those days. When she did speak again, her voice was hollow, as if a part of her mind was not there.

"I don't remember what happened next. I think I was in shock. I know I had lost a lot of blood. I remember standing in the snow and being shoved around and accused. I think I denied something, I'm not even sure what. Someone kept shouting at me. I was cold, and sick to my stomach, terrified, and bleeding, and I just wanted the screaming and terror to go away. I finally just told them whatever they wanted to know. I remember looking at Steve and realizing he was shouting at me to not say what I had just said. It was all like a dream, a very bad dream."

She paused for another long minute without speaking, her voice ragged. "The next thing I remember is a gun going off. I looked up and

Helaman was lying on the ground. This guard was saying, 'You are free to
go, and take your garbage with you so I don't have to arrest you for litter-
ing.' Mama, he had killed Helaman because of something I had said, but
I don't remember what it was!" she cried, burying her face in her hands,
her body shaking with sobs. It took her many minutes to compose herself.

"With that he and his troops drove away, and left us standing in the
darkness of the darkest night I have ever seen. I was grateful for the darkness because I couldn't see the faces of my friends. All I could hear was
their weeping and mourning as they picked up Helaman's body."

Her shoulders shook with weeping as she continued. "Mama, Steve
and I tried to help, but our Mormon friends, or who used to be our
friends, refused to even let us touch his body. They asked us to leave them.
Steve tried to tell them it was not my fault; he begged them to listen. But,
they just ignored him, and walked into the darkness until all I could hear
was their voices mourning their dead friend."

Bonnie was completely undone; her heart had broken and would not
be healed. Melody consoled her and waited for her to speak again. Finally
Bonnie continued. "I just stood there for a long time, sick to my stomach
and hating everybody. But mostly hating myself. In my mind and in my
heart, I knew I was responsible for Helaman's death. Steve tried to convince me otherwise, but I wouldn't listen. As far as I'm concerned, I am
totally responsible! I'm guilty of murder, and even worse—the shedding
of innocent blood!" she cried piteously, her voice filled with self-loathing.

"Oh, no, Bonnie. That's not true. You can't think like that. I'm sure
…"

Bonnie appeared to have heard nothing Melody was saying, but cut
her off to continue her narrative. "Later that evening we went to both our
apartments and found them locked and guarded. They wouldn't even give
us our own clothing. Even members we knew wouldn't let us in. We slept
that night in the alley behind Steve's apartment."

Melody decided to remain quiet, though her heart was crying out to
comfort her sweet and sensitive daughter.

"It was kind of ironic, actually. After that, everywhere we went we
were rejected and threatened. After four days surviving on rotting food
from garbage cans, we decided we could not survive much longer, and
held a fast."

"But, you were already starving," Melody protested.

"Yes we were, but we desperately needed Heavenly Father's help, and
Steve and I both felt we needed to fast. I was just numb, and felt like I
wanted to die; fasting seemed a type of poetic justice to me at the time."

She laughed ironically. "It was very difficult, because we were already hungry, but we fasted that whole next day. By the end of the day we were too weak to go find food, so we just knelt together in an alley and prayed for help. Our prayers were answered when we heard someone behind us."

"Who was it?" Melody asked breathlessly.

"It was Tarah, one of the members of the Church. We told her who we were, and told her to leave us alone."

"'I know who you are,' she said. 'We've been looking for you.'"

"Really?" Melody said, and slipped around the counter to put an arm around her daughter.

"Mama, we were so amazed, we asked her why they would try to help us.

'Because we love you,' she said simply."

"What a saint!" her mother marveled.

"I tried to protest, to remind her that I was responsible for Helaman's death. She just shushed me, and handed me a piece of bread from her pocket. I couldn't eat it. I wanted to die, and I just couldn't eat it. The fact that it came from someone who had also loved Helaman made it impossible for me to swallow the bread. I told her I couldn't eat her food."

Melody was crying. Bonnie patted her arm, grateful to not be judged, but merely listened to. She looked lovingly at her mother, and continued.

"'My dear sister,'" the lady told me quietly, 'it was wrong that you were treated unkindly. Two days ago, I held a special fast in the Church to help us find you and Steven. I personally decided that I would not break my fast until I had found you. So, you see, if you die from your fasting, then I will too.'"

"I cried out, 'But, I killed Helaman!' She just smiled at me, and said, 'Helaman knew his days were numbered, and spoke often of how few days he had left. We were not prepared for his death, but we were expecting it.'

"I told her that didn't alter the fact that my words caused his death! Then she asked me if I remembered what I said. I told her that I did not. Then she said, 'Neither do we,' and then she held out the bread to me again."

Melody put her arms around Bonnie while they wept together. "I opened my mouth like a little baby and let her feed me, Mama. There was such love and compassion, and genuine forgiveness in her face, that I let her actually feed me," Bonnie sobbed. "I have never felt such pure love from anyone in my life!"

"She must have been a wonderful woman, and filled with the pure love of Christ," Melody nodded at her with joy.

"Mama, do you know what? She was Helaman's *wife!*" Bonnie cried, as if the whole burden of her guilt was embodied by that single sentence.

Melody sat stunned, rigid with deep irony until fresh tears sprang to her eyes. They held each other for a long embrace.

"Mama," Bonnie said after she regained some control over her emotions. "Tarah and the other Saints took care of Steve and me for nearly a year. They fed us, and loved us, and taught us what it means to be a true disciple of Christ. If ever a group of people deserved to go to the Celestial Kingdom, they do."

Melody nodded through tears, and silently expressed her gratitude to God.

"A short time after that we were all captured and thrown into the prison where Daddy found us," Bonnie continued. "By the time he got there, we were all nearly dead from the beatings, from sickness, starvation, and exhaustion. We all longed for the peace and rest of being in Paradise with Christ whom we all loved."

Then Bonnie's face brightened. "But there was something incredible about that prison. Even though we were absolutely destitute, the one thing which we had in abundance was faith. I know you've heard how Daddy, Sammy and Steven used their priesthood to heal so many, and to even raise some of us from death. What you don't know is that the whole reason those miracles took place was because of their perfect faith in Christ. Those miracles were blessings long overdue those wonderful Saints of such purity. I just wish I could claim to be like them," she said sadly.

Melody straightened up, and took her daughter's hands. "My dear child," she said softly, her face a perfect image of gentleness and love. "I have several observations to make about your story."

"What?" Bonnie asked quietly.

"Do you have a testimony of Christ?"

"Oh, yes!" she cried passionately.

"Were you among those who were healed that night by Samuel and Sammy?"

"I was," she said softly.

"As I recall, you were suffering from a bleeding ulcer, which was in fact, life threatening."

"Something like that," Bonnie admitted.

"Is it possible that such a miracle could have happened if you were, in fact, such an awful person?"

"Oh but I am," she insisted.

"Just answer my question."

"I don't know," Bonnie said weakly.

"Yes you do. It *isn't* possible! In order to receive such a glorious blessing one must be worthy, through their faith in Jesus Christ. Oh Bonnie, none of us is worthy on our own; we all are sinners and fall short of the glory of God! But through Christ, you are worthy, I am worthy, and no one is worthy in any other way! I can feel the power of your convictions, Bonnie, and I can see the light of Christ in your face. Is it possible that light could be present in a person so unredeemable as you proclaim yourself to be?"

"I…"

"If you had it to do over again, would you do anything to contribute to another person's death?"

"No, never!" Bonnie cried.

"That's right. I know you wouldn't, because you would rather die that let anyone die in your place, or because of your words. Don't answer, because you know it's true. My dear Bonnie, I proclaim before you and all the world, and every angel who is listening, that you are free from the crimes that are burdening your soul!"

Bonnie blinked her eyes, a glimmer of hope emerging. "I wish I could believe…"

"Sweet Bonnie, you do believe! That's the point! You believe as firmly as any prophet of any age. Such belief comes from God, wrought by the atonement, through your faith in Christ. This makes you worthy, Bonnie! Let your heart rejoice, let it be lifted and soar unto the heavens. God holds no guilt against you, why should you?"

"Oh, Mama!" Bonnie cried, and threw herself again into Melody's arms. "I'm so sorry! I want to believe you, but even if it's true, Helaman is dead. Even if I didn't do it with malice, even if I am forgiven, I still spoke the words that resulted in his death!" she cried.

"Not everything is as it appears," a low voice said from near the door. They both started and turned toward the unexpected voice.

"Helaman!" Bonnie screamed for joy, and rushed toward him. Helaman caught her in his arms and held her as she sobbed. His eyes were filled with love and gentleness as he stroked her hair. Helaman appeared thirty years younger than when Melody had seen him the first time in England. But, there was no mistaking who it was.

When Bonnie finally got to the point where curiosity overcame her tidal wave of emotions, she pushed back from his embrace. Before she could voice a single question, Helaman turned to Melody.

"Helaman, how wonderful to see you again," Melody said happily, and accepted a warm embrace. "We were just talking of your tremendous help to Bonnie and Steven. Once again our family owes you a deep debt of gratitude, my friend."

"It was my great joy to be involved with Bonnie and Steven, and the other Saints of Cheyenne," he said with quiet enthusiasm.

"I thought they killed you!" Bonnie exclaimed, still in shock.

"Many people have tried to kill me," he said with a chuckle. "It's actually not that easy to do."

Bonnie took his hands into hers. "Oh Helaman, I have felt so awful all these years because I thought I got you killed! I thought . . ."

Helaman stopped her with a smile. "Oh, they did shoot me, my dear, and under normal circumstances, I would have been very much dead."

"So, what I said *did* get you killed—or at least, it should have?"

"That is correct," Helaman said soberly.

"So I am guilty," Bonnie said with lowered head.

"That is not correct," Helaman said again with equal force.

"But…"

Helaman patted her arm. "Let me explain, if I may. I only have a few minutes before I have to go. I was there in Cheyenne to accomplish several things. Only one of them was to help you and your wonderful husband. I promised your father Samuel that I would watch out for his family while he was on his mission. There were many other reasons I was there, too—not the least of which was to build up the struggling Saints in that city and to help them find the faith sufficient to be worthy to come to Zion. The only way I could accomplish that was through giving them a greater cause than their own hunger."

"Steve and I were that greater cause?" Bonnie asked, perplexed.

"You were a part of it. The larger task was teaching them Christlike forgiveness. For you and Steve, it was the process of abject humility, and powerful faith."

"Those were difficult and painful lessons," Bonnie said thoughtfully, her head lowered.

"Yes they were, and yet you learned them, and here you are, talking to an angel. So you must have learned them very well."

"An *angel?*" Bonnie gasped.

"Bonnie, honey," Melody interrupted. "I knew Helaman over thirty years ago."

"But, he's hardly thirty now!" Bonnie marveled, her understanding beginning to dawn.

Helaman turned to leave. "Your mother can explain it. I only came to complete my promise to your father, according to his faith," he said, and took a step back. As he did so, he seemed to become brighter, as if a light had come on within him that shone through his skin.

"Why did you come back, Helaman?" Melody asked. "You already got Bonnie safely to Zion."

"That is true," Helaman said. "But my job was not done until the scars in her heart were also healed. Now, Bonnie is whole in body and in spirit. My work with her is done," he said, and grew brighter still, until he vanished in a silent burst of light. Melody and Bonnie stood for a long time looking at the spot where he had just been.

Finally, Bonnie sank down on the couch. "I can't believe I've just seen an angel," she marveled, mostly to herself. Then she thought for a moment and asked, "How could he have been married to Tarah if he were an angel?"

Melody prayed silently for the right answer before she spoke. "Tarah was Helaman's wife when he was alive on the earth," she said, as the thought entered her heart with great force.

"You mean Tarah was an angel too? She really was his wife?" Bonnie asked in total wonder?

"*Is* his wife," Melody corrected quietly.

Both women sat silently contemplating these startling truths, which the Spirit was now confirming. It was Melody who broke the solemn silence. "Look out the window and tell me what you see," she said earnestly to her daughter.

Bonnie complied and knelt on the couch before the front window. It was late in the night, and Bonnie expected to see nothing but blackness. Melody drew open the blinds.

"It's still light outside!" Bonnie exclaimed in surprise.

"Oh, good," Melody said happily. "Your eyes are still open from seeing Helaman. Come quickly. I want you to see something before it passes."

"What?"

"Just come. It's wonderful!" Melody quickly led Bonnie out onto the street before the house. From where they stood they could see the partially-completed temple, even though it was over four miles away.

"It's lit up!" Bonnie exclaimed. "Is the electricity back on?"

"No, it's not electricity. Look closer. Can you see them?"

"You mean the people working on the temple? That's incredible! Mama, I didn't know there was a night shift. Where did all that light come from? That's amazing!"

"Bonnie, it is the glory of God, and those people working on the temple are not mortals. You're seeing a host of angels at work! The mortals are working inside, while the brilliantly-lit angels are working outside."

"Oh Mama, I can see them! There are so many! It's no wonder the work on the temple is going so quickly. I never knew. This really is the New Jerusalem, isn't it," she said with awe.

"You know it is," Melody confirmed.

"Yes, I do, I really do!"

Melody pointed to the street. "Now, look away from the temple. Look anywhere. Look at the end of the street by Elder Parker's home. What do you see?"

"Nothing," Bonnie said with disappointment.

"Keep looking, look with your heart, and with your faith. Tell me what you see," Melody urged.

Bonnie stared into the darkness, and then brightened. "People! I see people walking up and down the street. There are lots of them. Some of them are carrying books. Others seem to be searching from house to house." She turned to her mother. "Who are they, and what are they doing?"

"They are the righteous who are awaiting the resurrection. They are here to prepare for the coming of Christ to His temple. The books they are carrying are the genealogy of their families. They are preparing to have their temple work done," her mother said with a smile.

Bonnie was beginning to understand. "How wonderful! But why are they walking up and down the streets?"

"They are searching for their living relatives. When they find them they wait near them for the time when their relative's eyes and ears will be opened, and they can begin their long-awaited work in the Temple. This is a glorious time for them. See how they are all smiling. Listen, and you will hear their voices. Listen..."

Bonnie listened carefully and could hear a distant melody. It sounded as if the workers on the temple were singing. As she listened it became more distinct until she was surrounded by the most beautiful music. It was as if all of creation, the trees, the houses, the angels of heaven were singing with one accord.

"I hear them! It's all beautiful beyond description," Bonnie said as she listened, her hands pressed to her chest. "Why am I hearing and seeing all this? What does it all mean?"

Melody clasped her daughter's hand. "It means your eyes are opened, that you have become a part of Zion. It means that you are the pure in heart, because only the pure in heart can see the things of God. It means that you have a tremendous responsibility ahead of you. And, it means that the days of sorrowing are over. My dear, you just joined the innumerable company laboring day and night in preparation for the Lord's return!"

Bonnie let out a cry of joy. "It feels so—alive! I feel as if my very soul is on fire! I feel like if I don't start singing too, I'm going to explode with joy!"

"It is a marvelous feeling, is it not?" Melody whispered.

"Can everyone in Zion see and hear this?" Bonnie asked suddenly.

Melody nodded. "Some. Every day a few more. In time, everyone will, I believe."

Bonnie was so excited that she got up and started pacing. Then she turned back to her mother. "How did you come to see it, Mama? Who showed it to you?"

"Your father did, honey. It took quite a while for me to see. Of course, it was while we were still in Utah, and the heavens were not yet opened like they are today. But, it took me a long time, and much prayer and fasting to see with new eyes."

"What is the difference between here and Utah? Why are these marvelous things happening here and now? Why hasn't it always been this way?"

Melody thought for a minute. "I'm not entirely sure, Bonnie, but it has to do with the purity of the people. Even one telestial-minded person in a city can limit these types of spiritual manifestations. As the people collectively grow more righteous, the heavens open in response. In time, we will be ready to walk in the presence of Jesus Christ Himself. In time, there will be a wall around this city so that no unclean thing can enter in. Even one evil or worldly person in such a city would either be burned up by the glory of the Lord, or the Lord would have to depart. That's why the scriptures say that after the New Jerusalem is built, no unclean thing can enter in. Zion will be pure as much by the repentance and obedience of its citizens, as by the fact that those who will not repent will be required to leave."

Bonnie stopped her pacing and turned to her mother. "Oh, Mama, we have to tell everyone! I don't think people realize how wonderful the message of Zion is! We have to warn them. Is it too late to begin now?" she asked in a rush.

"Dear, it's early in the morning. Everyone is asleep."

"*They* aren't!" Bonnie said, pointing to those working on the Temple.

"Oh, they don't need sleep—but I do!" Melody laughed. "Come dear, let's get our rest so we can begin fresh tomorrow."

"I don't think I *can* sleep," Bonnie cried, but unwillingly let herself be led back toward their house, her eyes still upon the heavenly beings.

Melody laughed and gave her a good-night hug. "Everything in its proper order, Bonnie. Sleep now; warn later. Let me give you a warning, though, my darling daughter. You must say nothing of this until you are moved upon by the Holy Spirit to do so. Do you understand why?"

Bonnie stopped, suddenly sober. "Actually, I do. I had that exact thought just come into my heart. The teaching and warning must be done in its proper time, according to the timetable of God. I must wait for the proper moment, which may not come as quickly as I might want."

"That's right," her mother said soberly.

"Have you seen these things for a long time?" Bonnie asked.

"Several years now."

"It must have been very hard to not shout it from the rooftops!"

"It was at first. Now, I know there is a greater joy than shouting it from the rooftops."

"I can't imagine what *that* could be!" Bonnie said in astonishment.

Her mother gave her a kiss on the cheek. "As the Spirit accords, whispering it to someone you love, and watching her heart change as the truth of your words echoes in her soul. That is the greater joy."

Bonnie slid her arm through Melody's and walked with her back into the house, her heart full of joy. "I can see," she said, her eyes sparkling with joy, "that this truly would be the greater joy. Thank you, Mama. Thank you, and thanks be to God!"

"Hurrah for Israel!" Melody said with quiet fervor.

"I still don't think I can sleep," Bonnie giggled as they quietly closed the door behind them.

"Sounds like a good night to spend in prayer," Melody winked at her.

"It does indeed," Bonnie grinned.

Then they climbed up the stairs together, arm in arm.

THE STARS SHALL FALL FROM HEAVEN

Work was well underway on the interior of the temple. The entire interior floor was polished, white marble. Because gold was now plentiful, a six-inch strip of solid gold was laid around the perimeter of every room to set off the white floor. The walls held beautiful scenes carved in relief on the marble. Since there was no electricity, and at the direction of the Prophet, there were no light fixtures. The interior rooms were dark unless lit by lanterns or candles. Without understanding why, each exterior room had a perfectly round stone conduit a foot in diameter leading from the center of each room to the Holy of Holies. Below the large opening in the ceiling of the Holy of Holies would one day hang a large crystal chandelier. For now, work on the innermost rooms proceeded slowly due to the difficulty of working by lamp light.

Through the winter, a project was underway of which few of the Temple workers were aware. A huge kiln had been crafted outside the stone quarry. Its construction was entirely unique in that it was able to fire an object over fifty feet in height and the same in diameter. It had twelve forced-air furnaces around its base, and a circulation system inside to disperse the heat in a uniform fashion.

Just a dozen feet from the kiln a large temporary building was constructed. Inside, a mold of the spire was filled with an unusual mixture of sand, lime, crushed stone, flux and diamond and gold powder. The design was kept secret by guards day and night. Once the mold and mixture was dry, it was covered in an outer plaster several feet thick. The whole object was dried for weeks and moved on rollers into the kiln. It barely fit inside. It took one week to bring the kiln up to temperature. The services of two-hundred men and women were needed around the clock to stoke the mighty furnaces and run the blowers. Once up to temperature it was held at a steady 2500 degrees for eight hours. Thereafter, it took an additional week to slowly lower the temperature until it returned to normal.

Samuel was present when the doors of the kiln were opened to reveal a shapeless mass fifty feet in height and nearly that wide across the base. It was slowly, laboriously rolled out into the daylight. Its weight was massive, and caused the heavy planks laid for the rollers to groan and sink into the soil. Its surface was covered with gray ash.

Workmen began chipping away the exterior shell. When they first caught a glimpse of what was inside the shell, a cry of wonder arose from all present. Work proceeded quickly to reveal a crystalline structure of such surpassing beauty as to boggle the mind. Its appearance was glass-like, though not transparent. If one had to ascribe some color to it, one would be forced to pick opalescent white with a shimmer of gold. Anywhere light hit the structure it caused a shimmering rainbow of colors which appeared alive within it.

What was even more astonishing was the impossible delicacy of the structure. It was artwork of divine origin, more beautiful and astonishing than any masterpiece before produced on earth. Thousands of intricate curves, fluted columns, spirals and shapes too numerous to catalogue formed a colossal monument to the glory of God. And, this was only the base of the great spire. Even those who had shaped the model according to the plans were astounded at what had been created.

A month later, the upper section rolled slowly from the kiln. Formed in the exact design of the base, it was just as stunning, delicate and fragile in appearance. The final spire was a mere twelve inches in diameter and gracefully ended in a small platform upon which the twenty-ton Angel Moroni was to stand for all time. It was unthinkable, impossible and bizarre to even attempt to put the massive statue atop such a slender and delicate pedestal. Yet, it was the way the very creator of the earth designed it, and His children labored with absolute faith.

All the pieces of the spire were moved to the Temple site on huge wagons drawn by horses. Even if the modern world had used all its machinery and cranes, it would have been a daunting task to move these monolithic monuments to the top of the structure. Today, with little more than muscle power and faith, it should have been impossible. Yet, a stair-stepped ramp was built of scrap lumber that rose steeply from the ground to the roof. Another rose from the roof to the base of the spire. One hundred forty-four men and women, twelve from each of the tribes of Israel, stood around the glittering spire base.

On a signal, and with a shout of praise, they hoisted the spire to their shoulders. To Samuel's eyes, and in fact to many present, they also saw a legion of angels lift at every point and protrusion of the great spire. Less than an hour later it was situated atop the temple, spanning the opening above the Holy of Holies. Before lunch the ramp was expanded, and shortly thereafter, the upper spire was in place. A set of ladders was leaned against the spire and a dozen workers, and a thousand angels, carried the

Angel Moroni to its resting place atop the spire. They set it in place to a shout of "Hosanna!" that echoed across the valley for miles.

"Sisters, brothers—look at the windows!" a cry arose. Samuel turned his eyes toward the windows of the temple and gasped at a bright glow coming from every opening. A concourse of people filed slowly up the steps and into the partially-completed inner rooms. Each was lit by a column of light that seemed to pierce the darkness like a laser beam from the hole in each ceiling.

When Samuel arrived at the door of the Holy of Holies, he had to raise his arm to shield his eyes from the bright light. The room was ablaze with light so intense that the doors had to be closed to shield the mortal eyes among them from destruction. The great glass spire seemed to collect the power of the sun, rather the very power of the Son, and bring it undiminished into that holy room. From there, the light passed through the system of conduits to each room. In time, when the crystal chandeliers hung in each room, they would catch and disperse the celestial light into the rooms. The temple was, in fact, to be lit by the power of God.

From that day on the interior rooms were lit, and work within the temple progressed with accelerated speed. Gold was brought in abundance and lovingly laid according to the plans. Wearing protective clothing and goggles to shield their eyes from the brightness, workers covered the divinely designed floors and walls of the Holy of Holies with gold an inch thick. The circular column in the ceiling was overlaid with silver, inlaid with gold.

Even though the temple was not yet dedicated, and in reality mortals could enter the room that would one day be the holiest place on earth, it was nevertheless blocked off and guarded. This was done as much to protect some innocent from being blinded by the sheer brightness inside, as to begin its transition to the purity that must exist in order for the very God of heaven to dwell there.

The Holy of Holies itself was circular with seven broad steps leading to a raised platform exactly twelve feet in diameter. A throne of pure gold with white luminous cushions was constructed in the exact center of the platform, directly below the spire. Below this, on the next lower level, were twelve smaller thrones facing outward. Six positioned on the left side of the room, and six on the right. The next three levels were unoccupied. The sixth step held twelve altars facing the center of the room, again with six on each side. Each had dazzling white cushions upon which to kneel. In golden letters the names of each of the tribes were inscribed upon the altars. On the lowest level stood a large altar also with padded top. It had a padded ledge upon one side, sufficiently large for three people to kneel.

A veil of very thin material hung between this altar and the only door leading into the room. The veil had no openings in its fabric, and could only be passed by walking to the right or left around its ends. The veil would never be parted accidentally, so that some unprepared individual might inadvertently glimpse its inhabitants, and thereby be destroyed in the flesh. Though the veil was almost as translucent, once the glorious light was upon it, it was as impossible to see through as stone.

Every element of the temple had deep significance. The plans specified every design, every minute detail, every element of every part of the temple. The entire structure was a profound testament to the glory of God.

Scriptures were rendered in gold-overlaid stone. The murals on the ceiling of the Celestial Room contained prophecies of the entire future of the world. The trim around the doors leading into the Celestial Room contained the keys to entering the presence of God while in mortality. The patterns in the carpets taught concerning the earth and the eventual purification it would receive to become a great Urim and Thummim. The symbolic patterns woven into the veil of the temple spoke eloquently of the laws governing the veil separating men from God.

The chandeliers in each room were layered testimonies concerning the order of heaven, the government of God as it exists in heaven, and the place of mortal man within it. To understand the total significance of a single chandelier in that building would be to understand more than God had ever before revealed concerning the order of His eternal dominion. It was the first time that a glimpse of the beauty of that kingdom, which would later be called Celestial, had been displayed within the view of mortal man.

There was no detail in the temple that was random or without meaning. For hundreds of generations to come, the children of God would study the truths constructed into its very stone, layered with deeper and deeper meaning, and marvel at the workmanship of God in every age of man. Forevermore, angels would wander its halls, and gods in embryo would ponder its message as they prepare themselves to emulate the very God of all that is.

What was completely unknown to all, including translated angels and mortals, was that an exact duplicate of this structure stood at the heart of the Heavenly Jerusalem, the holiest of all places, the center place of the infinite and glorious Kingdom of God the Eternal Father.

Of course, all these vast and eternal correlations were obscure to the workmen and women who placed them there according to their instructions. Had they known the full meaning of what they crafted, and were able to implement it in their lives, they would have become gods themselves.

It was hard into winter and a light dusting of snow lay across the Missouri landscape as Samuel walked side-by-side with several brethren toward the Temple. It was just growing light, and the sounds of construction were again beginning to fill the air. It was cold enough that Samuel could see his breath. The brethren beside him were shivering and walking briskly to warm up. Without electricity, the only way to heat their homes was by burning wood or coal. Few homes were equipped to do so, and families spent their days and nights bundled up in all the clothing they possessed. Even though they were warm enough and had plenty to eat, there were problems with pipes freezing and other issues endemic to cold weather. Still, the joy of Zion was constantly upon them, and while they struggled with the affairs of their lives their voices were raised in frosty shouts of joy.

Four of the buildings forming the spokes of the wheel of the Temple were complete and in use for administration. It was toward one of these buildings Samuel turned as he parted company with the others. He spent a few minutes gazing at the Temple. Even in the dim light of early morning the spire seemed to contain lightning inside. At last he climbed the steps and entered the Temple. He removed his shoes and slipped on a pair of thick slippers.

President Johnson and most of the others were already seated at the long table. After singing a hymn, and a prayer offered, President Johnson stood.

"Brethren, it is with joy that I stand before you today and announce that we have received further instructions from President Andrews. But before I detail that, I want to introduce Sister Jennifer Evans, and Brother Tom Jamison."

The two people walked into the room, and the brethren stood as they entered. Four young women pulled a cart into the room and then departed, closing the doors behind them. The object on the cart was about the size of a television set and covered with a tarp. It was apparently fairly heavy, as the four who pulled it into the room were straining.

"Sister Evans, why don't you explain what you have brought to show us," Elder Johnson said, his voice taut with suspense, as if he could hardly restrain himself from blurting out the news.

"Actually, the original idea came from Tom," she began. "He came to me because I have a degree in electrical engineering, and together we were able to construct this prototype. I'm going to let him initially explain what it is," she said, and stepped aside.

Brother Tom Jamison was in his early twenties, with light sandy hair and freckles. He was slender to the point of being willowy, and stepped to the end of the table with confidence. "Without telling you the whole story for now, I want to say that this idea just spontaneously occurred to me the other day. I want to give full credit to Jesus Christ for it. Beyond that, it is probably better to just show you than to try to explain what it is." With that he and Sister Evans pulled the tarp from the object.

It was apparent from the first glance that their creation was inside the enclosure of a small refrigerator. Tom opened the door to reveal a device not unlike three cylinders on their sides stacked atop one another. Wires ran from the cylinders to a small control panel above them. Tom flipped two switches and a light came on. Having spent the last several years without electricity this stimulated a cry of amazement from those watching. Jennifer stepped behind the device and set an electric heater on top. Tom flipped a switch on the heater and the coils quickly turned red. A flood of warm air swept across the room.

"It's an electric generator. It functions on a completely unique principle. The process is actually very complex, but the Lord guided our efforts every step of the way. It uses the earth's magnetic field to produce electricity in the coils. In order to build this machine we had to first create a super-conductor which functioned at room temperature. That was the real triumph, and was only possible through God. Once we had that, it was simply a matter of constructing this device."

"What is the fuel it runs on?" President Johnson asked.

"There is no fuel," Jennifer answered. "It is like an electric generator that uses the earth itself as the armature. As long as the earth keeps spinning on its axis, the coils will continue to produce electricity. That's the best we can explain it at this time. It has no moving parts and a generator with three coils like this one would be sufficient to heat an average home. It is entirely safe and will run indefinitely if not overloaded."

"It is a gift from God," Tom concluded humbly.

There was an audible gasp from everyone in the room. "How difficult are they to make?" Samuel asked incredulously.

"Not hard, given the Lord's instructions," Tom said. "The hardest part is making the super-conductor wire. We have set up a small shop to produce it already. We should be able to produce about two generators a week at first, more as we get geared up. We hope to have one of these machines attached to every home in Zion before the winter is over."

President Johnson spoke next. "We are going to use the first few out in the tent cities. They are suffering from the cold more than those in homes. The next few will go to essential services such as refrigeration at the food stores. The next ones will come to the Temple to provide heat and light in the outer buildings. Then we will begin fitting them to businesses, and finally homes." He surveyed their excited faces with a grin. "Can I see a show of hands for all who approve this action?"

A hearty vote of approval followed. The two young inventors left the heater running and departed, smiling broadly. Even with his inability to experience discomfort from the cold, Samuel felt a thrill of physical pleasure as his body accepted the welcome warmth.

He paused and breathed deeply. "Now, Brethren, we have a far more pressing matter." All eyes turned from the heater back to their leader. "President Andrews, our Prophet, has given us an instruction from the Lord that must also be interpreted as a warning. He has instructed us to call twelve groups of twelve faithful priesthood holders. They are each to travel one mile from the Temple in every direction north, south, east, west, and equally spaced between those positions, until they form a two-mile perimeter around the Temple. We are to bring all our people within that two mile circle."

"What does it mean?" someone asked.

"President Andrews did not say. But, he did say we must have these brethren in place by tomorrow evening." This brought a rumble of anxious comment from the brethren. "Please, Brethren, your attention still. I have here a list of twelve men from this body who will preside over one of the groups. You are to call and have set apart the other eleven in your group and depart tomorrow morning." Again a flurry of comments and questions arose, all of which President Johnson ignored.

"Brethren, I was also instructed on a matter of utmost sacredness. Each member of these groups will be given an additional priesthood power under my own hand. Up until now the Lord has graciously given us the spiritual Priestly power of the Melchizedek Priesthood. As such we have been authorized to administer in all matters of the kingdom and establishment of Zion."

"The Lord has now authorized the transferal of the Kingly powers of the Melchizedek Priesthood. You will recall that in the Temple we are promised that we shall become Priests and Kings, Priestesses and Queens unto the Most High God. Today these brethren, in connection with their worthy wives, are to be given the fullness of the Priesthood with power to command the elements. Brethren, the times are upon us when we will defend Zion with pillars of fire. It is a great and terrible day. Let me read the names the Lord has chosen to preside over these groups," he said, and began to read.

Samuel's name was sixth on the list of leaders to be called. Immediately his mind began to fill with names of the eleven others in his group. He pulled a scrap of paper from his pocket and began jotting names as quickly as they came to him. He was pleased to see his oldest son, Sammy, his stepsons Theo and George, son-in-law Steve, and many from Alexei's people—Vladimir among them.

The following morning before the sun arose, Samuel, Melody and all those with them were assembled inside the temple to be set apart. The faithful priesthood holders with their wives waited reverently for their opportunity to be set apart, beginning with those called to preside. It was a marvelous gathering, and the Holy Spirit rested powerfully upon them. When the time came, Samuel took a seat before President Johnson who placed his hands upon his head.

"My beloved brother, Samuel Nephi Mahoy. By virtue of the holy Priesthood of God, I lay my hands upon your head and in accordance with your special calling by the Savior Himself, I give you the authority to confer the fulness of the Melchizedek Priesthood, which grants the power to command the elements and the earth according to the will of God in defense of His people."

"Great has been your service in Heavenly Father's name. You have been faithful in all things wherewith you have been charged. Now, lead in the defense of Zion. Let your faith be absolute, and you shall rejoice in this great opportunity to serve God. Though this profound power has not been exercised upon the earth by mortals since the days of the great Nephite Prophets, the keys have been held by every prophet and apostle since the Prophet Joseph, to be exercised at this time and those with the special calling you now bear."

"You have been privileged to hold this holy commission once again in this era. In time, this power will become commonplace. Today, it is unique and glorious, and it has been your privilege to be among the first to call upon this great power of God in this latter-day dispensation. Teach those you lead how to exercise this great gift. By your example shall Zion survive, or perish. In the name of Jesus Christ, Amen."

Samuel stood from the chair a little stunned. Even though he had exercised this great power many times since his translation, the authority to confer it to others was profoundly humbling to him. He knew he must have absolute trust in God as the safety or destruction of Zion depended upon his example. He smiled, embraced President Johnson and quickly departed to find the other brothers and sisters on his list.

It was not surprising that Vladimir was waiting for him at his home when he returned. He quickly explained and gave Vladimir half his list. They parted in search of the others. By late evening they had all had been found. All humbly accepted the call. Without exception, they derived courage from the fact that Samuel would lead them. With increasing certainty Samuel knew the words President Johnson had pronounced in the blessing to be profoundly true. If his faith was not sufficient to exercise this priesthood power, neither would theirs be. It was a burden more weighty than any he had known before.

It was a unique and unsettling idea, that even as a translated being, it would require all the faith he possessed to act in this new mission. His heart called out in mighty prayer, seeking strength he did not have. Even knowing he could not experience hunger, and in fact did not require food at all, he began a fast for the first time in almost a dozen years. To his surprise, his stomach knotted in a spasm of hunger. It was not painful, but it was sufficient to constitute a fast, and he rejoiced.

Samuel joined President Johnson in conferring the fullness of priesthood power upon each of the others. Samuel's group was assigned the area due east. With a strange foreboding hanging in the air, they set out before daylight the following morning and bid farewell to their loved ones and friends. By the time they departed all in Zion knew the time had come, and with one accord, they entered into a united fast and began crying unto the Lord with great faith for their safety.

After mighty supplication, the brothers and sisters walked the short mile to their assigned location. They stopped in a subdivision of middle-class homes and took up station in the center of the street. Others passed their group headed further east to spread the word of warning to gather into the circle of safety. By noon people were streaming past them, carrying bundles of their possessions.

The first indication of a threat to Zion came suddenly above them with such savageness that no one, including Samuel, was prepared. As evening approached it did not grow dark. It seemed as if the sun were rising in the east even as it was setting in the west. They watched with astonishment as a bright ball of light rose in the eastern sky. When they could actually see the source of the light it was immediately apparent that this was not the sun, nor the Son of God. It was some massive object approaching the earth, about a third the size of the moon in the sky, growing larger and larger by the minute. Samuel and his small group watched in awe as the celestial body entered the upper atmosphere. As it approached it suddenly burst into a fiery ball too bright to look at directly.

Panic filled his bosom as Samuel realized the magnitude of this calamity. The doom that was quickly approaching had the potential of wiping out all life upon the earth, let alone destroying Zion. Quelling his momentary panic, he fell to his knees and fervently petitioned his God, crying with all his energy for understanding and direction. He waited for the familiar feeling of calm to wash over him, and when it did not, he increased his strivings. He heard several of his group cry out in fear as if from a great distance away. He looked up into the eleven frightened faces surrounding him.

"My dear brethren and sisters, kneel with me in prayer. God will deliver us," he said, and with his own words, knew they were true. "When the moment comes, we will know what to do, and we will be spared. Until then, we wait upon the Lord. Have faith, and be at peace," he instructed, receiving a witness again that these words were profoundly true. Though his heart was pounding in his chest, an element of certainty settled upon him. Not the peace he had prayed for, but it was a beginning.

Samuel looked into the sky to see the great ball of fire streaking toward them. It was difficult to tell where it might impact. Though it appeared much larger, it was several miles across, but decreasing in size. Slowed by the atmosphere it broke into several pieces as it continued its westerly path, then arched away from them, turning slightly north. In what seemed to be an acceleration of its speed, it quickly fell out of sight.

"We are saved!" someone in his group cried.

"Not yet," Samuel said with absolute surety. He stood up from praying, as did all the others. Within seconds they felt more than heard the first wave. The earth trembled violently beneath their feet. Then, as if someone had shaken a huge rug, the ground started convulsing far away to the east. Within thirty seconds, all could see debris as large as houses being thrown into the air as the deadly earthquake approached in slow motion.

"Brethren, bring your arms to the square," Samuel said as the peace he had so earnestly sought finally swept through him. They did as he instructed. "In the name of Jesus Christ, by the power of His mighty priesthood, and through the merits, mercy and grace of Messiah, I command you to pass beyond us," he said in a quiet, commanding voice. The approaching wave of destruction rolled onward for another five seconds, then suddenly submerged. They felt it rumble far below their feet. They would learn later that it emerged about one mile beyond the temple and continued on its path of destruction. It again submerged just outside the Utah valleys, and appeared again beyond the Rocky Mountains. When it hit the coasts of California and Oregon, it had fanned out and picked up a 500-mile strip of the western coast at the fault lines, rolling it into the sea. Ocean water rushed in to fill the sudden void.

It would not be known until years later that the asteroid had fallen three miles off Long Island, New York. The resulting shock had lifted the ocean floor a mile from shore and rolled it atop the desolate cities all along the Eastern coast. Years later when people finally went to investigate the damage wrought, there was nothing but wilderness with no trace of mankind ever having been there.

"Praises be to God," one of the sisters cried out when it became apparent that they had been spared. The cry was echoed by all, and redoubled by the thousands within the two mile circle of safety.

"It is not over," Samuel said quietly. He did not know why he had said that until the sky grew dark in the east. It was a massive shockwave consisting of a dense cloud of sea water, mud and debris. It was potentially more devastating than the quake in that it could render the land uninhabitable for years, and darken the sun so crops could not grow for decades.

Without being told, all twelve couples faced the cloud now close enough they could clearly see flashes of lightning on its surface. It boiled toward them like the fist of Satan, accompanied by a continuous roll of thunder. They raised both arms over their heads.

"In the name of Jesus Christ, let the winds blow, and the mighty hand of God turn aside the destruction of the wicked, for there are no wicked here," they all cried in unison. It was the first time Samuel had heard twelve people speak an entire phrase as one, through divine inspiration. A thrill of faith and peace surged through him. A mighty wind instantly began to blow at his back, which struck the approaching cloud with great force, causing the approaching cloud to rear up like a charging horse thrashing its hooves.

After a moment the wind continued just above the level of the trees.
They watched the titanic forces battle for a long moment. Finally, the great storm parted, and passed on either side of Zion. They watched in calm wonder for many minutes as the winds continued to part the tide of destruction. For weeks thereafter the winds blew until the threat was gone. While all around them the land languished in darkness, the city of Zion was bathed in the warmth of sunshine.

Everywhere but in Zion and her sister cities, day after day further destruction from the sky rained down. Some days the asteroids were small and numerous and burned up in the atmosphere. Others were huge and struck the earth with great destructive power. During that time the priesthood of God stood guard along their perimeter which was expanded to five miles from the Temple, and nothing harmed their tranquility. It was a time of intense wonder for all, including Samuel. Miracles of divine intervention became so commonplace that people lived in a constant state of rejoicing. It was the greatest day of miracles ever wrought by the hand of God upon the earth since its very creation.

When Samuel and the other brethren walked away from their posts that day, the danger from this assault was past, and their faith in God was absolute. Where once they had trembled before the titanic forces of destruction, now they strode away in the humble majesty of Kingly Priesthood power.

A phenomenon no one had anticipated was that a few television stations continued to broadcast news of world events. How they had survived could only be described in terms of divine intervention, for every part of every continent, east or west, was one continuous scene of destruction.

As electricity became available in some homes, and with the widespread use of generators, pockets of people around the world availed themselves of these daily broadcasts to hear of the condition of the nations. What they reported was appalling and distressing to watch, for it chronicled the collapse and destruction of the entire fabric of society.

Unknown to the Saints was the fact that the remnants of the United States Army persisted in its involvement in the war. This was only possible because of the huge store of arms they had cached all over the globe prior to the collapse of the US economic base. Even though every notable nation in Europe and England had largely been overrun by Chinese and Russian forces, the tiny nation of Israel was yet intact in spite of relentlessly being under attack. This was so because nearly every western nation on earth saw tiny Israel as the only toe hold in the Middle East, and pressed every resource at their disposal into its defense. From the shreds of information the news media reported, it was apparent this resistance to the Ruso-Sino juggernauts was temporarily effective.

Also startling was the now apparent fact that the Russian push across Europe had been for the sole purpose of attacking England. For reasons every future history book recorded, Russia considered it a moral duty to destroy the British Empire and the vast system of world banking that had so long held the Communist nations in chains of poverty. Their assault on England was single-minded in its ferocity. They cut a ten-mile wide path of total obliteration from the English Channel to London, where their fury spent itself in destroying everything associated with culture, government and banking. Needless to say, the British Royalty ceased to exist—nor would it ever rise again.

It had taken the Russians and Chinese six years and six months to conquer England and its allies. Immediately after those days the war changed dramatically. The Soviets unexpectedly withdrew most of their forces from every conquered land except for vast tracts of Eastern Europe. Now that they were completely purged there of their former enemies, the agreement was that China would send wave after wave of Chinese to settle the land. Just as startling as this withdrawal was the fact that they left behind nearly half of their military hardware. At first everyone thought this an oversight, or some concession to local sovereignty. It was perhaps the most pernicious act the Russian-Chinese forces had perpetrated to date, and was born of Satanic brilliance.

Crazed by prolonged war, failing economies and the incalculable death count, the inhabitants of these lands picked up those weapons and began carving out little empires for themselves in hopes of securing some peace. Instead of gaining any security, they created a feudal system of small city-states jealous of every neighbor's holdings. The war that ensued was far more terrible than the former threat, in that families were divided by the happenstance of their physical locality. A prolonged war of father against son and mother against daughter ensued, ignited by a universal hatred that seemed to know no bounds.

This withdrawal of the Russian and Chinese armies from most of the Middle East and Europe dropped the checkered flag on the race to finally conquer Israel. With one accord the remnants of the nations of Islam united, picked up the scattered pieces of their armies, and attacked Israel with demonic fury. Faced by a far more determined assault than the Chinese or Russians had ever brought, the combined forces of the defenders of Israel were pounded back to within their own borders.

Their hatred was fanned to white-hot intensity by the recent removal
of the Dome of the Rock, and the nearly-completed reconstruction of the
Third Temple described by the prophet Ezekiel. The desecration of Islam's
holy shrine fanned their hatred, and it simply was not possible for them
to wage war any more violently. If anything, the assault waned briefly as
the collective spirit of Islam mourned what they considered an irreconcil-
able spiritual loss.

On the American continent a similar, though different, dynamic
occurred with the end of Russian and Chinese aggression. As if orches-
trated by an invisible commander, the nation fractured overnight into
a dozen tiny nations. Florida combined with Cuba to form New Cuba.
The Confederate States of Texas retained Texas, Louisiana, Oklahoma and
Arkansas.

South Carolina reformed the Confederate States of America upon
lines almost identical to those of the South during the Civil War. What
was left of the destroyed eastern seaboard above New York was annexed
by the new Canadian nation of Quebec. The former states of Utah, Idaho,
parts of Nevada, Colorado and Wyoming formed into the self-proclaimed
state of Deseret, with allegiance to their newly-elected Congress convened
in Salt Lake City.

Previously conquered by the South American Liberation Army,
California, parts of Nevada, Arizona and New Mexico split with their
mother countries and formed the nation of New Mexico. Immediately
upon this defection, a war commenced between this new nation, and
their South American motherland.

Under these circumstances it was hardly unexpected when each new
nation-state began sending ambassadors to Zion in former Jackson
County, at first inviting, then demanding Zion's political union with each
new nation. Because of the central geographic location of Missouri, and
because it was intact and completely undamaged from recent events, it
soon became the hub of anxiety among the new nations. They reasoned
that whoever controlled the powerful state of Zion controlled the corridor
to either annex other non-aligned states, or to defend against aggression
from the other nations vying for the vast resources and fertile farmlands
of central United States.

Every offer was politely refused. Every refusal brought a myriad of
threats for speedy retaliation. As the pressure mounted, only one question
remained: Would this Zion be righteous enough to maintain independence of every nation on earth, or would this generation falter?

The faithful knew that glorious answer.

A NEW DAY OF PENTECOST

It was never clear how President Andrews came to Zion—the New Jerusalem. All most knew was that he was suddenly there. It was a great joy to have the living Prophet among them at last. Somehow, Zion had been incomplete prior to his arrival. From that day onward he would remain in Zion. A special conference was scheduled for the sixth of April, only one week away.

Upon arriving in Zion, President Andrews immediately asked to see Alexei. President Johnson had inquired among his aids to find out who Alexei was. When he learned that Alexei was the leader of the Levites from Russia, he sent word immediately. When the worthy Levites arrived, men and women alike came with Samuel, carrying with them their sacred records in their carved wooden box.

Introductions were hardly over when President Andrews asked to see their scriptures, a note of anticipation in his voice. Alexei carefully presented the leather volume to the oracle of God. President Andrews removed the book with reverence and sat it upon the table. After studying the cover he said, "The Book of Levi."

"Is that what it's called?" Alexei asked excitedly.

"Can't you read English?" the Prophet asked casually.

"It's not written in English," Samuel said in reply.

"It's not... ?" he began, then sobered. "Forgive me. This is my first experience with ancient scripture, and I'm afraid I did not recognize the gift when it came. Of course it's not in English; yet to my eyes the words are as legible as if they were, though I can plainly see they are another language."

President Andrews's eyes filled with humble tears, and he silently gave thanks to his beloved Father. "Brothers and sisters, take a seat, and let me read you a page or two."

They found seats as best they could while President Andrews studied the words of the ancient scripture before him. He glanced up, and satisfied that everyone was comfortable, he slowly began. A scribe sat to his left and transcribed every word.

"The record of the People of Omish, children of Levi, sons of Moses, who were taken captive into Babylon during the reign of Nebedkenezer, king of Babylon. Written by the hand of Karush, servant of the prophet of God whose name was Issac ben Jacob, who was born in captivity in

Babylon one-hundred and twelve years following the defeat and fall of Jerusalem by the hand of the Babylonians."

"Praise be unto the God of Israel, and the hope of our salvation. Glory be to him, and to his son, Jesus Christ the Messiah, who according to our faith, and the words of our prophets, must come and be born of a virgin at Jerusalem in the meridian of time."

"We know by these words that in a future day some of our seed will return to Jerusalem and build it up again. But, we also know that our house will not be among those to fulfill this prophecy. For, we know by the word of God that we will be gathered unto a strange land, there to dwindle in quietude and oppression until the fullness of times are fulfilled, and we are called home to Zion, where we will build an holy city, a New Jerusalem, to our Savior, there to meet him at his return in Glory. This because of our continued faith, the former sins of this people, and the will of God in keeping our blood unpolluted that in the last day there may be those of the house of Levi to offer up again a righteous offering unto the Lord . . ."

It was late into the night when President Andrews's voice grew hoarse, and he had to stop. Rather than invite them back for further readings, he promised to work diligently to complete the work of translation of these sacred words scribed to paper where they could be had by all.

As Samuel escorted Alexei and Vladimir and their people back to their tents, the aged Russian walked slowly, his head lowered to his chest. Every now and then he would break his own silence by sighing deeply.

"Tell me what is in your heart," Vladimir asked his uncle.

"It is a glorious thing, what we have just heard. Did you hear that the first words of our scripture proclaim Jesus Christ to be the Son of God?"

"I did. I surely did," he allowed.

"Our people have awaited this glorious day for 2,600 years, and we are alive to see its fulfillment. It is a glorious day!" Alexei proclaimed.

"Praise God!" Vladimir rejoiced as they embraced.

"Praise God!" Samuel agreed, and the unseen keepers of truth seemed to cry in response, "Hallelujah!"

Springtime in Zion was joyful. The breezes were warm, the rains gentle and nourishing. Flowers were profuse and trees and grasses grew lush green. It was April 6th, the day of the special general conference called by President Andrews. A large tent would serve as their meeting place. No room inside the Temple was large enough to house the tens of thousands who wished to attend. A mediocre but competent sound system had been engineered, powered by generators outside the tent. A little ingenuity formed Zion's first television station, and the conference was broadcast in Zion, and in Utah.

Like a new day of Pentecost, the Spirit of the Lord was poured out in profuse abundance. The choir was angelic in its worship and praise, and the conference proceeded with outpourings of truth never before taught in such plainness.

A breathless hush fell across the vast assembly no matter where they were, as their now-aged prophet stood to address them. It was apparent that he had no prepared text, as he gripped the sides of the pulpit and gazed out into the throng.

"Such a righteous assembly of God's Kingdom has never before occurred, my beloved brothers and sisters of Zion," he began, his voice rich with emotion. "Those of you who choose to see with spiritual eyes, will note that the enormous numbers of people here is insignificant to the number of those from the spiritual realm. The heavens are opened, and the union between God's people and His very presence is nearly complete. In a not far-distant day the very Lord of Heaven and Earth will come to His Temple, and we will at last be one!" he proclaimed with fervor. The crowded whispered excitedly, and he waited for a hush to fall over them again.

"This is the era of time that every prophet of every age saw in vision, and yearned to participate in. This is the time. This is the place. This is the dawning of the Millennium. My brothers and sisters, and beloved from the unseen world, as the mouthpiece of God, I declare this day as the beginning of the thousand years of peace the world has awaited since the days of the Garden of Eden. Let all history record this day as the day upon which it began. Let the heavens burst open and rejoice; let the people shout for joy; let all creation witness the glory of God that shall soon cover the world as the waters cover the ocean floor. Rejoice, oh ye people of God, rejoice! I say, for today is that day of days! I proclaim this people Zion, the pure in heart! And I proclaim this land the City of the Living God! This day is the beginning of the Kingdom of God in its fullness upon the earth.

"Let every voice cry Hosanna!" The combined voices of men and angels echoed the words in such jubilation that the very ground beneath their feet trembled, and choirs of angels sang in anthems heard by all.

Then a long silence of nearly a full minute fell upon them, as joy too full to be expressed with words burned in their souls. Finally, his eyes moist and flowing, President Andrews looked across all assembled. "Let me here observe that the millennial reign of peace shall in the beginning rest only upon this blessed valley, and the everlasting hills of our pioneer home. Elsewhere wars still rage, and the hearts of men are cold and hateful. They will come with their armies thinking to take away our lives, our homes, and our peace. Yet, as long as we are the pure in heart, the Captain of our souls will fight our battles! We will stand in the robes of the holy priesthood upon the hills and the plains, and call upon the very elements to defend us. If necessary, we will call down pillars of fire to consume them, and send them back into their own lands."

His voice grew strong. "But, my dearly beloved, beloved family, this is not all. Even while they try to destroy us we will send our missionaries forth, armed with the full power of God to call them to repentance. These gloriously-arrayed missionaries shall sweep across the face of the whole earth one last time. Into every land on this globe they shall teach and baptize and invite all of God's children to Zion. For only in Zion, and her Stakes, shall there be peace. Against those who reject or who molest God's chosen messengers, they shall dust off the soles of their feet as a witness against them, and their destruction shall be swift and sure."

The prophet cleared his throat, speaking again with renewed clarity. "From among the Quorum of the Twelve, the finger of God has identified two who will dwell in Jerusalem, there to stand between the armies of Satan, and the children of His ancient covenant, as prophecy has long indicated they would. This very day they arrive there and begin their ministry of mighty works among our long-embattled Jewish brothers in Jerusalem.

The entire congregation sat up with anticipation. "With these words I hereby call twelve thousand high priests and priestesses from every tribe of Israel to assemble as quickly as possible, and to depart into every part of the world to glean the fields. You shall go two by two, without purse or script, without two coats, or two pairs of shoes. You shall go in the power of God, by the power of God, and shall be His instruments to call a world back from the very brink of destruction. The borders of every nation are down, and you shall go unhindered wherever the voice of God sends you."

The President raised his arms in magnificent gesture. "You may well ask, 'How shall we go?' seeing that all transportation has been destroyed by the unholy war still raging upon the face of the land. There are no ships upon the sea, and no airplanes in the air. There are but few automobiles and busses and trains that function. I will tell you how you will go. You will go in the power of God. Each of you shall fast and pray, and fall upon your faces before God until you shall hear His voice assigning to you that part of His vineyard wherein ye shall labor. Thereafter ye shall arise and simply walk in that direction, no matter if a great ocean separates you from your destination; and before many days, and perhaps in the blink of an eye according to your faith, you shall be there. From city to city shall you thus go, and from house to house. We have but a short time to bear this final witness to the children of God."

His voice lowered to a reverent whisper. "Your voice will act as a final testimony against the wicked. You will know when it is right to raise a person from the grasp of the grave, and you will know when it is not. Understand that you shall sorrow for the nations and people you serve. It will tear at your very heartstrings. Yet, you will have brought to the land of Zion and to the valleys of the Everlasting Hills, all those whose names the Lord has written in His Book of Life. When you have found, taught and purified those cut from Celestial cloth, you, my glorious brothers and sisters, shall bring them home. Bring them by the power of God! Take them two from a field, and one from the stall, and three from a family, and ten from a village. Bring them home to receive their blessings in Zion!"

His words rang with intensity. "Yes, we will go in haste! We will not, however, return in haste. It will be a gathering of many years. You will bring the children of God home upon your shoulders and in your arms singing the sacred songs of Zion. After your testimony comes the testimony of unquenchable fire, according to the will of the Great Jehovah."

"You shall not go to the heathen nations until after the Lord comes in Glory. Neither shall you any more than lightly pass over the nations of the Gentiles, as a final witness. But to the house of Israel outside the nation of Israel shall you go, preaching Christ, and Him crucified, and risen again the third day. Those you teach and prepare will largely be the Jews, the members of Christ's true Church who have lived faithful to their covenants, and those of other denominations who have dedicated their lives to Christ. We shall not teach anyone else."

Now his voice rose until it was almost a shout. "Unto those of faith shall you show forth mighty miracles, raising the dead, healing the sick, and causing the blind to see. Unto those with no faith shall you turn away. You shall go to teach, not to be taught. You shall not debate or convince by logic, neither shall you pause to persuade. But, those who can hear, will hear, and all others shall you leave without comment or explanation, for in the few days wherein we may glean the fields, we must hurry before the storms of winter begin."

The congregation was still, listening to one another breathe with pounding hearts at the divine message. "I say unto you this day in the hearing of the eternities, that this is the last time the Gospel of the Kingdom shall be preached on this earth before the Lord comes again in His glory. I declare that the times of the Gentiles are fulfilled, and from this day onward we turn our faces to the lost family of Israel. Thus let it be recorded in heaven.

"This I say in the name of Jesus, the very Christ, the Messiah, the great I AM, Amen!" he cried.

A mighty "Amen!" arose from the collective voices of the righteous of every age. In response, the very hills and valleys of Zion trembled with joy.

President Andrews remained at the pulpit, his hands shaking, his eyes raised toward heaven. After a moment, he looked out across the tens of thousands assembled to hear his words. He smiled lovingly down at them, and spoke again.

"It occurs to me that we have one other task to complete. Before the first missionaries leave to return with the children of God riding upon their shoulders, we must first dedicate the main building of this glorious Temple. It is now almost complete except for many furnishings we must still construct. All systems have been installed and are functioning as designed." He paused and continued with a little irony in his voice. "We don't fully understand what some of those systems are for, but they do seem to be functioning."

The crowd laughed with understanding, since almost all of them had seen or worked on the very systems he was referring to. This technology seemed to have a terrestrial purpose, and its design was remarkable and mysterious. They grew quiet again, and President Andrews continued.

"We will provide the interior furnishings and some trim after it is dedicated, as the Lord instructs. For this reason we will meet in the second floor assembly hall within the Temple at noon this coming Saturday. By that time our faithful technical people, who have in the past blessed our lives with innovative solutions to very demanding problems, will have an even better public address system functioning, or so they tell me." Louder laughter this time.

"In the Temple proper we will request the President of each tribe, and one hundred of their brothers and sisters to be invited by the President, according to instruction by the Spirit. The remainder of your people will meet in the outer temple rim buildings which bear their tribe's name, or upon the spot where that tribe's temple will eventually be built. A representative of the Quorum of the Twelve will be in attendance at each temple wing. This is the pattern for all future meetings. In this way, we will all participate in this and future glorious events. You may believe me when I tell you, this is only the first of many spiritual outpourings such as the world has not known since the city of Enoch was taken to the bosom of God."

His eyes searched the crowd of glowing faces. "Let all who are in favor may manifest it and say Amen!" he called with great fervor.

All arms raised and a single mighty "Amen" again echoed on both sides of the veil.

Several months had passed, and with great fervor and anticipation the Temple had been readied for dedication. The excitement in the air was palpable.

"But Mommy, why can't I go too?" four-year-old Helaman pouted at his mother, who was kneeling to plant a farewell kiss on her son's chubby cheek.

"Because you're not old enough to go to a temple dedication, honey. You have to stay here with your cousins," Melody said matter-of-factly. Then she brightened and ruffled his red hair. "Now don't worry—you're growing like a weed, and soon you'll be as big as Daddy. Then you'll be able to go with us!"

"That's right!" Samuel yelled from the back room. He was laughing as he strode into the living room and snatched little Helaman off the floor, tossing him high into the air. "Hey little Buddy, I think you're getting too big for me to do that much longer!" he said with a wink. He whirled his gleeful son around and around until they were both dizzy, then plunked him safely onto the couch. The boy was giggling so hard that Samuel decided his only recourse was to pull out the big guns.

"Oh no, Buddy," his Daddy warned, his voice low and ominous. "I think I feel some tickles coming on . . ."

"No, Daddy!" Helaman protested in delight.

Samuel's face was deadly serious. "Oh yeah!" Samuel suddenly pulled his hands from his back, tickle fingers flexing menacingly and moving swiftly toward Helaman's round tummy.

"No, Daddy—nooooooo!" Helaman screamed in delight. Finally, Helaman and his Daddy toppled on the couch in one another's arms, laughing hysterically.

Melody was giggling as she watched this exchange. "I sure do love that man of mine," she thought as they were walking together with their older children to the Temple. It would indeed be a day of days.

––––––––––––

Samuel, Melody and their family assembled with the others, and could hardly contain themselves in anticipation of what this day of dedication would bring. They had a good view, as they were seated just twenty rows back in the Temple. The room was built after the pattern established in the Kirtland Temple. Both ends of the long hall had a tiered stage with three pulpits on each level. Rows of seats on each level were separated by a breastwork handrail before them. The east end held the presidency of the Melchizedek priesthood, First Presidency and each of the Quorum of the Twelve who had come for this momentous occasion—though the Twelve were presently meeting with the various tribes. The west end was filled with the Presiding Bishopric, and presidency of the Aaronic Priesthood.

On the floor was seating capacity for exactly 2,400 people. These consisted of hand-crafted individual seats which could be lifted and turned around to face either direction. Samuel was quite interested in the fact that the seats were obviously old, and wondered if they had been "borrowed" from some other temple for the occasion. If so, they must have been brought to Zion by the power of God, since no trucking or transportation currently existed anywhere upon the continent.

They sang "Israel, Israel God Is Calling" as the opening hymn, and a choir augmented the singing with a thrilling obligato. There was no piano or organ, and indeed had there been one, it could not have been heard above the voices of the faithful. As they sang, a corridor of light opened on both sides of the eastern pulpits, and a row of men in flowing white robes walked to the seats reserved for the Quorum of the Twelve. These took their places during the song.

As soon as they were in place, another group of twelve men similarly took their places immediately before them. This latter twelve, though also dressed in long white robes, wore a style of clothing noticeably different from the first. Samuel took the occasion, as did many others, to turn and look behind at the Aaronic Priesthood pulpits, which had also been filled with visiting dignitaries from beyond the veil. As they turned again back toward the east, two final beings entered and stepped onto the stage from a corridor of light and took seats to the right and left of the First Presidency. The corridor of light closed and disappeared as they were seated.

Though all these men appeared as tangible as any mortal, they glowed in a way that testified that they were not from this mortal sphere. All assembled saw them. None among them thought it odd or incredible that heavenly beings had appeared. With universal faith, every heart burned with the Holy Spirit in a great outpouring of believing.

President Johnson offered the invocation after which President Andrews again took the highest pulpit.

"Beloved of every age," he began. "Those you see before you may need some introduction. Immediately before me, in the seats normally occupied by the living Quorum of Twelve Apostles, are seated the Twelve chosen by Christ during His earthly ministry. Immediately before them are the Nephite Twelve chosen by the Master shortly after His ministry there in the flesh.

"Seated upon the west podium are various dignitaries from the days of Moses who administered in the offices of the Aaronic Priesthood during their lives. In the highest pulpit are seated Moses, Aaron and Joshua. Before them are dignitaries from various dispensations prior to those times who I shall not introduce by name until they can declare their own dispensation in due time.

"To my right I present a distinguished visitor whom I have had the privilege of laboring with since we arrived in the land of Zion. He was known, and will be known among us, as Brother Joseph, the Prophet of the restoration." Joseph stood, with a smile so broad and genuine that it warmed Samuel's soul.

Brother Joseph was different in appearance than any photos or carvings Samuel had seen. He was, in fact, so much different that without an introduction, Samuel would not have recognized him. What occurred to him at that moment was that Brother Joseph's body was now resurrected, and in the express image of his combined spirit and body, and therefore slightly different in appearance than during his mortality.

After Joseph sat, President Andrews waited for a murmur of excitement to dwindle away.

"To my left, I am pleased to introduce another distinguished guest also instrumental in the establishment of Zion in this dispensation, Brother Brigham Young." A youthful Brother Brigham stood effortlessly and smiled in quiet acknowledgment. He was no longer the rotund man he had been during his mortality, but appeared to be barely old enough for the tightly-clipped beard he wore.

President Andrews continued with vigor. "It is my great pleasure to announce the recent commencement and completion of the great patriarchal council held at Adam-ondi-Ahman." A great murmur of ex- citement swept across the throng. President Andrews raised a hand for silence. "As the prophet at this time, I was privileged to attend and participate in that great council which took place at the break of day this last April sixth, being one year from our arrival in this valley."

Some actually began to applaud, which quickly died down as President Andrews raised a hand and shook his head.

"It is an understatement to say that the heavens are fully opened once again, and great are our blessings! Behold, my faithful brothers and sisters, behold the men of God seated upon the stands before you. I give you to know that each of these righteous men is a resurrected being. Each of them attended that great council at Adam-ondi-Ahman, and each has been faithful and true, and in time will become gods themselves. Let us give wonder and glory to our God."

The congregation was motionless.

"Let your wonder extend to the profound witness that what they have done, you yourselves are also doing, and in time will inherit alongside those we honor today. Let your wonder extend to praise to our merciful and loving Heavenly Father, and to his beloved Son, our divine Redeemer. All glory to Them! Let us raise a shout of hosanna unto God!"

"Hosanna!" President Andrews cried, and the crowd roared back, "Hosanna! Hosanna! Hosanna to God and the Lamb!" they all cried in unison.

It took many minutes for quiet to again fall upon them, for their hearts would not let their tongues be stilled. Many prophesied with voices of joy, many spoke in tongues, and many interpreted what was said. Some among them stared in open awe at visions and heavenly manifestations which only they could see. Samuel thought, "This is truly a Day of Pentecost!"

President Andrews waited until peace settled upon them once again. "Before this day is complete we will see and hear many things. First, Brother Joseph has agreed to address us. This is a glorious and unique opportunity for us!" he said, turning to smile at the Prophet. Then he turned back to the throng.

"Brother Joseph has asked me to instruct you in the new millennial order before he speaks. He also asked me to tell you that he joins us as a guest and by invitation. His dispensation and his stewardship extend beyond the veil, and are in fact never-ending. As much as we honor and love him, he takes no part in the present line of authority as it exists upon the earth today. That authority rests squarely upon my shoulders until I, too, pass beyond the veil."

The congregation nodded in renewed understanding.

"As he speaks to us, every word he says we will receive as counsel and wisdom. But nothing he says will be spoken by way of commandment to our dispensation. Such is true of every other heavenly being here today, and will always be the case. The one exception to this will be when the Lord Jesus Christ Himself appears. He then will govern upon the earth, and we will serve Him, and Him alone."

President looked lovingly upon his waiting friends. "Without further comment, Brother Joseph," he said, and stepped back.

Joseph stood. His was tall, his bearing noble. His hair was a sandy blond and his eyes were piercing blue. He wore a suit of exquisite white, cut in the exact fashion of the days of his mortal experience. He shook President Andrews's hand firmly and stepped to the pulpit. He looked at the microphone suspiciously, then allowed his gaze to sweep across those assembled. A breathless silence fell upon the Saints.

"Greetings, and God's blessings to you all," he said, his voice like an amplified clap of thunder in the large hall. He winced, and then grinned.

"I feel compelled to say, my beloved brothers and sisters, that this is the first time I have spoken using a public address system! It makes me feel like our good Alma over there, whose great wish was to speak with the voice of an angel, like the trump of God unto every people," he said in a voice that echoed loudly through the hall. A ripple of laughter flowed across the room.

Joseph then looked directly at one of the men seated to his left and said, "I believe I will suggest to our friend that he give this a try; it really is quite exhilarating!" This brought louder laughter from the people, and Alma turned in his seat to wave Joseph off with a fond smile.

Joseph grew more serious. "As useful as this technology is which you possess in such abundance, it is nothing, *nothing* I tell you, in comparison to what will shortly come upon you as the blessings of the millennial day quickly unfold before your eyes.

"During its history this nation has blossomed and prospered under the greatest mortal transportation system has ever constructed on this earth. I say to you that in a short time no one will even mention that system, except to hold it in contempt. The days will come when you shall desire to be in a certain place for whatever purpose is in your heart, and you will take one step and be there.

"For many years you have been able to speak and be heard on the other side of the world. As wonderful a missionary tool as this is, the days will shortly come when you shall face an assembly of beings so vast as to fill every square inch of space upon this planet, if they were all present here at once. Every single one of them will be thirsting for the truths you guard in your hearts. You will raise your voices and by the power of God, not by the power of electrons and transformers, you shall address hundreds of thousands—and millions eventually—and they shall clamor for baptism."

The congregation sat in rapt attention, their minds trying to formulate the vision that Brother Joseph was outlining so profoundly.

"The Church of Jesus Christ of Latter-day Saints, before it was torn down and scattered, was adding hundreds of congregations each year. In a short time, you will be adding hundreds of stakes each year. Your biggest challenge will be to teach and train them, and to keep up with the rapid growth of the kingdom. In time, you will cease to build chapels, and will only build Temples, for all will be worthy to enter them and worship there. The Family—a righteous father and a righteous mother who have been sealed under the Holy Spirit of Promise—will be the governing body of the terrestrial world, under Jesus Christ; and you will look to the ecclesiastical Church to receive the priesthood of God and the sacred ordinances."

Melody glanced up at Sam, and he looked at her with a meaningful smile. He squeezed her hand tightly as Brother Joseph continued.

"In a few days the Lord will send 144,000 High Priests and Priestesses into the world to bring the Elect of God to Zion. I say to you that after this great missionary effort, tens of thousands of the Elect of God will come to you, to this very Holy City, every day of the year, seeking the blessings of the House of the Lord."

The excitement at this announcement was palpable, with audible gasps heard from every corner. "You have hitherto built scores of temples. As the Gospel of Christ sweeps the nations of the earth in the not-too-distant future, you will build more Temples than today there are chapels," Joseph said, then fell silent. He gripped both sides of the pulpit and stepped closer to the microphone as if he were about to tell a great secret.

"Why am I telling you this?" he whispered. "Why awaken your minds and hearts to what will shortly come to pass? I will tell you why, it is because President Andrews requested it of me. But, even more importantly, it is because the success of this great work depends entirely upon your faith and obedience in these next few months and years. It has long been the case that God would reveal the fullness of His glorious gospel to worthy people, and those people would slowly drift away and apostatize. It has long been the pattern of mankind that each spiritual blessing is followed by a period of spiritual comfort, then apathy, and then apostasy.

It is such a prevailing pattern that you have grown accustomed to it, and even expect it."

He drew a deep breath. "My beloved Saints of the Living God, this must never happen again! Consider the great spiritual height you have achieved by the grace of God. This is the first time such marvelous spiritual manifestations have occurred so ubiquitously since the days of Enoch, and in fact have eclipsed those of that grand era, and my era as well. Consider the fact that scores of resurrected beings are sitting before you now in plain view. This has never happened in the history of the world!"

A thrill went through every soul as they surveyed the glorious models of righteousness seated before them.

"This being so, consider what terrible condemnation would come upon you if you allow yourselves to again fall into apostasy! Consider this, and mark my words—a great warning of God in your ears—know this: that if you ever turn back from these privileges, either in your own lives or as a people, the second coming of Christ will wipe this valley clean of inhabitants, melt this glorious temple to a pile of slag, and erase your names from the Lamb's book of life without a trace."

A few shifted in their seats, but all kept their eyes riveted upon their glowing speaker.

"Then, my friends, when Christ proclaims the work complete, there will be no one left of this great city present to hear His words. He will pass the scepter of His priesthood power to a more worthy people and the days of the Gentiles will truly, ultimately, everlastingly, be ended. Beware! Beware! Beware!" he cried. "I urge you to let nothing call you back into the world. You are now Zion, the pure in heart, and if you falter the whole of creation falters with you!"

He paused for a moment. When he began again his voice was soft.

"As glorious as it was to head the dispensation of the restoration of the Gospel, it was in part a failure. The forces of the evil one nearly succeeded in destroying the work of God before it truly began. What was the weapon the evil one used to nearly destroy us? I will tell you. It was pride. For the pride of our hearts we nearly failed. We came within a breath of losing all God had given us. But for the grace of God, and the labors of faithful Brother Brigham," he said, turning to look Brigham in the eye, "and many others like him, we would have lost our blessings altogether. But, God chose to extend to us mercy that perhaps we did not deserve, and called us out of the jaws of hell, and led us to the Everlasting hills of Deseret where we waited out the days of our divorcement."

A murmur swept across the throng.

"Mark my words, these *have* been days of divorcement. For over two hundred years we have lived under condemnation. This condemnation was nothing more than our own failure to believe what God had promised us. It took these many years for us to awaken our souls to our privilege of building Zion. The timetable of God patiently awaited our awakening to this glory."

His voice shook, and his eyes searched the congregation. "Why were we waiting? Certainly not for God to make up His mind, but for us to become Zion! We, through our pride and apathy, prolonged our days in the wilderness of Deseret that could have, should have been spent in Zion in millennial bliss."

"In some ways our long years in Utah were a refuge—in some ways a blessing, and in some ways a long exile. Had we done what you must now do, we never would have had to made the trek west to Utah. We could have stayed in this very spot, built this very temple, and called in the Millennium upon our heads over two hundred years ago! But the Lord, in His infinite mercy, grace and patience, allowed His people the time they needed to mature into the stature of Zion—all glory to God!"

He stopped short and crouched into the microphone, speaking in a near-whisper.

"I tell you there is one thing that the forces of evil cannot abide, will not tolerate, and upon which they unleash all the unholy power of their fury—and that thing is Zion. You can expect, you *must* expect to become a battle ground. But, this time the Lord will fight your battles, and you will defend your homes and your sacred religion by priesthood power, and Zion will prevail.

"Now, it is your turn to do what we could not," Joseph continued earnestly. "I tell you, I prophesy to you, I warn you in the name of the Living Christ, that the possibility of your failure looms as threatening as it did over us. Choose ye this day that failure shall not occur again. This is the last line of defense. Here we stand firm. Here we set our stakes in the rich soils of righteousness and raise the tents of the tabernacle of God. Here, as never before, do we defy the power of wickedness and for the last time, establish the Kingdom of God! Today is indeed the most glorious day the world has ever known, and we—you and I—are blessed beyond compare to be here."

He let a long silence ensue before continuing. When he spoke again he seemed resigned, and his voice somber.

"There is much more that I wish to tell you which the Holy Spirit directs to postpone until another day. I am sure, now that the veil between the heavens and the Earth is growing thin, that the opportunity to address you again will shortly come."

A new smile played on his lips, and he looked lovingly upon them. "Until then, my dear sisters and brothers, I leave my blessing upon you." He raised his hands high over his head. "I call upon the heavens to open above you. I call down the angels of His presence to guard you and teach you. I pray our Heavenly Father to bless you that your hearts will stand faithful and true in every trial, as I have every confidence and faith they will. In the name of Jesus Christ, Amen!"

A breathless silence answered his "Amen" as Brother Joseph lowered his hands and bowed his head. President Andrews stood and raising a fist into the air, all present cried with him, "Amen! Amen! Hurrah for Zion! Hurrah for Zion!"

The rest of the day was a spiritual ecstasy. When it came time to dismiss, it was nearly six p.m. President Andrews offered the dedicatory prayer. The entire prayer was but a single paragraph, not much more than could be said in several breaths. Yet, it was the most powerful of its kind ever uttered.

"Oh, God, our Heavenly Father. Great and Glorious is Thy Name. Unto Thee do we give all honor and glory, and unto Thee do we dedicate this great house, this holy Temple. Father, for thousands of years have we awaited this profound moment wherein we have built unto Thee a throne upon this earth. We give unto Thee the fruits of our labors, and humbly ask Thee to let Thy glory rest upon it as a pillar of fire by night, and an illuminating cloud by day. Let Thy beloved Son, our Master, take His place upon that throne in His own due time. Henceforth and forever, from this very place let His law go forth to fill the whole world, until His own words are fulfilled wherein he prayed, 'Thy will be done on earth, even as it is in heaven.' In the beloved name of Jesus Christ, Amen."

As the congregation sounded the hosanna shout, a sound like the rushing of a mighty river filled the Temple so that even above the sound of their shouts of praise it was plainly heard. Jesus Christ appeared above the pulpit in His glory, and every soul fell to their knees as they felt His infinite love for them, and His acceptance of the Temple they had worked so hard to build.

Suddenly, across the great throng, the Savior looked directly at Melody as she heard His voice in her mind. "Melody, wait three days, then come to me in my Temple, and bring your righteous Samuel. I will come to you in my glory, and administer the holy gift I promised a lifetime ago I would give you."

Melody was so stunned and delighted that she could only nod. Samuel turned to her and said, "I heard Him too!" He found himself inwardly dancing, for this was the greatest desire of his own heart for Melody, as it was hers as well. They had often spoken of it in reverence.

A moment later, a great ball of light then gathered around the pinnacle of the temple and a beam of light shot from the heavens onto the temple spire, a thousand times more vivid than a shaft of lightning. It reached into the sky as far as the eye of man could behold. So sublimely glorious was this pillar of fire that during the day it affected the air such that a shroud of mist boiled around it, illuminated from inside by the pillar of fire. At night the cloud dispersed, and the fire was visible for a thousand miles. Its brilliance was such that it gave the brightness of midday to the city of God both day and night.

Even though only righteous mortals were at the glorious dedication, not everyone had been given that gift Melody would shortly receive in the Temple. Hence, the Master could not yet walk the streets of His own city in His full glory. Appropriately, a warm blanket of faith-filled desire had laid itself over each soul, so that every member of Zion had turned his or her heart to seeking the greater blessings. It would, in a not far-distant day, become commonplace to meet the Savior of all mankind strolling upon the golden streets of Zion, surrounded in His glory and accompanied by angels, both mortal and otherwise. But that would not occur until every single inhabitant in that great city had received their supernal calling and election, and had been given greater glorious blessings associated with their personal missions.

As they were directed, three days later Samuel escorted his beloved sweetheart to the Temple, where they were thrilled to see Alexei waiting for them in joyful anticipation. After the dear friends embraced and briefly conversed, Alexei solumnly escorted them to the veil of the Temple. After a time, as they emerged through that sacred space Jesus Christ was waiting for them, shining with glory and light. He beamed at her, His blue eyes gleaming with eternal love and delight in her.

Melody gazed into His eyes, and had she not still been clinging to Samuel's arm, she would have fallen to her knees. Instead, she stood looking up at him, for he was nearly a head taller than she, her face glistening with tears.

"Come to me," the Lord said gently, extending his arms to her. In the blink of an eye Melody collapsed into His arms in utter joy. Then she sank to her knees at His feet.

"My God!" she cried out. "My Master! My friend! I remember! I remember you! I have always loved you!"

"And just as wonderfully, I have always loved you!" He replied with equal fervor.

Samuel watched all this with rapture of soul. What was utterly fantastic was that this was a meeting of old friends. There was the inescapable knowledge that Jesus was her Savior, but He was also Melody's oldest and dearest friend. First and foremost, this was a meeting of two people who fiercely loved one another. The Savior's demeanor and words to Melody were of infinite compassion and love.

Whether He held her for seconds or minutes Samuel could not tell. But, when the Savior released her, Melody was different. When she turned to Samuel again, her face full of life, her form was straight and vigorous, her eyes crystal clear and joyful. He caught his breath.

Jesus turned and gently led them toward the Holy of Holies, where His glory suddenly increased and enveloped them. He turned and again gazed deeply into Melody's eyes, and she felt His all-consuming love wash over and through her. Jesus then stretched forth His hand and said, "Look." The room opened to the vastness of creation as Melody was allowed to experience the great vision of all things, and her glorious part in it. Her soul seemed to expand into eternity, and she was enabled to comprehend every detail. She fell to her knees in worship and utter nothingness, now fully knowing for herself that her Heavenly Father, Heavenly Mother, and Jesus Christ are literally in and through all things; that their eternal love permeates every element and creature in the universe.

As she returned to her mortal frame, all she could do was weep, "My Lord, my God. Thank you."

Jesus lovingly raised her to Him and said, "My dearest daughter, what would you desire of me?"

Melody looked intently into His eyes. "Thou knowest what I have desired, Lord."

He smiled at her again, and nodded in acknowledgement of the righteousness of her request. As He placed His eternal hands upon her head, Melody's face became translucent with light as she received the blessing she had most desired in her premortal and mortal life—that of translation. She felt a surge of power and light electrify every cell of her body. The Savior then commissioned Melody in the work of the final gathering Israel and to receive all the powers and authority associated with this divine calling.

Samuel had never felt so much overwhelming joy as he did in that moment, watching his extraordinary companion receive her promised gifts.
After the sacred words were spoken, Melody turned to Samuel and with a
cry of joy, rushed into his open arms. As he held her, Samuel realized she
had transformed into the expression of her glorious premortal self.

Then the Savior's hand reached out and lovingly turned them toward
Himself again. They looked up at Him in humility and wonder, questioning what more He might desire. Calling them by name, Jesus Christ
spoke these astonishing words:

"My beloved children, I now bind you together, eternally and irrev-
ocably by the Holy Spirit of Promise, and pronounce this blessing upon
you and your posterity." Samuel and Melody clung to each other, and
wept freely as their merciful Redeemer ordained the fullness of priesthood
blessings upon them.

Samuel gazed upon his eternal bride with new eyes, and was astonished to realize he had never truly seen her before this moment.

AND THEY SHALL MAKE WAR AGAINST ZION

The first attack against Zion came one week after the dedication of the Temple. Apparently angered by Zion's refusal to join their nation-state, and the imagined need to control the land upon which the Holy City sat, the Confederate United States, in spite of heavy destructions, gathered an army of thousands just outside the city with heavy weaponry.

There was no warning. Saints were still walking around the Temple rejoicing, when the all-too-familiar scream of an incoming missile rent the air. The computer-guided weapon was targeted upon the great Temple itself. With no warning and no instructions, ten thousand arms came to the square. The shell exploded harmlessly a thousand feet above.

Samuel and Vladimir were the first to see the advancing army. Vladimir had been standing next to Samuel when the shell exploded. The faith-filled Russian turned to his old friend. "Samuel, I could use a lift." So saying, he looped his arm through Samuel's and they started to walk. Except for his beloved wife and Sarah, it was the only time Samuel had taken a mortal with him. It was also the case that he could not transport by the power of God in the view of other people. Yet, there was such an outpouring of pure faith among the people of Zion, that when Samuel turned his mind to the army outside their city, he and Vladimir were instantly standing upon a bluff overlooking a large mechanized army.

"Thank you, my friend," Vladimir said with a smile. "I have been wanting to do that for a very long time," Samuel grinned at him and clapped him good-naturedly on the back. Their faces immediately grew sober as they gazed upon the army. The two men were well within range and bullets began whining past them, kicking up dirt all around. Within a few seconds three other priesthood holders stepped beside them. The approaching army was a dozen miles outside the city, so all who joined them came by the same means. They waited patiently for more to arrive. For some reason, it seemed appropriate to have twelve brethren present before proceeding. Samuel turned around in time to see an old, white-haired man step out of nothingness and stride purposefully toward their group. He immediately recognized him.

"Dad!" Samuel cried out in joy, and leaving his position, ran to meet his father who had stayed in Utah.

After a brief embrace, Jim Mahoy nodded toward the group standing on the rim of the bluff. They joined arms and walked briskly toward them.

"It's fantastic to see you again, Dad! Is this the first time you have traveled by the power of God?" he asked.

Jim nodded. "I guess I took President Andrews's words literally. When the Spirit informed me that I was needed to defend Zion, I started walking that direction as fast as I could, knowing it would take me a month to arrive. I made no preparations, I just started walking as the Spirit directed. I walked only about two blocks and arrived at this bluff with you men facing an army. I presume I have come to Zion?"

"You have!" Samuel exclaimed.

Jim looked stunned, but overjoyed. "Amazing, over 1000 miles in a few blocks! What is the situation here?" he asked, turning his attention to the army arrayed beyond them as they stepped up to the edge.

"We were just waiting for twelve brethren to come," Samuel informed him. "Your arrival makes twelve exactly."

"All right then! Samuel, I'm new at this. Should we destroy them? Who's in charge?" Jim looked out again over the edge. "They have started coming toward us," he said calmly.

"Jesus Christ is in charge," a brother to their right answered, voicing their collective thoughts.

Everyone was silent until a young man in his teens spoke up. "I know you all know a lot more than I do, but I feel we should just send them home," he said without fanfare.

With a collective understanding born of revelation, they all looked at each other, discerning the truth of that inspired statement. Then they unitedly raised their arms to the square. "In the name of Jesus Christ, we command you to return home."

Their words were utterly simple. But what happened next was anything but simple, and in fact, difficult for even the most experienced brethren to understand. It was completely perplexing to the army. They had been advancing steadily toward the bluff, firing as they came. Now they were inexplicably advancing in the opposite direction. In an instant all Samuel could see was the backs of the soldiers. The soldiers blindly continued to fire for a full minute before realizing their former targets had disappeared from their sites.

It took nearly thirty minutes for the soldiers to determine that the bluff, and the few men that were upon it, were behind them. When they finally got turned around and oriented again, they began their advance toward the bluff once more, but instantly found themselves again firing in the wrong direction. Three times they attempted to turn their army around, and three times they found themselves retreating rather than advancing.

At this point they paused as if uncertain what to do. Unable to advance, and fearful to return without even having engaged the enemy, they waited without attempting to move. It soon became apparent to the brethren what the army was waiting for. On the horizon a trail of white appeared, streaking toward them not far above the ground. It had been years since any of the brethren had seen a fighter plane. Yet, there was no question this was what was coming toward them at many times the speed of sound.

"They are determined to defy the will of God, aren't they?" Samuel heard his father say.

"Defiance is a fiery rebellion," someone said from down the line of men.

In exact unison, all twelve arms came to the square. "In the name of Jesus Christ, let the flaming sword of God end the defiance of this enemy of Zion," they said as with one voice, the Spirit dictating the words.

No mortal eyes had ever seen what next occurred. A short distance before them, just beyond the bluff, a wall of fire shot into the sky as the jet screamed toward them. Samuel could see flashes of light as the jet belched rockets and machine gun fire at them. Too late to avoid the wall of fire, the jet attempted to pull up. The plane's roar was nearly deafening as the mighty engines strained to escape the flames. It slammed into the fiery wall and disintegrated in a burst of light, as the entire armament of the plane exploded simultaneously and fell to the ground where the army stood, speechless with fear. The blast was so fierce that it destroyed a dozen vehicles and hundreds of men of the advancing army, yet left the brethren completely unharmed.

Demoralized and disoriented, the soldiers broke into smaller groups and quickly retreated. For nearly an hour the rippling wall of fire continued to reach into the heavens. Every few minutes the retreating troops would look back at it in stark terror. It was nighttime when the last of the troops disappeared into the darkness, never to return. The wall of fire illuminated the land for hundreds of miles. Finally, the brethren turned their faces from the awesome spectacle of their fiery deliverance toward their homes. Instantly the great barrier evaporated. In the ensuing silence they suddenly realized the wall of fire had made a roaring noise not previously noticed. Several brethren observed that the trees and grass that had been directly within the fire were unscorched.

They knelt in a circle and offered profound gratitude to God for their deliverance. As they stood the brethren shook hands, and turned into the darkness. A few steps later they could not be seen.

Samuel, Vladimir and Jim Mahoy were the last to depart. Vladimir took a dozen steps along the ridge to allow some Samuel some privacy with his father, and to wait for his friend to bring him back home.

"Dad, how is Mom?" Samuel asked when they could finally speak.

"Your mother passed away a few weeks ago, Sam," the faithful family patriarch replied soberly.

Samuel gasped, surprised and shocked, and bowed his head in sorrow. He could not have known. Communication between Utah and Zion was limited to the weightiest of matters. "I'm so very, very sorry, Dad," he said finally, his eyes filling with tears. He held his father in a long tearful embrace.

Far to the west, the pillar of fire above the temple continued to lance into the sky, illuminating the ground all around them. Jim looked at his son lovingly, then shook his head, causing his full head of white hair to flash. "She was a righteous and valiant woman, son. But she was ill, and her passing was a great relief to her. There is nothing to mourn. I fully expect to meet her as a resurrected being not many days hence," he said quietly.

Samuel felt the pain of deep grief engulf him, and he missed his precious mother more than he could express. He almost felt cheated, and wished with all his heart that he could have seen her, just spoken with her one last time. His father's words, while hopeful, did not give his son much comfort. "Dad, I know what you're saying, but I really have no concrete feeling about how far off the resurrection might be. It might be years, even decades—who knows?"

He stopped then, realizing he was probably saying something that his grieving father didn't need to hear. "Of course, things in Zion are accelerating quickly," he said more hopefully. "The final scenes are playing out before our very eyes."

Jim turned from his son to look out across the landscape of trees and grass, illuminated entirely by the light from the Temple which was much purer, much whiter than sunlight, and seemed to emphasize every hue beautiful to the eye, bathing the landscape in glowing color. It was an impressive sight. Just standing on the soil of Zion fired his soul.

James Mahoy was eighty-four, and he felt as if his life should have ended long ago but for the pressing need for priesthood holders in Utah. The faithful women of the Church now outnumbered the men nearly ten to one. There was hardly time to get from one crisis to another. He spent all day, every day exercising his faith and his priesthood. He had been ministering in a tent city near Salt Lake City, when his beloved Laura had died. He barely made it home in time for her funeral. How his heart yearned for closure, for a last good-bye, for one more smile from the woman he had loved more than life itself. Without Laura, life did not seem worth living.

Still, it was quite possible he would live until the resurrection, and then what? Would Laura be so different, become so advanced, that she might not want him? Would her resurrected status take her off this earth and onto something else? Must he also await the grave before they could at last be together? He was still in good health, and having been given the power of the priesthood now so markedly manifest, he could reasonably live another twenty years or longer. Twenty years separated from his childhood sweetheart seemed like a prison sentence.

"It is indeed the era long awaited," Jim said with deep emotion, avoiding the subject that seemed more and more upon his mind. "It is an exciting time, a joyful time."

Samuel brushed the tears from his eyes, then spoke with as much energy as he could muster. "Will you come to Zion and live with me and Melody, Dad?" he asked. "You really should see your grandchildren again, and meet your beautiful great-grandchildren. And Dad, the Temple is incredibly magnificent! You've just got to see it from the inside!"

Jim looked kindly at his son. "I would like to, Sam, but I feel compelled to return to Utah. Things are much less settled there. The missionary work is enormous. We don't exclude anyone who comes, so there are many who don't even believe in God, let alone in His restored gospel. Yet, there is great faith among the saints, and marvelous blessings."

Samuel was genuinely disappointed. "Are you sure? We would love for you to be here in Zion with us."

Jim sighed and shook his head. "I would love to be with you, too, Sam. But I have a mission to fulfill that cannot wait." Then he looked at Samuel with a twinkle in his eye. "Besides, I doubt this amazing blessing of traveling by the power of God was meant for sightseeing."

"I suspect that's true," Samuel admitted wryly. "And the work in Utah really does sounds daunting."

"All the work of God is daunting, and all of it is joyous. But at least no one is launching missiles into Utah," Jim said with a tiny smile.

"Why is that? I would have thought Utah would have as many enemies as Zion."

"Not really. The leaders of the nation of New Mexico are very friendly toward us. They see us as the only Americans who cared about them while they were in their poverty. They have actually threatened to attack Texas, or anyone else who molests us," Jim exclaimed.

Samuel was surprised. "That's astonishing!"

"What is astonishing is how the works of God roll forward unhindered." Jim straightened up. "But I must go. I do love you, my son. Do not grieve too much for your mother. The time will pass, and we will all be together again. So, how are Melody and the children?"

"They are all fine. I know they miss you and their grandmother, of course." Samuel reported.

"Of course," Jim said quietly. He put a fatherly arm around Samuel's shoulder. "I am ever and always proud of you, Sam. My precious son—now a servant of the great Jehovah!" His eyes were misty. "You have brought me nothing but joy, you know—all your life." He looked at Samuel with tender eyes, took three steps, then vanished into the night.

Samuel stood for many minutes, his father's sweet words touching his childhood heart, as well as his grown-up one. He silently thanked the Lord for the supernal gift of being a Mahoy.

But, the Prophet said that as one of the 144,000, I should come along as your companion!" Melody proclaimed with undeniable logic. "The Prophet gave me this assignment as well, and I want to go!"

"Melody, I really am excited to be a missionary with you," Sam replied. "You are the Lord's servant, just as I am. But, what about little Helaman?" he asked.

"Helaman will be just fine for a month," Melody assured him. "He adores Sarah, who is the most responsible young woman I know. She can take him to kindergarten and pick him up, and then play with him afterwards. He'll think it's just a big holiday! Besides, with the way travel is these days, we can always pop home for a visit." She stopped and looked at him. "Can't we?" she asked, suddenly unsure.

"I doubt it," Samuel said in complete honesty. "Every mission I've been on for the Lord has pretty much made me stay until it's done."

"Oh," she said. She paused for a long moment, then continued with renewed determination. "Well, then I will just have to learn to get used to it. As your wife, and with this wonderful new gift, I'm committed to doing the Lord's work—whatever that looks like! So let's go get our passports!" she said, then gave him a kiss and hurried into the bedroom to pack.

Samuel laughed softly. "Hey honey, you don't need to pack, you know! The Lord allows us to create anything we need—so no toiletries required!"

She peeked her head out of the bedroom holding her toothbrush, and laughed. "I've got a lot to learn, that's for sure," she said with a grin.

It was late in the evening when Samuel and Melody walked away from the house and their little son, after long hugs and last good-byes. It was many times harder on Sam's tender wife than on himself. There was no doubt in his mind that they would eventually return home, but he did not know exactly when that would be. For Melody, leaving her son even for a few weeks, was much harder than she let on. But no matter the sacrifice or the outcome, she knew that she had personally been called to this mission by God.

When they were about halfway to the Temple and alone on the street, Samuel turned to his beloved companion. "Any thoughts on where we should go?" he asked.

"I just assumed you would decide that," Melody replied with a shaky voice. Her eyes were red. " I have no idea what we are supposed to do."

He reached up and wiped away tears gently with the back of his finger. "This is indeed unusual in that we have no specific assignment from the Brethren. In all such decisions like this it is preferred to make a joint decision with both companions—when we have a companion, that is."

Melody thought about this as she began walking again. About three steps later a look of resolution lit her face. "I know where we should begin," she said, her voice alight with happiness as the Spirit rested upon her.

"Tell me."

"Africa!" she pronounced with a sudden giddy happiness. She had been born in Africa, and the thoughts of returning thrilled her. She still had relatives there she hadn't seen for over twenty years. It had been nearly forty years since Sam himself had been there as a missionary.

"Yes! And more specifically, we are to go to Rhodesia," Samuel said with surety.

"More correctly, Zimbabwe," Melody corrected.

"That's right, they changed the name after the revolution," he said.

Melody sighed with relief. "Okay, I think I'm ready," she said as resolutely as she could.

"Here, take my hand and…"

Melody hesitated, "Wait! What do I do?"

"Just start walking to Africa," Samuel directed. "The three governing principles are first, the commission of God, second, your faith, and third, your destination must be where Jesus Christ wants you to go. Then, pray unto the Father and take a step."

She nodded, and they bowed their heads together. Then, without saying another word, Melody set her face southward and walked with purpose toward Africa. Taking his cue from her, Samuel joyfully strode along with her as they walked side-by-side to a continent on the other side of the globe.

The sky seemed to grow lighter as the road turned to red dirt and the trees became the desert tropical foliage of Africa. Less than a block later they were walking down a row of abandoned homes made of brick and stucco.

"We did it!" Melody cried and turned to give Samuel a big hug.

"Jesus Christ did it, but I must say you did it beautifully. Usually it requires more training."

He held her hand, and they walked in silence for a few minutes, trying to determine where they actually were. "Do you recognize this place?" Samuel asked Melody.

"I don't. None of this looks familiar to me. I know we are in Africa, but exactly where I can't tell," she allowed.

"Wait, what's this?" Samuel said, his attention riveted on something down the road. She quickly saw what he was looking at.

The column of men marching toward them were native Africans. They were waving clubs and machetes over their heads. They had spotted the two missionaries and seemed very excited. They broke into a run toward them.

"Our first teaching opportunity," Melody said with a steady voice.

Samuel was very proud of her for not suggesting they retreat; it spoke of her diamond-hard faith and courage in Christ. "Yeah, even people with clubs need the gospel, perhaps more than any other," he said wryly to her.

The men split and formed a circle around the missionaries, and a few passersby ran in the opposite direction to avoid any involvement. Everyone surrounding them was shouting so that no rational exchange was possible. Clubs and machetes were flashing inches from their bodies. Neither Samuel nor his fearless companion cowered or ducked.

This lack of fear sobered the mob somewhat, and they grew uncertain what to do when their usual methods had not worked. A man with a pistol strapped to his hip stepped forward. Besides being dressed in tattered shirt and knee-length pants, he wore dirty white tennis shoes without laces or socks. But, the most fascinating part of his apparel was the small gold cross hung by a gold chain around his neck. Against his coal-black skin, it shone like the sun.

Samuel stuck out his hand which the leader of the mob grasped reflexively. "We're here to teach you the Gospel," Samuel said with complete confidence. He noticed something miraculous about his own speech; the English coming from his mouth was being changed into a different language. The meaning of every word he spoke was clear to him, yet the sounds were foreign.

The man's grip tightened even as a perplexed look spread across his broad face.

Samuel nodded at his cross. "I see you are a Christian. Do you have any sick who have faith to be healed?"

"How came you to speak the language of my homeland?" the leader asked suspiciously.

"What you hear is the gift of God," Samuel replied. "You are all of different tribes," he said, turning toward the mob. "Which of you hear my words in your native tongue?"

A murmur of acknowledgment came from every man. "Is it possible for a man to speak many languages at the same time? It is only done through the power of God. Now, I ask again, do you have any sick who have faith to be healed? Our time is limited, and we must do our work and pass on," Samuel said without any indication of rudeness. It was simply the case.

The leader surveyed him for a minute before speaking cautiously. "My daughter is sick with a fever, and I fear for her life," he finally said. "Come, she is this way." Though he had said this, he continued to look deeply into Samuel's face for perhaps another ten seconds before turning and striding away. Sam and Melody followed, surrounded by the mob. The men were no longer threatening to kill them for now, but the missionaries knew that this could be a temporary state of affairs.

The group walked nearly a mile to a more prosperous part of town. Samuel was still not sure which city they were in, and chose not to ask. However, during his mission here over forty years ago he had seen the stark disparity between the very rich, and very poor. They were approaching a street lined with large trees, vast lawns and neglected landscaping that had once been beautiful. The homes were actually small mansions. Guards stood before each home. They marched into the gates of the largest home and up a cobblestone drive. There was a jet black Mercedes parked before the front door. The car was covered with dust and looked as if it hadn't been driven in years. Samuel concluded that even the very rich were walking now, as there was no gasoline at any price.

"Stay here," the leader ordered the mob before he took the first of six steps leading to the massive front door. "You," he said, pointing at Samuel, "come with me. The woman stays outside with my men. If you do not heal my daughter, my men will have their games with the white woman. Do you understand?" he threatened menacingly.

"I do. However, you do not," Samuel replied, taking a step closer to the leader and lowering his voice. "We are not here to play games, or to be threatened. Do you love your daughter?" he asked.

"I do," he replied, his eyes narrowing.

"Your action of keeping my wife as a hostage unless God performs to your satisfaction speaks of pitifully weak faith. Do you really expect to be able to threaten God to heal your daughter? Do you expect me, a man of God, to allow you to do this? If you truly desire the power of God in your home, you must quit treating God's servants as enemies. It offends the very God upon whom you are relying to heal your daughter. Now, I ask you. Do *you* understand?"

There was a moment when the man glared at him; then his concern for his daughter became evidently stronger than his pride. His face softened. "Forgive me," he said, his voice a little choked. He looked at Melody and motioned for her to follow. "Welcome to my home."

They entered the large front doors to find themselves standing on thick, dirty white carpeting. The foyer was spacious, and had a beautiful staircase going up one side. Their host followed a brown trail in the carpet to the left and up the stairs. Samuel followed behind Melody. Only one of the guards followed after them.

They climbed past paintings and delicate statuary to the landing. Turning left they walked down a short hall and into a large, sunny bedroom with bright windows and thin white drapes moving gently in a breeze. The canopy bed had a lacy top and curtains drawn and tied near the front. Melody thought it was like stepping back into a scene from "Gone With The Wind." The only deviation from that image was the fact that the room was filled with stench and smoke.

Near the foot of the bed someone had piled sand on the floor and shaped a fire pit. An African witch doctor sat cross-legged before the smoldering fire, chanting spells in an African language. It was interesting to Samuel that he could not understand the words of the witch doctor, even though he was probably speaking the same language as their host. The witch doctor was nearly naked but for a loin cloth that served almost no useful purpose. His skin was smeared with some liquid he was dipping from a copper pot beside the fire. His head was inside a hideous mask made from a crocodile head.

The most revolting aspect of the African shaman was the incredible stench of death that emanated from his body. Samuel had heard that these so-called holy men never bathed. He was also quite sure the dark liquid he was rubbing on his body was blood, probably human. A feeling of evil emanated from the man, who had stopped chanting to fix steely black eyes on them. Even within the mask, Samuel could feel the hatred that seemed to be emanating from him in waves. Melody swallowed hard, but she did not shrink.

The bed was surrounded by five women who were in a state of mourning. Though they had presently stopped, they had been chanting and

mourning when they entered. With a wave of his hand their guide or-
dered the women back. For the first time they got a look at his daughter. She appeared about sixteen. She was naked from head to toe except for a piece of the sheet laid across her hips. Her skin was glistening with sweat. She slowly turned her head when she perceived the white couple in the room, and blinked as if unable to believe what she was seeing. She reached for the sheet, but was not able to grasp it.

Melody let out a cry and pushed past the women surrounding the bed. She grabbed the sheet and yanked it up to cover the young girl's body. Melody placed a hand on her forehead and spoke in soothing tones. "We are God's servants," she said quietly. "My name is Melody, and we have come to heal you. Do you understand?"

"Yes," the girl said through parched lips, then added, "Thank you."

Melody merely nodded.

"Bring me water!" Melody ordered to no one in particular. In a few seconds someone handed her a glass of brown water. Melody looked at it with distaste. "Bring something that isn't polluted!" she ordered, and set the glass on a nightstand. This time the girl's father demanded angrily that everyone do as Melody had asked. A few minutes later they returned with freshly-squeezed orange juice. Melody helped the girl sip. She meekly allowed Melody to administer to her.

Samuel knelt beside her bed near the girl's head. "Are you a Christian?" he asked. She shifted large black eyes to Samuel.

She tried to speak, and had to try again to make a sound. "I am," she said in a whisper.

"I knew you were. Now I have a favor to ask," Samuel said, leaning near her face. "Will you please ask the witch doctor to leave?"

A look of disgust crossed her sweaty features, and in a voice devoid of strength, yet possessed of an iron will, she said, "Father, order the shaman to go, or I will die from loathing."

Her father seemed electrified by this statement, and ordered the witch doctor to leave. It took several minutes for the grumbling old man to gather up his "holy" possessions and leave the house. Someone stomped out the fire, and in a few minutes the breeze cleared the room.

"Now, please ask everyone but your father to go," Samuel said quietly. This was done with equal grumbling.

Samuel turned to her in earnest, a new feeling of love for her coursing through his soul. "My name is Samuel. I am a man of God."

"I'm Makki. I am a daughter of God," the young girl replied earnestly, though barely above a whisper.

"Do you remember the dream?" Samuel asked, unsure of what his words meant, yet certain they were the right ones.

Her large black eyes rolled up into her sockets slowly, then returned just as slowly. "Yes," she replied. "The two white crows sitting on the fence surrounded by black ones," she said feebly.

"You know the crow is the symbol of your people." Samuel replied.

"I have never seen a white crow," she said.

"What happened in the dream?" Melody asked her gently. The girl slowly turned her eyes toward her kind visitor.

"I was next to the white crows. They pecked me very softly on the head, then flew away. I became white, and flew away, but I came back with the others. Then, I pecked the bird next to me, and it turned white and flew away. Sometimes, when I pecked another bird it stayed black," she said softly. "It was very confusing. The ones who stayed black did not fly away." This explanation took several minutes with long pauses to catch her breath.

"We are the white crows," Melody told her softly.

"I know," Makki replied, her eyes filled with conviction.

Samuel placed his hands upon her head. Melody took her sweaty hand, and bowed her head in prayer.

Samuel spoke with authority. "In the name of Jesus Christ, and by virtue of his holy Priesthood, I command this disease to depart, and for you to arise," he pronounced.

Melody pulled the girl to a sitting position. "Makki, do you have the faith to stand up?" Melody encouraged her gently.

The girl's legs slid to the floor. The pasty look immediately left her face, and her skin grew warm in Melody's hand. With her other hand she held the dirty sheets against her chest. A look of joy crossed her features, and she gazed into Melody's face with calm wonder.

"Bring me clothing," she said to her father, who had watched all this with amazement. He hurriedly found her clothing and brought them. Melody held up the sheet as the girl pulled the dirty dress over her head. She stood and looked around the room. "I thought I was going to depart this world."

Her father cried out in joy, "Thank God!" He rushed to his daughter and held her tightly. Then he left the room, and appeared again with fruit and bread. "Here, you eat, my daughter!" he urged her. She gratefully chewed and swallowed a small portion, then turned toward Melody.

"You must tell me what God expects of me," she implored her. "I want to quickly learn these things and teach them to my people. I have the feeling that the time is very short." She looked at Samuel. "Is this not true?"

"It is true."

Makki smiled. "The Prophet sent you, didn't he," she said confidently.

Samuel nodded. "His name is President Andrews. We are working to gather in the faithful before our Savior returns."

Melody put her arm around the girl. "So, you know about our Prophet?" she questioned her. "Have you heard of the Church of Jesus Christ of Latter-day Saints?"

Makki's father stepped forward, his voice strained. "It is true. All my family were baptized into God's true Church years ago. It has been very hard since civil war broke out. I have tried to keep my family safe, but the Church has collapsed here. We have done terrible things. I'm afraid we are not worthy to be gathered," he said with deep sadness.

Melody smiled. "And yet here we are, come to gather you," she said with a happy shrug.

Makki took her father's hand. "My father is a good man. He has done some bad things, yes, but he is still good inside. The evil of these times has been hard."

Samuel placed a hand on her father's shoulder. "I know it is true. What is your name, brother?"

"My name is Mattias Sakka. I am a High Priest, or at least I was once."

Samuel laughed. "You still are. Were you the branch president before the Church collapsed?"

Brother Sakka frowned. "I am ashamed to say that I was the stake president," he replied slowly. "We had wards and a stake here. Many people believed. I did not know how to keep the Church going with so much warfare and bloodshed."

Samuel and Melody suddenly understood. "This is the reason we came to your home first, President Sakka!" Samuel exclaimed. "From this moment you must repent and resume your presidency. End the warfare among your people. Restore everything that you can. Return people's property. Rise up with faith and you will be the means of saving your stake yet."

Sakka's shoulders shook as he hung his head. "My brother, I do want to repent! This is my greatest desire! But can I ever be forgiven?"

Samuel gazed at him with discerning eyes, praying with all his soul for the Lord to confirm what he was about to say. When he received that confirmation, he spoke. "As a servant of the Most High, I declare to you, Brother Sakka, that the Lord will forgive you from this very moment, as you humble yourself before him. Today, at this moment, you can be completely clean through the blood of the Lamb! Repent mightily, my brother, go forward again with unwavering faith in Jesus Christ, and you will receive power to do all things!"

Brother Sakka sank into a chair, praying and weeping for sorrow of his sins. All else in the room was quiet except for the sound of his sobbings, until Makki drew aside to talk with Melody.

"What is your name, my sister?" Makki asked.

"My name is Melody."

"I have a question for you, Sister Melody. I dreamed that all of us will turn white and fly away," she said. "What does this mean, to turn white? Will our skin be white?"

"I believe that this white means purity of the soul," Melody replied.

Makki nodded with understanding, walked back to her weeping father and placed both hands on his bare chest. She gently picked up the cross hanging from his neck. "Father, it is time to stop the war. We must let these white crows peck us. Will you join me, or must I do this alone?"

President Sakka squared his shoulders. "I will go and do as the Lord commands," he said firmly,

Samuel smiled and took Melody's arm. "Very good. We will come back when you are ready," he said. As he and Melody walked downstairs, Samuel turned to his wife. "You have a remarkable gift of charity, my beautiful companion," he said in awe.

They walked out the door and vanished unseen from the street.

The warfare in Zimbabwe had nearly replayed the Nephite tragedy. Outnumbered hundreds to one, the whites in that small nation were systematically hunted down and killed. As the Nephites had done before, they eventually gathered into fortified villages where they could defend themselves as much as possible. Outside Bulawayo their place of refuge was a national park named Matchum Schlopee for the great white rocks scattered about like children's marbles. The rocks were almost perfectly round, some a hundred feet across, most less. The large number of these white boulders made it impossible to attack in a straight line, giving the defenders a considerable advantage. Inside the park a series of lodges and huts had been built years earlier for tourists that were now the inadequate refuge for hundreds of families.

"Hello, the guards!" Samuel called as they approached the first line of boulders. They were alone, and afoot. It was the middle of the day. This was obviously where the defenders had drawn their line of defense because of the obvious signs of savagery everywhere. Melody had to keep her eyes straight forward to keep from being sick. "Hello, the guards!" Samuel called a second time.

"Who goes there?" a voice called back from a short distance.

"We are servants of God, and have come to visit your people!" Samuel called back.

There was a long pause. "Whose side are you on?" the voice called back.

"God's side!" Samuel responded without hesitation.

"I mean, whose bloody side in the war!" the voice returned angrily.

"This is foolishness!" Samuel called back. "We are coming in. Shoot us if you must!" He looked over at Melody, winked, and took her arm as they confidently began to weave their way through the rocks.

"Do you think they'll shoot?" Melody asked with some hesitation.

"Not when they see we are also white, I think."

"You think?" she asked.

"We'll find out shortly," he replied.

Melody shot a glance at him. "I know it doesn't really matter if they shoot us or not," she said, staring nervously up at the menacing rocks above them. "But I have to admit that, even though I know I won't actually die, I do fear the pain of bullets ripping through my body."

Samuel put his arm around her waist, steadying her as they climbed. "My love, let us forget our fears and listen to what the Holy Spirit is saying. Fear is the opposite of faith. We can't have both at the same time."

"I know, and believe me, Sam Mahoy, I have faith! It's just that…"

"Stop where you are!" a man's voice commanded from above them. They both complied. As soon as they had stopped a man stood up atop a bolder to their left. He was aiming a rifle at them. "Go away," he commanded. "If you come another step, I'll shoot you both down!"

"Do you have sick and wounded in camp?" Melody called in reply.

"There are sick and wounded everywhere one looks these days," the man replied disdainfully.

"We have come to help them," she called back.

There was a pause. "Are you doctors?"

"No, servants of God," she replied.

"Got no use for God!" he spit back at them. "He's bloody well left this part of his earth. If you happen to see God, tell him we got no time for 'em! We got no use for you, either, an' we got no food to spare." They heard his gun cock. "I'm going to give you three seconds to turn around or you're both gonna die!"

Melody continued walking toward the narrow passage between the boulders leading into their camp. The guard chambered a round with a loud clunk.

"Stop!" he ordered. Melody continued forward. The man screamed in satanic hatred. "Anybody stupid enough to think they are servants of God needs to die!" From up above her there was a small "click."

"What?" the guard said as he lowered his weapon. He began slapping it to try to make it work.

"Shoot her!" he ordered to someone at his right. Two men stepped into sight atop the boulders. They quickly took aim and pulled their triggers. "Click, click."

"Are you coming, Sam?" Melody asked him without turning toward him. Samuel realized he had stood riveted to his position, fascinated by what was going on. He hurried to catch up. Neither of them said a word to the other as they walked along the single-lane dirt road, but he was thinking about her rebuttal to his instruction about fear and faith. After a minute he had to chuckle to himself. This tremendous faith was vintage Melody Mahoy, but he knew that she was just beginning to comprehend the power to which she had been ordained. Melody looked quizzically at him, but did not ask him why he was smiling.

As they walked past them, Samuel and Melody saw the guards spewing directions into the radio, desperately combing the area to find them. But the men's eyes were blinded, and Sam and Melody calmly walked past them, completely undetected.

The land beyond the boulders was flat, with massive, widely scattered trees. Tall grass and low bushes grew profusely. Before them was a man made lake not more than a hundred yards across and twice that in length. The lake was created by a low concrete dam a short distance away. The water from the lake was flowing over the top of the dam so that no part of the dam was actually visible. It appeared as if the water was going over a waterfall with a very long, straight edge. Because the water atop the dam was only a few inches deep, and moving slowly, it gave anyone walking across the dam the appearance of walking on water. It was a very interesting effect, considering who they were, and how they had gotten to Africa.

The walked across the dam and followed the road to their right. About a hundred feet further it turned left among the trees and brush. A short distance from the lake was a wide clearing surrounded by stone huts with thatched roofs. Several hundred people were going about their business tending to cooking fires and children. There were very few men among them.

Finally, a young woman with a child on her hip noticed them and walked toward them suspiciously.

"Who are you?" she asked, her accent much heavier than Samuel remembered from so many years ago. She almost sounded Australian. But, before they could answer, the same group of men came running into the clearing. In a matter of seconds, the missionaries were surrounded and their hands were quickly tied behind their backs.

"See you soon," Melody said ironically as they roughly dragged her away toward the lake. Samuel was pushed in the same direction by angry hands. He hurried to keep up with Melody who seemed to be receiving the brunt of their anger. A hundred things passed through his mind to say, to explain, accuse, or otherwise interrupt them, but nothing reached his lips. He was left to stumble along trying not to fall each time he was jabbed by the butt of a rifle. Though he felt no pain, he was certain their intent was to bruise or break his ribs.

As they approached the lake Samuel noticed an ominous sign for the first time. It read:

WARNING
MAN EATING CROCODILES
NO FISHING
NO SWIMMING
YOU HAVE BEEN WARNED!

They led Melody beside a small rowboat pulled up on the shore. They paused long enough to pick up a dozen stones and drop them into her pockets.

"Get in," the man whom they had first seen atop the boulder ordered. Then, without waiting for a response, shoved her into the back of the boat. She cried out as she hit her head on the boat's edge. Samuel's protests were answered by several blows to the back of his head. Those guarding him were too busy watching the drama at the lake to wonder why he didn't fall down unconscious from their blows.

"Take her out," the first man ordered. Two others jumped into the boat and in just a few minutes had reached the center of the lake. Samuel watched as a dozen large crocodiles splashed into the lake and swam after the boat. They apparently knew exactly what this meant from previous experience.

"I told you to go back," their leader said as he turned back toward Samuel. His voice was hostile with indignation. Not only did he feel no remorse for what he was about to do, he also felt perfectly justified.

"We came here to help…"

"Shut up!" he screamed.

"If you try to harm my wife, it will damn your soul," Samuel said calmly. For his reward the man slammed the butt of his rifle into his stomach. Samuel was too intent about Melody to remember to double over. He did not even observe the amazed look on his assailant's face.

Samuel watched Melody, who was sitting stiffly in the bow of the boat, facing him. He could plainly see a blue bruise above her right eye. Samuel knew her faith was absolute, as was her power and authority as a translated being. But he could not watch the terrible scene before him. Tears sprang to his eyes, and grief surged through him. He wanted to lash out, to fight them. He had no idea how much resistance he could put up, but knew it would be considerable. Yet, his own will was swallowed up in a greater will. He was not to fight, or even to call comforting words to Melody. He knew that this was Melody's mission, and that no matter how frightened she may be, she would fulfill it with dignity, and would come off conqueror. Samuel silently plead in prayer for his beloved wife.

The man completed his crime with icy hatred. "Throw her in," he ordered. Then turning back to Samuel, added, "Don't worry, you'll be with her in just a few minutes."

Samuel could not take his eyes off of the boat. It was close enough that he could have hit it with a rock. Melody struggled ineffectively for a few seconds before they pushed her out of the boat. She went over the side head-first and hit the water with a big splash. Her thrashing legs hooked the side of the boat. One of the men dived for her leg, but in his haste to throw it into the water, he fell overboard with a cry of surprise and terror.

With her hands tied behind her back and her pockets full of rocks, Melody quickly sank out of sight. The fallen man thrashed about wildly until he caught hold of the side of the boat. The man inside the boat caught his companion's arm just as the first crocodile hit, and he struggled to pull him into the boat. In seconds, the man was carried away, his cries for help a stream of bubbles coming to the surface beside the boat.

Samuel fell to his knees in grief, praying for Melody to be strong. He knew that she was at that moment struggling for breath on the bottom of a lake, and he could do nothing for her, or to allay the fear she was undoubtedly experiencing. Yet, among the many emotions he felt, anger was not one of them. He knew that God would judge them, and this he let carry away what might otherwise have become overwhelming anger.

The survivor in the boat sat looking into the crystal clear water for several minutes before beginning to row back to the dock. Samuel watched the boat slowly return. When it arrived the man stepped out of it and ran into the woods.

"The bloke who died was his brother," the leader told Samuel, his teeth clenched in rage.

"You can't really expect me to feel sorry for the man who just murdered my wife, can you?" Samuel asked in astonishment. In fact, Samuel did feel sorry for the man, but in a way that he could not understand.

"What you feel inside won't be bloody half as bad as what you'll feel on the outside, you blasted fool," his captor hissed, his eyes intense with loathing. "Throw him into the boat," he ordered.

After they loaded his pockets with rocks, Samuel let himself be led into the boat. An argument ensued about who was going to throw him into the lake. Everyone felt as if the lake were now cursed, and loudly refused to do the deed.

Finally, their leader drew his pistol and pointed it at the head of one of his men. "Into the boat," he ordered. The man's face turned red as with lowered head he reluctantly climbed into the boat. Under the threat of death he began slowly rowing toward the middle. When they reached the center of the lake Samuel's back was to the shore. He pondered if he should even resist.

When nothing seemed to be happening, Samuel turned to see a new look of fear on the guard's face. The man's teeth were clenched in stark terror as he stared back at the shore. Samuel turned around in his seat. From underneath the boat dock, a large crocodile was now rising up out of the water, lunging toward the men on the dock. The men were paralyzed with fear, their mouths open in silent screams. Samuel watched their leader aim his pistol at the creature that was coming toward them and fire nine rounds in rapid succession. His hands were shaking so violently that the bullets went whizzing across the water. Samuel wondered why one of them didn't hit the boat. Finally, the leader threw his empty weapon at the crocodile and began running awkwardly backward.

Samuel caught sight of something else moving under the water toward the shore, and his heart leaped.

"Back to the shore!" Samuel ordered. "Row back to the shore!"

"No!" his guard cried, and fumbled with the oars. Samuel easily pulled his hands from his fetters and moved forward in the boat. The man stared at him with huge eyes. Remembering his pistol, the man jerked it from his belt and leveled it at Samuel's head. Samuel swatted at the gun in a movement too swift to actually see. The gun discharged and landed twenty feet from the boat. The guard stared at his bruised hand that had seconds ago held a gun. He began thrashing around trying to get as far away from Samuel as possible.

"Sit still, or you'll fall into the water yourself," Samuel warned him. "We're returning to shore."

"No!" the man cried with insane fear. He then stood, turned and wildly ran off the bow of the boat. His feet were still running when he hit the water. He sank out of sight in a swirl of hungry crocs. Samuel took a seat between the oars, turned the boat quickly, and powered back toward shore with just a few strokes.

Samuel stepped onto the shore just as a moss-covered figure emerged from the lake and stumbled toward him. He caught her in his arms, and began kissing her. Melody's hair was tangled with weeds, and she was muddy from her waist down. She was the most beautiful sight he had ever seen.

"That mud is really thick!" she exclaimed as she drew back from his embrace to catch a breath. "And, it stinks!" she added, wrinkling up her face.

"My brave darling wife!" Samuel cried. "Was it terribly painful?"

Melody shook her head in wonder. "No, it really wasn't," she said, her voice breathless. "Oh yeah, I was scared at first, but then I remembered that the Lord has always kept His promises to me—and suddenly I didn't need air. I didn't need anything."

Samuel's eyes were wet as he gently brushed the mud from her glowing face. "The Lord is so faithful!" he exulted in gratitude.

Melody hugged him tightly. "It's so true! I will never be afraid again!" Her face was shining with absolute faith and trust. "My Redeemer will always deliver me from all sorrow and trouble. Of this I am now certain!"

Then she turned and nodded toward a group of men who had re-grouped from their terror and were coming toward them warily. "Let's do what we came here to do!"

Samuel turned and walked toward them. They stopped, and waited for him to arrive. There were about fifteen of them, including a few women who had come from the village.

"Where is your leader?" Samuel asked when he did not see the man who had ordered their execution.

"He ran away. We don't know where he is," one of the men who had not been involved replied. "And we don't agree with what he did. If he returns, we're going to try him for murder. Even though it appears he was not that successful," he added unsteadily as Melody walked up beside Samuel with squishing steps.

"Who are you?" one of the women asked. It was the same one who had first asked them that question when they had originally stepped into the village.

Samuel answered in her tongue. "We are sent by God to assist you. If you have any sick or injured who have faith in Christ, we will heal them. Then, we need to speak to anyone who is, or was a Mormon."

The woman stared at him. "A Mormon? I was," she replied slowly. "I was baptized when I was eight. Why, are you Mormons?"

"We no longer refer to ourselves that way," Samuel informed her. "The Church's new name will soon be The Church of Jesus Christ of Millennial-day Saints."

"Has the millennium begun?" she asked with both excitement and doubt in her voice.

Melody nodded. "In Zion it has! We are here to conduct all true believers to Zion. Are there any true believers here?" she asked.

"I am," a young man said quietly, and stepped forward from the back.

"So am I," a much older woman with gray hair said, "though, I'm not a member of your church." She stepped through the crowd of people until she was directly before Samuel. Her left arm was suspended by a sling. Her left hand was wrapped in a bloody bandage. She was dressed in a ragged dress that appeared to have been worn for months.

"What happened to your arm?" Melody asked her.

"I fell and broke it during the last attack," she replied, looking down at her arm. "It has since become infected."

"Since you are a true believer, in the name of Jesus Christ, and by the holy Priesthood I hold, I rebuke your injury. Take off your sling," Samuel instructed her.

"But I can't. It doesn't feel any better," the woman replied.

"Just take off your sling," Melody said, repeating Samuel's instruction.

"It is intensely painful to remove it," the old woman said, and turned aside. She walked slowly away, her head bowed. This brought a murmur from those assembled.

"Why couldn't you heal her?" the young man asked. "Can you heal anyone?"

"We cannot," Samuel replied. "But Jesus Christ can. She could still be healed. She just did not have the faith to do as I instructed her. It's easy to believe in Christ. It is often something else to believe Christ when He speaks to you. Through my voice, I gave her the words of Christ that would have healed her. It was her choice to not respond."

"That's bloody convenient," someone started to say, but was cut off by another who cried out as she came forward.

"My name is Eleanor Appleby," she said, offering her hand to Samuel, which he shook. She was so thin she almost looked like a young man, but her grip was strong and confident. "I'm not sick, but my oldest son is. He was shot in the last raid. My father was a righteous man. I have great faith in the priesthood. Won't you come heal him? Before it's too late?" she added urgently.

"I will," Samuel replied, and he and Melody began walking briskly with her toward the village, followed by several dozen people. As they walked Samuel hurried to catch up with Eleanor. "Is it possible that your maiden name was Knight?" he asked her.

"It was!" she replied, shocked. "How…"

"And, your mother's name was Elaine, and your father, Thomas?"

"How did you know *that?*" she asked, bewildered.

"Do you remember sitting on an Elder's lap and twisting his tie as he taught your parents the gospel many years ago? You were about seven years old."

"I do!" she cried and stopped walking to face him. "Are you…"

"Yes, I'm Elder Mahoy! I taught your family over thirty years ago. And my companion there is my wife, Sister Mahoy," he said happily.

Eleanor threw her arms around them both, laughing and crying at the same time. "I just don't believe it!" she said over and over.

She started walking again as she excitedly explained, "I have wanted all my life to meet you again." She turned to Melody, who was smiling behind them. "You can't believe how I was in love with your husband, Sister Mahoy. He was my first crush!"

"You were only seven years old," Samuel reminded her.

"Still, that love has endured all these years. It is such a coincidence that you are here!" she said.

"It's no coincidence at all. We are here to finish what I started over thirty years ago," Samuel told her with a smile.

"I believe you," Eleanor said, slowing her walk as her eyes brimmed with tears. "I only wish my parents were here to see you again.".

"What happened to your parents?"

"They were both killed in the battle near the church."

"I'm sorry. They were faithful in the church after I left?"

"Faithful? My father served as the first bishop of the Bulawayo ward. He died defending the church building. He was a great man," Eleanor said with pride.

"Do you have any brothers or sisters?"

"None. I'm the only one. They just had me. I think I was enough," she said with a laugh.

"And what about you? Do you have a husband?"

Eleanor shook her head. "He was also killed, though not defending the church. He died somewhere out in the bush fighting rebels about two years ago."

"I am so sorry. Was he a good man?"

"He truly was. I loved him very much. He was a member, but since the war broke out, he had very little time for the Church."

"Were you married in the temple?" Melody asked her.

Again Eleanor shook her head. "Sadly, no. The war had already begun before we were married. It made travel impossible."

Melody brightened and took her hand. "Then, we will get you to a temple where you can get his work done for him."

"Oh, he would love that. So would I!" Eleanor exclaimed joyfully. Then her voice lowered. "However, there's no chance that will happen in my lifetime," she said with a sigh.

"There is no such thing as 'chance' in the Lord's plans," Melody stated. This brought a questioning glance from Eleanor. She would have said more, but by this time they had reached the makeshift village. Eleanor conducted them to the second stone hut. As they approached, Samuel could see numerous white chips in the stone where bullets had hit.

The village was much larger inside than expected, with concrete floors and an open roof. It had been constructed by the park service during better times. Eleanor led them into the only bedroom and to a cot against the far wall upon which lay a teenage boy. His face was white and beaded with perspiration.

"His name is Moroni Appleby," she said, as she laid a tender hand on his arm. Melody put her arm around Eleanor as Samuel approached him.

"Moroni," Samuel said to the boy. "We are here to heal you. Do you have faith in Jesus Christ?"

"Yes," he replied weakly.

"Are you willing to do as I say?"

The boy looked at him carefully before he spoke. "Yes," he finally said.

"Take my hand," Samuel instructed. Moroni forced his hand to lift from the mattress with great effort. "In the name of Jesus Christ, and according to your faith, and by virtue of the holy Priesthood I hold, I command you to arise from your bed of affliction," he said quietly, yet with deep conviction.

Samuel straightened, still holding onto Moroni's hand. The young man attempted to raise up on an elbow, and failed. "Get up, Moroni," Samuel instructed quietly. Again he tried, and managed to get as far as one elbow, yet his strength was not sufficient to hold his head up. The sheet slid aside, and Samuel caught a glimpse of the bloody bandage on his side. Moroni's wounds were fatal.

"I'm afraid I don't... have enough... faith," Moroni said apologetically, and began to sink back onto his cot.

"No!" Eleanor cried. "Get up, son. Please, get up. Please have the faith. I beg you..." she wailed, her eyes overflowing with tears. Word quickly passed into the outer room of the failure inside, and was followed by angry words from the crowd.

"I ... can't," he said and was just about to crumple onto the cot when someone pushed past Eleanor and grabbed Moroni's other hand.

"Yes, you can!" a woman beside him cried. Samuel realized with astonishment that it was the woman he had first attempted to heal that day. Her left arm was no longer in a sling. She pulled Moroni to a sitting position on the cot while he cried out in pain. He stared at her with only partially comprehending eyes.

"Listen to me, Moroni," the woman said, kneeling before him while holding onto his arm to keep him from falling back onto the bed. "Look into my eyes and feel my faith in Christ. I tell you these people are from God. God healed me after I had faith to do what Christ wanted me to do to manifest my faith. It requires enough faith to do what may seem impossible. To me, it seemed impossible to take my arm out of the sling. To you, it seems impossible to stand up. But, you *must* do it. If you want to live, Moroni, you must not only *have* faith, but you must *exercise* your faith." With that she released her grip on his arm and stood.

"She is right, Moroni. It doesn't require strength for you to stand, it requires faith," Melody said to him. "If you want to live, then stand. Let your faith do the impossible, not your body."

A look of determination crossed Moroni's ashen face. Almost immediately that look turned to calm, then peace. With a slow, yet steady movement he levered himself to his feet. He turned toward his mother and crossed the distance between them with two steady steps.

"Mother!" he cried, and embraced her. "I'm healed!"

The room filled with cries of joy and happiness. What was quite odd was that the room beyond had emptied of curious onlookers. They were alone for the moment.

The older woman turned to Samuel. "By the way, my name is Elizabeth, but I go by Liza. I'm going to go get the others," she announced. Turning toward Melody she asked, "How long can you stay with us?"

"Only a little while. We must hurry."

Liza turned to Moroni's mother. "Eleanor, you know those from your church. You get them. I'll get the others I know have faith. We'll be back shortly," she said happily, and hurried from the room. Eleanor forced herself from her son and followed Liza out the door.

When everyone had arrived there were eleven people in the room besides Samuel and Melody. A tall man dressed in shabby clothing leaned against the wall, nodding kindly to them as they entered the room, and speaking words of encouragement to each.

After Melody had offered an opening prayer, Samuel stood before them.

"My brothers and sisters. Thank you for coming. We have very little time. I apologize for making this meeting brief. The reason we must hurry is because angry men will return soon. By then their anger will be sufficient that they will try to kill you as well as us. If you do not have enough faith to die for our dear Savior, now is the moment when you should leave. It is entirely your choice, but if you wish to live, you should leave quickly."

Samuel said this with as much force as possible without shouting. He let the silence linger into a full two minutes. Finally, a middle-aged man and his wife stood and left the room, slamming the screen door behind them.

"Now we can begin," Samuel said with relief in his voice. "Everyone here has enough faith to die for the Savior. I am going to tell you in great plainness what you need to know. Everything I tell you is the truth. While I tell you these things you will know they are true by a powerful burning in the bosom. When I am done, we will leave your village and begin our journey to the New Jerusalem in America."

He cleared his throat and began. "First, Jesus Christ is the Savior and Redeemer of this world, and of each person here. That means He can save you, here and now.

"Second, Joseph Smith was a great prophet of God who restored the true and everlasting Gospel of Jesus Christ to the earth in 1830.

"Third, the Church of Jesus Christ of Latter-day Saints is that Church, and is the only true and living Church upon the face of the earth, with all the authorized keys and priesthoods of the Lord.

"Fourth, these Saints of the Church of Jesus Christ have returned to middle America, to build the Temple of the New Jerusalem to await the second coming of Christ.

"Fifth, we have come here to your land to find and gather all the faithful to Zion, the New Jerusalem.

"Sixth, those of you who have not yet been baptized in the Church, will have that opportunity as soon as you arrive in Zion.

"Seventh, only the pure in heart can enter Zion. Therefore, you must examine your hearts, repent and prepare your souls, or you will not be allowed to enter there. It is a holy city, and all who dwell within are holy. Already the enemies of Christ have attacked with their armies and have been turned back by pillars of fire."

"Eighth, in not many days hence Christ will come to His Temple in Zion. We will be there to greet Him, and will walk the streets of Zion by His side. For this reason you can see why only the pure in heart can enter Zion."

"And, lastly—it is time for us to leave here. Our enemies are organizing their attack as we speak. I must ask you each to answer this question. Do you believe all I have told you?"

A chorus of "Yes!" filled the small stone cabin. Samuel waited until the Holy Spirit bore witness that each had spoken truly.

"We will leave by the back door. Melody, will you take the lead?"

"I will," Melody replied with a sure voice. "I would like everyone to find a companion and join arms with him or her. Watch the back of the person in front of you, and don't allow yourself to fall behind, no matter what you might see. Remember how your faith and your willingness to do the impossible healed you? It is the same now."

Melody looped her arm through Liza's. "Ready? OK, here we go," she said, and strode out the door. The tall man in the corner picked up Eleanor's young daughter and seated her upon his shoulders. Eleanor took her healed teenager's arm with joy and determination, while Samuel brought up the rear.

A narrow trail wound from the back of the hut and lead straight to the lake. They passed by an outbuilding, and into the trees.

"They're not here! They've escaped!" they heard a familiar voice cry out.

"They must have gone out the back way!" another voice called. A rifle fired to their right, and again off to their left. As the believers walked quickly along they could hear shouts of anger and curses from both sides and behind them. Ahead of them was the lake. There was no way to escape. They walked along as quickly as possible, their minds fixed upon their faith. Ahead of him Samuel heard a voice begin to sing "Come, come ye Saints, no toil or labor fear, but with joy wend your way…" His own voice joined in that holy anthem that seemed even more appropriate now, in the last few moments of their safety, than it ever had for two hundred years.

"There they are!" voices cried. "The lake will stop them. We've got 'em now! Close in! Don't let any of them past!" they heard. "Don't shoot them! We've got better plans for them!" another yelled in rage.

Seconds later the lake came into view, and Melody continued her unbroken stride. None in their small group faltered, even knowing they could not survive more than a few seconds longer. They knew their destination was in God's hands, and they cared not where it might be.

"Here they come!" a voice cried, and a shout of "Hosanna!" followed. The trees quickly grew greener, and dense. The soil beneath their feet changed from red to brown, and the lake before them became a bubbling fountain, with a majestic Temple behind it.

"Go inform the Brethren," the tall man said to a young lad who was standing open-mouthed on the street facing the Temple. The lad obediently hurried away, and the tall man gently gave Eleanor's daughter back to her mother. Then he began shaking the hands of each newcomer, and rejoicing with them.

"Welcome to Zion," he said with joy as he heartily greeted each dusty traveler. They stood wide-eyed with hearts pounding, gazing at the shining city before them. "Welcome to the New Jerusalem—City of the Living God!" he cried.

Samuel left Eleanor weeping for joy in the care of another translated sister of Zion. Then he approached the tall man, and bowed his head. "Thank you for your service, Lord," he whispered so that no one else could hear.

Then Samuel and Melody joined arms and walked toward home.

"Now, that's what I call missionary work!" Melody exclaimed, her face aglow with joy. She knew from that moment that there was no work sweeter.

It had taken them five days to find and bring their little group to Zion. Theirs was the twenty-third group to return. Amazingly enough, the first group had returned a scant six hours after the first missionaries had departed. All over the world people had been prepared by uncountable legions of angels to answer the call to return to Zion. It was simply their duty to find them.

As Isaiah had prophesied, "And they shall bring Thy sons in their arms, and Thy daughters shall be carried upon their shoulders." Truly the 144,000 in all ways fulfilled the scripture, "Kings shall be thy nursing fathers, and their queens thy nursing mothers." In a way marvelous and unexpected, the prophecy of Isaiah that Israel would "come with speed swiftly: none shall be weary nor stumble among them; none shall slumber nor sleep; neither shall the girdle of their loins be loosed, nor the latchet of their shoes be broken" was being fulfilled before their eyes.

Samuel and Melody left on several more missions in the following year, as did thousands of other missionaries. Each of their experiences in gathering the elect from the four quarters of the earth was similar in power as their first together, and every one as miraculous. Very few of them were without incident, and none were without opposition. In every instance Jesus Christ worked anonymously alongside the missionaries, although most did now know it was Him; and those who did, never discussed it.

And this is not all. Whether they came to Zion or not, or were ready to accept the gospel in its fullness, Jesus did not tire of ministering to all His beloved sons and daughters. He met them in their individual needs, wherever they were, and bestowed whatever light they could assimilate. His faithfulness and infinite love were extended to every soul, in every corner of the earth. All of Zion marveled at the grace the Lord poured upon the earth in preparation for His coming.

During the next year, groups of faithful returned almost hourly to Zion. It required every ounce of energy that the City could summon to keep up with the influx of people. Besides housing and feeding them, there was the absolute necessity of teaching, baptizing, and leading them through the process of being ready to receive temple ordinances. All those not ready yet for the Temple were taught outside the City until they were prepared to commit to and live the Millennial Law.

As busy and demanding as all previous years of life in Babylon had been, it was nothing compared to the intensity of what was occurring in Zion. While in Babylon their labors had produced only fatigue and sorrow, the Zion-dwellers were continually empowered with energy, spiritual strength, and seemingly boundless love.

The Final Harvest was indeed the work of angels, and the most joyous to the soul.

THE LORD WHOM YE SEEK

This marvelous missionary effort continued day and night for exactly three and one-half years. On the very day the last missionary couple returned home to stay, the Temple was finished. All the interior furnishings were completed and installed. All the many veils, including the one before the throne in the Holy of Holies, were hung. Every piece of artwork was finished, every decoration overlaid with pure gold, gems and other precious materials, and every fingerprint lovingly polished away. It was by far the most perfect building ever built on earth. During those glorious years the pillar of fire continued to blaze above the Temple. Its effect was so marvelous upon the people that they ceased to think of the sun in the heavens as their source of life and light. It was Christ who illuminated their souls, their minds, and their land.

One might have thought such a manifestation of God's divine sanction would have discouraged the enemies of Zion from attacking. For whatever perverse logic those of evil intent use, at first had the opposite effect. Almost every month, some new army brought a force either large or small against them. Without exception they were repulsed by the power of God. Eventually, the tales and terror of Zion spread so wide that none dared to approach her for hundreds of miles.

By the time the great missionary work drew to a close there were over a million inhabitants in Zion. Expanding in all directions, outlying cities had been founded, laid out, and built. Without exception, every structure built prior to the millennium was torn down, its materials salvaged and refurbished to build new and perfectly for the Lord. Since there was no need to accumulate wealth, those things that would have otherwise been considered of immense value became commonplace. Once they became commonplace, they became abundant. The lamp posts, park benches, and statues of Zion were cast of pure gold. For a mile in every direction of the Temple, the streets were made of the same material as the spire of the Temple, thus giving the streets the color of gold, and the appearance of fine crystal. With the holy light of the Temple reflecting upon the streets, walking upon it gave the feeling of walking on water, as if one could look into the pavement and see to the center of the earth, or to the edge of eternity.

As peace spread itself across the lands of Zion, gross desolation of war continued its rapine of the earth. Decimated to near extinction, the armies of the world had no difficulty finding weapons with which to fight, for the face of the whole earth was littered and heaped with them. One had only to stoop to find the means of killing another.

The very evening that the last missionary returned home, the pillar of fire suddenly flashed off as if someone in heaven had turned off a celestial switch. It was nighttime when this occurred, and the sudden darkness was seen and felt by all. With one accord the people rushed into the streets to gaze at the darkened spire of the temple. They each fell to their knees and wept for the loss of His great gift. As powerfully as they prayed, nothing penetrated the heavens, and the Holy Spirit refused to lighten their hearts. Tears ran in rivers upon the golden streets of Zion. For three days the darkness continued unabated, and only silence was heard from the heavens. Though the sun rose and lit the world on its normal course, for those in Zion, it was the blackest of nights. The only explanation they could imagine was that their Savior was no longer in Zion. What it meant, or why He had departed was the subject of intense speculation.

As Samuel and Melody were praying together that night, Samuel heard the voice of the Lord in his mind.

"Come to Jerusalem, my son. You are to assist my two Apostles in their mission."

Samuel immediately turned to Melody with tears in his eyes. "I must go, my darling."

Melody threw her arms around his neck. "I know, Sam. The Lord just told me you are needed in Jerusalem!"

The eyes of the world were now fixed upon Israel. Led by Supreme Commander Aleksander Sarkus, the United World Order considered Jerusalem and its vast resources the key to solidifying its control of the world. Surging from the east, Russia and its conquered Islamic states were also determined to destroy Israel, along with the infidels of the west. The long-prophesied stage had been set.

In the land once familiar with the sandaled feet of the Savior, the war over Jerusalem had now reached its climax. Reduced from a thriving city of over one million to a struggling one hundred-thousand, the survivors of Jerusalem clustered behind hastily-constructed barricades, fighting against the tide of certain extinction. They found themselves surrounded by two vast armies of millions of soldiers and armaments. But unbeknownst to their enemies, the besieged people of Jerusalem were suddenly given a glimmer of guarded hope.

Three years prior to that day, hour, and minute, two strangers in business suits had walked into the walled city. Without introduction, without apology or explanation, they had simply taken up residency within the city. Unknown and unnamed, they had said nothing of their mission, but were quietly preparing the people.

It had been months before that the two strangers first began holding meetings among them. In any time prior they would have been arrested and expelled from their synagogues. Yet, without a formal national, state or local government to intervene, they quietly began teaching belief in Jesus Christ as their true Messiah. At first, very few cared; in fact, it seemed refreshing to speak of God instead of war, even though their doctrine seemed to oppose Judaism. After a year there were a thousand or more Jews who had not only heard the two strangers preach, but who hoped against hope that they spoke truly. The strangers baptized no one, and did not offer to. They simply preached in voices of great conviction concerning Jerusalem, and its preservation, or destruction, according to their own belief in this Jesus whom their fathers had long ago crucified.

By the end of the second year, three thousand or more had heard, and hoped. Yet, all who believed their words did not do so with the intent of rendering obedience. Like their fathers who had crucified Jesus, most of those remaining sought the life of those who now came in His name. This was not because they believed the two strangers to be liars cut from dark cloth; it was because they believed them to be exactly whom they claimed to be: messengers sent by the Christians to turn their hearts, claiming to preserve their lives from annihilation.

As the two strangers now observed a barrage of rockets raining down toward the people, they calmly raised their arms to the square. The missiles suddenly veered sharply, screaming away from their targets and returning to their point of origin, exploding in huge fireballs. As waves of tanks and soldiers tried to penetrate the barricades, a wall of heavenly fire came forth as thousands tried to push through it, perishing instantly in the flames. Most did not know where this heavenly help was coming from.

Commander Sarkus was furious that his attacks had failed, and his assaults grew more vicious. Week after week the Jews were pushed back, but unbeknownst to them, were largely preserved by the godly powers of the two strangers. At the very minute the pillar of fire above the Temple in Zion flashed out, with reckless hate the forces of Commander Sarkus launched a final offensive. U.N. snipers cruelly murdered the two strangers, who were Apostles of the Lamb of God. In that hour the hostile forces of the army overran the barricades and thrashed through the streets of Jerusalem in an orgy of slaughter and rapine not seen since the times of Caesar, as the people fled to the back half of the city.

It was the abomination of desolations spoken of by Daniel, and again by Christ himself. The surging armies systematically sought and murdered every living soul they could find. Theirs was not a mission of conquest; it was a demonic orgy of complete annihilation. For three days it seemed there were no devils in hell—they were all roaming the streets of Jerusalem. Stone by stone, the mostly completed temple at Jerusalem was being dismantled by frenzied hands.

Perhaps the greatest irony of the whole conquest of Jerusalem was the presence of many reporters and television cameras. The whole world, now unitedly under the rule of the seductive Commander Sarkus, watched the destruction of the Christian missionaries and the long-hated Jews with satanic rejoicing. They declared holidays and gave gifts to one another in celebration of the death of the two Christians who had so long kept the brave armies of the world at bay. As was prophesied in scripture, Commander Sarkus, the long-foretold Anti-Christ, in gluttonous pride defiled the very steps of the temple in Jerusalem as he entered the holy sanctuary. Laughing and mocking God, he declared himself to be the god of all the earth. He abated destroying the last of the Jews, savoring this moment so they could despair in his ultimate triumph.

Now that the two Christian strangers were dead, the world watched their bodies lie in the bloodied streets of Jerusalem for three days. They gleefully reasoned that now the war could finally at long last end, because the last enemy had been subdued. They were right, but they were also terribly wrong. It would shortly end, but they were wrong about which enemy would finally be subdued.

On the third day, a light broke through the dense cloud cover over Jerusalem. It was the first of April, and a cold rain had fallen all throughout the night. With the largest mass of the Jews having already been killed, the final order to destroy them was now given. The slaughter began at a diabolical pace.

The city exploded into chaos, and the terrified Jews started fleeing with their families westward out of the city. The soldiers pursued them with heavy gunfire into the Kidron Valley, and soon trapped them against the Mount of Olives, where the Jews faced certain annihilation.

In this moment of the Jews' greatest peril, the sun suddenly burned a hole through the rumbling clouds. A shaft of light fell upon the two disheveled bodies lying in the city. No sooner did it touch them than they were instantly resurrected in a burst of light. The remaining soldiers there shielded their eyes as the two glowing men stood upright, looked directly into the TV cameras, and then were taken up into heaven. The last image the cameras captured was the soles of their feet as the dark clouds of early morning closed around them.

No sooner had this occurred than everyone within miles of the city looked up to see the two glorious strangers rising into the sky. Samuel could plainly see the astonishment on their faces as they saw an even brighter burst of light from which their Messiah emerged in glory. The surrounding army also saw the man descending, and turned their mass of weaponry toward Him.

Samuel could not believe his eyes as dozens of rockets streaked into the sky, all to explode harmlessly far below the Savior's feet. The army in pursuit of the refugees on the ground turned their automatic weapons skyward and emptied their magazines into the air. After that they picked up rocks and bricks and threw them at the sky, their faces twisted in demonic fury. They were actually attempting to make war against the returning Messiah!

The Lord began a steep descent rapidly toward them. In breathless wonder they watched as the Lord drew near and finally settle upon the Mount of Olives. At the exact moment His foot touched the ground, a mighty earthquake shook the earth such that all upon it fell to the ground, decimating the impending army. Beneath the Lord a chasm opened, dividing the mount into two jagged halves nearly a quarter mile apart.

The quaking of the earth ceased suddenly, and those near the wall stood only to find themselves immediately under attack again. A hundred men, women and children fell in death every step they took. Seeing the glorious being standing above the opening in the earth beckoning to them, the survivors surged toward Him and into the cavity that had once been the sacred Mount of Olives.

Their numbers were now very few, and dwindling steadily under the ferocious hail of bullets and rockets. When the last of their numbers finally entered into the canyon below them the Lord held out His left hand exactly as He had His right, and the beam of light which burst from His left hand brought unquenchable fire and destruction upon the pursuing

armies. Whereas the light from His right hand had been totally silent, the
flame from His left roared above the threshold of hearing. Samuel had
never heard the sound of devouring fire, but it was horrendous, as if all
the oxygen on the planet were being sucked through a tiny hole.

In utter astonishment, Commander Sarkus fell to the earth, clapping
his hands over his ears in writhing pain, and cursed God as he was being
consumed by divine flame. Moment by moment the purifying fire thundered across the wastes of Jerusalem, devouring everything as it went:
buildings, trees, streets, armies and tanks, rockets, guns, the living and the
dead. Nothing escaped—nothing.

As the fires of retribution rolled outward as if in slow motion, the Lord
descended into the cavity of the Mount until He stood among those few
survivors. Samuel and all those present knew their exact number, and
they were fewer than five thousand. At that moment the words and music
to a new song entered the minds of those accompanying the Savior, and
they lifted their angelic voices in song. In a language unknown, yet so familiar, in voices made perfect by the power of the resurrection, they sang
with one heavenly accord. The music was as vast as eternity, yet simple
and holy. It both overwhelmed and soothed the soul.

The filthy and bloodied Jews remaining looked around them in wonder, taking in the majesty of what their senses were bringing to them.
Then they pressed slowly toward their Messiah who stood in glory before
them. They came forward and fell down upon their faces in prayer and
solemn gratitude and rejoicing. For they knew, at long last, their conquering Messiah had returned. The long wait that had begun the day their
forefathers had departed Egypt was finally over.

An older man, apparently a Jewish leader among them, was the first
to arrive at the Savior after crawling to touch their rescuing Messiah's
feet with a trembling hand. No sooner did his finger touch divinity than
he turned to his people, and in a surge of triumph too grand to be kept
inside he cried out:

"He lives!" The cry was taken up like an anthem chant, and every voice
joined in. This was not a dream—"He is here, He lives!"

As the old one's eyes fell upon the Messiah's feet, a look of confusion
mingled with his expression of joy fell upon him. He straightened upon
his knees, and in boldness asked, "Lord, what are these wounds in Thy
feet?" Then looking up added, "and in Thy hands?"

This question had the immediate effect of arresting the attention of
all present. Everyone turned their faces in wonder toward His hands and
feet.

The living Christ tilted his hands so that His palms were toward their faces. "These," the voice of a thousand rushing rivers said in perfect mildness and love, "are the wounds with which I was wounded in the house of my friends. I am Jesus Christ, whom your fathers crucified."

The people fell back in horror.

"Oh, my Lord, my God!" the old man closest to the Lord cried out in anguish. He fell backwards in horror. "My God, forgive us! Forgive us!" he wailed in abject sorrow so deep it seemed as if his soul might depart his body.

"I forgive you," the same kindly voice replied. "Ye are they who were the most believing of my people. Ye are they who did not persecute those whom I had sent among you." A hush of bewildered reverence swept through the crowd, and they all crumpled to the earth in awe.

Jesus gently reached down and lifted the trembling old man to his feet, enfolding him into His bosom of infinite love. Then He spoke to the others. "Arise. Come forth unto me. Feel the wounds in my hands and my feet, and let me heal you. The long separation of my old covenant people is accomplished. The debt is paid and I am come to cleanse you and make you whole and clean again. Come unto me, ye lost sheep of Israel, and I will gather you as a hen gathers her chicks under her wings. Come unto me ye heavy laden, and I will give you that peace which surpasses the understanding of man. The first shall be last, and the last shall be first."

A cry of joy arose from those kneeling before him, yet their joy was burdened with grief. The tears that streaked their filthy faces were partly for having rejected Him for so many generations, the loss of many loved ones, and the relief of deliverance and joy they felt in their glorious Messiah.

Their Messiah knew their pain, and His own face was burdened for their sorrow. "Fear not," he said, his voice so soft that it entered the heart more forcefully than the ears. "They only sleep, and the time of awakening is at hand."

"Mama!" a small voice cried from the entrance to the canyon. "Mama!"

"Natali?" a mother's voice cried out in wonder too impossible to be hope. Samuel watched a ragged mother press her way through the throng as all eyes watched her. She ran to a tiny figure standing alone and scooped her child into her arms. While she cleansed her baby's face with tears and kisses, she literally ran back toward the Savior.

"See, see Natali! It is the Messiah. He has delivered us! He has raised you up!" she cried in a voice that was almost a shriek of elation.

"I remember him," the little one said, and took three bold steps toward her Lord as soon as her mother set her upon her tiny feet.

"Hello, Natali," the voice of infinite love said in perfect mildness. In answer, little Natali rushed into His open arms with a silvery laugh of childlike innocence.

At that moment a man's voice cried in joyous wonder as he embraced his wife who had fallen from his arms in death mere moments ago. She was whole, and together they walked toward their God. Samuel watched, unable to keep tears of wonder, joy and sweet emotion from his eyes as every individual there received the loved ones who had just died in the final assault as the Lord descended to deliver them. Their deliverance was complete, perfect, and immaculately joyful. Samuel had never seen such a tender scene. Then, something happened that was miraculous and healing. Many accompanying the Lord felt His silent invitation to go forth among these struggling souls.

Samuel stepped forward and watched as one of the translated sisters with whom he worked, lifted a corner of her sleeve and gently wipe the face of a teenage girl. The grime of years as well as scars, scabs and bruises of body and soul became clean in a single stroke. She bent forward and dried the girl's tears with her kisses.

Then another angel put her arms around a gray-haired man's shoulders, and when he looked up slowly, she kissed him on the cheek. She joined him in prayer and spoke words of love and consolation.

Samuel lifted a child, all alone and stricken with grief into his lap, and the words of love and healing flowed freely from heart to heart. All this and a thousand other ministrations were done while the Savior walked slowly through the people, blessing, healing, comforting and fulfilling promises made seven millennia earlier. It was a scene of infinite tenderness beyond human understanding.

A cry of joy and praise flowed over those angels standing above this sweet scene, and they burst into song. Long and worshipful, it flowed out across those below. Samuel had never heard such spontaneous purity. For a long time they sang in complete, perfect worship.

Their long-promised Messiah then said to His people, "Lead me to My house that I may cleanse and sanctify it unto the Most High God."

The people shouted with joy, and surged around Him as he walked in the midst of them toward the temple. As they entered the Kidron valley, many graves were opened and scores of the righteous of ages past arose to join the heavenly throng. As they neared the walls of Jerusalem, their Messiah raised His left hand toward the sealed-over Golden Gate and the surrounding bricks turned to dust to form an arched opening. As they entered the holy sanctuary He turned with tears in His eyes, purified and ordained them saying, "The time has fully come that the sons of Levi may offer again an offering unto the Lord in righteousness."

Suddenly, a stream of living water burst forth from under the temple into the valleys below. The water danced and sparkled as it healed everything it touched.

Then, almost as suddenly as it had begun, it was over. Every tear was dried, every pain healed, and every wound closed. With one single accord, Samuel and all with him rose with the Savior into the air, as 5,000 now-glowing Jewish faces strained to catch one last glimpse of their Messiah. Then Christ and His company were gone.

In as little time as it took to ponder what had occurred, Sam found himself with Jehovah coming toward the familiar vistas of Zion, and the Holy Temple of the Most High God.

It was still dark in Zion, and all around the Temple the people of God had kept a constant vigil upon their knees. Melody, her family, and a multitude of the pure in heart had spent many days in fasting and prayer, camping on the Temple grounds, and pleading with the Lord to restore the Temple light. The first hint of morning had begun to show in the Eastern sky when Melody suddenly arose to her feet.

"He's coming," she said as if to herself.

"Who's coming, Melody?" Sarah asked, perplexed.

Melody could not find other words to describe the magnificent feeling that had suddenly burst upon her. "He's coming!" she said more forcefully. Turning to others kneeling nearby on the grounds she repeated, "He's coming to His Temple!"

"Who?" a hundred voices asked her, yet her heart was so filled with rapture that she could not answer. She could only point into the eastern sky at a pinprick of light and exclaim, "Him!"

Every eye turned toward the dot of light moving toward them with perceptible speed.

"It's another missile!" someone proclaimed. "Gather the brethren, quickly!"

"No, it's Him. It's Christ! He's coming to His Temple!" Melody cried with fervency.

Friendly hands patted her back, and a few tried to gently restrain her. Someone mumbled something about Melody being old and weary. She hardly felt their touch as she began jumping from one foot to another.

"Hallelujah!" she cried. "Praise be to God! He comes!"

Then they saw the light. "It's another missile! We are under attack! Let's call upon the power of God to defend us!" some cried.

From other places around them they heard, "Wait, I can see someone in the light!"

Melody's eyes were fixed upon the light as it rapidly approached. In her mind, she could plainly see the personage standing in the light. Her heart soared to the highest joy at the sight.

"Hallelujah!" she cried over and over.

Others began to see. "It *is* He!" they cried. "Look into the light. See! It is the Christ! He is coming to Zion! He is coming to the Temple!" The people cried together, "Hallelujah! Praise be to God!"

By now every eye could see the face of Christ. Though He was in reality still far away, His face and form were plainly visible. His robe was white like the pillar of fire that had once arisen from the Temple. He wore a red sash about His waist which hung to His bare feet. His face was solemn, yet compassionate and infinitely beautiful. He looked at them all, and smiled.

A mere moment later Jehovah was above them, standing in the air just below the clouds. Behind Him were angels and glorified beings in the attitude of rejoicing and praising their God. This was the long-foretold prophecy: Christ was coming to His Temple in the New Jerusalem!

Jesus looked down upon those assembled around the Temple. His countenance softened as he saw them, and His smile warmed every soul. As His hallowed foot touched the first step of the outermost building, the entire structure began to glow. He stepped through the great doors, and an instant later the pillar of fire lanced again from the Temple spire into the heavens. The light from this glorious pillar re-illuminated the landscape for hundreds of miles in every direction.

The Lord was in His temple, never to depart again! The skies rolled back together from opposite horizons, as if a scroll was being rolled into itself, and blue sky and billowing clouds once again drifted above them. The multitude of angels descended, and combined with all present in a spontaneous shout of exaltation:

"Hurrah for Israel, Hurrah for Israel!"

Samuel was walking among the Temple crowd, searching for Melody and his family among the thousands of rejoicing worshippers, when he felt two little arms clasp him tightly around the legs. "Daddy!" his little son Helaman shouted with boyish happiness. Samuel laughed and tossed his son high into the air, while Helaman giggled with delight.

Melody threw her arms around her husband, and affectionately kissed him. "Hey, stranger! I'm thrilled you're finally back! Oh darling, you could not have chosen to come back on a more glorious day!" Samuel's eyes flooded with tears as he held his beloved wife once again, and felt her glorious spirit communicating with his. Their souls were now both complete, whole, and one. They embraced tenderly and long, yearning to never be separated again.

Then Samuel saw the face of someone he had not seen in many years.

"Mother!" he cried as his long-deceased mother stepped forward from the crowd to greet him. He fell into her arms and felt the familiar warmth of her motherly touch. To his eyes she appeared exactly as he remembered her in his childhood—a beautiful young woman in her mid-twenties. He heard Melody laughing to his right, and turned in time to see her clasped in the arms of her own mother, whom she had not seen since her youngest childhood. He knew that Melody had dreamed of this moment all her life.

"Sam," a silvery voice said behind him, and he spun around to find himself face-to-face with someone most dear to him.

"Dawn! Oh Princess!" he cried, new tears springing to his eyes, his voice caught in his throat. She embraced him in joy, repeatedly speaking his name.

"Dawn! Is it really you?" Samuel cried again.

"Oh Sam, I have longed to see you these many years!" she cried. Then unexpectedly, she asked, "Where's Melody?"

For the first time Samuel pondered the improbability of this very situation. Did he love two women? And yet, Melody was the love of his life! At that moment of confusion and hesitancy, he saw Melody moving quickly toward them, her eyes not upon Samuel.

"Dawn!" she cried. "I... I think I remember you! We have been friends for eons of time, haven't we?"

"Yes, Melody! And I still adore you, my friend!" Dawn cried, tenderly embracing her.

"What?" Samuel exclaimed, his mind reeling happily. The odd thing is that even though he didn't remember many of the details, he knew they were right.

Then Dawn turned as a young man approached. She took his arm, beaming at everyone around her. "Sam and Melody, I want you to meet Nathan."

Samuel reached to shake the young man's hand, and a distant pre-mortal memory crystallized in his mind. He started to understand for the first time why Dawn had come into his life and then departed so quickly.

Melody hugged them both, and spoke excitedly. "Don't you remember, Samuel? Before we came to earth, Dawn and Nathan were our dear friends. They had consecrated themselves as eternal companions, and actually gave us the courage to do the same. When we found out that Nathan was required to be born long before Dawn, we wanted to help them. Dawn needed to have the ordinances, and she desired the opportunity to bear children. You and I offered to delay our love to give them those gifts. Father and Mother granted us permission to do so."

Dawn and Nathan nodded happily. "That's right," Dawn said, looking at Nathan with shining eyes.

"You remember all this?" Sam asked Melody incredulously.

"It is an isolated memory with me," Melody assured him. "But what I do remember is bright and pure! The Lord had promised Dawn that He would give you to be her husband on earth who would love and care for her until Nathan and she could be reunited."

"Yes, and I will always be eternally grateful to you, Samuel," Nathan added earnestly.

At that moment, Samuel knew that he had always loved Dawn deeply, but had never planned on spending eternity as her companion. He felt a rush of tremendous peace enter his soul. This was right! This was the only way that eternity could be perfect. He felt Melody slip to his side, and the four friends gathered in a simultaneous embrace.

Then Samuel felt someone approach, and looked up as a familiar young woman ran to Melody, smiling and laughing as she reached to embrace her. He knew immediately this was the precious daughter they had lost so many years before.

"Mother!" Star said with such overwhelming love in her voice that Samuel's heart felt as if it might jump from his chest. He took a step forward, and Star flashed him a brilliant smile. Then she turned back to Melody. "Mother, I have awaited this moment for a long eternity. I love you!" she cried, and after looking at Samuel with loving eyes, she reached out both hands and laid them lightly on her mother's arms. In the blink of an eye she changed, grew smaller and closer to Melody. Samuel could not see exactly what took place, except that a moment later Melody turned toward him, her face alight with joy. She held up a tiny baby girl in her arms.

"Oh, Star, my precious baby girl! I have missed you so long and so terribly! Welcome at last to my arms, my child," Melody cooed softly as she brushed the baby's cheek with her finger and kissed her.

From that day on Zion was different, both in reality, and in the minds of its inhabitants. All knew that Christ was now an inhabitant of Zion. And all knew that the days had come when Christ would finally walk the streets of Zion and greet them with loving words and an embrace.

Zion was at long last, in name and in fact, the City of the Living God. A wondrous thing occurred from that day onward: it became at first gloriously unique, and then commonplace to see Christ walking slowly along the streets of Zion.

One may ponder what such a thing as living with the Lord might be like, yet never in a lifetime really imagine it. For when He now walked among His Zion people, Christ chose to come without His glory. He came as a man, a friend, a loving brother who laid aside His vast and incredible glory to personally minister to His people, answer their fears, and dry their tears. Every part of His being among them was unexpected, and wholly delightful. He called each person by his or her first name, expressing His individual love for them. He invariably thanked them for services rendered in His name. Though with one accord the people fell at His feet to worship Him, feeling completely unworthy, He often raised them up, and asked them to wait until He was in His Glory for such adoration. For now, in this setting, He was a friend among them, not above them.

Almost without exception, each who met Him initially called Him "Jesus." The Lord kindly informed them that "Jesus" was not actually His given name. His mother had called Him "Yeshua"—commonly known as Joshua in English. He informed them that among His friends, He preferred to be called His given name.

No matter who they were, everyone who met Yeshua instantly recognized who He was. Some ran to Him, others lowered their eyes in regret for past deeds long ago abandoned. To these particularly He came, lifting them up, blessing them, filling them with love such as they had never before known. The diseases He healed were now those of the soul, rather than of life or limb. There were none sick in Zion, for illness had long ago been vanquished. But there was sickness and impurity of the soul which had nothing to do with unworthiness, or sins unrepented. The debilitating diseases the living Christ healed were remaining emotional scar tissue upon the soul. With a touch of His hand and a gentle word, He healed them all. None could doubt their worth after experiencing His incalcula- ble love for them—no one.

As intently as they desired to again greet the Lord, Samuel and Melody were in a unique situation wherein they had already been in Christ's presence, and had heard the words of life spoken to them from the Savior's lips. There were many from all nations who had just been gathered into Zion, and who had great need for the healing and gifts of grace that only He could give them. So they did not openly seek opportunity to be with him.

At dusk one evening, Samuel was walking with Melody and little Star when his whole being told him the Master was near. Melody felt it too, took his hand and together they ran toward the lush garden before the Temple. There they saw Him withholding His glory, standing near the edge of a fountain, and holding a young man in His arms. Nearly a dozen small children stood around him, their eyes so fixed upon His face that the young man was nearly unseen by them. Beyond the children stood a small semicircle of adults in various postures of adoration and worship. It was a scene of supernal tenderness and glorious peace.

Samuel and Melody walked quietly to the outer ring of people and watched. Melody held up Star to see Him, who waved her chubby little arms and cooed with delight. Samuel glanced at his wife and saw her face streaked with tears. When he looked back at the Savior, the young man had stepped away. As if time stopped at that moment, the Lord looked directly at Samuel and smiled. In an effortless movement the Savior stood and smoothly walked toward them.

Even though Samuel remembered with vivid detail his glorious previous encounters with the Lord, he would never tire of those piercing eyes that seemed to contain all of eternity in their supernal blue. The people parted as Yeshua came, and He excused Himself with kind politeness as He passed. Many reached out to touch Him as He went by. Samuel felt Melody wrap her arm tightly through his and press her body against him.

"Hello, Samuel!" Yeshua called, still a step away. He extended both arms, and Samuel fell into His embrace. Every sense, every sensation, every emotion was even more poignant than he had recalled. The joy that flooded through him seemed to cause his soul to melt. "I am so grateful," the Savior said as he released Samuel, "for all you have done in my name. You have served me well, my son. Thank you."

"Master, it is I who owe to you all thanks, and honor, and glory!" Samuel replied, as if the burden of his joy could be entirely summed up by these few words.

"You are most welcome," the Lord replied genially, a gentle smile upon His face. The words "Knowest thou the condescension of God?" came strongly into Samuel's mind. His soul cried out with perfect understanding. Here was the mighty Jehovah, the Creator of heaven and earth, the Firstborn of the Father, the Savior of mankind, preeminent and most glorious of all Father's children, standing without His glory upon a city street thanking *him*—think of it—thanking *him* for all *he* had done!

With this, Yeshua turned to Melody, who transferred Star to her father's arms.

"My beloved Melody, it is so good to be with you again. You have labored in love as my servant and my friend. You have done all I asked of you—and more. Thank you," Yeshua said earnestly.

Melody fell to her knees. "Oh my dearest Lord! You do not owe me thanks. Anything good I might have done was only through your kind grace and empowerment. It is you who are righteous, Lord—-not me."

Yeshua smiled broadly at her. "You have been obedient to my voice, my daughter. You fully consecrated your life to me and to the Father. This is our greatest joy."

Then He turned to the child in Samuel's arms. "And I see you have your little one again."

Melody smiled radiantly at Samuel as she lifted Star from him and in a single motion, turned and gently pressed the child into the Savior's arms.

"Star! Dear Star!" Yeshua laughed, holding the child first at arm's length, then folding her little body into His bosom. Star giggled happily, her hands reaching for his face. He lowered his face to let her little fingers explore His beard and cheeks. He laughed again and kissed her; then raising His eyes to heaven, He said something most startling. "Father, I thank you for this little one whom you have given unto me. I pray you to bless her, and release her tongue that her parents may hear their baby's joy."

"Hosanna!" Star's little voice cried out. "Hosanna to God, and the Lamb!" she cried. All who stood nearby pressed around to hear this infant whose voice spoke articulately of her adoration for her Savior. Yet, nothing more then came from her voice except the laughing and cooing sounds of her infancy.

At that moment it seemed appropriate to take their child back, and Melody gently received her from Him. As if in explanation, Yeshua said, "Her glorious spirit within her cried out with such joy that the Father wished us to hear. It was a wonderful blessing. Praise be to thee, Father!" He exclaimed happily.

Yeshua then turned back to those surrounding Him, and waved a fond farewell. Their time with the Lord today was now finished, since there could be nothing of greater impact than what had just taken place. So the Zion-dwellers obediently dispersed, often turning backwards that their eyes might linger upon their Savior for as long as possible. Slowly, ever so slowly, they walked homeward. Yet, as they neared their abode, it felt to them as if each step had taken them farther away from Home.

FULL CIRCLE

The next evening Dawn came to visit Samuel and Melody. She explained that she had requested this special visit, which had been graciously granted by Father. As she entered their home, Dawn brought with her a spirit of sweet peace and purest love. The three of them spent the evening happily speaking of their former mortal lives, their eternal connection, and rejoicing in Melody and Samuel's beautiful experience with the Savior the day before.

As they spoke of eternal things, Samuel was startled by the advanced truths that Dawn knew and shared with them. Now a resurrected being, she understood mysteries he had never imagined. Her life beyond the grave had given her a thirty-year head start wherein she had absorbed knowledge of the things of God beyond Samuel and Melody's comprehension. Dawn was very careful about what she told them for no other reason than some things could not be explained, but had to be seen, felt and experienced to be understood. Even so, the thoughts she shared with Samuel and Melody were mind-boggling.

The three were still talking excitedly when the sun edged above the horizon of a new day, and Star began to cry for breakfast. Melody stood and stretched, although not a bit tired as she started down the hall to get the baby.

"Melody," Dawn urged, "stay here and let me get Star."

Melody laughed. "No need, my friend. I'll be right back," she assured her. She returned in a minute.

"Here's my little sweetie," Melody said happily as she walked back into the living room. Melody wore a thick white bathrobe, and Samuel marveled at how beautiful she was. Her hair was a vibrant auburn, her face clear and youthful, and her eyes bright. Melody's spirit radiated from her body in a nearly-tangible halo all around her.

She sat beside Samuel and discreetly began nursing Star. She was beaming with happiness and motherly contentment. After a few minutes she called for Sarah, who bounced down the stairs to retrieve Star while the three friends took a walk in the fresh morning air of Zion.

Samuel, Melody and Dawn walked from the house and out into the pale light. The sky was a panorama of pinks and golds spangled across a canvas of rich blue. The streets of crystalline gold glittered richly in the warm light. All around birds were taking up their morning song like a choir of angels singing their prayers. Samuel felt completely, permanently at peace. His heart beat with joy.

"What does it feel like to be a resurrected being?" Samuel finally asked Dawn as they walked slowly down the golden street toward the Temple. It was an odd question, but one that had occurred to him with considerable force. Never before in his life had he been in a position to ask such a question, and the framing of it in his heart sent a thrill of wonder through him.

"It feels like nothing I ever imagined," Dawn replied. "One thing I didn't realize when I was mortal was that the human body is always in pain! You know—a leg hurts, your finger hurts, your tummy hurts, headaches, backaches, side aches, cramps, sprains, cuts, burns. The body is designed to be in continual pain. The first big difference I noticed was the total absence of pain, and yet I still have a physical body."

"I've noticed a lack of pain, too, since being translated," Melody told her. "But I'm told being translated is considerably less powerful than resurrection."

"In many ways, I envy you both, and your mission!" Dawn admitted. "But do you want to see something amazing?" she asked.

"Yes," they both cried.

"It's this," Dawn said, and turned toward them. Stepping closely, she held out a hand between them. She looked in both directions up and down the street, as if concerned that someone might be watching. Satisfied they were alone, she looked back at her hand. It quickly changed to a whiteness rivaling the pillar of fire over the Temple.

Samuel and Melody were astounded. "Wow!" Samuel said in childlike amazement.

Dawn lowered her hand as it quickly changed back to the color of normal flesh. "It's actually an effort to keep it from showing. I have to continually be aware to keep it inside. To be honest, if it were possible to feel discomfort in such a perfect body, I would have to say that keeping the light inside is uncomfortable. I feel like I need to go to some private place and just let myself shine for a while."

"I would like to see that. I can't imagine anything more beautiful!" Melody allowed.

"I can't show my glory on this earth," Dawn said softly. "I don't belong here anymore."

"What do you mean?" Samuel asked.

Dawn sighed and turned to walk again. "It's difficult for me to remain here. I'm no longer a mortal, and must go where people like myself go. But before I do, Nathan and I must wait for our sealing, as soon as we can arrange for two mortals to do it."

Samuel looked startled. "You mean, mortals still have to do the temple work for you? I hadn't expected that."

She sighed, then laughed. "Me either, actually. The temple belongs to the mortal world, and to mortal ordinances. I already have my sealing ordinance in place, so my sealing will be transferred to Nathan and me as soon as his ordinances are completed. When we get sealed, we will stand by as mortals perform these sacred ordinances in our behalf."

Dawn stopped to look intently at them. "Nathan and I were hoping you two would do this for us," she asked quietly.

Samuel looked at Melody, and they both nodded.

"Yes, of course!" Melody told her with a grin.

"We would be pleased to do that," Samuel responded happily. "I'll make the arrangements immediately."

Dawn seemed relieved. "Nathan and I have waited thousands of years to be together. Thank you so much," she said with tears in her eyes.

"We are honored," Samuel replied.

Dawn shook her head. "I didn't mean just for the temple work. I meant," she paused to glance shyly at Samuel, "I meant, for taking care of me during my lifetime, and for loving me through everything, and not giving up on me. Even though I know you could have."

Samuel stopped walking to consider his words, while Dawn waited patiently. "It was my honor to love you, and I always did. But shortly before you passed away, there was some part of me that knew our life together was by design a temporary arrangement." He looked at Melody, who gave him an encouraging nod. "After I married Melody, I understood that even more fully. Somewhere deep in my soul, I knew we each had another assignment that would bring us even greater joy."

Samuel regarded Dawn with deep gratitude. "I will always love you, too, and remain grateful for our life together."

Dawn nodded and smiled brightly. "Me too, Sam. I feel so grateful to you, and to God!"

"Isn't it crazy?" Samuel replied in earnest. "I don't understand all the reasons that God allows us to go through what we do on earth, and why everything doesn't turn out as we thought it would—but I do praise Him for every experience! I would not have wanted my life to be anything different than what it was—or what it is now."

Melody giggled. "Well, you two, I can honestly say that I would never change a thing in my life, either—as crazy and convoluted as it was at times!" she grinned.

Sam remembered something. "Oh yes, and I never got to thank you for the gift of the diamond that enabled us to bring Alexei's people to Zion!" he exclaimed. "That came just at the right time!"

"It was my fun surprise for you! Little did I know how you would really use it," Dawn laughed.

They walked along in quiet contemplation when Melody suddenly asked, "Dawn, I have a feeling that we have loved one another long before this life. I wonder how long we have actually known each other?"

Dawn shrugged. "I have not yet been given a full memory of the pre-mortal world, either, but I do know it is longer than Sam and I have known one another."

Samuel shook his head, bewildered. "That seems very odd, and very wonderful," he said. "I wonder what forces brought the three of us together?"

"It was love," Dawn told them in a voice colored with wonder. "It was a love so strong that we were willing to make any sacrifice to ensure each other's eternal happiness."

"I believe that," he agreed. "I'm not sure why, but I know it is the truth."

"It will be fun to remember all those things one day," Melody nodded.

The three friends had arrived at the exquisitely-crafted Temple grounds and sat together on a park bench under a sprawling tree, their backs against the outer wall of the Temple. They talked deeply about their profound blessings, the challenges they had faced, and the glorious events that had brought them to this very moment in time.

Then Dawn took Samuel's hand, and said, "My friends, I must go soon. But before I do there is something else of my experience in the world of spirits that I think you might enjoy knowing."

"Please tell us!" Melody urged her.

Dawn drew an excited breath and began. "I received instruction in things you cannot even imagine. I was taught the order of the Gospel as it applies to eternity. See, we have only known the Gospel as it applies to this dispensation, and to this telestial world. The Gospel is actually eternal in its scope, and infinitely vast in the possibilities it affords us!" she said, grasping his hand more tightly.

"The gospel, or the grace and law of Christ, gives us the power to step into any realm or thought process; mere thought becomes reality. Do you understand that? This is the reason that obedience has always been the key to every blessing. We have to learn obedience to God's law, because the time will come that if we were not pure and flawlessly obedient to divine law, we could obliterate portions of existence by our unworthy thoughts."

Sam stared at her. "Wow, I have never contemplated that!" he exclaimed.

"Consider this," she continued. "The time will come when to merely think a thing will be to create it. To desire will be to immediately receive, and to wonder will be to immediately know. I have experienced this in part, and it's so staggering that I can hardly describe the phenomenon."

She took a deep breath, trying to convey her thoughts in a way they could understand. "You see, we have always known that Father lives in a dimension where time does not exist. I was once given the privilege of experiencing that dimension, in a limited way. When a being is in that realm, *all* things are present—you literally see all things at once! I could see yesterday, or a million years ago as easily as I could see my present moment."

Samuel nodded his head, not fully comprehending, only knowing what he had experienced as a translated being. He and Melody nodded for her to go on.

"But here's more truth: Not only do you see, but you comprehend and understand all things frontwards and backwards—infinitely," she exclaimed. "Father is all-powerful because He loves infinitely and knows everything that can be known. He is all-knowing because everything is quite literally before His eyes. He is all-powerful because He understands what he sees, down to the most minute detail. He comprehends, obeys, and lives in accordance with every eternal law."

She smiled at them, perceiving their thoughts. "And yet, because of His infinite capacity, He is able to give his complete focus to every child and every one of his creations at the same time. The human mind cannot understand this, but for God, it is actually very simple for Him to govern His vast domain."

Samuel was hanging onto every word. "Dawn, that is exciting, and most comforting to me," he said. "It's funny—and I've never told anyone this—but I always secretly thought that with the universe that God has to maintain, with children as numerous as the sands of the seashore, and with everything that is required of Him, I thought that perhaps His life could get far too complicated—even for Him!"

Dawn smiled at his confession. "Oh Sam, you are so endearing!" she said warmly, winking at Melody. "God's life the most wonderful existence in the universe. Rest assured on that!"

Sam nodded. "Thank you, Dawn," he said quietly.

She continued, her eyes glowing. "But this is the real truth above all truths," she continued. "God is God not because of His vast power or knowledge, but because of His never-ending, all-encompassing Love. He is God because His love caused Him to take that infinite power and understanding, and turn it into a means of salvation for every one of His children, and for each of His creations. It is this incomprehensible love that is the very substance of our Heavenly Father and Heavenly Mother, and of their Son, Jesus Christ. It is this love that drenches all Their creations—from the greatest to the least. It is this infinite love that makes God, God."

Dawn grew silent as she perceived that, though incomplete, she had said as much as she was able. She stood and turned to face the center spire of the temple as it glowed softly above them. Samuel and Melody stood also.

"By the way, do you know what the pillar of fire is for?" Dawn asked, breaking a long silence between them.

Sam shook his head. "You know, I hadn't really thought there might be an actual purpose to it other than to testify of the glory of God."

"One thing I have learned is that besides being symbolic, everything has a purpose. Nothing is incidental or casual. The pillar of fire is somewhat like an elevator shaft," Dawn told them.

"Really? How is that?" Melody asked.

"All things operate by application of some law. This pillar is an implementation of an eternal law, too. In a symbolic sense it represents the presence of Christ upon the earth. But in an actual sense, it is a physical means by which we come and go upon the earth. It is one of the ways that the heavens and the earth are joined."

Dawn stopped speaking, and they each remained silent for a long time. Then Samuel spoke. "So, is this where we say goodbye?" he asked.

"Only for a short time."

Melody turned to go, then whirled around suddenly. "Sam Mahoy, why don't you play the piano anymore?"

"Probably because I have been way too busy hanging out in Jerusalem," he replied with a chuckle.

Melody burst out laughing, and Dawn smiled, but continued firmly. "Let me make you a promise then. I will return to hear the next song you write," she said. "Is it a deal?"

Sam smiled at her. "Deal." He took Melody's arm and they turned toward the door.

"Please give Nathan our love," Melody called back to her.

"I will! Farewell," Dawn said fondly. She regally walked through the ornate Temple doors and toward the fiery spire which would bring her home.

Then she was gone.

Samuel and Melody strolled together toward the gate of the temple. Then Melody turned and kissed him lightly on the cheek.

"What a wonderful morning this has been! Dawn is a beautiful friend," she told him sincerely. She pulled her jacket around her. "I'd better go home now and take care of Star," she said. "I have the feeling you need a few minutes alone here at the temple. See you in a bit?"

Samuel nodded, knowing she was right. Melody took two steps and disappeared into the morning light. It made Sam smile to watch her use a privilege she had been given as translated priestess.

Sam presently got up and slowly walked into the Temple, his mind surging with new understanding, wonder and delight. There was no sadness in his soul anywhere to be found.

When he passed the open doors to the grand assembly hall his eyes unexpectedly fell upon a large white grand piano sitting in the middle of the hall. All around it the chairs had been moved back so that it appeared to be sitting by itself in a sea of empty chairs. He paused, wanting to touch it, to run his fingers across the silken keys, to hear, even in the briefest way, the long-loved wonder of music as it emerged from his fingers and found its way into the piano and to his soul. However, this was the Temple, and he highly doubted the propriety of doing so. Then he was startled to see someone standing close to him. He looked up to see a familiar face.

Except for the fact that this young man stood several inches above the floor, Samuel would have thought him a mortal temple worker dressed in white suit and tie. The young man smiled, and with his left hand, motioned toward the piano. It was all the invitation Samuel needed.

"Thank you, Helaman," Samuel said, and winked at his dear friend. "You knew I needed to express the music in my soul this morning, didn't you?"

Helaman looked at him with deep adoration and love. "That's what family is for," he said with a smile. "Enjoy this moment, my friend and fellow servant in Christ," he said as embraced Samuel, stepped away, then disappeared into thin air.

Samuel raised the lid of the piano and found himself looking into an instrument of unusual construction. In days long gone by, he had often studied the workmanship of the old grands, but this was unlike anything he had known. Taking a seat upon the upholstered bench, he raised the lid to find himself looking at two rows of keys, rather than one. The nearer row was the familiar black and white piano keys he had always known. Above that, and slanted toward him, was another keyboard unlike any he had yet seen. It was laid out in a pattern similar to the black and white keys, but these keys were all the same level, with no raised keys.

Samuel ran his fingers across the surface and found the keys only separated by slight grooves. As he touched them they did not move downward as expected, but immediately a rich tone emanated from the instrument with striking clarity. He again ran his fingers across the upper keys and listened to the ringing tones it called forth.

As he experimented, Samuel quickly learned that any combination of keys made a beautiful tone. There were no bad chords or notes. He placed both hands on the upper keys, and intuitively played a short rhapsody. He slid his fingers upward on the keys toward the black, and heard the tone go minor. He increased the spacing slightly between his fingers and found rich harmonies of seventh's and ninth's. His musical mind came alive! This was an instrument of instruments! Having spent mere minutes with it he knew it as if he had labored at it for centuries.

But there is a hunger that old memories bring, and his fingers ached for the former tones and keys he had come to love so well. In the few seconds it took to move his hands from the upper keyboard to the lower, he had time to wonder, even fear, if he could still even play the piano at all? He had loved it so well, rejoiced in it, touched people's lives with it, wooed and won his Love with it; the idea of discovering that the gift may have died frightened him.

Samuel cautiously placed his fingers upon the familiar keys and found they were not forgotten. Like the moment one comes to know Christ truly is their everlasting Savior, sweetness flowed through him, his heart burned brightly, and joy swept through him. He threw back his head and let his heart take free command of his fingers. They flew across the keys with boldness and surety. Not only could he still play, but he could play as he had never done before. It suddenly occurred to him that in the almost forty years since his change he had not played the piano simply for the joy of music. This was his first time in all those years, and he found that his fingers were tireless, flawlessly obedient to his mind, and superbly responsive to his will.

But far beyond this, he felt his soul open to that familiar place from where his music sprang, and for the first time in his life he understood. This was not so much a connection with the divine, though he knew it was a gift from Heavenly Father. No, this was a connection with who *he* was.

For the first time in his life, Samuel realized that the music which played in a stream of seemingly endless symphonies in his heart, was but a pinprick opening in the veil that had obscured Samuel from himself. This music, whose harmonies thrilled him so, these precious feelings that brought his soul so close to pure worship, these surges of love so powerful they could only find expression in music of surpassing beauty—even the words that upon occasion had startled him with their crystalline clarity— these were all a remnant, a reminder, a small glimpse into his divine soul.

No sooner had these thoughts surged sweetly through his mind than the memory of his life, of Melody, his children, of Helaman, of all those he had ministered to, and all those whom he had loved beyond the power of words to tell, entered his mind. The music then changed; it grew light, joyful and expansive. It began like the sound of a distant bird singing morning vespers, then slowly grew in passion and intensity, dancing upon harmonies of which he had never conceived before. It was alight with melody, and awash with celestial beauty.

Then, the words came as if he were listening to them: words that flowed too quickly for him to speak, too perfectly for him to utter, and too glorious to write down. He gasped, and his fingers came to an imme- diate stop. Suddenly, as surely as he knew any truth, he knew this: he had known and loved this music long before his mortal birth. This very music was the crowning achievement of his former self, and of someone else eternally important to him. This music was his and Melody's.

As he sat looking at his fingers stilled on the keys, Samuel suddenly understood that this glorious music was the anthem that defined the very essence of who both he was, and who Melody was. It was their shared musical passion which had joined them to one another permortally, and now lit the fire of their eternal future. This music expressed the entire content of their lives—past, present, and forever; it was the symphony of their souls, powerful in content and prophetic in scope. To sing this song was to know all things. It was to love as Christ loves.

In that moment of silence, Samuel realized that he was not yet ready. Like waiting to be given the sealed portion of the Book of Mormon, Samuel knew he must wait for the fullness of that perfect music to manifest itself in him. Sitting in that empty hall of the Temple, surrounded by the swish of silken robes of unseen visitors, he wept. He placed his hands on his head and cried tears of joy. And, with every sob of happiness he knew less and less why he was weeping. Perhaps it was because he had come so close to knowing everything. No, this was not a matter of "perhaps." He wept because he had glimpsed for a moment who he was, and who Melody was; and it was far more than his still-primitive frame could contain.

Samuel slowly closed the lid on the great piano and stood. He bowed his head for a moment and fervently thanked Father for the music in his soul, for this life-changing moment, and for an eternity of music yet to come. He stepped away from the room and walked toward home. He realized that he was not ready to write this music—not for any lack of love, but for lack of eternal perspective.

A finite man cannot write infinite music.

"What's wrong?" Melody asked the instant he walked into the house.

Samuel stepped to the couch, deep in thought. "Nothing, darling." He sank down, then looked at her with longing eyes.. "I just tried to write you a new song. But I couldn't express the overwhelming feelings of my heart—the infinitely precious music that is *you!*"

Melody beamed at him, touched to her core. "Samuel, a song for me? You've never written me a song before!"

Samuel shook his head. "Oh Melody, I wanted it to be so perfect! And for one second, it almost was. But I am so limited, still so limited! I sat at that piano in the temple and realized my nothingness—more today than ever before. And yet, I also know that you and I were and always will be eternal soulmates. My darling, we have been blessed with things few mortals can imagine."

He stopped for a moment, feeling the warmth of the Spirit as he spoke. " I don't know why our lives took such different paths before we were finally allowed to come together—but I do know that everything is exactly as it should be."

Melody sat beside him, and snuggled deeply into his chest. "Yes, my love, everything really *is* as it should be." Then she whispered with deep emotion. "Oh, Sam, I have never been happier in my life than I am right now." She threw her arms around him. "And you, Samuel Mahoy, are the most precious blessing I have received in this mortal existence—except for my Savior!" Her eyes were glowing. "I adore you, my Angel!"

Samuel kissed her tenderly for the millionth time, when something new and unexpected flooded his soul and spirit, taking him by surprise. At that moment he felt more pure love, more exquisite passion, and more reverence for this godly woman than he had ever known in his life—for anyone, at any time.

Overwhelmed by the intensity of what he was experiencing, Samuel kissed her neck, her face and her lips over and over, murmuring profound words of love that she hardly understood, but wept to hear.

ANGELS OF FIRE

On the sixth day of April at the break of day, Samuel heard the clarion sound of a trumpet, and he rushed into the street. Still far away, he could see a pinpoint of glory growing brighter as it approached the City. His heart raced wildly, and he shouted, "Hosannah!" as he ran inside to get Melody and his family. The Spirit told him plainly that this was The Day of Days for which they had for so long been waiting: the coming of Christ in His Glory, the Day of Cleansing, the Dawn of the Millennium!

The King of Kings came toward the earth slowly, and all of Zion gathered in the streets to watch His glorious descent. Today His coming was accompanied by magnificent signs in the heavens. A billowing cloud of glory surrounded Him, electrifying the heavens and the earth; a heavenly choir sang resounding hosannas to His name! From the moment of His appearance, upon the horizon they could see infinite shafts of light reaching out from His glorious personage to lift those to Him who were worthy to rise, and worthy of resurrection.

As He came toward the earth the sky convoluted, almost as if it were being rolled up into a scroll. Beyond the blue edges, like a silken curtain had been lifted, one could see into the depths of eternity. To look into the heavens was to behold the glory of God, and to see a vast array of beings, some of whom were praising the holy name of Jesus, and some who were cursing their consequences. What was being rolled back was the veil of mortality which had so long covered the earth. To Samuel's eyes, the sky—one of the elements of the earth's telestial atmosphere—was being superseded. When it was fully gone the earth would no longer be a Telestial world, but a Terrestrial home for the righteous.

This was the Great Day of Days when the Celestial-worthy dead would come forth, one and all. Previous to this only a select faithful few had been resurrected. Today, the long-awaited day of resurrection had fully come!

Christ passed slowly overhead, looking directly into the eyes of those gazing up at Him from the streets of Zion, and communicating His profound love to each one of them. Samuel immediately felt the pull of gravity release him, and he rose up to join his Savior once again. His joy could simply not be contained, nor did he have words to adequately describe this day to future generations of children. If it were possible for any experience to be grander than anything that had happened to him previously, this experience was.

Everyone ever born on the earth with garments now unspotted through the blood of the Lamb and who had been rendered worthy of a Celestial reward, was lifted up to meet Him in the air. The celestial dead were resurrected, their mortal bodies perfected, cleansed, healed of wounds and illnesses of body and spirit, made gloriously beautified, and brought forth triumphantly to join Him. Samuel tearfully joined Melody, their parents, their children, their brothers and sisters, relatives, missionary companions, eternal friends, and fellow-servants in Christ.

It was both a great and a terrible day. Nearly every mortal who rose left loved ones standing upon the ground weeping in deep distress; for those left below knew that the hour of their preparation was past. They had rebelliously procrastinated their repentance one too many days, and had not partaken of the gifts of grace that Christ had so freely offered to them. This knowledge was terrible indeed.

Those who rose had their eyes fixed upon their triumphant Savior, upon loved ones rushing to join Him, and upon the sweet consolation to their mortal suffering. Those who rose all rejoiced in their precious Redeemer, knowing that it was only through His great atonement, through their choosing to obey the Holy Spirit's whisperings, through consecrating all that they were and ever would be—that they were able to rise. They praised God to be clothed in the robes of His righteousness. They each knew they were worthy only through Christ—through His merits and not their own, through His mercy, through His grace. It was a great day of humility for all—both for those who rose, and for those who remained.

Looking behind him, Samuel could see a long, continuous flow of spirits coming from the heavens toward the earth in flowing robes of faithfulness in Christ. Each spirit moved quickly toward the earth, which had willingly given up the elements of their mortal body. Those elements very quickly reassembled into a perfect form, and their joyous spirit stepped into his or her perfected body, emanating with glory and light, never to be separated from it again. Many would throw their heads back, raise both hands high and give a shout of ecstasy as they stood momentarily upon the earth, or reached to embrace a loved one nearby. Immediately thereafter, each would be caught up to join the others in the heavens as they followed Christ in His triumphant return.

Then the Light touched Samuel's body! In that moment, he realized that this was his time to come forth in his long-awaited resurrection! The change that occurred in that fraction-of-a-second was like each cell being electrified by a billion volts of electricity, and each volt bringing a tingle of perfect elation. He watched as light burst from his skin—and in that moment not only his body but his perception of everything changed. His vision now included profound truths previously obscured from his view.

Samuel felt the veil lift from his mind, and though he could not remember everything about his long premortal life, in a flash he saw his own magnificent spirit, which had always been an intimate part of God himself. This knowledge astonished him to the core. Then he comprehended even more profoundly the excruciating and infinite sacrifice that Jesus Christ had wrought for him personally, which at the same time made Samuel more fully realize his own utter nothingness without Christ. He saw who he truly was in the full light of Truth—the nothingness and the magnificent greatness, simultaneously. He wept in humility and joy.

With this new knowledge, Samuel looked in complete adoration toward his Yeshua, by whose power he now stood. New memories then emerged, held back from mortality until this day. What he remembered first and foremost was pure love—unrelenting, infinitely compassionate love which his Brother and Friend had always felt for him. It was like liquid manna to Samuel's soul, the pure essence of life. He comprehended an eternity of their association, their deep friendship, their glorious work together, and their mutual obedience to Father's will.

Heavenly Father! Heavenly Mother! Suddenly his mind was opened to a new and vast panorama of a long and glorious association with his Heavenly Parents. "Oh Father, Mother—how I love you!" he immediately cried out. His heart swelled with unbridled joy and intense longing as he remembered. Yet, today this memory was only a glimpse. The veil still stood largely sentinel to his premortal life. Samuel was apparently not ready yet to know the very beginnings of his own existence, nor the mysteries concerning the origin of all that he called heaven. But for now, this was enough.

Samuel realized with a sudden jolt that Melody was near him. She approached in full glory, and he marveled at her celestial stature, her beauty and her incomprehensible power. She was by every definition a goddess. Her clothing was as bright as the sun. A circle of glory surrounded her head that in every way resembled a crown. As she approached, he found himself alone with her in a vast sea of light. He gazed into her face, and gratefully saw the same tender and familiar smile he had always known. In wonder he contemplated her physical glories, and her enhanced and perfect being, although her features were still recognizable as the Melody he had loved in mortality. But now she was a daughter of pure light, of glorious divine femininity, of infinite capacity and fully-endowed power—and he marveled at the exquisite goddess before him.

"You are a Queen!" Samuel whispered in near worship.

Melody embraced Samuel long and fervently. "All glory to God, who has redeemed me through His grace," she said humbly. Then she released him with a broad smile.

Samuel laughed aloud. There was nothing in his soul but exquisite joy.

Suddenly, Helaman came into view, looking all of twenty-four years old, as he had earlier in the Temple. Samuel cried out for joy and embraced him warmly. "Helaman, my dear friend, this is the glorious dawn of the Millennium for which we have so long prepared! How can I ever thank you for patiently teaching me, and for watching over my family as you did all those years? I will be forever indebted to you—Grandfather!"

Helaman stood tall, and embraced Samuel with joy. "You are indeed a grandson to be proud of, Samuel. It was my honor to serve you and our family!"

Then Bonnie and Lisa joined Sam and Melody, and their entire family excitedly surrounded Helaman, each expressing deep love and profound gratitude for him being the hands of heaven in bringing them all home. These were eternal ties that they knew would never be broken.

"Tham!" a small voice cried out behind him, and he spun around to find his mother Laura leading a small redheaded child by the hand. Samuel fell onto his knees as his baby brother ran into his arms. "Tham! Tham!" he cried repeatedly.

"Jimmy!" Samuel cried. "Oh, Jimmy! I'm so sorry I didn't look down when I drove over the ditch. I just didn't..."

"Tham," the little one interrupted. "It wath not your fault. It wath Heavenly Father'th plan, and we all played our role in it. Let uth rejoith, Tham. Leth's praith God that the time has finally come when we can be together again! Now Mother can raisth me, as she was promisthed!"

Samuel felt his heart healing from years of anguish. "Jimmy, now that you are here, I do rejoice! Oh little brother, you look like a two-year-old, and you're talking the way you used to!" he proclaimed joyfully.

"It may take thome getting used to for both of uth, Tham," Jimmy said, his face next to Samuel. "A few minuteth ago I wath an adult! Now I'm two yearth old, or at leatht my body ith! And I thtill have a lithp!" he said with a grin.

Sam laughed and ruffled his little brother's head like he had so many years ago. With this, Jimmy pulled something out of his pocket, and put his little arms behind his back to keep it a secret.

"I brought you thomething!" Jimmy cried with such happiness that his voice actually squeaked.

"What, Jimmy?" Samuel asked, his eyes sparkling with love.

"Thith!" Jimmy proclaimed and brought from behind his back a long silver flute. He laid it carefully in his big brother's hands. "I thlept with it every night until I could give it back to you," Jimmy said pointedly. He was referring to the nearly 80 years since his burial.

Samuel took the shiny silver flute and turned it over in his hands. It was indeed his flute from so many years ago. Every dent and scratch was very familiar.

"Play my favorite thong," Jimmy said happily. "Play, 'I am a Child of God,'" he said, his voice effervescent with happiness.

Samuel raised the flute to his lips, and played a single note. It was sharp and clear and seemed to reach beyond this world into eternity. Suddenly, a thousand flutes, and a million angelic voices sang the same note as if his had opened some great reservoir holding the music of heaven. Crystalline and beautiful it came. From the depths of his soul he played while kneeling right there on the clouds of heaven. Jimmy laughed, threw back his head and in a voice of a two-year-old, yet with the heart of one infinitely older, sang, "I am a child of God, and He hath thent me here…."

The music had hardly ceased when Jimmy suddenly jumped into his big brother's arms. Samuel stood smiling as Jimmy dangled from his neck, chortling with two-year-old glee. It seemed as if nothing could be more perfect.

At that moment Samuel's eyes shifted across the vast throng of glowing people in the throws of joyful reunion. He saw a beautiful woman walking toward him. Samuel's first thought was to feel amazed she was coming toward him, and secondly, to wonder who this divine creature was. She was so graceful and elegant, so glorious and stunningly beautiful that for a moment he wondered if a goddess had joined the throngs of happy mortals. As she came others saw her glory, and stepped aside, reverently bowing their heads or reaching out to touch her shimmering garments as she passed. These she seemed not to notice, for her eyes were fixed upon Samuel. He had had but a few moment's experience being so near resurrected beings and could not know for certain, but the glory surrounding this soul's resurrection attested to a noble mortal life far superior to most, including his and all whom he loved.

Jimmy slid to the ground just as she stopped directly before Samuel. She placed a hand affectionately on Jimmy's head, which won a beaming smile from him. Samuel couldn't even think of anything to say to this glorious creature. Her eyes were the most perfect blue he had ever seen. Her hair was very light brown, the color of spun gold, her body glorious beyond any mortal definition of perfection.

She smiled at him, and his heart skipped a beat. He almost found himself lapsing into a lad's shyness, which surprised him. Then, gaining control of himself to some extent, he smiled back, then became shy again. She was simply more glorious than anyone he had yet seen, except Christ himself.

"You don't recognize me do you?" she said simply, her smile warm and loving.

"I'm sorry," Samuel replied, his attention and curiosity now completely captured.

"I'm Catherine," she said. Samuel's mind immediately fastened onto a long-ago memory.

"You mean little, blind, deformed Catherine with the angel's voice?" he asked in wonder.

"That's who I was," she beamed. "I've changed a little since then."

"In every way!" Samuel replied. "I'm sorry so many, including myself, couldn't see your beauty then."

"Most, including myself, didn't see it," she answered. "But, more than most, you did. You gave me a chance to glimpse my own inner beauty. You didn't realize it, of course, but singing that song at Christmas, and feeling the outpouring of the Spirit upon everyone there, and suddenly knowing for the first time in my life that there *was* something beautiful inside me, was *the* most important moment of my life. I never stopped singing after that! I have come to thank you for what you did."

"I didn't know…" he began, his mind fumbling for an appropriate response, not wanting to invalidate her feelings, but also not wanting to take credit for something he actually had no idea he had done.

"That is exactly the point," she interrupted him. "You didn't know. You had no reason to know, or to care, or to give me a chance. You did it because you heard the Lord's whisper, and because you were gentle and kind. Your obedience gave me the first real chance I had in my life. I never did go far with my singing. Only a few people could see past my ugly exterior, and it always remained a beauty hidden within. I never married or had children. The only thing I did was to freely forgive, and to love and trust my dear Savior."

Then her face lit up with joy. "But, that one moment you gave me fired my faith, my hope, my love and my happiness for the remainder of my lifetime. Throughout my life I remembered it again and again, and it brought me hope when nothing else could. It was my personal test to be trapped in that body, and though rejected and alone, to remain faithful and return kindness for pain. It was my test—and I passed it, all glory to God! What you gave me, Sam, was a boost enough to see me through all those lonely years."

She stopped and regarded him gratefully. "I know you feel as if it was nothing. But, to me it was everything."

Samuel took a tiny step backward, and bowing slightly from the waist, said, "I am deeply honored to have been a part of your life. It is obvious it was a life of extraordinary righteousness. I am humbled," he said in total honesty, his eyes upon her feet.

At that moment Dawn stepped into their circle of light, holding Nathan's arm. Samuel's mind flooded with clear memories. "Nathan!" he cried and rushed into an embrace with his friend. "Although Dawn introduced us before, until this moment I had not fully remembered you, my beloved friend! It is so marvelous to be with you again!"

Nathan embraced him fiercely. "Samuel, now that you remember, we can speak about these things! I watched everything you did on earth! You were faithful and have done everything you said you would do. Perhaps you don't remember this, but we had several wagers on the outcome of your life. I admit that you won them all—and I owe you everything, buddy!"

"What did we bet?" Samuel chuckled, still clapping Nathan on the back.

"It wasn't so much of a bet, as a hope," Nathan admitted. "You had a difficult life laid before you, and I knew so much of my happiness and hopes with Dawn depended upon you. Do you remember now that we asked you to take care of Dawn for me? You said you would, and you did!"

Samuel's eyes grew larger as new understanding filled his mind. "Yes, I remember that I promised I would wait to be with Melody so that I could take care of Dawn. I knew that Dawn would leave me as soon as her life's mission was completed, and if I was faithful there would still be time for me to marry Melody!"

Dawn stepped forward with a smile. "Sam, I will always love you for what you did for us. You brought me into the covenant, loved me, and allowed me the gift of giving life to two beautiful daughters. We are eternally grateful for you and Melody being sealed for us in the temple." She turned to Melody, bursting with curiosity. "So, Melody—do you remember more clearly now, too?"

Melody stepped forward and threw her arms around Dawn. She began to laugh softly as she clung to Dawn's neck.

"I remember that this was all my idea!" Melody cried joyfully between tears and laughter.

"Yes, it was," Dawn said with a smile. Then she turned and kissed Samuel on both cheeks. "Thank you, Sam."

He grinned happily back at her. "God is so good," he said simply.

Dawn took Melody's hands in her own. "Friends forever," she said fervently.

"Friends forever," Melody rejoined. Then Dawn and Nathan stepped away and were gone in the throngs of people rejoicing all around them.

Melody sank into Samuel's arms. Samuel shook his head as if trying to clear it. "Everything is so different than I ever imagined—and yet it is the perfect outcome," he whispered softly into her ear.

Melody laughed, almost giggling. "I know! Some of it would be a shock if it weren't all such a vast blessing. Oh Sam, I think ours is one of the greatest love stories of all time! What you—what we—did for Dawn and Nathan made our present joys truly possible. It was sacrifice that turned the key. And she and Nathan will now always be our precious friends—forever!"

Samuel laughed in joy. "It all astounds me. And yet, what astounds me most is that you can remember those things much better than I do," he said, still grinning.

"Oh, you will catch up to me one of these days, sweetheart," Melody said with a wry grin as she nestled into his arms. "But for both of us now, these memories will bring us peace. Sweet, sweet peace."

Samuel nodded, and then drew her up gently, one hand on her waist and the other held out to her. "Nothing could be sweeter than this. Come, my darling, and let's dance! I believe that now I can finally keep up with you!" Melody caught her breath, gave him her hand, and they whirled off together in a cloud of eternal bliss.

The Resurrected Lord, all His holy angels and those who had just participated in the Morning of the First Resurrection passed completely around the globe, completing their passage well before midday.

At exactly noon another trumpet sounded as they began circuiting the world a second time. This time there were no choirs singing. As Christ passed over, His glory reached out in a seemingly-solid sphere to touch the earth below. Samuel and Melody watched in wonder as all around them Mother Earth stirred and yielded up her dead. This was the beginning of the Afternoon of the First Resurrection, wherein the Terrestrial spirits of all periods of time came forth. These spirits were resurrected with a lesser degree of glory, so that their glowing countenances might be compared to the brightness of the moon.

In the moment it took for the resurrected spirits to rise from the ground to the heavenly throng, each mind was opened to his or her new resurrected status, much as had occurred to Samuel when he had been resurrected. They began to learn who they were and what their lives might become. From there, a company of angels met each of them, conducting them to family and friends. Because of their enormous numbers—billions upon billions of them—the stream of angels guiding them to their loved ones appeared endless. Samuel had no idea where they were going, or where their new home might be, whether on the earth or somewhere else; but he knew it was glorious beyond description.

Finally, all who were redeemed through the grace of Jesus Christ were caught up into the clouds of heaven to meet Him. Samuel looked upon the earth and saw millions of unclean people still upon it, cowering in terror, and hiding in the ruins of their cities or in caves and forests. He saw them viciously curse God for being unfair and ruthless. He saw them turn upon their neighbors in abject violence. He saw a numberless concourse of evil ones who had been infesting the earth since that day when they were cast out down to it, and he watched in sorrow as they moved to inhabit the mortal bodies remaining there. A thousand evil spirits tried to crowd into one mortal body until the person was thrashing upon the ground.

Jehovah descended quickly with a fierce look of righteous retribution. Again His voice was heard: "Let the devil and his angels be bound!" A wail arose from the earth as in an instant the wicked spirits of the damned were swept from its surface and carried away. Their hatred and evil were at long last gone from the earth, only destined to return for a brief and futile battle a thousand years from hence.

"It is good!" a mighty voice rolled across all the earth. Samuel looked upon the Savior to see a serene look of peace replace the expression of retribution that had been there before. In a voice like the heralding of heavenly trumpets, Christ spoke the words, "Let the earth be cleansed by fire!"

Suddenly, the glory of Christ ignited the ground immediately below them and released a fire of purifying intensity upon the earth. Faster than a fiery flood it spread, devouring everything telestial in its path. People,

590 animals, art, music, technology, buildings and anything telestial simply vanished in the cleansing fire. Gone were the cities, the mighty works of man, the pride and haughtiness of the world—everything meaningless was gone, and all forgotten. All that remained was the exquisite beauty and serenity of the newly-born terrestrial world.

Samuel, Melody, Helaman, Dawn and Nathan, and all the glorious hosts of Christ let forth a mighty cry of triumph, and the Earth opened her mouth with joy: "Hosannah! Blessed be the Name of the Lord!" A trumpet sounded three times, and the voice of God in the hearing of all creation said, "Let the earth rest!"

And for one thousand years of peace, it was so.

THE END

ABOUT JOHN PONTIUS

It was never John's intent to write LDS books or a doctrinal blog or website, but he decided early on to obey the voice of the Lord and discern His will in his life. Hearkening to the Lord's voice was not always easy, but John's difficult journey ended in a far better place than he ever dreamed possible.

After living thirty-three years in Alaska, raising a family there, and building several careers, the Lord sent John and his family to Utah. John and his wife, Terri, who is the love of his life, both grew up in Utah but spent the majority of their lives in "the mission field." Returning to Utah was like coming home and brought them nearer to additional family, children, and grandchildren. Together they have eight children and twenty-one grandchildren.

John had many opportunities to speak at firesides, write books, and begin and maintain his blog, *UnBlogmySoul*. He accomplished many unexpected and amazing things that only the hand of the Lord could have brought to pass. The Lord's hand took John places he did not want to go, but when he actually got there, he recognized them as his "far better land of promise."

John passed away peacefully in his home in 2012, after a lifetime of service to the Lord Jesus Christ.